The C

CW01628384

Jane Barry, wh
copywriter since
Director of one c
cies. She contributed theatre reviews and articles to Broadsheet and Granta while at Cambridge and in 1980 was one of the winners of the Lancaster Literary Festival International Poetry Competition for her poem 'Mr Rochester'. *The Cavendish Face* is her first novel.

JANE BARRY

The Cavendish Face

FONTANA PAPERBACKS

First published by Fontana Paperbacks in 1983

Copyright © 1983 by Jane Barry

Made and printed in Great Britain by
William Collins Sons & Co. Ltd, Glasgow

CONDITIONS OF SALE
This book is sold subject to the condition
that it shall not, by way of trade or otherwise,
be lent, re-sold, hired out or otherwise circulated
without the publisher's prior consent in any form of
binding or cover other than that in which it is
published and without a similar condition
including this condition being imposed
on the subsequent purchaser

To all my friends without whom
nothing would be possible

PART ONE

THE VOICE IN THE GARDEN

CHAPTER ONE

Yes, of course I remember the first time I saw my Cousin Felix. And, if I did not, merely to touch the scuffed leather binding of my mother's diary would remind me.

My cousin, Felix de Lisle, my Aunt Jessica's favourite son. He had commanded a company of two hundred and eighty men on the Somme and, one day in November when the battle was petering out and his company had been reduced to forty-three, he had caught a German bullet in the spine. At the casualty clearing station they had given him twenty-four hours to live, at the base hospital they had awarded him the Military Cross and told him he would never walk again. And now it was February 1917, and he was coming home.

Monks Last had been in a turmoil with it for a week. Every day my Aunt Jessica's voice could be heard uttering imperious and contradictory instructions from some quarter of the house. A nurse had been engaged, not pretty like my governess, Miss Ashe, who had been inexplicably sent packing a fortnight ago with her chin quivering and tears flowing unrestrainedly down her soft pink cheeks, but a dumpy, middle-aged woman with a slat-eyed Fenland face and a black moustache, who smelt strongly of onions. Magnus, the head gardener, hunching his shoulders against the knife-sharp February wind, had struggled in with whatever blooms he could find, winter jasmine, sprigs of early almond blossom, survivors of the frost. And Mrs Wix, in the kitchen, weather eye out to stop me filching sultanas, would talk of nothing else to half-there Marjorie as she stirred cake mixture.

'The poor Captain. Such a tall, good-looking boy he was. The light of her Ladyship's life.'

Then, to me: 'But of course, Miss Christabel, you'd never have seen him. Him going off to do his duty before you came. Though it's strange he never did come back on leave. Not even when his father died.'

'Strange,' echoed half-there Marjorie as she scrubbed the potatoes.

'Strange indeed,' said Mrs Wix, 'with her Ladyship being so

devoted to the Captain and needing both her sons to support her at a time like that, him more than the other I shouldn't wonder.'

'Strange indeed,' echoed half-there Marjorie.

And while they contemplated mournfully the strangeness of it I crammed a handful of sultanas into the pocket of my pinafore and slid away.

Perhaps, caught up in my own private turmoil, I was the only person at Monks Last on whom the coming home of my Cousin Felix impinged but little. It could, after all, render my own situation neither better nor worse. From my first day under her roof Aunt Jessica had made it plain that, though my mother had been her sister, no blood connection could reconcile her to shiftlessness and weakness of character. And she had ever since dedicated herself to driving out of me whatever hereditary traits my mother had passed on – the only inheritance it had been in her power to grant me. I was rude, I was noisy, my nails were dirty, my hair unruly, I would never find myself even a passable husband, my eleven-year-old presence was an affront to the sensibilities of a household which had long ago ceased to ring with childish laughter and had, in any case, always held firmly to the dictum that children should be seen and not heard.

It had, I surmised, been my Uncle Arthur's idea to bring me to Monks Last after my mother died. 'The poor child. She is, after all, my dear, a blood relation, and now she has no one.'

'And nothing to live on,' I could imagine my aunt replying tartly.

'Well, my dear, I don't think we can blame your sister for that. Montague Ward was never a provident man. I'm sure his last consideration was for what would happen to Adele if she were suddenly left a widow. And now there's only the child.'

'There are always charities.'

'But she is your blood. And that gives us a duty beyond charity.'

My Uncle Arthur was a kindly man, but years of marriage had taught him that survival lies in the line of least resistance. So, having accomplished my arrival at Monks Last, he left the rest to his wife, retiring from the battle zone to the musty, tobacco-laden peace of his smoking room, where he would spend hours pottering amongst his books and papers, pretending, so Aunt Jessica said, to manage the business of the estate. And it was there the butler, Grover, found him one afternoon, whisky decanter at his elbow, cigar still smouldering in the ashtray, propped quite upright in his great shabby leather wing chair, stone dead.

The de Lisles were not, as the Wards, thanks to the depredations of my father, had been for so many years, poor. As well as the Norfolk estate, my Uncle Arthur had owned land in South America and an estate in Ireland which he had sold when he had judged the political situation there to be beyond recovery. Once property and money had been divided between his wife and sons, the baronetcy and the management of Monks Last passing to the elder, Meredith, there was a small sum left in trust for me, to continue my education and keep until I was either married or twenty-one. And so my Aunt Jessica, who had suffered me from my ninth birthday, was now burdened with me until I was of an age where some foolish young man might be persuaded to take me off her hands. The unlooked-for and irksome nature of this burden she caused me to remember daily.

It had not been so bad when Miss Ashe was there, dear Miss Ashe, who was as perplexed by the intricacies of geography and mathematics as I, but who could play the grand piano in the drawing room so that the notes sounded liquid and translucent like the cascades of some sparkling waterfall, and who was so delighted to find even a pitiful imitation of the same dexterity in me. Miss Ashe would laugh and put her arms around me and ruffle my much-despaired-of mane of carrot-coloured hair and kiss me, so that sometimes the loss of my mother seemed a little less insurmountable. But Miss Ashe had been sent packing because of something that had happened two weeks ago when my Cousin Meredith had stolen into the conservatory at the tail end of an impromptu botany lesson on sub-tropical flora, and Miss Ashe had been still laughing after I had gone, and Aunt Jessica had walked in and found them.

So now there were no lessons, and nothing to be done with me, and little enough for me to do with myself. On days when the wind dropped I would brave the cold to try to make friends with the half-starved wild kittens lurking in the stables, or watch old Magnus fretting over the frost-blackened stumps of Aunt Jessica's favourite roses. But more often I would sidle into the steamy warmth of the kitchen and feast on the rich, yeasty smells that came from the oven and watch the pots simmering on the range, and surrender to the soothing tide of Mrs Wix's gossip, which washed in its ceaseless ebb and flow over half-there Marjorie and the kitchen cat, and the meat dishes on the dresser and the cured hams hanging from the ceiling, until even the kitchen clock seemed to tick more slowly. And sometimes half-there Marjorie would give me leeks or carrots to chop or Mrs Wix would offer me the mixing bowl to lick clean. And frequently a couple of hours would go by before she would suddenly look up at me and say: 'My goodness, Miss Christabel, you'll get me into hot water with her Ladyship one of these days!'

And then I would be off, to other parts of the house.

The object, I had long ago learnt, was to keep out of everyone's way for as long as possible. If you were careless and were stumbled upon, you were taken to have nothing to do and given intractable pieces of the Old Testament to learn by heart, or penwipers to make or Latin verbs to conjugate. The chairs in the library were good and deep; curled up, I could stay there undetected for hours, endlessly re-reading *Pride and Prejudice* or swooning over Shelley. The drawing-room Bechstein was a ceaseless temptation; but, even played quietly, it was out of the question unless everyone was away from the house (why else was the schoolroom provided with a tinny upright piano if not for the inept strumming of children?). And, when I tired of slipping ghostlike in and out of empty rooms, there was always the schoolroom itself and all that remained to me of my mother: a battered walnut secretaire, two strings of pearls that hadn't, in the end, needed to be pawned, a Stephenograph of Grace Darling, a lavender sachet, two volumes of poetry – one of Keats and one of Elizabeth Barrett Browning – and the three slim, leather-bound volumes of my mother's diary.

The secretaire had a secret drawer which only I knew how to open and shut by operating a concealed spring at the back: in it I kept the pearls, the Stephenograph and the lavender sachet. The Elizabeth Barrett Browning was very handsome, red morocco with the spine tooled in gold, while the Keats was clothbound with a broken spine and dog-eared pages that fell out when you opened it, and an odd inscription on the flyleaf, the name Dinu Radescu and a date, 1905. Both books I had read from cover to cover; but I had only recently begun to read my mother's diary.

At first it had been a comfort merely to have it, to sit at the secretaire and look at the configurations of that loved, familiar writing, and imagine her sitting there, in the dingy back room at Weymouth with its faded curtains and wilted armchairs, writing letters or frowning over bills, trying to puzzle out how the money could be made to stretch if all the lodgers left when winter set in

– she had not kept a diary then; perhaps she had been too busy, or simply too tired. The three volumes I possessed began when she was my age and ended just before I was born. They seemed at first sight merely a detailed record of inconsequential things, and, besides, my eleven-year-old eyes found the writing in the last two volumes difficult to construe. Yet, in all that welter of writing, smudged here and there where the ink had run (or blotched with what I would realize much later could only be tears), there must be something more than just a sentimental significance. So I had begun to trace my twelve-year-old mother through dancing lessons and tea with long-dead aunts, to see if she had written anything about herself and Aunt Jessica which might provide some answer to my present predicament.

And thus it was that, when the word came that Blackitt had picked up my Cousin Felix from the station and that the car had passed the lodge and was even now coming up the drive, I was in the schoolroom reading my mother's diary, having been apprehended loitering in the hall ten minutes before and summarily banished.

I ran to the window when I heard the scrunch of the tyres on the gravel and pressed my nose to the glass. I had a perfect view of the drive in front of the house with the two stone steps leading down to the barren vista of lawn, dotted here and there with rusting croquet hoops and cut off finally from the surrounding fields by a windbreak of blighted trees.

The long black snout of the Rolls-Royce edged ponderously forwards and then, with a creak of the handbrake, jerked to a stop. I could imagine them all, lined up on the front steps, trying not to shiver, their breath steamy in the cold air, their hands raw, Grover and the footmen and Jenks the valet, Mrs Wix and half-there Marjorie and the maids, and Cousin Meredith, whose asthma had prevented him from playing for his country in the Greater Game, and Aunt Jessica clutching at her shawl with the effort of not showing her excitement, and the dumpy nurse.

There was a second when everything seemed suspended. Then Blackitt got out of the car, looking up inconsequentially at the leaden sky as if he expected rain, and walked round to the nearside door. Aunt Jessica came suddenly into view from the right and from the left the nurse, advancing with the wheelchair. And then, very slowly, two hands first, straining with the effort so that I could imagine the knuckles were white, then two long, stiff legs, then one hand going back for a moment to find a stick, my Cousin Felix emerged. The nurse edged the wheelchair forward, Aunt Jessica moved to take his arm. But, without his making any sound or gesture that I could see, they fell back suddenly as if they had been brushed away. He stood, for an instant, a gaunt, pale man, his British Warm draped over his shoulders, his head bare, his right hand clenching on the stick. Then, drawing himself up to the full extent of his long lean height, he began to walk towards the front steps. He walked stiffly, carefully, my Cousin Felix, like an old man, as if the fibres of his tall straight body were held together not by any cohesion of nerves and muscles but by an indomitable effort of the will, and the few yards of gravel that separated him from the house seemed suddenly to expand and distort until they were infinite.

I watched until he had finally passed out of my line of sight. My Cousin Felix, returning from the war. In 1917 he was twenty-two.

CHAPTER TWO

Diary of Adele Cavendish. Volume the First.
Sawstead Hall, Hampshire.

14th September, 1892.

My darling M has come at last, and now there are only two and a half days until the happiest day of my life. He is at this moment in the library with Papa, no doubt discussing the final details of the marriage contract; I am to have £10,000 settled upon me, in addition to the thousand a year that was left to me by my Great Aunt Cavendish. Yet how strange Society is, which must make of marriage a business arrangement when all the world knows its sole foundation is love.

My dearest M! How tall and strong and handsome he is, how manly and honourable. And yet what inexpressible tenderness in his smile just now as I ran to greet him, how reverent his lips as they impressed themselves upon my hand. He is my true and noble lord, my parfait gentil knight. Regarding him thus, permitting my hand still to remain a prisoner while his eyes, despite my blushes, sought mine with such a worshipping, passionate glance I feared they would devour me, I found myself thinking once again: 'This is but a dream and, should I pinch myself, I shall awake and discover I have only imagined him.' He is, indeed, so wonderfully romantic he might be the hero of a novel come to life – those novels by Ouida and Miss Marie Corelli which, though Mamma expressly forbids them, dear Rose smuggles up to my bedroom, where I may wickedly, rapturously indulge myself in the solitude of the small hours. Oh, with his fine, aristocratic features, he might be Chandos, or Bertie Cecil from Under Two Flags, languid, nonchalant and yet with a latent recklessness about him. Certainly he has Bertie Cecil's eyes, handsome Spanish eyes with unfathomable depths, although his hair is dark, not chestnut, and he has the most dashing black moustachioes besides. And as for his devotion to honour, his nobleness of mind – why, his very bearing speaks of them. Indeed, I believe I shall never meet a finer, more upright, more handsome man, unless it be my very own dearest Papa.

To think last September I had barely put my hair up, and now I have been presented at Court and had my first Season and, to crown it all, in two and a half days I shall be a married woman, respected in Society, with my own household to run. Dear M, it is indeed a dream come true. What raptures, what ecstasies we shall share.

And yet there are so many things I do not know about you, the little things a wife must know in order to please, like Mamma understanding Papa cannot abide the smell of lavender wax and must have the tweeny iron his newspaper before it is laid by his place at breakfast. Dear Mamma, to counter that giddiness which, woefully, Papa so often detects in my nature, has these past weeks striven to impress upon me the awesome solemnity of marriage; how a woman must enter that state with religious dedication, for upon her the wellbeing of her husband and children, the moral atmosphere of her home depend; and how, above all, she must hold to her modesty and purity of mind, for in a woman's modesty lies our natural safeguard against man's baser passions which tend to immorality and domestic strife. But with all her years of devotion to dear Papa as my example, how shall I fail to know my duty? And, with love as my teacher, that which your innermost heart has not yet revealed to me, dear, darling M, I shall assuredly be quick to learn. Oh, but it is all so unbearably exciting!

J arrives tomorrow, with Sir Arthur and the dear baby. I wonder how she will take to M? I cannot doubt but that, like everyone else, she will be quite won over by his charm; and yet she is so very strict and severe in her judgements that sometimes she almost frightens me. What does Papa say when he chides me for my dreamy nature? That she is the prudent sister and a good example.

Oh well, I shall lull myself to sleep tonight with such romantic dreams of my darling M.

15th September, 1892.

Dearest M! When you tried to kiss me this morning in the rose garden and I scolded you for such impropriety, particularly when we were in full view of the gardener's boy, your smile was so tender and your gaze so passionate I quite forgave you. Oh, in two days you may steal all the kisses you please!

J and Sir Arthur arrived at noon. I must say J is very cold and unromantic. Although Sir Arthur may not have your handsome looks and figure, dear M, he is very kind and considerate and sees that she wants for nothing. Yet she treats him almost with contempt, making him fetch and carry like a footman. She is cold with baby Meredith too, showing no interest in him when he was brought down in his petticoats after tea, although the rest of us petted and made much of him. I was again in some trepidation as to her verdict on my poor darling, but when, witty and brilliant as ever, you charmed a reluctant smile from her at dinner, I told myself all would be well. I should have known my sister better.

After dinner, when you were tête à tête with Papa over the port, Mamma had gone to fetch her Berlin work, and J and I were momentarily alone, she suddenly said, à propos of nothing: 'I cannot think why Papa did not let you marry that dull curate over at Stockbridge. You have not a brain in your head, which makes you perfectly suited for a country vicar's wife. What will become of you married to an adventurer, heaven only knows.'

I stared at her, mortified. 'The Reverend Green has foul breath and hair growing out of his ears,' I said. 'And besides, darling M is not an adventurer. He may not be a baronet like Sir Arthur, but he is second cousin to Lord Ambleside and has an inheritance from his grandmama. But if he were a pauper I should not care. I should love him all the more because of it.'

'Love?' said J sarcastically. 'Only a fool marries for love.' With which she pursed her mouth shut in that decided way she has and would say no more.

Poor J. Can it be that she alone of all the world has never felt love? You and I, M, shall have between us such a surfeit that, warming her with it, we shall count her an ice maiden if her heart is not a little unthawed.

16th September, 1892.

Oh tomorrow, tomorrow! The whole house throbs with it, the maids in a ferment, Mamma driving Mrs West and Cook to distraction with last-minute instructions; even Papa appears quite on edge. This evening as I played the piano while Mamma sang 'Pale Hands I Loved Beside the Shalimar', I wept a little secretly to realize I should be leaving my own dear home. But now, when I think of my trousseau, already packed, when I think that tomorrow at first light Rose will lay out my white kid slippers and Grandmama's veil and the dress with its leg-o'-mutton sleeves and froufrou of organza embroidered with seed pearls – oh, my hand trembles so much I can hardly hold my pen.

But these are the last words I shall write in this diary, the record of my childhood. This is my happy ending. Tomorrow I shall start a new diary for a new life.

For tomorrow at ten o'clock, I, Adele Hermione Cavendish, shall become Mrs Montague Ward.

CHAPTER THREE

I did not see my Cousin Felix again for some weeks, not until the day after Aunt Jessica found the diary. He remained in his room and the only visible signs of his presence were the frequent visits of Dr Blair, and the nurse rushing up and downstairs with trays. But, just as his coming had turned the house upside down, so his being there informed every part of it too with a strange restlessness, as if somewhere an invisible wire were being slowly pulled and stretched.

In the absence of both nanny and governess I was now permitted to take breakfast and luncheon with the family in the dining room and I would often come in to find Aunt Jessica and my Cousin Meredith in the midst of a conversation which they would suddenly, on noticing me, break off.

Only once, at breakfast, when I had slipped in silently and was helping myself to kedgeree from the serving table, did they fail to detect my presence soon enough.

'He must learn to accept,' Aunt Jessica was saying. 'He will never be very much better than he is now. Dr Blair has said it, I've said it to him many times. He must simply learn to accept it.'

My Cousin Meredith shifted his copy of *The Times* slightly as if he were trying to set up some sort of wall against the conversation. 'My dear brother has never been much given to accepting things,' he said.

'If only he would talk to me. Oh, of course he wouldn't with you. But to me, he would talk to me about everything before he went away. You were always much closer to your father, but Felix and I—'

Meredith moved his paper again and sighed. 'Yes, Mother.'

'It's even doubtful if he'll be well enough to go back up to Cambridge in the autumn. Not that I'm entirely sorry. He could help you manage the estate.'

'Felix has no interest in running the estate.'

'But he has a good head on his shoulders. He wouldn't let everything drift from day to day like your father did. And you're no better, in fact you take after your father in every way. How often have I—'

Meredith thrust the paper aside in exasperation. 'Very often, Mother. And I happen to think—'

But here he noticed me hovering by the serving table, and they both fell into frosty silence for the rest of the meal.

Mrs Wix, of course, was more forthcoming, if only in the context of her running battle with That One, her now habitual term for Nurse Blunt, who came demanding this and that from the kitchen at all hours and had thus committed the unforgivable crime of upsetting Mrs Wix's routine.

'You mark my words, Miss Christabel,' she would say, as she rolled out pastry and dusted her hands smartly together to get rid of the flour. 'That One's days in this house are numbered. Take last night, if you please. A right old rumpus there was, according to Mr Grover, who had it off Mr Jenks.'

'A right old rumpus,' echoed half-there Marjorie from the sink.

'There's the poor Captain having one of his nightmares from the shell-shock and shivering and screaming as if he was still out there in France fighting the Boche, and there's her Ladyship trying to go and comfort him, and That One says, calm as you please, that the Captain's given her strict orders whenever it happens that he's to be left alone and no fuss made. Trying to shut her Ladyship out of the room in her own house and away from her own son, indeed! Well, her Ladyship won't take that lightly, I can tell you. I've seen her read the riot act just because dinner was a quarter of an hour late.'

Whether because of the battles with Nurse Blunt or the general sense in the house of everything shifting, as if solid foundations had suddenly been replaced with quicksand, my Cousin Meredith and Aunt Jessica seemed to change too, to become exaggerated versions of themselves, Cousin Meredith drooping his shoulders and labouring with his breathing as if the weight of his body had become almost too heavy to bear, and Aunt Jessica, ever more imperious, subjecting everything to the relentless penetration of her hard eye as if she feared some impending disaster which only her being in several places at once could avert.

And that was how she found me with the diary. She did not usually trouble to come up to the schoolroom, but on this particular day, sensing the wisdom of sanctuary, I had been up there for several hours and, I suppose, discovering me unaccounted for, she felt the need to find out why.

I was sitting at the secretaire with my back to the door. She walked straight in and stood in the centre of the room, uttering my name like a military command. I jumped and in a moment of foolish instinct tried to push the diary out of sight between the desk flap and my knees.

Her sharp eye caught the movement instantly.

'What are you doing? What are you trying to hide?'

'Nothing,' I said. 'Nothing, Aunt Jessica. I was just reading.'

'What are you reading?'

I hesitated.

'Well come here, child. Show it to me.'

I got clumsily to my feet, clutching the diary to me, hesitating still.

Her lips twitched impatiently. 'Show it to me.'

I held it out to her and she snatched it. For an instant she flicked through the pages, then her face went first white, then crimson with rage.

'Where did you get this?'

'It's my mother's diary.'

'I can perfectly well see that. I asked you where you got it.'

'It was with her things. She left it to me.'

She took a step towards me, waving the diary menacingly. 'And did she leave you any more of this rubbish? Well, answer me. Is there any more?'

I thought of the other two volumes hidden for safekeeping under the seat cushion of the old armchair no more than five paces from where Aunt Jessica stood and willed my eyes not to betray me by drifting in their direction.

'No,' I said. 'May I have it back now, please?'

Her face turned a shade deeper red. 'Of course you may not have it back.'

'But it's mine,' I said, feeling my voice beginning to rise.

'It's rubbish. I shall give it to Grover and ask him to see that it is burnt.'

'No! You can't! It's mine, mine!'

'Control yourself, Christabel!'

'Oh no! Please, please, no! It's mine!'

She made to turn away from me. I rushed forward and caught hold of her arm. 'Please, please!'

She brushed me away. I looked at the diary clutched firmly against her bosom and something within me snapped. I fell upon her, screaming, tearing at the black stuff of her dress, trying to prise the hard fingers apart. She fought me with her other hand, twisting my fingers back till I cried out with pain, but still I would not let go. She caught me by the mass of my hair and wrenched my head back. I jerked myself free and sank my teeth into her hand. She let out a screech of pain and anger and the diary fell onto the floor between us. I was faster but she was taller and stronger. Wrenching the diary from my grasp she pushed me away from her and ran to the door. I rushed after her and fell upon it kicking and screaming as it slammed shut. I heard the key turn in the lock and footsteps retreating down the corridor. I continued to scream and cry long after the sound had died and there was only empty silence. Then, at last exhausted, I slumped down where I stood and lay there crying quietly until I had no more tears left.

Hours seemed to have passed and dusk was gathering. I thought suddenly of the other two volumes of the diary. If the existence of the one she had found filled her so inexplicably with anger she would not take my word for it that there were no more. I knew Aunt Jessica. She would not rest until she had rooted out the others.

I went to the armchair and felt under the cushion to reassure myself. Yes, they were still there. But it was nowhere near safe enough. They would never escape a search once I had been released from my imprisonment and sent to bed. I thought of the secret drawer in the secretaire. Even Aunt Jessica knew nothing about that.

Although the diaries were not bulky, the drawer was shallow and it took a great deal of pushing and squeezing before I was finally able to release the catch and it sprang back into concealment. I knelt there for a moment, out of breath, pushing the hair from my eyes, gazing at my new hiding place with satisfaction. Then I went and sat in the armchair in darkness and waited, until Aunt Jessica eventually appeared to send me to bed. There was, she said, no point in my apologizing to her (it had not, in fact, been in my mind). Behaviour of my sort could not be forgiven on the strength of a few easily-mouthed words. My nature was at fault and, although she despaired of ever succeeding, sterner steps would be taken to correct it from now on.

So, when I was summoned after breakfast the next morning and told that I was to be sent down to the village where I would see Mr Apthorpe, the vicar, about filling the lacuna in my education occasioned by the banishment of Miss Ashe, I assumed that this was simply the first step in the process of my correction.

The housekeeper at the vicarage collected me half an hour later and I sat for the whole morning on a hard chair in Mr Apthorpe's study, listening to him stuttering and stammering about the virtues of Greek and Latin. The housekeeper fed me luncheon there, cold, fatty ham and boiled cabbage, and then I was taken, all unsuspecting, back.

To avoid Aunt Jessica's scrutiny, I rushed upstairs immediately and went straight to the schoolroom. But when I opened the door I stopped on the threshold in disbelief. For there was nothing there. Nothing at all. Not the old armchair nor the upright piano nor the rickety oilcloth-covered table, not the books, not the blackboard and easel, not the map of the world that had always hung crooked and still left a mark, not the tattered Brussels rug, not even the curtains. And not my mother's secretaire. While I had been at the vicarage every stick of furniture had been removed from the room. And with it, every trace of my poor gentle mother.

My disbelief turned suddenly to a choking anguish. I rushed downstairs again. Aunt Jessica was in the smoking room talking to Meredith.

They both looked up at me as I burst in, Meredith staring in astonishment at my wild eyes and flying hair.

'My mother!' I gasped. 'Everything in the schoolroom! All my mother's things!'

Aunt Jessica fixed me with a cold eye. 'Please pull yourself together, Christabel. Since you will take lessons from Mr Apthorpe from now on, you do not need a schoolroom.'

'You've taken all my mother's things!'

'On my instructions Grover has had the rag and bone man from the village collect all the schoolroom furniture. It wasn't good for anything. The only piece that was your mother's was that hideous old bureau. It wasn't any more worth keeping than the rest.'

I stared at her. 'But you didn't even ask me.'

She gave a tight little smile. 'My dear Christabel, before you can expect to be consulted about things you must demonstrate by your behaviour that you are worthy of it.'

I could feel myself beginning to cry and suddenly I did not want to cry in front of her and show her that she had won. I turned on my heel and ran blindly away, on down the hall and down the corridor that led to the green baize door and through and on and down the short flight of stairs that ended in the open door of the kitchen.

Mrs Wix was standing at the kitchen table cleaning a chicken.

'She's thrown away my mother!' I cried. 'She's thrown away my mother!'

'Dear Lord, Miss Christabel,' said Mrs Wix with her hands half inside the chicken. 'Whatever is the matter?'

And I said again: 'She's thrown away my mother!' And half-there Marjorie started to laugh because I wasn't making any sense. And I began to cry where I stood, in great, jerking sobs I could not hold back any more.

Half-there Marjorie stopped laughing. Mrs Wix, wiping the blood from her hands, came and put her huge arms around me, crushing my face into the starched pillow of her bosom.

'The poor motherless child,' she said. 'Well, don't stand there gawping, Marjorie. Make her some hot milk.' Then she sat me in a chair at the kitchen table and between sobs I tried to explain. But, since every time she pronounced that she was sure her

Ladyship had good reasons for doing what she did it only made me cry the harder, she finally contented herself simply with shaking her head and pouring into my milk a little of the sherry she drank while she worked, 'for medicinal purposes'.

And I, sensing that she did not understand, gradually stopped crying and sat there in silence, sipping the sticky-sweet milk and stroking the cat, until she judged I had been there too long for safety and sent me out to the kitchen garden to fetch parsley and sage for the stuffing.

It was on my way back that I came face to face with my Cousin Felix. I had taken a circuitous route to see one of the stable cats who had given birth to kittens under the laurel bush on the west side of the house, and as I rounded the corner I came suddenly upon him.

He was sitting on one of the wrought-iron chairs on the terrace with a rug over his knees, working away with a pencil and a drawing pad. He seemed to be sketching a view of the lake and the folly. He looked up as I came suddenly out of nowhere and our eyes met, so that it was too late for him to pretend he hadn't noticed me and for me to slink away. We hung for a moment suspended by the awkwardness of the encounter. And I became instantly aware that what Mrs Wix had said was true. My Cousin Felix was handsome, undeniably so.

He had that face we all have in our family, the Cavendish face, which Aunt Jessica used to say was descended from the Stuarts and which you could see in the family portraits she had brought to Monks Last after my grandparents had died: straight thin nose, high cheekbones and a mouth a little too wide to be completely in proportion. But, whereas in my Cousin Meredith it was blurred with discontent and overeating, in Aunt Jessica beaky and imperious, and in me, so I would be told later, pretty, but in an unfashionable Pre-Raphaelite way, in my Cousin Felix it had assumed all the best properties of its original: dark hair, cool grey eyes, a clear-cut firmness of feature. But yet there was something in the arrogant line of the jaw, in the patrician aloofness of it, that disconcerted and frightened me too.

I bent surreptitiously to hitch up the wrinkles in my stocking, suddenly aware of how tall and gangly I was for my age. 'I'm your Cousin Christabel,' I said.

'Yes,' he said. 'I know.' He said it almost without expression, as if the information could hold no trace of interest for him. But at least he did not use that condescending tone that most strange adults resorted to when suddenly confronted with the unwished-for fact of my presence.

'They say you were a great hero in the war,' I said.

He had an odd way of looking, as though he could see through me and beyond me, as if he had seen too many things he did not wish to see and had disciplined himself to cut them off from his plane of vision. 'Do they?' he said.

'And will it be over by Christmas?'

'Over?'

'The war. They say every year it will be over by Christmas.'

He suddenly let back his head in a long, loud laugh, a laugh that had no trace of humour anywhere in it. And I, catching a glimpse of his sketching pad, saw that he was not drawing the folly at all, but a strange conjunction of tin hats and planks of wood and arms and legs which had a monstrous disembodiment about them. And clutching tightly my bunch of herbs and gathering my skirts around me I ran the whole way back to the kitchen.

CHAPTER FOUR

The battle between Aunt Jessica and That One finally reached its natural conclusion in mid-April. Aunt Jessica would do any further nursing herself and Dr Blair was on hand to administer morphia injections should they still be needed. We saw more of my Cousin Felix after that, at mealtimes, or sketching mysteriously in the garden. At the dining table he was a strange impersonal presence, polite but withdrawn, like a guest who has never been completely put at his ease. He still had that way of looking through and beyond things which added to the feeling of his detachment. But there was something else, too, I thought, watching him covertly, something in the taut face and carefully empty eyes which suggested that his detachment was bought only by a daily effort of the will.

Aunt Jessica had a special way of talking to him, honeyed and almost flirtatious, which was reserved for no other member of the family, and which sat oddly with her harsh manner and sharp voice. Looking at the two of them, I found myself wondering whether she saw the person we saw and whether there was, or ever had been, any resemblance between the adored child of her mind's eye and the polite, impersonal stranger sitting next to her. He took it all, the constant injunctions not to tire himself, the reproving clicks of the tongue if he had overstretched himself and was evidently in pain, took it without obvious irritation. But he did not assent to it either. And sometimes I thought I could hear in the lilt of her special voice and the carefully-measured cool of his responses an undercurrent, the growing swell of two opposing tides, so that you could almost catch in Aunt Jessica's special voice a hint of desperation. I thought I agreed with Meredith. My Cousin Felix was not a natural accepter of things.

He moved more easily now but his dependence on the stick obviously frustrated him. Once when I was chasing after the stable kittens I came upon him in the disused grain store with Routledge, the blacksmith from the village, and one of the grooms, inspecting a curious construction of iron bars. I peered fascinated round the door as my Cousin Felix tested his weight on it, swung upon it until his face was creased with pain, then regained the floor and straightened himself with evident satisfaction. I would see him from a distance, too, on my way back from the Reverend Apthorpe's, limping determinedly onwards, a mile from the house, his head bare, his face set relentlessly to the wind.

And there were other things. One day a carter arrived from King's Lynn and unloaded a number of mysterious packages. Then Mrs Wix told me a week or so after that the Captain had installed himself in one of the attics with an easel and canvases and was painting furiously. 'A terrible mess, Mr Jenks said, paint everywhere and everything smelling of turpentine. And such strange pictures too, by all accounts. Not nice country scenes, like you'd expect from a gentleman like the Captain, but all reds and yellows and oranges. All fire and burning, Mr Jenks said they were. Like Hellfire.'

Of all this Aunt Jessica disapproved unremittingly. But she was also curiously powerless to stop it. One luncheon-time my Cousin Felix limped in late and seemed more forthcoming than usual. Aunt Jessica did not remark upon his lateness as she would have done had it been Meredith or I. But she leant forward, scrutinized him critically and said: 'You look tired.'

He gave her an unexpectedly open smile. 'Yes,' he said, unfurling his table napkin. 'I am tired. I walked to the village today.'

Her face tightened. 'You should have asked Blackitt to take you in the car.'

At the other end of the table, my Cousin Meredith sighed and bent himself with deep concentration upon the cold mutton.

The triumph died in my Cousin Felix's voice. 'The point,' he said, 'is that I didn't have to ask Blackitt to take me in the car.'

'But you know what Dr Blair said.'

'I have no idea, Mother. I gave up listening to doctors some months ago.'

'You won't even let him give you anything for the pain. You wilfully reject all our efforts to help you.'

'Does it help me, Mother, to be in a perpetual drugged stupor?'

'And then there's that infernal construction in the stables. I want it pulled down, I want you to stop punishing yourself like this. Yes, Dr Blair agrees there has been a small improvement. But he's also told me in no uncertain terms that if you go on like this you will simply push yourself into total collapse. Do you want to be a helpless cripple for the rest of your life?'

'No, Mother,' said my Cousin Felix very quietly. 'But if I didn't know better I might be tempted to think you wanted it.'

There was a small electric silence. My Cousin Meredith looked up from his mutton. I waited to be sent from the room, but Aunt Jessica was oblivious of me. They faced each other, she and Felix, her eyes glittering, his no longer empty of expression. For a moment I thought the unheard of was about to happen, that she was going to cry. Eventually, swallowing hard, she said: 'I realize it's simply the pain that makes you so cruel. Of course I want you to be well, my darling. But you must accept that there are limits, and learn to live with them.'

My Cousin Felix was perfectly silent. My Cousin Meredith heaved another deep sigh.

'And anyway,' she said, changing tack, 'you have no need to go to the village. I suppose you went to see that wretched man Routledge again. I don't know what you're thinking of, allowing the fellow to become so overfamiliar.'

'His son was in my company.'

'Yes, and he showed me the nice letter you wrote from hospital saying the boy had died bravely in action. You've done all that was necessary.'

'Necessary, Mother?' My Cousin Felix was suddenly very pale.

'I wish you would forget about this wretched war. There are at least six Routledge boys. One more or less can't make much difference. You're still alive. And that's what matters.'

My Cousin Felix's face was white. There was a small screech of wood against wood as he pushed back his chair. 'No, Mother. It is not what matters. What matters is that through the sheer incompetence of Meredith's politicos and our glorious generals there are acres of France and Flanders sodden with the blood of Corporal Routledge and thousands like him, shell holes slimy with the shattered bits of them, trenches stinking with their half-buried remains. That's what matters. The fact that I am still alive to remember the stench and the squalor and the utter waste of it matters not one jot! Least of all to me.'

We watched him limp from the room. There was another silence. Then my Cousin Meredith got up and went over to the sideboard. 'It seems to me,' he said, helping himself to more of the mutton, 'this blasted war has made my brother lose his sense of humour.'

Spring turned into a summer of intermittent rain. General Haig began the third Ypres offensive which would bring our army eventually to Passchendaele. Meredith, walled-up behind his *Times* at breakfast, speculated on the collapse of the coal industry if British convoys could not outwit the U-boat patrols in the North Sea. And my Cousin Felix continued to improve, so that even Aunt Jessica was forced to admit he would be well enough to go up to Cambridge in September and resume his Tripos. But the all-pervading tension in the house still grew, seeping out from beneath closed doors, swirling in the wake of half-heard conversations, spiralling into the space of silences like a fine smoke, until the air was thick with it.

Aunt Jessica abhorred Society, but in order to lure Felix away from the village and his curious pursuits in the attic she began upon a whole series of house parties. It was a good time for me. Lessons with the Reverend Apthorpe had been discontinued, though whether finally because of my incompetence at Greek and Latin, or because of the interesting trick I had perfected, with the aid of a piece of broken mirrored glass found in the stables, of deflecting the sun that shone in through his study window directly into his eyes, I never absolutely discovered. It was now decided that in September I should be sent away to a boarding school in the south of England. I viewed the prospect with mixed feelings: on the one hand, what little description of the institution I had been given made it sound like a prison where discipline and moral rectitude were all; but, on the other, I should be out of Aunt Jessica's eye. Meanwhile I experienced a curious freedom. With the house so full and busy, there was little time to monitor my comings and goings. And on days when there were picnics or walks to the marshes I had the house to myself and could play the piano in the drawing room gloriously, noisily, for hours on end.

It was on one of those days at the beginning of September, a week before I was due to be packed off to school and under a month before Felix was to go up to Cambridge, that I knew the storm which had been gathering over us would break.

The men were off shooting in Kite's Wood, the women played tennis and Aunt Jessica discussed the War Fund Bazaar at Mr Apthorpe's, and I was in the drawing room struggling with a Chopin *ballade* when I was suddenly uncomfortably conscious of someone else in the room.

My Cousin Felix, in white flannels, was standing in the doorway, leaning on his stick. My hands went hastily to close the piano lid, but he shook his head and, coming into the room, stretched out on a chaise longue near the piano and lit a cigarette.

I was all at once acutely nervous. I had not played in front of anyone since Miss Ashe. I began the piece again, willing my fingers not to stumble over the notes. And then a strange thing happened. I became aware of him listening. I had such a vivid sense of it, of the notes forming, clear and abstract, in someone else's mind, that I began to do what I had never been able to before, to forget about the mechanical activity of my fingers and my feet on the pedals and to hear for myself the liquid, perfect abstraction of the music. And in the flow of it, in the measured gentleness of its *pianissimos*, in the cascading fall and ripple of the treble and the thunder of the base, it was as if the whole room were caught up, furniture, rugs, chandelier, the grandfather clock ticking in the corner, Felix lying on the chaise, my hands playing, caught up and distilled until there was only that fine pure abstraction and the two of us listening, and a deep, mysterious peace.

I came to the end and let the last chord fade, ringing, away. There was a profound silence into which fell only the sound of the clock and the small distinct plop of a peony petal from the vase near the piano landing on the Aubusson rug. I glanced round. He did not move or look at me. I turned to the Military Polonaise, which I could play tolerably well, and began again. Almost simultaneously, or so it seemed, there was a clatter and a shriek of laughter outside in the hall, and the house guests began filtering in for tea. I carried on playing, but my fingers were leaden and mechanical now, struggling against a rising buzz of conversation.

I heard a man saying: 'So I told the blighter: "Fifteen years I've been a member of this club and you refuse to serve me butter. I don't care if there's a war on. You bring me some butter sharpish. Or you'll find out what's what."'

I stumbled and stopped. Aunt Jessica was sitting beside Felix on the chaise longue. They were turned to each other, profile to profile, heads raised, and in that juxtaposition of family similarities, proud features, hard jaws, there was such a sense of opposition that I almost caught my breath. It was Aunt Jessica who looked away first.

'That's quite enough of that noise, Christabel,' she said. 'Go and brush your hair and wash your hands for tea.'

The break came the next day. The house party had dispersed in the morning, and in the afternoon I had taken the Shelley from the library and gone in search of my favourite reading spot, under the apple tree next to the water butt in the walled kitchen garden. Propped against its trunk in the sun, I was almost asleep when I heard the sound of voices from the other end of the garden.

Peering round the water butt I saw Aunt Jessica and my Cousin Felix, a tall black figure and a tall white one, walking down the grassy aisle between the blackcurrant bushes and the strawberry bed. He had his jacket slung over one shoulder, she carried the rug and the small secateurs she used for dead-heading the roses. At first, because her voice was higher and travelled further, I could only make out distinctly her part of the conversation.

'Talk? Yes, of course we must talk. You've no idea, my darling, how all these months I've prayed for you to say that. We used to be such good friends, you and I, before you went away.' Here she made a little movement as if wanting to link her arm with his, but the way he was carrying his jacket prevented her. 'You can't imagine how lonely it's been, just with Meredith and that wretched child. I've so longed for you to get this whole miserable business of the war out of your head. The war's over for you. Now we can forget it and start again as we were.'

He said something which I still could not quite hear.

She laughed. 'Well, of course not precisely the same. We have so many plans to make about what happens when you come down from Cambridge.'

They had arrived at the bottom of the strawberry beds a few yards from the water butt where the central path of the kitchen garden intersected theirs and where there was a weatherbeaten wooden bench on which Magnus used to sit occasionally and brood. They sat on it now, oblivious of my presence. With the water butt between me and the bench I could not see them but I could hear both of them clearly.

'That's why I needed to talk to you,' he said. 'I have decided not to go back to Cambridge.'

There was a small pause in which she seemed to catch her breath. Then she said: 'Oh, my dear, I'm so relieved and glad!' I had never heard Aunt Jessica's voice express such positive pleasure. 'There's so much to be done here. Meredith simply can't manage the estate, he's as hopeless as his father. When I think of the death duties and the government piling taxes upon us because of the war, I'm sometimes amazed we still have two pennies to rub together. But with you here—'

'Mother. Don't misunderstand me.'

Her voice changed. 'Misunderstand?'

'I know I've hurt you over the last few months.' His voice was very low and level. 'I would try to avoid hurting you again if I could.'

She gave a little tight laugh. 'Oh, my darling, you could never hurt me. You know you are the only thing I live for. If you'd died out there in No Man's Land I think I would have died too. All the terrible endless waiting, nearly three years of it, waiting, praying, dreading the telegram. I would have sacrificed a thousand Arthurs or Merediths to keep you safe, I would have given my own life—'

'Mother,' he said quietly. 'Please.'

She was suddenly angry. 'Well, if you're not going to Cambridge and you're not staying here, what do you intend to do with yourself?'

'I think I shall probably go abroad.'

'And leave your family, leave me, leave everyone who loves you? Oh, dear God, why?'

'Because I very badly need to be alone.' He paused. 'I think I've changed somehow. The war's altered so many things.'

'Nothing has changed here.'

'I know, Mother,' he said softly. 'And I am suffocating with it.'

There was a pause. Then her voice came back, stripped of the last traces of honey, an angry growl. 'I don't know how you could be so cruel! You never wrote, you never came home on leave, and now this!'

'I didn't write,' he said, and now I could hear an undertow of anger in his voice too, 'because I had nothing to write about.'

'But I wrote to you. Every week.'

'Yes, screeds of it. Backbiting about my father, complaints about Meredith. Dear God, Mother, there was enough ugliness where I was without increasing the total.'

'You never thought how I suffered. Even when Arthur died you didn't come home.'

His voice was taut with the effort of control. 'We were at the front, Mother. There was a man in my company whose three-year-old daughter was dying. He hadn't had leave for two years. I could hardly refuse him and then take leave myself. Besides, my father was dead. There was no way left for me to show him the respect I'd failed to show him while he was alive.'

'Because you loved me more? Because I couldn't help loving you more than him?'

'Is that love, Mother? I think what frightens me most is that I have no idea any longer what love is.'

There was another pause in which she appeared to marshal her forces. When she came back her voice was all sweetness again. 'Let's not quarrel, my darling. All of this is simply because you've been so ill. Tomorrow you'll feel quite differently about it. And besides, you're nowhere near well enough to go away anywhere.'

'Mother, I am perfectly well enough.'

'When you're still in so much pain all the time? Come, my darling, let's not talk about it any more.'

He rose to his feet. 'You're right, Mother. If we can't talk sensibly about it, then let's not talk at all. I need to go. And I will go. That's all there is to be said.'

He had turned in the direction of the door that led from the kitchen garden to the terrace. She followed after him, her body suddenly hunched, her hand outstretched to catch his arm.

'Oh no, no, my God, no!' I heard her cry, in a voice quite unlike Aunt Jessica's. 'If you could only understand. If you could only know all the suffering, if one day I could tell you. Oh, please God, my darling Felix, don't leave me, don't leave me now!'

Her voice drifted for a moment on the breeze, then died as she disappeared after him through the garden door.

My Cousin Felix did not appear at tea, nor had he arrived in the dining room for dinner by the time Aunt Jessica had found my fingernails were dirty and sent me up to bed. But she herself had so completely resumed her usual air of harsh command that it was impossible to imagine her capable of that lost, pleading voice I had heard in the garden.

However, when I came down to breakfast the next morning it was to a different scene. My Cousin Meredith was hunched behind his usual defensive wall of newspaper, but Aunt Jessica was pacing up and down the dining room with an air almost of frenzy. She did not even notice me.

'He said nothing. Oh, he mentioned yesterday he wanted to go. But not like this. Not without saying anything. I suppose he said nothing to you?'

Meredith withdrew from *The Times* for a moment. 'Dash it, Mother, is that likely?'

'Blackitt says he caught the seven o'clock train. He drove him to the station. And you had no idea?'

'I am not, as they say, my brother's keeper.'

'Just to go. Not even to say goodbye. I don't think I can bear it!' And suddenly tears she had not shed at my mother's funeral nor even when my Uncle Arthur had died began spurting down her face.

Meredith laid aside his *Times* with a deep sigh. 'Mother, you really should know Felix by now. He's the only person I've ever met who's as obstinate and self-willed as you are.'

Aunt Jessica gave a cross between a sob and a snort and rushed from the room.

It was only later I discovered from Mrs Wix that my Cousin Felix had left that morning to go to Paris and become an artist.

CHAPTER FIVE

Diary of Adele Ward. Volume the Second.
Albemarle Street, London.

19th September, 1892.

Oh, was ever anyone so wretchedly miserable! I had thought by now to have begun to write that after one night under this roof we should be embarked for Switzerland – I longed to see the mountains and the Alpine chalets, which they say are for all the world like cuckoo clocks. But M is gone. He has been gone for one whole day and two nights now. And it is all my fault.

I did endeavour to heed Mamma when, with many modest blushes of her own, she gently prepared me for my duty. I understand that a woman, while she may not expect gratification for herself, must submit unselfishly to her husband. And I did submit at first to all his kisses though, since he had sat up long with the port, his breath, usually so sweet, was rank and his lips ungentle. But then a fever seemed to come upon him so that his face no longer shone with the noble beauty of my own true knight, but was red and coarse and savage; so that his breathing came in fits and starts and his fingers bruised my flesh; so that his hands, tearing at my nightgown, abandoning all respect for my modesty, sought to touch improper parts of my body. Whereupon I began in horror to struggle and to cry out and he hit me across the face and I struggled all the more till, pushing him backwards, for he was unsteady with the liquor he had drunk, I was able to tear myself free and rush for the sanctuary of the dressing room, slamming the door fast and locking it.

Oh, can this be anything but some terrible dream from which I shall presently awake? I long so for my own dear M, whose voice is tender and whose touch is gentle. I know it can only be womanly weakness in me that has changed him so, and I am resolved, when he returns, to throw myself upon his mercy and beg his forgiveness as a loving wife should. When he returns? Oh, should I not say, if . . . ?

20th September, 1892.

M came in just before teatime saying he had spent the two days of his absence at his club and, though his face was pale and there were dark circles under his eyes, he seemed once again the M I worship and adore. On seeing him, I could not restrain my tears and fell at his feet as I had resolved to do, imploring him to have patience with me. Yet he only stepped aside, very cold, remarking that he wished he had known I was neurasthenic before he married me. Observing, however, that this only made me weep the more, he became in a while more gentle, and patted my hair and told me I was a silly child and must stop crying, and that perhaps he should make greater allowance for me since I was after all very young and had had only a country upbringing. And so, after a time, our old loving tenderness seemed to spring up between us again and, fondling my hair, he kissed me lightly on the lips, which made me flinch a little at first, though he was kind enough not to observe upon it.

So now we are to have a <u>fresh beginning</u>. We shall go to Switzerland as we had planned and nothing shall ever again mar the sweetness of our love. We have dined together and been very gay all evening, and if it was only haddock and cold mutton, for I have not quite mastered the art of instructing Cook yet, he made no remark upon it. Rather, he plied me with a <u>great deal</u> more champagne than is good for me and told me again and again how he adored me until I was dizzy with it (though he did tend towards the conclusion of the evening to talk about racing and horses somewhat too, as I have noticed he is in the habit of doing when he has drunk wine, but it is my <u>duty</u> as his wife to make his interests mine, not always selfishly to be desiring to hear him sing my praises).

Duty. Did Mamma ever fail in her duty to Papa, and have they not enjoyed many years of blissful happiness together? As I sit here writing at the little walnut secretary in my room while M lingers downstairs over the port, I am resolved to fulfil the wifely duty my love urges upon me, <u>whatever the cost</u>. And if my heart thumps wildly as I listen for his footfall on the stair, and if there is perhaps in its movement a small tremor of fear, I tell myself it is only a foolish woman's weakness.

21st September, 1892.

Merciful Heaven, is it possible for one man to be two people, as with Mr Stevenson's Dr Jekyll and Mr Hyde? Or is this the true meaning behind Ouida's thrilling descriptions, this the reality which their languor, their ecstasy, their sublime oblivion, seek to disguise? It cannot be this for which Lucille swoons in the arms of Lord Strathmore, for which Ariadne pines in madness for Hilarion.

I could have borne anything had he not struck me as he did the last time, struck me, when I screamed, about the face again and again, not heeding my cries, rather driven by them to wilder excesses of his vile passion, swearing that I could go to the d——l before I unmanned him. At length, although my struggles served to protect me from the unspeakable extremes of his lust, the frenzy of it seemed to reach some conclusion, for he gave vent to a foul expletive and I felt his body grow heavy upon me. Using all the force I could muster, I wrenched myself free and fled again to the dressing room. But this time he was not to be resisted, this time I saw that he would force the lock and drag me out, despite my sobs and prayers for mercy. I had just sufficient strength remaining to me to push a small chest across the door where, falling upon it in a dead faint, I added my own weight to render it an effective obstruction.

This morning, when I at last ventured out, he was gone from the house. I am keeping to my room to conceal the sight of my red eyes and bruised face from the servants. Though I have bolted my door I fear, should he come back, this will afford me little protection from his insensate passion. I have no one to turn to, for a newly-married woman is not expected to pay calls for a month after her wedding, and besides I have no friends in London, only acquaintances; even dear Rose is no longer with me, for M declared his wife should have nothing less than a French maid, although she is insubordinate and spears my scalp with pins when she is dressing my hair. Oh, how I long for Mamma and darling Papa. I am alone and utterly helpless, and despair what will become of me. For I still have ringing in my ears M's last words before I fainted.

'D—n you to H—l! At least the old General's money enables me to go to Cremorne and buy myself a wh—re!'

PART TWO

THE WHISPER IN DEATH'S ROOM

CHAPTER SIX

'Oh, Christie,' said Lady Dilly Tollemache, arms and legs flailing wildly like a winged bird earthbound, 'I shall never get the hang of this if I'm the last unmarried girl left in the whole of London!'

I was laughing too much to go on winding the gramophone. It groaned to a stop, spitting out its needle. Dilly came to earth with it, puffing and heaving.

'It's all very well,' she said indignantly, 'for you to find it so amusing. You know you dance divinely.'

'Oh, don't be absurd, Dillo,' I said, wiping away a tear. 'Have you watched me waltzing? You know I was the tallest at school and always had to be the man at dancing class. Well, now I seize all my partners forcefully about the waist and guide them round the floor.'

Dilly giggled. 'That must disconcert them.'

'I should say it does. And if I'm lucky they don't ask me again.'

'Men!' said Dilly, with a trace of venom. 'Oh well, I suppose I'd better have another go.'

'Try it with the back of a chair this time,' I said. 'Then you'll at least get the feet right.'

'And you're not to let the gramophone run down, just because your arm gets tired. It's even more difficult at six different speeds.'

I put in another needle and we tried again. But this time two minutes of Dilly's heaving bottom and flying legs were enough to reduce us both to helpless laughter.

'It's no good!' she said, flopping into a chair. 'I'll never do the Missouri Walk like Dolly. Or the Vampire, or the Jog Trot, or the Elfreda. I'm just not built for it.'

Dolly was Dilly's elder sister, willowy where Dilly was plump, pale where Dilly was inclined to be rosy, and with the sort of deep cornflower-blue eyes that could melt a man at a hundred yards. Dolly was a year older, had already come out, and represented to both of us the acme of sophistication.

'Anyway,' continued Dilly, having paused to reflect, 'I'm not sure why I bother. After all, Crikey was born with two left feet.

He completely destroyed those new pink satin pumps of mine last night. They look as if I'd gone hunting in them.'

Crikey was actually the Hon. Gilbert Renton, the youngest son of Lord Strathclyde. But, because it was his usual response to everything from the newest jazz to the trouble in Turkey, we had taken to calling him Crikey.

'Archie's just as bad,' I said. 'And he sticks his tongue out when he's concentrating.'

Dilly giggled. 'Oh dear, Christie, what's to become of us? Dolly says we're very lucky, when you think how few eligible young men there are because of everyone being killed in the war. She says we're fortunate to find any partners at all.'

'I'm sure I shouldn't care,' I said, 'if I didn't.'

'Oh, but that's dotty, Christie. Whatever would you do if you didn't get married?'

'Study music. That's all I've ever wanted to do.'

Dilly pondered this for a moment. 'I must say I've never understood why your aunt wouldn't let you go in for that scholarship Miss Lassiter suggested.'

I shrugged my shoulders. 'She said it was a waste of time.' I had long since stopped speculating on Aunt Jessica's motives.

'Dolly says you're bound to marry Archie, even if he is frighfully *nouveau*. She says your aunt will make you, because Archie's father is so beastly rich and bound to get Lloyd George to sell him a peerage and, what with you having absolutely nothing, it's really a lot more than you could reasonably expect.'

I laughed. 'I wouldn't marry Archie Cadwallander,' I said, 'if he was the last man on earth.'

Dilly giggled. 'He is perfectly awful, isn't he? Though I'm not sure he's quite as bad as Crikey.'

'Archie has white eyelashes,' I said, 'like a pig.'

'Crikey squints.'

'Archie can only talk about politics.'

'Crikey can't talk about anything. Unless it's cricket.'

'Archie's quite impossible after a few glasses of champagne.'

'Crikey's insensible.'

We both sighed deeply.

'Oh, Christie,' said Dilly, 'aren't men the absolute end?'

'The lower depths, Dillo.'

'Too utterly ghastly.'

'Positively grim.'

Dilly heaved another, even deeper sigh. 'I wonder what it feels like,' she said wistfully, 'to be in love.'

Dilly was, and still is, my best friend, and the principal reason why my four years at St Monica's (motto: Duty before Pleasure) had not been an unrelieved nightmare of ragging, black marks and dressing-downs from the Head. Both Dolly and Dilly had been at St Monica's, but Dolly had been Chief Monitor, a leading light in the Debating Society and the repository of all the school's hopes at hockey and cricket. Dilly and I, on the other hand, as Dolly would frequently tell us, were a complete let-down to the side and a positive danger to school morale. Recognizing ourselves as kindred spirits from my first month, we united in our incompetence at games, our failure at exams, our love of practical jokes and our total inability not to get caught in the act of playing them. And if anyone was insensitive enough to remark upon Dilly's predilection for chocolate or the fact that I never seemed to stop growing, then whoever was not under attack at the time would make sure the aggressor got short shrift.

It always surprised me that people could not see Dilly was pretty. Oh, of course she was not like Dolly. But then did prettiness consist only in blonde curls, carefully veiled eyes and calculatedly pouting lips? Dilly's face was all softness, and when she smiled it was with such an embracing generosity that you almost missed the glint of mischief in her eyes. She was, I think, since the death of my mother, the first person I had ever completely trusted. Yes, if it had not been for Dilly, and Miss Lassiter, the music mistress, who would connive wickedly to get me excused from all kinds of irksome duties in order that I should have extra piano lessons, my introduction to the noble aims and high ideals of St Monica's would have been much more difficult to bear.

So, gradually, it came about that I spent most of my time with Dilly. Aunt Jessica readily assented to my staying with her at Critchley Castle for the school holidays and, when Dilly's mother, the Countess of Mountalban, suggested that once the two of us had left school I should join the Mountalbans in London for the Season and be presented, it was one of the few agreeable plans she did not oppose, since the possibilities inherent in it, of marrying me off and out of the de Lisle family once and for all, were obvious.

Accordingly, there we were, Dilly and I in 1922, debutantes. We had taken in the Private View at the Royal Academy and even looked at some of the pictures, we had yawned through Ibsen at the Old Vic and longed for revue at the Comedy, we had favoured the Guards Enclosure at Ascot with our most delectable hats and numerous garden parties with our insatiable capacity for strawberries and cream. We had longed to take our shoes off at cocktail parties and fought to keep them on at coming-out balls. We had seen three very drunk young men with chamber pots on their heads trying to swing from a chandelier, and a tall woman in weird robes who had been something to do with Mme Blavatsky levitate herself a full six inches off the ground as an afterdinner entertainment; and once at a nightclub, a very, very long way away, we thought we had seen the Prince of Wales.

And after countless fittings at Mme Fifirella's gown shop, after deportment lessons at Mme Vacani's Dancing Academy, court curtseying in regimented order with tablecloths for trains, we had survived the moment of our Court Drawing Room, survived it although Dilly said the two of us, one so short and plump and the other so tall and thin, looked, in our long white gowns, our trains the regulation two and a half yards from the shoulder and our veils, crowned with the uniform three ostrich plumes, too, too absurd to be true. And yet, despite the long wait in the jam of sleek motorcars in the Mall, despite the anxiety that the lords-in-waiting at the entrance to the Throne Room would pole out our trains with their ivory poles in quite the wrong place, despite the ordeal of the curtsey and the necessity of walking out backwards without hitching anything up, we had managed to come through without disaster, and Dilly didn't actually giggle, although she swore she went purple trying not to, and I didn't put my heel through my train until just after I'd backed out into the anteroom. And afterwards there was the buffet supper with a string orchestra playing Gilbert and Sullivan, and our pictures taken by Hoppé, and three hundred other girls who had suffered their feet to be trampled on night after night too, and had listened to men who talked only about cricket and had had strawberry juice spilt down their favourite afternoon frock.

So now, although our coming-out ball at Critchley Castle was still a few weeks off, we were out in Society in earnest. And we had somehow acquired Crikey and Archie Cadwallander along the way.

Crikey had risen up like a miasma at a charity ball, had been introduced and, apparently finding no way of extricating himself from the stilted conversation that ensued, had been lingering in

Dilly's wake ever since. Archie Cadwallander was less of an accident. My Cousin Meredith had given up the unequal struggle with Aunt Jessica over the management of the Norfolk estate, had consigned it to the care of an agent, married, and become a Conservative MP. Archie Cadwallander's father was a steel magnate and by all accounts a man of considerable influence in Meredith's northern constituency, and Archie, although he was supposed to be up at Oxford, had attached himself to Meredith and was frequently to be found in the London house 'giving old Meredith a hand with constituency business, don't y'know'. Apart from the occasional stiff family dinner, I did not see a great deal of Meredith, despite his now being in London much of the year – his wife, Sybil, a sharp, diamond-hard woman from a good Conservative family who might have been pretty were her mouth not set in a permanent downward curve, had modelled her management of Meredith on Aunt Jessica's example and had absorbed as part of the lesson a thorough dislike of me. So I was unable to tell whose inspiration, Meredith's, Sybil's or Aunt Jessica's, long-distance from Norfolk (my aunt loathed London and never came down if she could help it), had put the idea into Archie Cadwallander's head. But one thing, alas, was certain. There it was, an *ideé fixe*, that I was the only girl in the world for him and that, if he clung to my side, limpet-like, despite Dilly's giggling and my evident lack of enthusiasm, I should inevitably come to this conviction too, as if I had absorbed it by osmosis.

I felt sorry for Archie, in a way. It was not his fault that we had nothing to say to each other, or that I overtopped him by three inches in my stockinged feet. While I was anxious to shake him off, I didn't actively wish to be unkind to him. My heart would sink whenever conversation languished into a series of meaningful pauses, and I would start chattering madly, about anything, everything that came into my head, for fear that the strangled silence presaged the embarrassment of a proposal. His periods of absence up at Oxford brought a welcome respite. But these were becoming increasingly fewer.

Tonight, for instance, Dilly and I, in handkerchief-skirted pastel silk chiffon, our lips brave with scarlet lipstick, our faces white masks of rice powder, were to launch our sophisticated new selves on a supper party at the Cunningham-Cowpers' and afterwards go on for dancing at the '43'. And along with the inevitable Crikey, Archie, who should by rights have been sipping sherry in some peaceful Oxford quad, was due to accompany us.

'Oh, I do wish I were in love!' said Dilly, coming out of her romantic reverie. 'Dolly is. Hopelessly, passionately, so she says.'

'Who is it this week?' I said. 'Not that appalling American?'

Dilly laughed. 'Oh no. She wasn't in love with him. Or any of the others.'

'But she was engaged to Ralph Buchanan.'

'And to that awful man with the laugh like a horse whose hair oil smelt of friar's balsam.'

'And to Lord Bathgate.'

'Yes,' said Dilly impatiently, 'but that's different. Dolly doesn't usually fall in love with men. She sort of picks them up and puts them down again, like a cat does mice. But this is the real thing. She's absolutely certain.'

'How does she know?'

'You get a kind of churning feeling inside, apparently.' Dilly clutched her stomach as if anticipating it. 'She says it's absolutely divinely wonderful.'

'Well, go on,' I said. 'Who is he?'

'She says he's dark and very tall, and madly handsome. With eyes like cold steel.'

'Yes, but what's his name?'

'That's just it,' said Dilly. 'That's what makes it all so romantic. She doesn't know.'

'Oh really, Dillo!' Recalling Dolly's power of searching out from any situation what she required of it and extracting it piecemeal like a whelk from its shell, I found this hard to believe.

'She's never even spoken to him,' said Dilly. 'She was in the Kit-Kat Club two nights ago and she dropped her handbag, and he picked it up for her.'

'And she felt this churning feeling?'

'Instantly, she said. And when she got back to her table and asked the people she was with, they didn't know him either. Isn't it too, too mysteriously romantic?'

'But he could have been anyone,' I said. 'He could have been a waiter.'

'No. Dolly says he was definitely someone.'

'But suppose he's someone your mother doesn't approve of?'

'Oooh, Christie,' said Dilly delightedly. 'Wouldn't that be fun!'

We both considered the fun of it for some moments. Then Dilly said, apropos of nothing: 'Do you know, Crikey kissed me last night.'

'Oh,' I said, with interest. 'What was it like?'

'All wet and slithery. Like a fish.'

Sighing, we both fell into contemplation again.

There having been a temporary lull in the dancing, a fat man and two negro girls in glittering dresses had joined the '43' orchestra and were singing 'Dapper Dan from Dear Old Dixie Land'. The American was attempting to look deep into Dolly's eyes, while she stared straight ahead of her, blowing out little bored clouds of smoke culminating in a perfect smoke ring. A desultory conversation was drifting round the table, while Archie talked to Crikey across me and Dilly and I exchanged despairing faces. Then, suddenly, I felt the American stiffen beside me. I looked across at Dolly. Her eyes were no longer blank, but concentrated with great intensity towards the door.

A strangely assorted group of people was drifting in, amidst something of a stir. Waiters bowed, chairs were hurriedly drawn back, and for a moment most eyes in the room were riveted on them. There was only one woman amongst them, a tall sleek snake of a woman with oddly slanted dark eyes set in a dramatically pale face to which only the mouth gave colour. She shimmered in, a torch of flame georgette, looking, with regal indifference, neither to the left nor the right of her. Behind her pranced a little man, wiry and agile as a monkey, surrounded by a deferential retinue of four or five beautiful boys. And, with his hand touching the woman's elbow in a gesture both negligent and proprietorial, came a tall dark man, younger than his companion, perhaps by six or seven years, elegantly dressed and strikingly handsome, matching her air of royal command with a languid detachment that seemed to take up the room for an instant with all of us in it, then casually let it fall again, finding it devoid of interest.

It was on the tall man that Dolly's eyes were focused so intently.

'Who are they?' someone asked.

'Why, that's Anna Rostova,' said the American, surprisingly. 'She's over here to dance with the Tarantin Ballet.'

'Anna who?' said Archie.

'Anna Rostova, the prima ballerina.' The American laughed. 'I didn't think there was anyone alive who hadn't heard of Rostova. Or the Tarantin Ballet, come to that. They're the rage of Paris. I saw them in New York last spring and everyone went wild for them.'

'They're positively the newest thing,' said Maisie Cunningham-Cowper. 'Quite divinely avant-garde.'

'Ballet!' said Archie with some disgust. 'Bunch of effeminate blighters jumping up and down in woolly combinations. I'd rather have Bea Lillie, don't y'know.'

The singers had gone, and Mme Rostova and the tall man had risen to dance, although there was no one else on the floor. They moved easily together, without talking, as if they had been long accustomed to it. And in their faces, in her Oriental mask and in his cool patrician profile, there was a blackness as though separately, independently, they existed somewhere far beyond the clatter of waiters and popping of champagne corks, somewhere an infinite space was filled only with the searing wail of the solo saxophone playing the Blues. They made, despite the disparity in their ages, a handsome couple. And yet there was about them, too, I thought, the thrill of the demimonde, the whisper of exotic and extravagant lives flourishing darkly in the hothouse decadence of the hours after midnight, that spice of Bohemianism which one went to the '43' precisely in the hope of savouring. He danced well, complementing the woman's easy grace. And in none of his movements was there now the slightest trace of a limp.

'Who are the others?' Maisie Cunningham-Cowper was asking. 'Who's the man dancing with Rostova?'

'Oh, I can't say,' replied the American. 'But I guess the little guy must be Vladimir Tarantin himself. The company's here rehearsing for their London season. They say they've got works in the repertoire that have never been performed outside Paris before—'

'Oh, don't be so boring, darling!' Dolly said, standing up, her hand in his but her eyes on the dance floor. 'I want to dance.'

Dilly and I stared after the hauteur of Dolly's retreating back. Then Dilly glanced again at Rostova and her partner.

'That's him,' she stage-whispered across Archie. 'That must be him! Dolly's divinely mysterious man!'

I sighed. 'Alas, no mystery, Dillo. That's my Cousin Felix. He's by way of being my family's black sheep.'

CHAPTER SEVEN

'He doesn't look like an artist,' said Dilly a week later at a cocktail party. 'I've always imagined artists to be scruffy little men with paint in their hair.'

'Oh do stop staring at him, Dillo,' I said irritably. 'He's bound to notice soon.'

'Dora Chantry danced with someone the other night who said he's an Expressionist. Does that mean he paints pictures of naked women?'

'A great many artists,' I said, 'have painted pictures of naked women.'

'Constable didn't,' objected Dilly. 'Or Gainsborough. Still, I supposed if he's a really advanced artist one wouldn't be able to tell if they were naked women anyway. Have you seen any of his pictures?'

I shook my head.

'I wonder what they're like.'

I remembered Mrs Wix and laughed. 'Hellfire,' I said.

Dilly rolled her eyes. 'Gosh!' she said. 'How divine! Oh I do wish you'd introduce yourself to him, Christie. He is a close relative, after all.'

'But I don't know him, Dillo. I've only ever spoken to him once.'

'You said he was at Monks Last the whole of that summer.'

'Well yes, he was there. But in another way he wasn't. If you see what I mean.'

Dilly's tongue clicked against her teeth. 'Sometimes, Christie, I do think your family is most peculiar. Anyway, he must know who you are.'

'I don't see why. I was eleven when he went away. I hope I've changed a little since then. I don't suppose he even recognizes me.'

This last was certainly true, for he chanced to look round a moment later and met our eyes. He held mine for a second before I glanced away and, whereas there was perhaps a trace of puzzlement on his face as to why we should find him such a focus of attention, there was not a glimmer of recognition. I remembered the way his eyes had seemed to edit inimical detail out of his field of vision and imagined they would still be just as carefully empty. And there was, besides, a gloss about him now, I thought, continuing to watch him covertly as, caught by the Dowager Duchess of Rosslair's inquisitorial lorgnette, he deflected its glint with that cool, impersonal politeness of his – charming, or yet perhaps too distant for charm: a mica-bright polish which suggested that whatever lay behind the eyes had long ago been closed away fast and sealed over with an impermeable shell.

'Anyway,' said Dilly, 'I think you're a horrid spoilsport. You have it in your power to solve the whole beastly business of your family feud and us not being able to invite him to our coming-out, and you won't use it. At this rate how is Dolly ever going to reduce him to a heap of quivering jelly?'

I sighed. Since that night at the '43' I had come to regret admitting my relationship with Felix de Lisle. I could not comprehend how someone who had been in Paris for five years and to whose existence we had all that time remained happily oblivious could now occupy such a central position in our lives. It was true that his name had started appearing in the Society columns, usually linked with Mme Rostova's. And he did seem to be highly thought of as a painter amongst those who prided themselves on an understanding of the avant-garde. Indeed he was to have an exhibition at the Hayman Gallery towards the end of the Season and everybody who was anybody, according to Dilly, was going to the private view. But Dolly's interest in him and Dilly's interest in Dolly's interest seemed now to take up the greater part of our conversation.

Dolly, who when she wanted something had the sort of determination that wins lost wars and sends men willingly to death in impossible crusades, had that evening managed an introduction through the unfortunate American, who transpired to know someone who knew Tarantin and thus knew Felix vaguely – a kindness for which Dolly rewarded him by promptly dropping him flat. But surprisingly she was not yet making much headway. Oh, her eyes would grow round and hard like sapphires when she entered a room, as if by sheer concentration she could extract my Cousin Felix from the crowd and compel him, mesmerized, over to her; by careful manoeuvring she had trapped him a couple of times in passing conversation and once he had even danced with her: but the presence of Mme Rostova on his arm at those fashionable houses where the admission of such a personage would add a frisson of daring and sophistication to the gathering raised a considerable obstacle. It seemed that Dolly would have to hold her forces in reserve for our coming-out dance, to which Mme Rostova was positively not invited. And then the intelligence came that Sybil and Meredith deemed it unsuitable, in view of his rupture with the family, that Felix's name should appear on the guest list.

Dilly's frustration knew no bounds. It was bad enough that I, though a blood relation of this new and tantalizing addition to the ranks of Society's eligible men, could furnish no worthwhile gossip about him. And now, just at the moment when by claiming our kinship I could throw myself into the breach and help the course of true love run smooth, I was proving in all respects a broken reed. But alas, though I was sorry for Dolly, I was secretly by no means as certain as Dilly that her sister's jelly-rendering powers would work on my Cousin Felix. I could not see him wandering submissively after Dolly with her wrap or sitting alone at nightclub tables while Dolly enjoyed herself elsewhere, as the American and Ralph Buchanan had been wont to do. And besides I could not envisage how, whatever I did, I could overcome a veto that carried the combined force of Sybil's and Aunt Jessica's disapproval.

'But it's your coming-out, not your beastly family's,' Dilly would say impatiently. 'You could invite him personally. Then Sir Meredith and the awful Sybil could go and whistle.'

'But I've explained, Dillo, I really don't know him.'

Then Dilly would sigh. 'Christie, this isn't in the least bit like you. He is your cousin when all's said and done. Anyone would think you were frightened of him.'

'Of course I'm not.'

'Well then, it's all too, too simple. You act as the dove wafting the jolly old olive branch amongst your potty family. Then Mumsie can send out our invitation and he'll have to invite us to his terribly exclusive private view to see his divine pictures of Hellfire.'

I was beginning thoroughly to dislike my Cousin Felix. I resented the way his mere existence had created in my life such unlooked-for complications. It was not, I told myself, that I was frightened of him, for that would be absurd. But I did feel a very natural embarrassment at the thought of thrusting myself upon a complete stranger and making claims upon a familiarity that might exist in blood but had no foundation in reality. And, besides, my Cousin Felix was a de Lisle. I had determined that when I could grasp my independence I would steer a wide berth from the de Lisles, and that meant keeping away from the de Lisles I did not know just as much as from the ones I did. Apart from that, my time was now almost as thoroughly taken up with avoiding my Cousin Felix as it was with trying to escape Archie, so that sometimes I could feel my whole body tensed, reflexes tuned to dart through doorways or vanish behind pillars at the sight of an unwelcome back or a face in the crowd.

Strangely, it was through Archie that I finally extricated myself from my predicament. He had muttered something about Moral Tutors two weeks before and had vanished abruptly to Oxford. But one afternoon just after tea, when Dilly and I were recouping our strength for the evening's entertainment, he reappeared at the Mountalbans' quite unexpectedly.

He looked, I thought, a less buoyant, devil-may-care Archie than usual.

'What's the matter, Archie?' I said. 'You haven't had a smash in your new motor?'

He shook his head. 'Got sent down, old girl.'

'Oh, Archie,' I said.

'Going to be round and about all the time now. In town, I mean. Thought you'd like to know.'

'That's sweet of you, Archie,' I said, as sympathetically as I could.

'The guv'nor wanted me to go back North and learn to run the firm, don't y'know. But your Cousin Meredith's offered to take me on as his secretary for a bit. Decent chap, Meredith.'

'Yes,' I said. 'That is kind of him.'

Archie's face had gradually suffused with crimson, right to the tips of his ears. He swallowed hard. 'Jolly decent,' he said.

I suddenly had again the awful presentiment that he was about to propose. 'But what happened, Archie?' I asked quickly. 'Why did you get sent down? You didn't plough your exams?'

'Yes,' he said. 'But it wasn't that. Spot of bother, don't y'know.'

'Bother?'

Archie's round pink and white face had not yet had time to acquire the lines and wrinkles that would have made it expressive, but a small furrow appeared between his eyebrows, seeming to signify distress. 'Yes,' he said. 'After the eights, well, we had a bit of a beano, don't y'know – and I suppose – well, all the chaps had had a fair bit to drink – and, well you know how these things are – the cox was only a little chap so we threw him into the Isis.'

'Yes?' I said, feeling myself suddenly grow cold.

'Well, the idiotic little blighter didn't come up again.'

'Oh, Archie,' I said.

'Went down all right. Just didn't come up. Never mentioned he couldn't swim.'

'Oh, Archie,' I said. 'That's terrible.'

'I'll say. Going to be an inquest, apparently. Only hope the guv'nor can put in a word with some of his cronies in the House, keep my name out of it.'

'Archie,' I said sharply, 'that's terrible, too.'

'I know,' he said. 'Had wanted to get up a party for the College Comem. but of course that all went to blazes.'

I stared at him, speechless. Catching the expression on my face he changed the subject. 'Bumped into that cousin of yours yesterday.'

'Oh?' I said, still slightly stunned.

'Rum sort of chap. Met him at Meredith's.'

'But Meredith won't have anything to do with Felix.'

'Not any more. Instructions from a higher power.'

I stared at him, perplexed.

'Seems your Cousin Felix motored up to Norfolk two days ago and made his peace with your aunt. Welcomed back into the bosom of your jolly old family with open arms. Can't say poor old Meredith seems best pleased by it. But what your aunt decrees, weaker vessels must obey, what? Bit of a dragon, your old aunt.'

I was still staring at him. 'I didn't know you'd met her.'

'Your Cousin Felix drove her down here. I forgot, you're expected for dinner on Sunday. Inspection of the ranks, don't y'know.'

I went, dutifully, to dinner at Meredith's house in South Audley Street. Archie was also invited, but apart from that it was exclusively a family gathering. Sybil de Lisle, arching her elegant neck upwards as if this were the only way that the whole of me could be properly taken in, remarked with acid-drop sweetness what a wonder it was that I seemed never to stop growing. My Cousin Meredith, who had taken to a monocle, raised it hurriedly to his eye like a man putting up a shield and gave me the kind of grunt, halfway between a snort and a sigh, that he reserved for troublesome situations with which he hoped he would not have to be bothered. Aunt Jessica and my Cousin Felix were standing before the mantelpiece in the drawing room. Seeing them again together, I was once more struck by the same strange juxtaposition of family features, and by the almost girlish radiance with which she smiled at him – as if, in the embrace of that smile, she could isolate him from the rest of us, annexing him for herself. My Cousin Felix, presented with his long-lost girl cousin, took my hand lightly for a moment, raising his eyebrows with what I thought was a faint perplexity.

Over dinner the conversation was inevitably of politics, of Lloyd George and Asquith and whether the growing restiveness of the Conservatives would cause the Coalition to fall. My Cousin Felix said little, except at one point to remark dryly that he was sure the million men who still had no jobs after coming back from the Front would be comforted to know that, in the light of greater concerns, their problem was numerically acceptable. Listening to Meredith going into the attack, with Archie making suitable baying noises at his heels, and wondering whether Archie really was trying to edge his knee closer to me under the table, I wished there were space to ask Felix about Paris and Tarantin and why he had come back to England. But then like everything else about my Cousin Felix, his conversation was entirely impersonal and, with the consciousness of Aunt Jessica's fiercely exclusive gaze upon him, I dared not venture such an intrusion. Still, one thing was certain. The prodigal was well and truly returned. I lost no time in confirming the fact to Dilly, and permitted myself a little private rejoicing that the whole ridiculous invitation problem was at last solved.

I should not have allowed myself such false optimism.

'Dolly's in the most frightful bate,' said Dilly, in the back of the Rolls-Royce on our way home to Berkeley Square after the final fitting for our ball frocks.

'Oh,' I said. 'But Felix has accepted for our coming-out. And since he's going to be one of the house party at the Castle everything's set for her to move in for the kill.'

'She's not speaking to him,' said Dilly.

I groaned. 'Why ever not?'

'She says he's snubbed her. She says she's never been so snubbed in all her life.'

I wondered how someone could be so effectively snubbed by a person with whom they had only had four or five momentary encounters.

'It's the invitations for his private view.'

'But they arrived two days ago.'

'Yes, for you and me. But not for Dolly. She's not been invited.'

I reflected for a moment. 'Well, it's obviously a mistake. In fact, when you think about it, he knows who I am and he's met Dolly, but he's never met you. He probably thinks you and Dolly are one and the same person. Particularly as you both use your nicknames anyway, and they sound alike. The Lady Cordelia Tollemache on our ball invitation could be either of you. It's quite a natural mistake.'

Dilly sighed. 'Men don't make mistakes about Dolly. Even quite natural ones.'

'Anyway, she can go instead of me. I really don't care about Cousin Felix's private view.'

'She won't go unless she's invited. And she's being a perfect bore about it, flouncing around, snapping at Mumsie, accusing me of taking her chrysoprase earrings, screaming at Robinson until the poor girl's in tears. I think underneath it all she really is quite unhappy. Men just don't ignore Dolly. At least, they never have before.'

I stared out of the window for a while, watching Piccadilly slide by. 'I suppose,' I said eventually, 'you want me to sort it with him.'

To my surprise, Dilly shook her head. 'Dear Christie, that's sweet. But no. I know how you feel about your peculiar family. And I've been quite ashamed at having teased you so much before. Besides, she says she won't go now, even if she were invited.'

We were turning into Berkeley Square. I thought how little I wanted to be beholden to any of the de Lisles, but also how very beholden I was to Dilly and her family. I did not want to ask for favours from my Cousin Felix, and I did not suppose that even if I were successful it would do Dolly much good. But I would have attempted anything for Dilly. And also, I thought, perhaps Dilly was right after all. Perhaps I was behaving as if I were frightened of my Cousin Felix. And whatever else I had determined about the de Lisles, one thing was certain – I was not going to spend the rest of my life being frightened of them.

'I'm sure she would go,' I said, 'if she were invited in the right way.'

The chauffeur opened the doors, and we climbed out.

Dilly wrinkled her nose. 'Only if he asked her himself,' she said. 'And was truly abject about his mistake.'

'Abject?' I said. 'I can't guarantee that. But for the rest, I promise to try.'

Dilly threw her arms around me and kissed me on the cheek. 'Oh, Christie, how too, too wonderful! You really are an absolute dear!'

CHAPTER EIGHT

Diary of Adele Ward.
Albemarle Street, London.

14th September, 1893.

Today, puzzling over the household books, which I despair of ever making balance, I chanced to remember that it is almost a twelvemonth since M and I were married. What a girl I was then, what dreams I had! And now? Well, I have my household to manage and my fashionable London life. But the servants continually pilfer or are insubordinate, preferring to take M's commands above my own; and, however brilliant the Season's balls and supper parties, they all seemed stale and empty. Indeed, I found myself regarding the fresh faces of the debutantes with positive envy: they still have their dreams, their hopes of ecstasy. Oh, M and I have arrived at a state of truce: he is considerate towards me and is, I suppose, a good and faithful husband, although, as now, he is often absent and believes me too feather-brained to share his interests. And perhaps that is what love is – married love – this routine of dull evenings and empty days, this polite formality of separated lives. Yet, when I think of my dear Mamma and how darling Papa worships her, even after so many years, I cannot believe that this is all. How I long still for that other love, that bright, pure love I dreamed of once; and how, when I chance to pick up a novel and read of the passionate strivings of a Thelma or an Ariadne, do I long to share their rapture, so that sometimes I find the page moistened by a few foolish tears. Perhaps, if I could bring myself to . . . But no, such dreaming will not do, I must return to those pestilential household books.

Have been interrupted in my task by a most shocking occurrence. Mrs Andrews came to inform me, as she is bound in her capacity as housekeeper to do, that Jenkins, the parlour maid, is in a certain condition and must be sent away. When, thinking out of plain charity something must be done for the unfortunate girl, I asked that she be brought to see me, Mrs Andrews, giving me a most peculiar, almost pitying look, replied that Jenkins was a bad lot and should be got rid of without more ado. But I held my ground for once, and the girl was fetched from below stairs.

Jenkins is a pretty girl, fair, about my age, and inclined to be cheeky – though since she shares this trait with all our servants, I had not given particular thought to it until today. Now that discovery absolves her from the need to tighten her stays it is evident, however, even to my eyes, that she is enceinte. I asked her if she had followers, which of course to all the maids is strictly forbidden. She replied only with the most extraordinary, insolent laughter.

'If there is a young man,' I said, 'perhaps he could be persuaded to marry you.'

She seemed to find this suggestion even more risible. 'Not unless he's a bigamist, he won't.'

'Well, since that's the case,' I replied, 'we must pursue the only other course we may. Mrs Andrews tells me you have a sister in Wales who will take you in. I shall give you five pounds to cover the journey and other expenses.'

'Five pound?' All at once she ceased laughing and a curious, vindictive leer seemed to spread across her features. 'Five eff—g, s——g pound! It's worth a b——y sight more than an eff—g fiver if you want me to keep quiet about it.'

I stared at her dumbfounded.

'Well, who do you think done me up then? Who do you b——y think my married gentleman follower is? All hands he was, when I was dusting or bending down to the umbrella stand. More hands than one of them Indian statues. And one day his hand slipped, didn't it?' Here she patted her belly, sniggering repulsively. 'Well, more than his eff—g hand, by the size of me now, wouldn't you say?'

I crushed my handkerchief to my mouth. 'How much money do you want?'

'So's not to arouse interest in my – ahem! – interesting condition?' Again she made that flaunting gesture with her belly. 'Fifty eff—g quid!'

I had some money of my own put by but was obliged to make up the rest with every penny that remained of this month's housekeeping. The girl has been despatched immediately without a character. M returns tomorrow from his three-week absence in Ireland and, though I fear his blind flashes of temper extremely, I must confront him with it. As his wife, what other course is left to me?

15th September, 1893.

M returned this morning in high good humour. He had invited two companions for luncheon so I was obliged to postpone all mention of Jenkins until they had taken their leave. Indeed, I was grateful for my stay of execution, for my courage of last night had quite deserted me and, were it not for the matter of the housekeeping money, for which I shall be brought to account, I should have been tempted to keep silent on such a distasteful subject. M, not merely unfaithful, but lowering himself with a servant girl? Nevertheless, with much trepidation, I stumbled through an account of my interview with Jenkins.

He immediately flew into a great passion: I was unable to keep the respect of the servants, I let them cheat us at every turn, I could not even manage the housekeeping books, I was weak-brained and gullible, and now, on top of everything else, I had allowed some little chit of a housemaid to inveigle money out of me with a pack of lies specially concocted for the purpose, without – and this was the worst of all – ever questioning her story, although it reflected damnably upon the decency and honour of my own husband. Even allowing for my weak and nervous disposition, my faithlessness was unpardonable.

I retreated, mortified. For his accusation was just. I had accepted the veracity of the girl's accusations without question. The tears began to flow down my cheeks.

'Forgive me,' I pleaded. 'It is true I am sometimes wretched and confused. Only swear on your honour that I was mistaken and I shall never doubt you again.'

'Swear on my honour? To my own wife? By Jove, you've talked to the little trollop. A girl of that class! G–d, her bastard could be anybody's.'

I was arrested in my sobbing. 'But it could not be yours if there were nothing improper between you.'

He became at first very red, then very white, then his lips curled in a cold sneer.

'And what, dear wifie, if there had been? By G–d, do you think I take pleasure in living in this d——d ice-palace? At least the little slut has red blood in her veins.'

Running from him, I gained my bedroom where I have lain, stupefied, for some hours. I have tried so hard to fulfil my duties as a wife, although it seems I have failed in all of them. Yet where is that love, that pure dedication of the soul which would aid *me in my duty?*

As I was writing he came to me in my room. The sneer had gone and he was once again, as in moments he still can be, my old M. Taking me in his arms, he begged me to forgive him for his anger, which had been inspired solely by my doubting *him. And, indeed, seeing his eyes filled with tender affection, I once again reproached myself for my mistrust, for could this M, so gentle and solicitous, truly be capable of lowering himself so vilely? When he kissed my cheeks where the tears had been and told me he loved me, I was overwhelmed with remorse and promised, between sobs (for my eyes had begun to brim over afresh) that I should be from henceforth a better wife to him.*

'I know you will,' he said. 'And to help you, my dearest, I shall lighten your load. I shall take over management of the housekeeping books.'

I looked at him, startled. 'But I mean to improve – I swear I shall. After all, it is my duty –'

'You have no other duty, dearest, than to overcome this nervous disposition of yours. Remember, you are very precious to me.'

Very precious. *I can recollect the delicious sensation with which his words filled me, and how my heart melted at his tender expression. Yet it is curious that now I am alone and the image is fading I cannot help feeling* wretched *and* confused *again. Such a feeling I had a year ago when he swore that his reference to the low women at the Cremorne Gardens was made only in the heat of the moment.*

CHAPTER NINE

'I wish,' said Dilly, inspecting her complexion critically, 'you'd been able to talk to him before tonight.'

From the open window, drifting across the lawns of Critchley Castle and mingling with the alarmed screeching of peacocks, came the shriek of a saxophone, the clatter of cymbals, the pregnant discord of a jazz band tuning up.

In three-quarters of an hour a thousand people, most of whom we would not recognize and many of whom we would never have met, would assemble downstairs and in the Castle grounds to celebrate our coming-out. There was to be dancing in two marquees, dinner in the banqueting hall (the menu included both roast swan and boar's head), a string quartet in the Italian Garden, Jack Buchanan as cabaret, a Charlie Chaplin picture projected onto the ruined ramparts to entertain us when the dancing flagged, limitless champagne and a Royal Highland Fusilier to pipe in the dawn. All we had to do, once we had performed our duty of standing in line with Lord and Lady Mountalban to greet the guests, was to dance ourselves into exhaustion. And all I had to do was to take my Cousin Felix onto one side and remind him tactfully that he hadn't invited Lady Dolly to his private view.

I surveyed myself anxiously in the dressing-table glass. I was not sure I agreed with Dilly that cyclamen crêpe de Chine provided a dramatic contrast with red hair. I did not think I looked any more like Cupid than I felt.

'I would have asked him,' I said, 'if he'd been anywhere to ask.'

It was true. Just when he was needed, my Cousin Felix had been missing from London for a week. Perhaps he had gone back to Norfolk with Aunt Jessica.

'I'm not even sure he's here now.'

'Oh, he's here all right,' said Dilly, casting aside the looking glass in a gesture of despair. 'I saw his Hispano Suiza out by the stables, and Robinson bumped into his man taking his bags up to the Chinese Room.' She sighed. 'Why is it, do you think, that no matter how religiously I use all Mme Rubinstein's preparations I still end up with a spot on the side of my nose?'

I tweaked at my hair in disgust. Perhaps I should have it shingled like Dolly's. 'I think you look lovely,' I said. 'No one in their right mind will be scrutinizing your nose.'

'You are a dear. Dolly says this frock makes me look like a lampshade. And it would be too wonderful to fall in love tonight.'

I laughed. 'I don't think I should want to fall in love if it made me as grumpy as Dolly.'

Dilly giggled. 'Yes, she does look as thunderous as the last act of *Götterdämmerung*. I do hope she isn't going to ruin everything. And I have my suspicions about Archie and Crikey too.'

'Suspicions?'

'I caught them earlier being very furtive in the billiard room with a large cardboard box.'

'Perhaps it's a present.'

'Tied up with string and with holes punched in the top? They're up to something, I know they are.'

Dilly joined me in the looking glass and we both dabbed a little more precautionary powder on our noses. Our reflections appeared so lugubrious that we simultaneously broke into laughter.

'Oh well,' said Dilly, with a swirl of her fan. 'Forward into the fray!'

'I say,' said Archie. 'When are you going to spare a chap a dance?'

The early part of the evening was whirling past for, since it was our ball, it was incumbent on as many young men as possible to dance with us. I caught glimpses of them all from time to time, as I tried to keep my silver sandals out of peril and replied for the twentieth time that, yes, I was having a wonderful evening; of Meredith and Sybil looking weary with that air elders and betters so often adopt at the sight of too many young people enjoying themselves, of Crikey furtively stowing his mysterious cardboard box under the flap of the big marquee, of Dilly getting her feet trodden on yet again, of Archie, always Archie, becoming, I thought, rather too early rather drunk, and of Dolly, languishing sulkily on the arm of Charlie Devereux, whom she had taken up as a stop-gap for the evening. She had swept down to cocktails like a force-nine gale, cut my Cousin Felix dead – although, since he was absorbed in a conversation about Vermeer with Lord Mountalban, I am not sure he noticed – and had lavished upon

Charlie for a full ten minutes a totally uncharacteristic and exclusive concentration until she had observed it to have no effect on its true audience. But now her face looked as if she had drunk sour milk. And I could not see Felix anywhere. Oh, I had glimpsed him once or twice earlier, dancing first with Dora Chantry and then with Venetia Mainwaring. But when, marvelling how small men are attracted to tall girls like moths to a flame, I had seized the chance to look around for him over the top of my partner's head, he had completely disappeared.

'I say!' said Archie. 'What about sparing a chap a jolly old dance!'

'It's Daddy's fault,' hissed Dilly, when she and I had managed to manoeuvre our partners to within talking distance. 'He's taken him off to look at the pictures in the Long Gallery. Knowing Daddy, they'll be ages.'

I looked across at Dolly. She was sitting with Charlie Devereux at one of the little tables round the edge of the dance floor and Charlie was easing his arm very slowly and stealthily around her shoulders. Suddenly, blowing out a smoke ring and looking straight ahead of her, she stubbed out her cigarette with great precision on the back of his other hand. Then she got up and walked away.

'Oh dear!' said Dilly. 'And if that weren't enough, look at Crikey and Archie!'

I spotted them on the next turn, near the band. Crikey was whispering something. Archie shook his head then appeared to wink, tapping the side of his nose significantly.

'You're right,' I said. 'They are up to something.'

'Oh dear!' groaned Dilly as she was whirled off across the dance floor out of earshot.

'I say, old girl,' said Archie's voice when the music stopped. 'Mayn't a chap at least take you in to dinner?'

Despite beckoning from Dora Chantry and Miles Millington and a wave from the Mainwarings, Archie had settled us in the banqueting hall far away from anyone we knew.

'Glad to have a chance to talk to you at last, old girl.'

'Archie,' I said, 'what are you up to?'

He went instantly pink all over and I realized with dismay he had misinterpreted my question. 'Well, it's difficult for a chap, don't y'know. Difficult to express himself. When delicacy is required.'

I took a mouthful of roast swan. It tasted, I thought, rather like a cork bath mat in the hands of a cook who believes most things are better for a little extra time in the oven.

'I mean, Archie,' I said, 'what are you being so secretive about?'

His ears were growing ominously pink now. He downed his champagne in one gulp. 'No secret, old girl. Never kept it a secret. Just finding the right words a bit of problem, don't y'know.'

'Oh Archie,' I said, looking round frantically for some means of escape, 'don't be silly.'

He had gone crimson to the very roots of his hair so that his white brows and lashes stood out in relief like a photographic negative. 'Nice of you to laugh it off like that, old girl. But true, all the same. Never been an eloquent sort of chap – not like Meredith, speeches in the House, all that sort of thing. But there are some moments when a chap's just got to find the words – I mean – when a girl and a chap like each other, don't y'know – well, I mean to say . . .'

He took another gulp of champagne and seized my hand. I could not think how to stop him.

'Archie, of course I like you—'

'There you are then! And there isn't anything I wouldn't do for you, old girl – I mean – well, I think we should—'

'Archie,' I said in desperation, 'I can see Dilly beckoning to me. I've got to go.'

'Go?' he said in astonishment, releasing my hand. 'But, old girl, you're only halfway through dinner.'

'Yes, I know. But it's obviously some kind of crisis. I simply must go.'

He looked down into his champagne glass, crestfallen.

I felt suddenly sorry for him. 'I'll keep you a dance,' I said as I rose to my feet.

'Promise?'

'Promise,' I said.

It was cool and empty in the Italian Garden. Most people still seemed to be dancing or in at dinner. The string quartet was playing Mozart and I sat on the stone steps leading down to the lawn, suddenly blessedly alone, breathing in the night air and listening to the sounds of disorganized merriment all around me fade and merge into the clear sweet symmetry of the music. The piece had just come to an end and I had just persuaded myself that, no matter how many times Archie proposed, no one on earth, not even Aunt Jessica, could force me to accept him, when I realized I was not alone after all. There was a tall man, a little way out beyond me, standing as still as one of the statues, so that I noticed him only by the sudden glow of his cigarette as he threw it away, and by the white flash of his shirt front as he turned to walk towards the steps.

I scrambled hastily to my feet and saw with consternation that it was my Cousin Felix. In my preoccupation with the problem of Archie I had forgotten the problem of Felix and Dolly, and now, confronted with it all unawares, I felt a pressing urge to escape.

'My dear Christabel,' he said, coming up the steps to join me, 'I thought your card would be full. Perhaps, then, if you are not dancing, you would dance with me?'

I was so taken aback I almost refused him. But he offered me his arm and I was forced to take it and walk with him out of the Italian Garden and across the lawns to the big marquee, trying all the time to compose in my head a suitable speech about Lady Dolly's fondness for art as we walked. Alas, in vain. By the time we had reached the dance floor my mind was a complete blank.

The orchestra was playing an old-fashioned fox trot. He held me, not as boys of Archie's age did, clinging on tightly as if they feared drowning and only their grip on me could save them, but lightly, easily, so that it scarcely seemed he was holding me at all. I felt no impulse to obey my old dancing lessons and grasp him round the waist, nor was there any fear that he would tread on my feet. Yet, perhaps because of my mission or perhaps because every time I was confronted with him I was struck anew by how complete a stranger he was to me, I began to suffer such an overpowering trembling in my legs that I was in grave danger of treading on his. I was suddenly aware, too, that my eyes were directly in line with the second black pearl stud on his shirt front and that I should, if I wanted to talk to him, have to look up.

I looked up.

'May I—?'

'Are you—?' we said, both at once.

He laughed. 'Please go on.'

I said the first thing that came into my head. 'Are you back in England for good?'

He laughed again. 'For good?' He made it sound as if the idea of doing anything or staying anywhere for good was such a patent absurdity he had never considered it. 'No. I'm designing a ballet for Teddy Tarantin. For his Paris season. I shall go back there in the spring when rehearsals start. If not before.'

'Oh,' I said, thinking of how to turn the conversation towards art. 'And your exhibition?'

'The critics will savage it, a few society matrons will tut-tut over it, and perhaps I may sell one or two canvases.' He was smiling, dismissing it. 'Have you seen the Tarantin Ballet?'

I had forgotten how little he seemed to like talking about himself. I was beginning to despair. 'I've never been to the ballet at all.'

'Then you must persuade someone to take you when Tarantin opens at the Alhambra. You will enjoy the music.'

Music. 'I'd love to hear Stravinsky,' I said, despite myself. 'They say it's very strange, not like music at all.'

He was laughing again, and I knew the conversation had taken completely the wrong turning and could not think how to bring it back.

'Now may I ask you a question?'

I looked up and met his eyes for the first time. They were not, as I had supposed, empty of expression but glinted with a detached amusement.

'Yes, of course,' I said.

'Now that I know who you are, my funny little skinny cousin, perhaps you will tell me why you keep running away from me as if you had seen a ghost.'

I stopped dancing and stood, transfixed for a moment, staring at him, first mortified, then filled with fury that he should have been mocking me all the time, mocking me, worse still, where I knew I so eminently deserved it. Then, suddenly, it occurred to me that this was the perfect opportunity to rid myself of the problem of Dolly and my Cousin Felix and his pesky private view, once and for all. I opened my mouth to speak. But as I did so the music stopped and Archie was beside me, seizing my arm.

'Sorry, old chap,' said Archie. 'But she's definitely promised the next one to me.' And he whirled me away so fast to the other side of the dance floor I did not even have time to catch sight of Felix's face.

I turned upon Archie the full force of my anger. 'You're drunk,' I said.

'Not drunk, old girl. Been drinking, but not drunk. No need to fix me with that basilisk stare.'

'Tipsy, oiled, sozzled, drinking, drunk, I don't care which – you're the absolute and utter limit!'

He gave me a look of pained innocence. 'What have I done, old girl?'

'And don't call me "old girl".'

'Look here, what have I done?'

I was so angry, I told him – about Dolly and Felix and the private view and Dilly's and my plan, everything.

'And now,' I said, 'you've ruined it.'

Archie gave a puzzled frown. Then his face seemed to brighten. 'Didn't I say I'd do anything for you, old girl? No idle boast, don't y'know. You wait here a tick and watch me.'

I stared at him in horror. 'No, Archie. No!'

But he was already gone, back across the dance floor in search of Felix. I saw them together a few moments later, Felix with his back to me, Archie clearly explaining. At one point Archie must even have gestured at me, for Felix looked round. I turned my head away hastily, burning with embarrassment, glad that he was too far away for me to read the expression on his face.

After a while Archie returned, wreathed in self-congratulatory smiles. 'Spoke to the blighter. Everything taken care of. Complete misunderstanding, apparently. Hayman Gallery sends out the invitations, made a bit of a bish of it. Didn't I say I'd do anything for you?'

For a moment I was speechless. Then I said: 'How dare you! How dare you humiliate me in front of him!'

Archie gave a snort. 'Dratted Bohemian! Know he's your cousin and Meredith's brother and all that. But the blighter's a traitor to his class. Anyway, now I've done you a favour, old girl, how about doing me one, what?'

I stared at him, again bereft of words.

'Give a chap a kiss, old girl. Just one little kiss.'

'Give us a kiss,' said Archie, as the mournful face of Charlie Chaplin flickered palely against the ruined ramparts that were all that remained of medieval Critchley. 'Just one teeny, weeny kiss.'

'I've asked you to leave me alone, Archie. I've asked you to stop following me.'

'Just one little kiss, that's all. I've done you a favour, now you do one for me.'

Perhaps Archie had, after all, done me a favour, as he so irritatingly persisted. His distinctly unsubtle approach to the problem seemed to have had almost instantaneous results. A few minutes after the conversation with Archie, Felix had been seen talking to Dolly, and later they had danced together several times. In fact, watching his dark head bent towards her gold one, I could not think why I was not better pleased. Perhaps it was because I now had Archie to contend with, Archie who would not go away. My only hope was that he would get so drunk he would fall down. But, for a small man, Archie seemed to have unjustly large reserves of staying power.

'Jus' one li'l kiss.'

'Archie, you are persecuting me.'

I kept my face fixed rigidly on Charlie Chaplin, who seemed to be having trouble with a baby and a dog. Suddenly I felt Archie nuzzling wetly against my shoulder. I stood up abruptly, casting my shadow across both baby and dog, obliterating them, so that there were mutterings from behind me. Archie lurched forwards across my chair.

'Archie Cadwallander,' I hissed, 'I would not kiss you if by some miracle you were suddenly transformed into Rudolf Valentino!'

'Gosh,' said Dilly, taking off her left shoe surreptitiously in the darkness behind the big marquee and massaging her foot. 'Isn't it divine about Dolly? You're really too wonderful, Christie!'

'Not me,' I said grimly. 'Archie. And I'm never speaking to him again.'

'Archie? Where is he?'

'Strung up on the ramparts for all I care. I've been trying to lose him for hours.'

'And I'm trying to find Crikey.'

'Good gracious, Dillo! I thought you were enjoying yourself.'

'So I am. And that's why I want to find out what the wretch has in that cardboard box. And when I do, I'll—'

I did not immediately discover what Dilly would do to Crikey, because at that moment screams came from the large marquee. We rushed to the entrance. There seemed to be pandemonium inside. Couples were running from the dance floor, men were flapping their arms and legs about wildly as if to fend off a sudden plague, women were jumping onto chairs and tables and clutching at their skirts. The dance floor seemed to be seething with a darting, quivering shower of whiteness, like live confetti.

'Oh, my goodness!' said Dilly.

'White mice!' I said. 'There must be hundreds of them!'

'That wretched Crikey!' said Dilly. 'I'll wring his miserable neck!'

I looked down at my feet as something white flashed towards me. I swooped down, quick as a hawk, and picked it up.

In a matter of moments Lord Mountalban's steward and an army of footmen had appeared to restore order. They swept away the mice under the tent flaps out into the darkness, with napkins, with trays, with empty champagne bottles, anything that came to hand – one even brandished a pikestaff he'd hastily seized from the panelled walls of the banqueting hall. The screaming stopped. And I was all at once aware that the orchestra had gone on playing stoically throughout.

'Where is the miserable wretch?' squealed Dilly. 'Where is he?'

'Not he,' I said. 'They. Archie was in it, too, up to his neck.'

'They'll both be up to their necks in something else once I get hold of them. Something that'll make boiling oil seem as soothing as a Turkish bath.' Dilly was jumping up and down with rage. 'Just show me where they've got to!'

'Look over there,' I said.

They were in their old corner, beside the band, sniggering drunkenly together.

Dilly made to move, but I restrained her.

'My need for revenge is greater than yours,' I said. And very carefully I opened my cupped hands a fraction so she could see my trophy. She retreated with a squeak.

'Oh, Christie! How horrid! Put it down.'

The mouse surveyed us both with a bewildered air. Its body nestled softly in the palm of my glove and I could feel its heart pounding as its little pink nose set its whiskers atwitch. I stroked it gently behind the ears.

Dilly took another look. 'Well, yes, on second thoughts perhaps it is rather sweet.'

'And useful,' I said. 'Wait here for a moment.'

I picked my way carefully along the side of the dance floor to where Archie and Crikey were still convulsed with triumphant snickering. Crikey did not appear to notice my approach. Archie had slumped down in a chair with his back to me.

I waited till I was directly behind him. Then: 'Archie!' I said. And as he turned I yanked his stiff collar back with one hand and rammed the other hand, closed tightly around the small furry body to protect it, as far as I could down the back of his neck, inside his shirt.

Archie appeared for an instant suspended in total stasis. Then he yelped, leapt to his feet and began slapping and thumping the upper parts of his person. I could imagine the bewildered scuttle of those cold pink feet tickled abominably. Still jumping and yelping, prancing in circles in grotesque parody of some primitive war dance, vainly appealing to Crikey who, in common with other startled onlookers, could do no more than stare at him mouth agape, he began to make frantic swatting motions at the centre of his back. The movement seemed to liberate the mouse, for on his next pirouette he was seen to be tearing dementedly at the studs of his shirt front. Now he was pulling out the back of his shirt between the division of his tails, now, emitting a yelp more anguished than before, clutching at the front of his trousers, now shaking his left leg and hopping on his right, jerking at the flapping material of his left trouser bottom and taking violent swipes at his sock suspender. Until at last there emerged on his left patent-leather pump two enquiring red eyes and a pink nose. Then both were gone in a split-second flash of white.

A small titter went up amongst the onlookers. Archie stopped jumping up and down and looked about him. His face was an apoplectic crimson, his top stud had burst and his shirt hung down beneath his tails. Suddenly his eye lit upon where I had retreated with Dilly, and he began to blunder towards us.

'I say, old girl, that's a bit thick! A bit bloody thick!'

Dilly and I were still doubled up with laughter. 'Oh,' gasped Dilly, 'but revenge is sweet!'

'Do a girl a favour,' Archie spluttered, 'and how does she pay you back? Puts a handful of rabid rodents down your neck. Well, we'll see about that, old girl.'

Still laughing, I dodged behind Dilly, darted out of the marquee and began to run across the lawn. Behind me I heard muffled swearing as Archie, in pursuit, became entangled with a guy rope. I stopped and turned back to look at him. He had struggled to his feet and was lumbering on obstinately towards me. He looked so absurd, that I shook helplessly with another wave of laughter.

'No laughing matter!' he said, level with me now. 'When you do a girl a favour and she pays you back by making you look a bloody idiot!'

And he grasped hold of my arm.

Suddenly his fingers were hurting me and there was an expression in his eyes I had never seen before. I stopped laughing.

'Let me go, Archie.'

'Did you a favour,' he said, tightening his grip and pulling me towards him. 'Now you do me one.'

With a violent jerk I wrenched my arm free and began to run, in earnest now, across the lawn and through the Italian Garden, towards the terrace and the safety of the house. I should have outpaced him, drunk as he was, but the heels of my sandals kept sticking in the grass. I could hear him behind me, heaving and bellowing, gaining on me, gaining on me fast. He caught up with me on the terrace just past the ornamental fountain and, seizing me from behind, spun me round and forced me backwards till I was pinioned against the wall. Virginia creeper swished into my eyes, the jagged stone of Critchley Castle cut into my back, my feet sank into the mud of a flowerbed.

'Did you a favour!' he bellowed, thrusting my shoulders harder against the stone and forcing his leg in between mine. 'Now you do one for me!'

I started to scream but he clamped his lips down fast upon my open mouth. I tasted his saliva, felt to my horror the invasion of his tongue, violating my mouth, choking me. I could not see, I could not breathe, no matter how I struggled I could not free myself from the mad, blind grip or the thrust of his leg forcing itself ever forward against me. I wanted to scream, I wanted to be sick. I tried in vain to wrench my lips free and bite his tongue.

Then suddenly someone had him by the neck and was pulling him off me, someone was shaking him by the scruff of the neck as a terrier does a rat. I wiped the sticky smear of him from my lips and opened my eyes. His body slammed hard against the wall beside me and began to crumple slowly from the knees.

'You may look like a pig, Cadwallander,' said my Cousin Felix, 'but you don't have to behave like one.'

I stepped out of the flowerbed. Felix surveyed me coldly as I tried to smooth down my dress.

'You're all right?' he asked.

With a roar, Archie stopped crumpling and reared up from the wall. 'You blasted cad! You keep your hands off another chap's girl!' And, lurching forward, he swung out wildly at Felix with his right fist.

My Cousin Felix must have stepped aside to avoid the blow, but if he did, it was the merest hint of a movement, like someone flicking a speck of dust from his sleeve. Missing his mark, Archie lost his balance, careered out of control across the terrace, and fell face first into the ornamental fountain, where he hung suspended, his upper arms supported by the marble rim, his legs dangling, his head invisible. There was a gurgle. Then his body went limp.

'It seems to me, my dear cousin,' said Felix de Lisle, 'that you should be a little more discriminating in your choice of friends.'

Then, with a look of disdain which seemed to take in everything from my mud-encrusted sandals to the wreck of Archie, he turned and walked away into the Italian Garden.

I stood for a while, trying to shake off the mud and restore my hair to some semblance of order. Distantly there came the sound of bagpipes, and for the first time I realized that the festive glitter of a thousand Japanese lanterns had been quenched by a harsh, clear dawn. I went to look at Archie. Although he was quite unconscious, his nose and mouth hung just above the level of the water and, all at once remembering the little cox who had gone down but had not come up, I left him there for the gardeners to attend to, and went in to find some breakfast.

CHAPTER TEN

'My dear!' said the Dowager Duchess of Rosslair, her lorgnette not three inches away from what, despite its distorted perspectives and aquamarine hues, was, to Dilly's delight, undoubtedly a picture of a naked woman. 'I scarcely think this is suitable. Particularly when there are so many young unmarried girls present.'

'The point,' said a little man with a goatee beard, 'is not to represent the object but to dissociate the subject to be represented from the object itself, the representation.'

'It's called being modern, dear,' said Phoebe Millington, 'like all this dancing to jazz and drinking cocktails and nice girls smoking in public.'

'The artist seeks, not the slavish imitation of Aristotelian reality, but the reality within himself, which, subsuming the prosaic reality of the object, imposes upon its form a new dimension, an existential reality which transforms our whole perception of reality itself.'

'Tell me, Mr de Lisle,' said Lady Dolly, eyes wide, 'where do you get your inspiration? Could a particular person ever inspire you, do you think?'

'*Mon dieu!*' said Mme Rostova. 'These little pale English flappers. How the sound of their so-nice, well-bred voices drains one just to hear it.'

In a summer of cold and rain it was suddenly a blazing day, shimmering with heat and golden with the pollen dust from the plane trees in Green Park, and inside the Hayman Gallery the air was stifling as the bright denizens of the Season jostled shoulder to shoulder with moneyed Americans imported by Reuben Hayman and a flock of men in pince-nez and frock coats who, from the way they flapped and squawked like carrion birds around the paintings, I took to be critics. The crowd moved like water in a sluggish stream, making little eddies here and there where the prominence of celebrity caught its stagnant flow around Rostova, around Tarantin and his retinue of gilded boys, but most of all frothing and swirling about my Cousin Felix. And at the perimeter of the vortex I saw from time to time the broad brims of two elegant hats, the cream silk of Lady Dolly's and the osprey-plumed jade of Rostova's, two ensigns on the flag ships of opposing fleets, sail into view as if bound on a collision course then, just as the clash seemed inevitable, put about.

My Cousin Felix had followed up his apology for the shameful omission of the Hayman Gallery the day after the ball with two dozen red roses and a card inscribed simply with the initials F St J de L. The flowers had encouraged us to believe he might call in the interval, but when he did not it was easy to find explanations. 'After all,' said Dilly, 'he must be very busy with his exhibition – making sure they hang the pictures straight and that sort of thing.' At any rate, Dolly, immaculate in the pleated cream georgette panelled with charmeuse it had taken Robinson two hours to press, pale as a lily except for the sapphire flash of her eyes, seemed undeterred.

The day after the ball had brought other consequences too, I was reminded by catching sight of Archie skulking in a backwater. He had not appeared at breakfast the next morning, but had slunk off early back to London, and I had not exchanged a word with him since, although I had been aware of him at a distance in crowded rooms like this one, favouring me with hangdog looks. I had, however, been given a thorough dressing-down by my Cousin Meredith about the mouse. It did not matter that Crikey and Archie had let loose a couple of hundred mice upon our unsuspecting guests: that was boyish high spirits of the sort that won wars and made centuries not-out at the Winchester-Eton match. But for properly brought-up girls it was different: one did not go round inserting mice into young men's evening dress unless one wished to be considered 'wild'. And wild girls rapidly acquired the reputation of being déclassé and did not end up wives. I wondered fleetingly if my Cousin Felix had related to his brother the sequel in the flowerbed, but it was evident from Meredith's lecture he had not, and for that I was grateful. For, in truth, though perhaps not for the reasons Meredith believed I should be, I was rather ashamed of myself.

It was, I suppose, because I felt obscurely that I had done Archie a wrong. Oh yes, of course he had been disgustingly drunk and had behaved abominably. But perhaps he would have behaved better had I just occasionally paid him the courtesy of taking him seriously. I had come to think of Archie as I had observed other girls to think of their younger brothers: tiresome, but essentially harmless. But Archie, despite his blushes and his bumbling, was not harmless. In Archie, beneath his absurd affectations, there ran a brute strain which, I supposed, once you stripped away their notions of chivalry and fair play and honour, was common to all men. And I, unconscious of its needs, had taunted him into declaring it. For though I was perfectly used to him pulling out chairs and filling in empty dances and threatening to propose after too much champagne, though I had come to consider him with a lordly air, as a king might his court jester, I had never for one moment thought of Archie as a man.

So, I had listened to Meredith in unprotesting silence. I had not even confided the flowerbed episode to Dilly, although she continually pressed me to explain why Archie and I were no longer speaking to each other. And I was profoundly thankful that my Cousin Felix's habitual indifference precluded any possibility of gossip. Yet I wished wholeheartedly, too, that it had not been he of all people who had caught me in such a predicament and, as a sudden ripple in the Hayman Gallery's human tide disclosed him for a moment, an elegant, dégagé figure amongst the frock coats, I was never more grateful that the surge and swell of too many hot bodies crammed into one place would prevent any chance encounter with him as effectively as it had becalmed Archie.

'Oh goodness!' said Dilly, fanning herself with her catalogue. 'I shall expire in this crush, and I've lost my parasol and I've lost Dolly and if that revolting little man with the beaver steps on my foot again I shall kick him in the shins. And what about the pictures? Apart from the crowd parting like the Red Sea for old Bunty Rosslair to declare her disapproval of the nude, I haven't caught a glimpse of a single one of them.'

It was, indeed, impossible in such a press of people to take in any detailed impression of my Cousin Felix's paintings. Apart from the nude I had seen from time to time, as heads moved and groups fragmented and reformed themselves, a study of an old, gnarled peasant at a dissolute café table, two or three portraits of Rostova and one of Tarantin – there seemed from the catalogue to be a notable absence of self-portraits in Felix's exhibition and, near me, a huge canvas in which detail seemed to have been pared away almost to abstraction, entitled, according to the catalogue, *Dawn Gunfire 1916.*

But if individual paintings vanished elusively behind picture hats and impeccably-tailored backs the presence of the work as a whole dominated the room like an assault. They blazed at you, those paintings, as the sun blazed outside, with a fierceness of colour, of leaping reds, of searing blues, of scorching shafts of white and light, so that somehow, set against their twists and distortions, against the savagery of their brushwork, we, all of us, chatting about Henley or the Verrinders' garden party or the Surrey-Kent match at the Oval, seemed dwarfed a little.

'Oh, isn't it divine!' squeaked Maisie Cunningham-Cowper. 'Isn't it all too utterly modern!'

'Prefer a nice hunting print myself,' said Miles Millington.

'Or,' said Crikey wistfully, 'a decent portrait of W G Grace.'

'I've never seen a real artist's studio,' cooed Lady Dolly. 'I should so like, Mr de Lisle, to come one day and watch you work.'

'I say, old girl, must have a word. Can't go on like this, what?'

I had been looking absently across in the direction of Tarantin who, turning, seemed to fix me, alarmingly and for no reason I could think of, with his eye, when Archie's voice at my elbow made me jump.

'Oh Archie,' I said. 'Not here.'

The crowd seemed suddenly to part, pressing us to the wall and then closing ranks behind us, so that we were isolated together with no escape. We stood in the glare of *Dawn Gunfire 1916*. Despite myself, despite Archie, the painting stopped me dead for a moment. I saw now, not abstraction, but a flat and stunted landscape beneath a vastness of sky shot with flame, rent with the barrage of shellfire as if by some man-made aurora borealis, in whose electric blues and reds and saffrons there was a grim parody of nature's dawn. It was at once beautiful and horrifying. Hellfire.

'Want to apologize, old girl.' His face had attained the crimson hue it always wore in moments of crisis. His shoulders drooped, even his knees seemed to give a little, so utterly had he assumed the posture of humble dejection.

'I forgive you, Archie,' I said. 'So long as it never, never happens again.'

He had perked up. Now, as if puzzled, he said, with a little laugh: 'Oh, can't promise that.'

I was taken aback. 'Can't you, Archie?'

'Well, a chap's got to have the occasional beano, don't y'know. Not going to sign the Pledge or anything like that. Still, shouldn't get beastly drunk in front of ladies. End up with them not speaking, what?'

I stared at him.

'Woke up next morning fully dressed and soaked to the skin. Renton said he had to fish me out of some bally fountain. Didn't say how I got there, though.'

In spite of myself, I burst out laughing. The amount of alcohol he had drunk had obviously combined with the blow on his head to give him amnesia.

'Do you remember the mouse?'

'Mice!' His face brightened perceptibly. 'Jolly good wheeze that. Got 'em all jumping. Remember the mice all right. Just don't remember how I got into the bally fountain.'

'You were trying to hit my Cousin Felix.'

He was suddenly beaming. 'Gosh, was I? Defending your honour, what?'

'Something of the sort.'

'Good show.'

There was a pause, during which he gulped and became pink and serious again. 'Look, old girl, there's something I've been meaning to—'

'Archie,' I said firmly, 'you have apologized, I have accepted your apology. There is no need for anything more. And I want to look at the pictures.'

'Don't care for your Cousin Felix. Don't care for his dratted pictures either.'

'That's as may be,' I said. 'But if you don't leave me in peace to look at them I swear I'll withdraw my undertaking to speak to you forthwith.'

I turned back to the vast canvas with its blighted land and apocalyptic sky. Now that the crowd had thinned I could stand farther away from it and take in its entirety better. There was something about the sheer ferocity of it which drew me, fascinated. And yet it puzzled me too, for, looking back over my shoulder at my Cousin Felix, head bent towards Rostova's osprey plumes, I found a contradiction in the coolness of him and the searing heat of the painting which I could not square.

'Ah,' said a rich voice beside me. 'The little cousin.'

I turned and discovered myself confronted with Vladimir Tarantin.

He was alone, unattended by his usual entourage, and, seeing him close to for the first time, I thought more than ever, with his bright black eyes and his lined, mobile face, he looked like a monkey – a commanding and illustrious monkey perhaps, but a monkey nevertheless. There was about his whole appearance something at once distinguished and farouche. Though his hair was jet-black with a curl that resisted lavish amounts of brilliantine, he could, as the lines and creases chased each other in a smile from the corners of his eyes to the curve of his wide, thin mouth, have been any age from thirty to fifty. Nonetheless, I found myself smiling too, for although he had called me little I overtopped him by about four inches. The bright eyes picked up the cause of my amusement instantly, setting in train another dancing migration of lines as, showing two rows of large, evenly-spaced teeth which glinted here and there with gold, he threw back his head in a laugh.

'Forgive me. But the resemblance of the face is impossible to mistake. Even half-hidden under that most becoming hat.'

He introduced himself to me. And as he was taking my hand and bringing it to within a fraction of his lips I saw for an instant in those bright, sharp eyes an inquisitorial flash which suggested, to my perplexity, that he had not abandoned his retinue and found himself standing beside me in any way by chance. I felt myself blushing, to my chagrin, for I knew he would detect in a moment my unease.

'So. Everyone else is talking about their hunters and their stockbrokers and looking each other up and down in their so-English way. But you, Miss Ward, are looking at the paintings. You must be careful. Such eccentric behaviour will get you taken for a bluestocking.'

I smiled at him. And again there came that questioning, curious flash. Vladimir Andreyevitch Tarantin clearly took an autocratic stand with his friends; there was evidently not a corner of their lives, even the triviality of an obscure female cousin, that could be allowed to remain untrammelled by his supervision.

'You like the paintings?'

'I think so,' I said.

'You sound in doubt. Perhaps like your English friends you prefer a sensible picture of a rustic scene or a horse?'

I laughed. 'No, Monsieur de Tarantin, it's not that. It's just that they are so – ' I glanced for a second at the distant figure of my Cousin Felix, 'they are so very unlike him.'

'Ah!' He gave a sudden flourishing gesture which made the silk handkerchief protruding from his coat sleeve flutter like a banner. 'Then you do prefer the sensible horse. You make things too simple. No one, dear Miss Ward, is so simple. Not even an Englishman. I will tell you a story.'

He paused to dab his corrugated forehead with the handkerchief, then tucked it back into his sleeve.

'One summer in Paris I have an injury to my knee – to support the body's weight and also the weight of another dancer much inflames the nervous tissue, you understand – so I go to a man I know who is not a doctor but works miracles which make the doctors like *canards*. And there too is a young Englishman, very tall, very beautiful, so injured by the Kaiser's bullets and yet so determined that he will not for the rest of his life hobble like an old man. And I watch this Englishman fighting so much pain, willing himself that he will cease to feel it, and I think to myself, ah, this is your English sang-froid, your so-famous stiff upper lip. So when this young man tells me he is a painter I think not very much – with these perfect manners of the English gentleman, so perfect and cold-blooded, he must, you understand, be a dilettante who will soon go back to his country estate and forget such impossible ideas. But one day the young man tells me he has a painting hanging in the Salon des indépendants. My heart sinks because, of course, you know what I am expecting – '

'Horses,' I said.

'Exactly so. But when I go to look I see instead such a painting – a painting like this one – a painting like a scream.'

We both turned unconsciously to the canvas that loomed over us and, for a second, I fancied it seared our faces with its burning.

'Your nice tame English horses, they are painted from the outside. But this man paints from what is inside himself and he is not at peace with what he sees. And then I realize it is not so simple. In my thoroughbred, well-groomed English friend is something turbulent and dangerous, like the wild stallions of the Camargue. It is as if he is, like me, an exile, a stranger in a foreign country always trying in vain to match what this so-civilized world makes him with what his heart tells him he must be – '

I had watched Tarantin, fascinated, throughout this discourse. For, as he talked, the scrutinizing gleam had disappeared from his eyes and in its place had come a heat, as if he had absorbed it from the painting. Unaccountably embarrassed, I looked away and was caught again in the glare of Felix's picture, recoiling now from the nakedness of its pain.

'So I make him my protégé,' Tarantin was saying, his eyes no longer on me at all, but focused upon my Cousin Felix, where he stood in conversation with Lady Dolly, focused with all the fervour of that rapacious, suffocating desire. 'I begin to create him as I have created so many others – musicians, painters, choreographers, dancers, even Rostova who thinks herself great but was nothing, nothing before me. I shall create in Felix de Lisle a great painter. We are making a ballet together. It will be all fire and burning, you will see. And then next year he will exhibit in Paris, Druet or Vollard will show him, there will be none of these English peasants and their horses. So long as he will not fight me with that cold English will of his, I shall create for him *le monde entier* – '

'*Merde!*' drawled the voice of Rostova behind us. 'Do I hear the Great God Tarantin in the act of creation again?'

Tarantin's face went instantly through another of its mercurial changes, the lines flowing together in channels and tributaries until there emerged from the confluence a smile which at once radiated the utmost charm and yet glittered with malevolence.

'My dear Anna Nikolayevna, allow me to present Miss Christabel Ward – the little cousin of our friend. *Elle est assez ravissante, n'est-ce pas, tout le portrait de notre cher Félix?*'

He had adopted, I noticed, a proprietorial air towards me, as if, having subjected me to the necessary inspection, he could now subsume me beneath the general fabric of his intimacy with Felix.

'*Charmante,*' said Mme Rostova, with a long appraising glance that seemed to take in every particular of me from the single camellia on my hat to the hem of my muslin dress. 'The little English rose in white. So sweet. So utterly innocent of fashion.'

I shifted uneasily under her gaze, as I had beneath Tarantin's. Her eyes were level with mine and I saw now that they were not dark, although they seemed so against the pallor of her face, but a greenish yellow in which the pupils glinted as small and bright as pinheads. She was dressed from head to foot in green too, with more jewellery than was suitable for the occasion, crystal cascading at her throat, diamonds glittering about her ears and on her fingers, so that the whole effect, enhanced by her sinuous gestures and the way she held her body as if she were languidly uncoiling it, was of a glossy serpentine shimmering. If Tarantin were a monkey, she was undoubtedly a snake. As she spoke her tongue seemed to flicker between sharp teeth. In spite of the heat, two large, white fox furs hung about her shoulders, like prey.

'We were talking, dear Anna Nikolayevna,' said Tarantin, 'about how I should create *cher Félix.*'

'Perhaps,' said Rostova, in a voice that seemed to slide out slowly from somewhere deep in the back of her throat, 'he does not wish to be one of Tarantin's creations.'

'Then he is listening, dear Anna Nikolayevna, to someone who is not his true friend.'

Rostova gave Tarantin a long, slow smile that was almost equal to his in malignancy. 'Perhaps,' she said, 'he knows the Great God Tarantin not only creates, but also destroys.'

Tarantin returned the smile in full measure. 'I destroy no one, Anna Nikolayevna. Why should I when I may see them do it for themselves?'

Watching them, teeth bared, eyes aglitter, tasting, it seemed, a bitter pleasure in the venom of a contest I could not understand, I wanted only to get away, glad that their passing interest in me appeared to have abated – for that it was no more than a thing of the moment, that I would cease to exist for them again the minute I was out of their view, it did not occur to me in my foolish innocence to question. So I was relieved when Reuben Hayman, a little silky man who was forever rubbing his hands, materialized to announce that one of the rich Americans had bought six of Felix's paintings and gave me the opportunity to slip off.

Now that the crowd had thinned out, Lady Dolly was able to monopolize my Cousin Felix.

'I do so wish,' I heard her say, 'that you would paint my portrait while you're in London.'

He laughed. 'My dear Lady Dolly, I could never do you justice.'

'But you could try,' she pouted. 'I should so like it.'

She was standing directly beneath a full-length painting of Rostova in rehearsal clothes at the *barre*. The vividness of it, the way in which it appeared to shimmer as Rostova shimmered, capturing so perfectly the bright serpentine gloss of her, seemed to eclipse Lady Dolly so that beside it, in her pale dress and her pale hat, she looked suddenly indistinct, like an image that has been partially rubbed out.

'I should never dare even to try,' said my Cousin Felix. 'You should consult Sir William Orpen.'

'But I want you,' she said, her voice sounding shrill, as if it too had been drained of tone and shade. 'And I know I could persuade Daddy to give you the commission.'

'I'm afraid I don't take commissions.'

'But he'd pay you handsomely. You needn't worry about that.'

My Cousin Felix's face was perfectly expressionless, but his hand went to his pocket for his cigarette case in a little restless movement I would have taken warning from. 'My dear Lady Dolly, this is an absurd conversation.'

But Lady Dolly was not looking for warnings or even listening. As if drowning in the great wash of colour all about her, her small pale figure seemed to struggle, then go taut with the sheer effort of imposing her will. 'But you sell your canvases. You paint for money.'

'While I live to paint, thank God I don't have to paint to live.'

'Besides, it would be such an opportunity for you. Everyone in London would see my portrait and want theirs done. Then you could paint only beautiful things. Not like that ugly old man in the dirty café.'

My Cousin Felix, lighting his cigarette, looked briefly in the direction of the study of the man at the café table and raised his eyebrows. 'The old man is beautiful.'

Lady Dolly gave an impatient little moue of disgust. 'A repulsive, wrinkled, filthy old peasant!'

'He is beautiful because of the wrinkles, because he has a face and all the joys and miseries and struggles of his life are written in it.'

'You think that's beauty? Then you'll never have any success. There isn't a person in the whole of London who wouldn't prefer to look at a painting of a beautiful woman.'

My Cousin Felix drew deeply on his cigarette. And though when he spoke his voice was light, I heard in it now an undertow I remembered well from that long-gone summer afternoon in the kitchen garden at Monks Last.

'I won't debate aesthetics with you, Lady Dolly,' he said. 'But I will make you a promise.'

She stepped eagerly out of the blinding brightness of Rostova's portrait and suddenly her eyes seemed to show sapphire again.

'I shall paint you.'

'Oh, I knew you would!'

'I shall paint you, Lady Dolly, when you are eighty. And when you, like that old man, have a face.'

CHAPTER ELEVEN

Diary of Adele Ward.
Albemarle Street, London.

21st March, 1894.

Whatever M says about my neurasthenic disposition, today I must steel myself to be strong. But what if they attach our furniture as they threatened? What if we are both arrested and thrown into a debtors' prison? The shame of it, the wretchedness, the dishonour!

Today I have discovered why M was so anxious to relieve me of my housekeeping duties. First Cook informed me that the butcher will give us no more credit, then a dun arrived from the wine merchants saying they must foreclose if our account is not met. And when I unlocked M's bureau and examined the housekeeping books I found it is the same everywhere: not a bill has been paid since he took upon himself the management of them. But worse, far worse, occurred after luncheon, when two coarse-looking men in bowler hats pushed their way past Bradley, the new parlour maid, and began to cross-question me in the most disagreeable and hectoring manner. Much of what they said I could scarcely comprehend, for I was near to fainting with shock, but it appears they were bailiff's men!!

Oh, how useless it is to be a woman! I pay calls, leave cards, work at my embroidery, trifle with my sketching pad, for that is what I have been brought up to. But of the world, the real world outside this house, I know nothing. Never once has M confided in me or told me how we stand. He never did so, and since the affair of Jenkins, his silences, and his absences, have grown longer. Yet I must remember my duty as a wife, I must not be so quick to judge as I was before. Oh, how I pray he has some reasonable explanation.

M returned from his club, or the Tivoli, or the Criterion – I no longer dare speculate as to his haunts – soon after eleven, a little the worse for drink and surprised to see I had not retired. He seemed not a whit surprised, however, at my account of the day's unwelcome callers, but jumped at once to his usual form of defence, which is attack: it was all my fault, I am heedlessly extravagant, I must have a new hat once a week and order my gowns from Worth or Lucile, I must keep a Victoria as well as a brougham, I must have a footman to attend me whenever I pay calls.

I found to my astonishment an icy calm had stolen over me. I pointed out that many, if not all the little luxuries he had singled out for condemnation, he had not only insisted upon as indispensable for one who held the position of his wife, but were also paid for by me out of my income of a thousand a year. Whereupon he became suddenly very quiet and thoughtful: then all at once fell at my feet and buried his head in my lap in total abasement.

So, gradually, when his pleas for understanding and forgiveness had abated somewhat, it all came out: he has taken several bad 'plungers' at the racecourse recently; he has lost money at billiards and backgammon and indeed by wagering on anything that could make a wager; but worst of all, he has incurred heavy losses at cards, which debts must be honoured if he is not to be publicly disgraced. He craved forgiveness for his one shameful lapse with Jenkins, for which there could be no excuse, but for which I must surely show mercy since he has after all been considerate of me. And he ended by imploring me to tell him if I could not find it in my heart to love him still, just a little.

I was again astonished, for though I know it is my duty to love him, it is no longer a question I can answer. However, I could not bear to see the man I had once regarded as so noble and strong humble himself before me. So, stroking the hair on the nape of his neck, the hair I used to think curled so dashingly and deliciously, I tried my utmost to comfort him. We could, I declared, remove to a smaller house in a less fashionable part of Town, let most of the servants go; I should willingly make any sacrifices necessary to repay our debts, even, with his guidance, undertake the housekeeping again and, until our heads were once more above water, we could live very reasonably on my thousand a year.

All of a sudden he became very animated, springing up from my lap and beginning to pace to and fro. 'You forget, my dearest, that I am a gentleman. Life in a squalid villa in Balham or Battersea? G—d, how could I hold my head up at the Club again, how could I forgive myself for forcing such degradation on you? And to exist on my wife's income? By Jove, you must believe I am the worst sort of cad!' Then, in his pacing, he seemed to arrest himself. 'But, on the other hand, if you could lend me the money – to extricate us from our present difficulties, you understand . . . if your lawyers could be persuaded to advance you something – '

For the third time I surprised myself, for I heard myself answer in a little hard voice that was not mine: 'No!'

He became suddenly very cold. 'Dearest, you truly do not understand. You are my wife, what we have we share. If I can't meet my IOUs to Majoribanks at the Club I shall be forced to resign. You may not be prepared to save me by sharing your inheritance, but by G–d you'll share in my disgrace. No decent house will ever admit you, your friends will shun you in the street, your own Papa will ponder seriously whether he may still acknowledge you as his daughter. And why, my dearest? Because husband and wife are one in the eyes of Society, though you, it seems, believe you are a law unto yourself.' He ceased pacing and clutched his forehead. 'Dear G–d, haven't I made allowances for your extravagance, your feeble-mindedness, your failures in the smallest duties of a wife, let alone—?'

'Stop!' I cried. 'Please, oh please, stop!'

But he did not stop. He continued, on and on in the same vein, until I agreed: he could see my lawyers, have his five thousand, prepare the papers tomorrow and I would sign them. For he is right. Husband and wife are one, his disgrace is my disgrace, I have no position except his position, no life except his life. To what other purpose did dear Mamma's patient teaching tend in those halcyon days of innocence before my wedding night? It is my <u>moral duty</u>; every dream I have treasured, every high ideal in every novel I have read instructs me so. But without love? Oh, without love . . .

CHAPTER TWELVE

It was unanimously agreed that my Cousin Felix was 'entirely horrid' and thenceforth not to be spoken of again.

'And anyway,' I said, 'I'm sure Dolly would soon have tired of him. After all, Meredith has two sons now, so he'll never inherit the baronetcy. And although he does have money, he certainly can't run to the necessary one hundred thousand pounds a year.'

'Still,' said Dilly, brooding, 'you must admit he was more interesting than Charlie Devereux.'

But, in any case, we had, with the end of the Season, moved out of his orbit. The Mountalbans had proposed that I go with the rest of the family to Deauville, and Aunt Jessica, presumably optimistic that autumn would remedy my summer's omission to become engaged, had given her consent. After Deauville we had gone to Scotland for the shooting, and after the shooting had come Christmas at Critchley. And at Christmas Dilly had married.

She had met him at Deauville, a young lieutenant on leave from India, fresh-faced, looking rather less than his twenty-two years, and yet, despite his cherubic innocence, with that same glint of mischief that would light up Dilly's eyes at the first hint of pretension or pomposity. I asked her about the churning feeling and she said, yes, it was there all right, but there were other things too, not just that he didn't talk about cricket or tread on her feet – in fact he professed to be so bad at dancing he had given it up altogether, a renunciation to which Dilly very readily agreed – but that he was so extremely, straightforwardly, unabashedly nice that being with him was like being with a friend. And, remembering that as I watched them come down the aisle of Critchley Castle chapel to the strains of Mendelssohn on Christmas Day, their faces pink and glowing with their sheer delight in each other, I own I felt a distinct twinge of envy.

The speed of Dilly's marriage had been occasioned by Robbie's need to return to India and his regiment soon after the honeymoon, so as she was gaining a friend I was, at least in the day-to-day sense of having someone to laugh with and confide in, losing one. The time had come to take myself in hand.

I had had plenty of respite to think that autumn. The October meeting at the Carlton Club at which the Conservatives had renounced the Coalition and brought about the fall of Lloyd George had taken Meredith North to fight the General Election and Archie had, of course, loyally followed him. Free from their pressure, I knew now what I must do. Accordingly, I wrote to Aunt Jessica before Christmas outlining my plans: if my allowance would stretch, and it seemed to me after careful calculation that it would, it was my intention to take digs in London, find myself a piano teacher and try to win a place at the Royal College of Music. I could not see how she could oppose me, since she had already tolerated my absence for so long, and since it could all be managed without any additional expense.

I had reckoned without Aunt Jessica. She wrote back by return of post saying that it was quite out of the question that I should, at my age and unmarried, live alone in London, and that, in any case, there was no point in my studying music since it would at best only fit me to become a teacher, an occupation completely unsuitable for someone connected with the de Lisles, albeit from the wrong side of the family. I was to return to Norfolk immediately after Dilly's wedding.

I studied the letter for some time. I could not believe she really feared my simple ambitions would blot the family escutcheon. It seemed to me she had responded from sheer perversity. It was she who ordered the destiny of individuals within the family and I was to understand that it was arrant presumption on my part, as her least favourite member of it, to challenge that. I felt she must, after reflection and when she had become accustomed to the idea, see reason. After all, she could not really want me back at Monks Last, and the effect of my plans would be, in the end, that she could comfortably wash her hands of her responsibility for me. I wrote again, a long, deferential and carefully-argued letter in which I hoped my determination nevertheless shone through. She again replied by return of post. The only suitable course for a young woman in my position was to get married. There was a perfectly eligible young man anxious to marry me. She not was forcing me into anything but simply laying before me the choices that were open to me. I was to marry Archie or return to Norfolk.

I wrote back saying that I would do neither. She wired me to inform me that until I saw reason she was cutting off my allowance.

Feeling that I could trespass no further on the generous hospitality of Lord and Lady Mountalban, I had gone, directly after Dilly's wedding, to stay with the Cunningham-Cowpers in Gloucestershire for a week. Here I laid my final plans. It was inconvenient to be without the allowance, but surely no more than inconvenient. In one sense it would even be better, for I should no longer be beholden to the de Lisles for anything. I would earn my own living, pay my own way and, by hard work and judicious saving, I should carry myself through my music studies. I should be independent at last.

And so, packing a small suitcase with sensible clothes, tweed skirts, blouses, suitably anonymous cardigans, and afterwards throwing in two afternoon dresses and an evening frock, just in case, I locked the rest of my wardrobe and possessions in my large tin trunk and, without breathing a word of my intentions or my true destination to anyone, caught the train to London. There, depositing my trunk in the station left-luggage office, and taking a firm grip on the suitcase which now contained my sole equipment for survival, I went in search of a room and a job.

That I found both relatively easily – admittedly at the cost of aching legs and two blisters the size of pennies, one on each foot – but easily nonetheless, should, I realize, not have encouraged me to over confidence. But, foolish in my innocence, I took it all as an omen of my inevitable success.

The room was in a hostel for young women in Bayswater. I shared it with two other girls, Jenny and Mary, both in their twenties, and older than me. We each had an iron bedstead with a flock mattress, a rubber undersheet and two grey blankets, a deal chest of drawers for our clothes and a small looking glass. There was oilcloth on the floor, a chamberpot under the bed, to be emptied, Jenny informed me, by the last person who used it, and jugs of hot water to wash in, unless we felt strong enough to brave the communal bathroom with its sluggish taps and stained bath. The establishment also provided us with a clean sheet every fortnight, breakfast of bread, butter and tea every morning, and supper every evening (usually more bread with jam or dripping), and pudding twice a week. The room was bitterly cold, particularly at 6.30 when the bell went for us to rise, and grey with a pall of intractable London grime. But I did not mind. I told myself it was simply an uncomfortable version of my boarding school, and besides, it was cheap.

I did not mind Jenny or Mary either, despite the fact that they would burst into fits of raucous laughter every time I opened my mouth.

'Oh, my!' Jenny would scream. 'Aren't we the toff!'

'M'Lady,' Mary would rejoin, flouncing up and down and pursing her lips in extravagant mimicry, 'would be obleeged if the butler would bring her breakfast in bed this morning.'

And their mirth knew no bounds when I thought I had found insect bites on my legs and arms.

'Well, we did tell you it was Dirty Dinah's old bed, ducks. Never liked to sleep alone, did Dirty Dinah. If she couldn't find herself a Russian Duck she'd take the bed bugs for company, she wasn't particular.'

Jenny and Mary did not seem so particular either. But then it was hard washing underclothes in rough soap and cold water and even harder to find somewhere they would dry. And the exigencies of the basin and ewer on those icy mornings, combined with a natural reluctance to undress in the full view of others, tended to make a quick lick and a promise the only practicable form of toilette. So when Jenny, fondling their silver-initialled backs with a hungry longing, drew my brushes through her lank hair or Mary appeared in one of my afternoon frocks from another assignation up the Dilly with someone I took to be her young man I told myself it would be ungenerous of me to be put out by it. And anyway, borrowing seemed to be a rule of the house, without the obligation to seek permission first. I contented myself with joining in their laughter and with liberally dousing my bed in Keating's Powder while they were both out of the room. And if I was secretly rather glad that my chinchilla coat, although it would have kept out the chill of my daily walk to work and made a much-needed extra bed-cover, was safely locked away in the Paddington left-luggage office, I also felt such thoughts were distinctly unworthy.

My job was as a shop girl at Mme Raoul's hat shop in Wigmore Street. For twenty-six shillings a week, plus a promised 6/6 commission when I had learnt my trade, I was to sell hats from 9 a.m. to 7 p.m. with an hour for luncheon – or dinner, as she called it – and a half day on Wednesday. My uniform was a black dress with a white lace jabot which made me look like a parlour maid, and at all times I was to be clean, neat and pleasant and above everything to remember, come what may, that the customer was always right.

It had sounded so simple. But under the tuition of Mme Raoul, an imposing woman with the uncertain temper of a bulldog, I was to discover that the selling of hats involved such a mixture of Machiavellian cunning, Disraelian eloquence and Uriah Heep-like humility, not to mention the patience of Job, that perhaps Mme Raoul was right when she described it in her fractured French accent as 'ze fine art'.

We were, as purveyors of exclusive *haute-couture* millinery designed in Paris for ladies of high breeding and quality, not given to the vulgarity of a sale in January, as were the department stores. But we harboured, nevertheless, amongst our stock a number of models which had, to the disgust of Mme Raoul, lain gathering dust for far too long. This old stock, regardless of its suitability to the needs or preferences of my customers, it was my duty to sell. And that this was not just a question of my smiling pleasantly and being as helpful as possible, Mme Raoul made abundantly clear on the first afternoon of my first day.

''Eavens, girl!' she screeched, the moment I had closed the ruched-netted glass of the shop door upon the retreating and empty-handed figure of my first customer. 'I show you what to do, you watch, but do you once pay ze attention? You do not stand there like ze pudding, telling madame "yes" and "no". You tell her in zis creation she is elegant, bee-ootiful, in zis marvel from Chez Raoul she will be the delight of 'er 'usband, ze envy of 'er friends, ze very embodiment of ze chic Parisienne!'

'But she looked ghastly in it,' I said.

'Zat is not ze point!' she spat. 'Ze customer does not come to Chez Raoul for ze truth. She come 'ere to buy ze creations. You will flower things up for ze customer!'

'Ze customer does not come 'ere for ze truth!' mimicked hunchbacked Elsie later in the workroom, where, seizing a moment when there were no customers in the shop and when Mme Raoul had vanished into the back office, I had retired to rest my aching feet. 'She's no more French than I am. That accent's like her hair – straight out of the dye bottle. You listen carefully, love, and you'll find its roots are showing.'

And, to my amusement, Elsie was right, for the next day when Mme Raoul, in full flowery spate over the glories of a jewelled toque, observed me leaning against a pillar surreptitiously easing my feet, she abandoned the flowers momentarily to let out a screech that owed more to the sound of Bow Bells than it ever had to the Champs Elysées.

Elsie was little and pale, and I was glad she had told me she was only twenty-five before I had had the chance tactlessly to betray my assumption that she was very much older. She worked to support an invalid mother and five brothers and sisters, and when she talked of her family, her thin hands never stopping for a moment but pinning, sewing, twisting, tweaking, her voice vibrated with pride and affection like the old tin kettle brewing up to boiling point on the gas ring in the corner. I liked to sit in the tiny, steamy workroom listening to her talk when I could, watching those deft hands coax velvet into folds, organza into the petals of a tea rose, gossamer veiling into a fine mist above a broad golden brim of straw, little, pale, twisted Elsie, magicking out of air the magnificence of Chez Raoul's creations. We were allies in adversity, Elsie and I, in those brief moments of snatched respite when Mme Raoul retired to the office to take, so Elsie swore, a snifter from her silver flask of gin, the aroma of which she masked with violet cachous. And, when Elsie was screamed at for being behind with an order or I had a quarter of an hour's pay cut for being five minutes late, we would exchange meaningful looks and Elsie, choking with the little dry cough she had, would spit out a mouthful of pins and proclaim darkly: 'She'll get what's coming to her one day – the old cow!'

Still, it was work and it would get me where I wanted in the end. All I needed now was to find a piano and a teacher. There was an old upright piano in the hostel sitting room. I had not dared to try it yet, as there had always been other girls in the room talking and smoking whenever I had put my head around the door. But I wondered whether, if I plucked up enough courage to ask the Warden, she would give me permission to get up very early in the morning and practise while no one else was around. I would need first to get my energy back, for I found, with the unaccustomed rigour of standing all day, the absence of meat from my diet and the difficulty of getting to sleep in a freezing bed, I felt constantly exhausted. But I had no doubt that would pass when I became used to my new life. The question of the music teacher was a more vexing one. My 26/- did not stretch far once I had paid for dinner and my bed and board. But when I had got into the way of selling ze creations my wages would be augmented by commission. And besides I had with forethought in the autumn saved what I could of my allowance for emergencies, some £20 which nestled for safety between the crêpe-de-Chine folds of my underwear in the top drawer of my dressing table. All I needed was determination and my plans for the future could not fail to work out.

I had been thankful that Chez Raoul was not the sort of shop likely to be frequented by people I knew – its power to preserve the mystery of my whereabouts had been my main reason for choosing it. But, one morning after I had been working for ten days and had survived the loneliness of a solitary Sunday, I saw two customers step over our threshold and was dismayed to recognize one of them as Miles Millington's old aunt. Quickly I slid behind a pillar and was making for the sanctuary of the workroom when Mme Raoul's voice rang out: 'Attend to ze ladies, if you pliz!'

Lowering my eyes, I slunk back.

Phoebe Millington's friend wanted to try one of our pull-on velour models – 'so chic for the country or *pour le sport*'. We had them in several colours and I was able to make a play of pulling out drawers and handing new shades over my shoulder with my face averted.

I was relieved to observe that Mme Raoul had retired to the office for her mid-morning reviver, for this new manifestation of my failure at salesmanship would certainly have brought her close to a seizure.

I had only one thing to count on: my complete invisibility as a shop girl. For I had very quickly noticed that while my manners, attentiveness and mistakes might be remarked upon, the particulars of my face would go quite unobserved. Mercifully, this seemed to work in my favour: though Phoebe Millington's eyes did once stray towards me they did not linger, and I ushered the two women out of the shop congratulating myself not only on preserving my incognito but also on having sold the friend one of Chez Raoul's oldest velour hats, which would surely restore some points to my credit.

Alas, perhaps it was time my ridiculous optimism was punctured. (Or perhaps it was a judgement on me for the hat.) For when I returned from luncheon the next day it was to be confronted by an irate Mme Raoul.

'My girls do not receive ze personal visitors in zis salon!' she rasped, expelling a gust of hot violets into my face. And, standing aside, she revealed Archie, hat in hand, loitering sheepishly near a pillar.

'S–s–sorry, old girl,' he stuttered. 'Had to come, moment I knew where you were.'

Mercifully at that instant two women in sables swept into the shop and Mme Raoul, torn between reprimanding me and the scent of a sale, finally fell prey to the vision of flowering up several of ze oldest and most intractable creations, and left us.

'Been dashed worried, old girl. Dammit, it's not on, running away like that, what?'

'Archie,' I whispered, 'keep your voice down. You'll lose me my job.'

'Bloody silly! Girl like you doesn't need a job. Want to look after you. Love you, old girl—'

'Please, Archie—'

'Dashit, got to get the words out. Won't let you stop me this time. Want you to – marry me.'

In the genteel hush of the salon his voice bellowed. The two women in sables looked round in amazement and Mme Raoul's eyes popped.

'Archie,' I said, as gently as I could, 'it's very kind and sweet of you, and you will make some girl a splendid husband. But not me. I don't want to get married. Oh, Archie, understand. Not me. Not me.'

There were little beads of sweat upon his upper lip, his brow was furrowed with the effort of concentrating on his purpose, and I suddenly knew that he was not listening to me, that his thoughts had never taken him farther than the moment of confronting me, so that he had no contingency plan for failure and must stand his ground until I had been persuaded to see things his way. I felt deeply for him but I could not say the only words that would help him, and I saw with despair that Mme Raoul was now opening the door for the two sabled ladies, who had not made a single purchase.

'Oh, Archie,' I said, as he stood, ramrod-stiff beside the pillar, 'I'm so sorry.'

But at that moment he seemed at last to see Mme Raoul advancing on us. As if all of him had suddenly become unglued with the unsticking of his resolve, he appeared to crumple, his shoulders drooped, even his knees seemed to sag. And, making a little helpless clutching movement at his hat, he bolted for the door.

I was certain, even while I watched the ruched net shiver as the door slammed shut, that his visit would not be without repercussions. He knew where I was now and he would tell others, perhaps come back himself. If I had not, in all these months, succeeded in discouraging him, I had no reason to suppose the mere fact that his intentions and my rejection of them were now set out openly between us would work where everything else had failed. He had the backing of Aunt Jessica and Meredith. Where I deflated him, they would buoy him up, where I protested the seriousness of my resolve, they would dismiss my actions as the product of a girlish whim. I did not want him to return because, above all, I did not wish to be forced to hurt him again. But I also feared in earnest for my job. Mme Raoul had lectured me this time and, apart from docking my wages a further quarter for the minutes Archie and I had spent talking, had otherwise let me off. But it was not difficult to gauge her mood, should the episode occur again. I tiptoed round the salon, praying that I might be efficient and invisible, holding my breath and casting apprehensive glances through the net at the street outside, waiting for the inevitable.

I did not have long to wait. Late next morning, as I was sneaking a quick sip of stewed tea with Elsie in the workroom, Mme Raoul exploded through the door.

'Mees Ward, I 'ave told you I do not permit gentlemen visitors in ze salon! You will pliz to get rid of 'im now.'

My heart sank, and I silently cursed Archie for his obstinacy. I followed her submissively into the salon.

But the man who stood at the far end of it, his back turned to the room, looking out through the grimy net at the street, was not Archie. My footsteps slowed. For there was no mistaking that tall straight back, or the air of indifferent elegance with which the dark, velvet-collared chesterfield swung negligently from his shoulders.

My Cousin Felix turned towards me. He was not smiling. And I knew at once that he had been sent by Aunt Jessica to force me to return to Norfolk.

CHAPTER THIRTEEN

I felt suddenly such an overwhelming sense of panic that I almost turned and ran back to the workroom. But Mme Raoul was behind me, barring my way. I advanced two or three reluctant steps towards him.

'I can't talk to you here,' I said.

'I have no intention of talking in this place,' he replied quietly. Then, turning to Mme Raoul, he said: 'Miss Ward is my cousin. I had hoped to take her to luncheon at one, if she is free. Perhaps you would forgive me – ' and here he looked at his watch – 'if she went five minutes early.'

There was in his voice, despite its utmost politeness, an undertone that did not brook denial. Mme Raoul hesitated. I watched for a split second the protuberant eyes absorb every nuance in line and cut of the elegant handiwork of Messrs Locke, Turnbull and Asser and Lobb, computing them into pounds, shillings and pence with the speed of a cash register, before she nodded. Then, all at once, as if I were a creature bereft of will or decision, I was being bundled into my coat and hat and escorted out into the street like a prisoner under guard. My Cousin Felix's Hispano Suiza stood at the kerb. He waited for me to settle myself into its pigskin depths, then closed the door on me firmly and climbed into the driving seat without a word.

I took a deep breath and willed myself to be sensible. After all, he could not force me to return to Norfolk against my wishes, and he would never persuade me to go of my own accord. 'Where are you taking me?' I said.

'I thought Claridges.'

'Oh.' So he really did intend to give me luncheon. 'That would be glorious, but – '

'But what?'

His face was set upon the road, swinging the long silver-grey bonnet of the car out to overtake a horse-drawn grocer's van, and I could not read its expression.

'Well, I'm afraid it would take too long. You see, I must be back by five to two. Otherwise she'll dock my money again. Or worse, give me my cards.'

Still I could not read his face. 'Then I'm in your hands,' was all he said.

There was a chop house in a side street just round the corner where I sometimes went for a bowl of soup when my stomach cried out against yet more bread and dripping and the part of me which controlled my exchequer was weak enough to listen. It was an establishment notable for its attention to economy rather than to elegance or gastronomic pleasure. But still, the place was fast and near the shop, and I would also have the advantage of being on my own territory – for as I grew calmer I could see, in the face of his general air of commanding the situation, I should need every advantage I could muster.

To my embarrassment, we caused some surreptitious turning of heads as we entered. I had not thought how ill-assorted we looked, I in my shop girl's black, he so tall and striking, with that aura of patrician hauteur the clientele of the chop house were more accustomed to see drifting out of Mayfair clubs into the sleek fastness of chauffeured limousines; the shop assistant and the gentleman, keeping a secret tryst across the gravy-stained tablecloth, the sheer stuff of threepenny novelettes. He seemed to impress our waitress too, for she came to present the menu almost immediately, vigorously whisking away the crumbs left by the previous diners with her napkin.

We both ordered the soup and I chose the mutton chops, he the fried fish. He opened his curved silver cigarette case, took out one of the oval Murattis he smoked, tapped it against the silver and struck a match. In the flare of the sulphur, his face was as impenetrable as ever. I supposed he must be irritated by his errand, or bored, or both.

I watched him draw upon the cigarette. 'Why you?' I said.

'There seemed no alternative. My mother, as you know, prefers not to leave Monks Last. And since the House isn't sitting, Meredith is busy in his constituency explaining why Bonar Law hasn't put an end to unemployment. I was the only person left in London.'

He drew again on the cigarette. It was a clever choice of Aunt Jessica's, I thought, a masterstroke. I knew how to cope with Cousin Meredith. He would leap in directly, lecturing, hectoring, would become fixed and obstinate if he were challenged but was helpless against silent resistance. But Felix was another matter. Not only was it impossible to tell what he was thinking, but he had annexed silence to his side, waiting for me to explain myself, to tie myself up in words until I had accomplished my own downfall.

The soup arrived, brown and glutinous, but hot nonetheless. I was irritated to discover that my hand trembled as I raised the spoon to my mouth. I decided at last upon cold reason. I must put my case sensibly, practically, without panicking. Though it had not worked with Aunt Jessica perhaps, as an echo of his own cool reasonableness, it was my only hope with Felix.

'I'm sorry you've been put to this trouble,' I said. 'I didn't want anyonc to bc worried or bothered about me. And I'm perfectly all right, as you can see. I have a job and somewhere to live and I'm getting on splendidly.'

Abandoning the soup, he surveyed me again with that cool, quizzical look of his, tips of fingers together, like a doctor disinterestedly observing symptoms in a difficult patient.

'You must understand my mother's point of view, Christabel. She has a responsibility for you as your guardian. She simply cannot allow you to disappear out of her—'

'Control?' I asked, interrupting despite myself.

'Out of her sight. Out of reach if you should get into any trouble.' He pushed the soup plate away with faint disgust. And from the gesture, and from something in his voice, I took suddenly not irritation or boredom alone, but a distaste for the job he had been given.

'But I'm not in any trouble. Everything's going brilliantly. I have a job, a room, I'm saving money, next week I'm going to find a piano teacher—'

'A piano teacher?' He sounded puzzled.

'Well, I'll have to work like mad if I'm going to get into the Royal College. And I can't do that without a teacher.'

'The Royal College of Music?' He looked genuinely surprised.

'You mean she didn't tell you?'

'No,' he said thoughtfully. 'She didn't tell me.'

'She probably wouldn't—' I stopped myself. 'She probably just forgot. But that's why I'm doing all this. I may not have enough talent, but I'd never forgive myself if I didn't try. My music teacher at school always said if I worked I might be quite good.'

'Yes,' he said, and all at once there was an odd, absent look in his eyes. 'I remember. That dreadful summer. The funny little red-haired ghost who was always vanishing whenever anyone else appeared. Chopin. One of the *ballades* – or was it the Military Polonaise?'

It was my turn to look surprised. I had not imagined he had recalled even my presence at Monks Last. I wondered if he remembered too that while he had lain upon the chaise longue listening to me play he had been secretly planning his own independence.

'It's the only thing I want,' I said. 'I don't care about being poor, I don't mind about losing my allowance. I'll do anything so long as I can study music.'

The waitress appeared to replace our plates – mine empty, his brimfull – with the next course. My Cousin Felix looked circumspectly at the fish, lifted his fork, hesitated, then lowered it to the table again. The mutton chops had a grey, congealed look and a tired smell as if they had been much warmed over. But, since it was the first time I had seen meat for nearly two weeks, I fell upon them eagerly. My knife and fork flew, filleting, dissecting, taking up every morsel of meat and soggy cabbage as if they had been rare delicacies, chasing after the last lump of potato and ripple of gravy, until my plate was licked clean. Letting loose unwittingly a small sigh of satisfaction I looked up and observed that Felix was surveying me with some concern. I blushed. I had been quite unconscious of how fast I was eating.

'May I order you something more?'

The unexpected solicitude in his voice made me curse my hunger for having given itself away. I could not afford to let my guard slip, not now when he seemed, I was almost certain of it, to be reassessing my situation.

'No. No thank you.'

'Pudding then?'

I nodded. The pudding was apple pie, and I ate it with a measured slowness while he smoked a cigarette and lapsed into thought again.

Eventually he said: 'I think perhaps I could persuade her.'

I looked up, astonished. 'Persuade Aunt Jessica?'

'About the music, yes. I think so.'

I had hoped for a willingness to listen, perhaps even a concession or two, but this seemed like a total change of heart. I stared at him. 'Would you? Oh Felix, would you really?'

'I give you my firm promise to try.'

Try? Why, he was the only person in the world who could succeed. If he spoke to Aunt Jessica, why, her agreement was almost an accomplished fact. And to think I had imagined him my enemy when he had turned out to be the most powerful ally I could have.

I looked up at him, and for the moment the quizzical expression in those cool eyes no longer alarmed me.

'Oh, Felix, I'll never forget it, never, never. I'll go on being grateful as long as I live. Oh, I'm so grateful I could kiss you!'

He laughed. 'My dear child, there is no need to get overexcited – I haven't succeeded yet. But you have my promise.' His face was suddenly serious again. 'And now, in return, I require something from you.'

I was still reeling from what seemed his complete volte-face. 'I'd do anything to repay you,' I said. 'Anything.'

'After you have finished work you will come back with me to Cheyne Walk and we will make arrangements for your return to Norfolk.'

I stopped with my spoon halfway to my mouth and stared at him. Surely I could not have misunderstood him. Hadn't he just said he would help me against Aunt Jessica, help me stay in London?

'You will collect your wages and tell the woman at the hat shop you will not be coming back. My man will go to wherever you live and pick up your things. And we shall put you on a train tomorrow morning.'

I felt suddenly chilled. 'No,' I said.

'But my dear Christabel, you must realize there can be no other way.'

'No!' I said. 'No, no, no!'

'I have given you my promise about the music, and now you must do this for me in return.'

I looked at that closed, impenetrable face and knew how right my first instincts had been, how wrong I was to have trusted him, even for a second. 'No. You tricked me. I won't go back. Your promise means nothing if I go back!'

He sighed. 'My dear child, you are being ridiculous.'

I felt the panic rising in me again. 'If I go back she'll never let me return to London. You can talk to her all you like, but once she's got me where she wants me, she won't listen. She'll force me to marry Archie Cadwallander.'

He took another cigarette from the silver case and snapped it shut with an irritated click. 'Christabel, you are beginning to sound like someone from a Victorian melodrama.'

'All I want is to be independent. Is that so very bad? I've

proved I can look after myself, I've proved I can manage perfectly well.'

He laughed. 'My dear little cousin, next time you pass a looking glass perhaps you should examine yourself. You are all skin and bone and obviously starving hungry. Your face is as white as chalk and you have big black marks under your eyes. You work ridiculous hours in that sordid little shop and then you go back to God only knows what squalor in the evenings. How long do you imagine you will survive on your own, a mere child?'

'I was seventeen last birthday.'

'You are still a child and sooner or later you will discover one Season doesn't altogether equip you to take on the world.'

I was beside myself. 'What does Aunt Jessica imagine – that I'll be carried off for the white slave trade? I can keep myself out of trouble.'

He raised his eyebrows. Though his eyes were impenetrable there was in the curve of his mouth a faint smile, a superciliousness that made me certain he was remembering the incident with Archie at Critchley Castle. In desperation I glanced up at the clock on the wall. 'Oh my goodness, I must go. I'll never get back to the shop on time!'

He drew upon his cigarette. 'I think, in view of your attitude, we will change the plan. It will be more sensible if you don't return to work but come directly home with me.'

I looked at him. His face was a mask now as though, having arrived at his decision, he had withdrawn from any further discussion of it.

'Oh please,' I said. 'Couldn't you go back to Aunt Jessica and say I wasn't at the hat shop? Couldn't you say you'd never seen me?'

He gave a sigh, as if I were beginning to try his patience. 'Christabel, there is no point in arguing. You really have no choice in the matter.'

'Because Aunt Jessica won't allow it?'

'No,' he said, stubbing out his cigarette abruptly. 'Because I won't allow it. You will come with me now to Cheyne Walk.'

I watched him being charming to the waitress as he paid the bill and thought I hated him more than all the other de Lisles put together, even Aunt Jessica who, though she was implacable in her opposition, never sought to disguise it beneath smooth words and spurious promises. I thought of getting up from the table, suddenly that instant, and running for the door.

But no, it was too public, there were too many people to create obstacles, he would find a way of stopping me somehow. Indeed, though his touch on my elbow was light, as he escorted me out into the street, I knew the moment I tried to break and run it would tighten like a vice. I was, in broad daylight and under the guise of all the normal gallantries a man pays a woman, ushering her through doors, taking her arm, interposing himself between her and the road, a carefully-guarded prisoner.

He settled me into the car again, slamming the passenger door shut like the door of a cell. But this time, as he walked round to the driver's side, I felt for the handle and tested it surreptitiously. It was not at all stiff.

The car pulled out of the side road and into the traffic of Oxford Street. Neither of us spoke. We took our place in a procession of cars, between a Baby Austin and a taxicab. Distantly, in the stream of traffic approaching in the opposite direction, I saw a bus and in front of it a brewer's dray piled high with barrels, ribbon-decked horses plodding steadily forward. Our progress, too, was sluggish, but nevertheless not yet slow enough. I held my breath and waited. We were almost opposite Selfridges now, on the other side of the road. Ahead of us, in the direction of Marble Arch, there came suddenly the expected squeal of brakes. The Austin braked, we braked, behind us the taxicab braked, the brewer's dray drew almost level with us. I pushed down on the door handle with all my strength and, hurling myself out into the path of the oncoming horses, avoiding the hooves of the leading pair by inches and narrowly missing collision with a yellow Bugatti which was trying to cut past them on the inside, I flung myself across the road, darted along the crowded pavement and dived in through the swing doors of Selfridges main entrance. The store was packed with shoppers up in town for the January sale. I worked my way towards the crowded epicentre of it, away from Oxford Street, away from the entrances until I was lost in a welter of cheap household linen and lingerie and bales of last season's cretonne.

I had scarcely drawn breath let alone looked back, but I knew he would not be following me. It would have outraged his dignity to chase me across the road, but, even if he had wanted to, he had been trapped by the necessity of staying with the car, of moving on when the traffic moved. I had escaped.

But it was a blow, nonetheless. I could never go back to the hat shop, and I had lost nearly a week's wages into the bargain. Still, I had retained my independence. I was more determined than ever now, and after all I had my savings to fall back on, carefully hidden in my underwear drawer. And although they had found out about the shop, no one knew where I lived. I would wait an hour or so, until Felix must without doubt have given me up, then leave by a side entrance and walk about until it was evening and I was allowed back into the hostel. Then I could decide what to do.

At eight o'clock, weary, footsore, but unmolested, having finally killed time in a picture house, I returned under cover of darkness to the hostel and went straight up to my room. Jenny and Mary appeared to have come back from work and gone straight out again and I was mercifully, blissfully alone. Despite its stained oilcloth and mean furniture, I felt this room was sanctuary now, my hope of survival. I went to the top drawer of my dressing table and, opening it, put my hands in amongst the smooth folds of crêpe de Chine to feel for the four crisp five-pound notes that constituted my savings.

The drawer was in disorder and my money was gone.

CHAPTER FOURTEEN

It was an agonizing dilemma.

On the one hand I needed the money now, desperately. I had, I discovered after counting, only 3/6 left in my purse: 3/6 suddenly between myself and starvation until I could find myself another job. And there were my lodgings to be paid for and, even if I were successful, a whole week to be got through before I should have money again. I had never in my life, even during the time at Weymouth when my mother had gone grey fretting over how to stretch our meagre subsistence, been utterly penniless before.

I needed my savings. But I realized I would do better to give them up for lost. For how could I not focus suspicion first upon my roommates, Jenny and Mary? And yet was that fair? Yes, in the matter of clothes and personal possessions they seemed to believe what was mine was theirs. But would I not have been perfectly free to borrow anything from them if I had wanted to? It did not follow that the borrowing of a couple of frocks should extend itself to taking money. Our doors did not lock and any one of the girls in the hostel could have let themselves in while we were out and hunted through our drawers. To someone living with the utter despair I now so suddenly understood real poverty to be, twenty pounds was a considerable sum of money. It had been foolhardy, not to say unkind, to place such irresistible temptation in what I realized with hindsight was an obvious hiding place. Anyone could have yielded to it – indeed, in the circumstances in which we lived perhaps it was only surprising that no one had sooner. So why did my suspicions keep coming back to Jenny and Mary? Why did I keep reminding myself that they, above all, had the time and the opportunity, they more than anyone were most likely to be rummaging through my drawers? They were, in my new life, apart from Elsie, my closest approximation to friends. What right had I to think such ill of them? Or, even if my suspicions were justly founded, what could I achieve by taxing them with the theft? And I could prove nothing. It seemed to me that all my conjectures and suspicions served only to make me more despicable to myself and to worsen my plight.

It was bitterly cold. Even in my coat, sitting bolt upright on the edge of the bed, my arms clasped about me for warmth, I shivered. A distant clock chimed. I counted the strokes carefully until they stopped at twelve. Ten minutes later I heard voices and giggling in the corridor, voices I recognized and which suddenly filled me with dread. I turned to face the door as it burst open.

'Oh Lor!' sniggered Mary. 'What's up with her Ladyship then? Been to a funeral by the looks of her.'

They were staggering a little, supporting each other as they clung together in the doorway giggling. I could smell the alcohol on their breath. Mary, her serge coat swinging open over my evening frock, her thick black hair, escaped from its combs, falling across her face, looked flushed like overripe fruit, her mouth sticky with carmine lipstick, her eyes luminous with excitement and a strange triumph. Beside her Jenny, too short for my afternoon frock, seemed pale and shrunken. There was, I thought, in her eyes, meeting mine, an unease, the first traces of uncertainty.

I forced a half-smile of welcome. 'I've lost my job,' I said.

Mary burst into raucous laughter. 'Her Ladyship's lost her job! Oh my, what a tragedy! That brings tears to my eyes, that does.'

'Oh, go easy, Mary,' said Jenny, and the uncertainty was there too, in her voice, growing. 'The poor thing looks done in.'

'Poor thing? She doesn't have to work. What's a job to her?'

'I have no money,' I said.

'Then you'll have to sponge off one of your rich relatives. Or pawn a diamond tiara. Or do what we do, ducks – go on the game.'

'The game?'

Mary was doubled up. 'Oh, hark at her!' she spluttered. 'What game do you think I mean, dear? A nice spot of lawn tennis or croquet? Or a little roulette on the French Riviera?'

'Leave her alone,' said Jenny, and now she looked thoroughly ill-at-ease. 'You can see she's upset.'

'So her Ladyship's upset, is she?' Mary swung round upon me and suddenly her face was transformed, her mouth crooked with hate, her eyes ablaze with it, her voice like a rasp. 'Well, she knows what she can do about it then. She can go back to her toffee-nosed family and stop bothering the likes of us. Her and her upstage ways – "Such fun, darlings, seeing how the other half lives!" Well, we don't want her sort spying on us, trying to make us feel small. She can bloody well hop it back to her bloody stately home and leave us alone!'

Her right arm flew out in a hot gesture, pointing my dismissal, and with it flew her handbag, a small envelope of scuffed leather, skidding across the oilcloth floor and coming to rest not two yards from my feet. Its fastenings were undone, and out of it spilled lipstick, powder compact, keys, some boiled sweets, a dirty handerchief. And three clean, crisp five-pound notes.

For a moment all three of us were transfixed, staring at the open bag and its contents.

Then I got up from the bed. 'Where did that money come from?' I asked, keeping my voice with difficulty light and even, taking two paces towards the bag.

'None of your business!' Mary swooped down and snatched it up, cramming the scattered objects back into it, thrusting the notes in with them, pushing them down as far as they would go as if the action would make them invisible. 'An American film star gave it me because he liked the colour of my eyes. What's it to you?'

I took another two paces towards her. I could feel myself beginning to shake with anger. 'It's my money, isn't it?'

'I got it fair and square off my young man for services rendered.'

'He would never give you so much.'

'Oh wouldn't he just? What a bloody insult! What the flaming hell do you know about it?'

'I know it's my money,' I said, moving towards her again. 'And I'd be grateful if you could give me back what's left of it.'

We were close now, both of us taut, still, trying to outface each other.

'It's nothing to do with me,' stuttered Jenny, edging away from Mary to the safety of her corner of the room. 'I told her she shouldn't touch it.'

'You stupid bitch!' snarled Mary. 'You keep your bloody trap shut!'

Jenny cowered. Mary whirled back at me, her chin thrust out, her eyes defiant.

'So what if I did take it? What right have you got to it anyway? You didn't earn it. Your people got it from riding on the backs of working people like mine. I'm just taking from the rich and giving to the poor. What's twenty bloody quid to you anyway?'

I made an effort to swallow my anger. 'Please,' I said, as reasonably as I could, 'I think I understand. But it's not as you imagine. That's all the money I have in the world.' And, putting out my hand, I took another step towards her.

The sudden movement brought the tension between us to breaking point. She flung herself upon me, pushing me backwards by the throat. I staggered and fell, jarring my head on the bedframe. She threw the handbag at Jenny, then leapt upon me again, tearing at my hair, clawing at my face and eyes with her fingers. I felt wet blood on my cheek, felt anger and fear rising within me. I grabbed her hair and pulled it back hard, rolling over until I was on top of her with my hands at her throat. Then I felt Jenny from behind me, tearing at my arm, twisting it behind my back while Mary's hand pushed up into my face. The three of us rolled over again, a snarling, scratching, seething knot of bodies. Jenny's fists pummelled my neck and back, Mary's knee jabbed like fire into my stomach. I was winded, I could not breathe, I could taste my own blood. And then suddenly there was a voice shouting at us, bellowing, commanding us to be still.

The Warden stood framed in the doorway, her face like thunder.

We untangled ourselves slowly, Mary and Jenny retreating to their own corners of the room. I lay in the middle of the floor, clutching my stomach, trying to get my breath back, trying in vain to get to my feet.

The Warden was a tall woman. With her dark serge dress, and her steel-framed spectacles glinting sternly in the dim flicker of the gaslight, she looked the very embodiment of harsh justice.

'Who started this?' she asked sharply.

There was a pause. Then Jenny said, pointing at me: 'She did, Miss. She started it.'

'That's right, Miss,' said Mary, pushing the hair out of her eyes. 'She started it. I caught her trying to steal some money. And when I went to stop her she started fighting.'

The Warden looked down at me. 'Is that what happened, Miss Ward?'

I struggled slowly to my feet.

'That's what happened, Miss,' said Jenny.

'She was trying to steal my money, Miss,' said Mary.

The Warden looked at me severely. 'Well, Miss Ward? This is a very serious allegation. What have you to say?'

I looked back at the Warden, then glanced at Jenny and Mary, who avoided my eye. There was no point in telling the truth. I had been brought up with the idea that one did not sneak on one's fellows, for one's own sake as much as for theirs. And anyway, if I told my side and was believed, what good would it do? Jenny and Mary would be arrested, Mary would probably be sent to prison, there to be labelled, hardened and set upon a path of self-destruction from which, if she were simply let be, good luck or her own common sense might otherwise save her. I, on the other hand, had, through the unfair lottery of fate, much more chance of survival, whatever happened. In one sense, Mary was right – twenty pounds, in the end, was not so important to me.

I felt suddenly overwhelmed with exhaustion. I staggered, under the Warden's arraigning eye, to my bed.

'Miss Ward,' said the stern figure in the doorway, 'I have asked you a question and I must have an answer. Did you steal, or attempt to steal money from Miss Larkin?'

Mary was studying her nails now, pretending inconsequence. Jenny was staring out of the window. Her face was ashen.

I looked at the Warden and said nothing.

'Come along, Miss Ward. This could be a police matter. I must have an answer.'

I held her gaze unwaveringly, silently.

She took in the other two for a moment with a hard, assessing glance. When she came back to me her face was grim. 'Very well. Since you will say nothing, I must assume your guilt. As you are obviously of previous good character, and as no theft has actually taken place, I am disposed to be lenient with you this time. But I cannot have uproar and brawling under this roof. You will pack your bags and leave here first thing tomorrow morning. Until then, I do not wish to hear another sound from this room.'

And, shooting all three of us a look heavy with warning, she went out, closing the door behind her.

There was silence for a moment.

Then Mary, turning towards me, gave a harsh laugh. 'I suppose you think you've got one over on us,' she said contemptuously, 'being such an angelic little martyr and not squealing to Old Drybones. I suppose you think we'll come and fawn over you and tell you what a saint you are. Well, you've got another think coming. Do you know what you are to me? Soft, that's all. Soft. Like a worm, to be trodden underfoot.'

And she pursed her lips and spat, with great force, in my direction.

I felt my eyes grow wet and burning. So I was to pack and leave the next morning. I would not wait, I would not bother to pack, they could have everything if they wanted. I would not wait, I would go now.

It was as if the very air was frozen, so that it had become thick, palpable, a swirling, clinging shroud into which the vapour of my breath vanished instantly. Tiny particles of ice stiffened my eyelashes, and froze the congealing blood on my cheek. The frost seemed to have seeped through even to my lungs, for from time to time I coughed harshly, painfully, the sound echoing weirdly in that thick darkness.

I stumbled on, bereft now of all sense of direction, unaware of how many miles I had walked, only of the necessity of not giving way to my exhaustion. And yet I was glad of the fog. It concealed my presence, wrapped me fast in its chilling blanket, keeping me safe from other night prowlers. Once, before it had settled so densely, I had been nearly stopped by a policeman who thought I was a woman of the streets. And later two drunken men had shouted that they would give me a good time, and when I had ignored them and simply walked on faster, they had chased me until I had managed to shake them off by hiding under some bushes.

I had formed no firm plan of where I was going or what I would do when I got there. Every so often I would try to run a little to get the blood flowing in my limbs again, although I increasingly lacked the energy for such an effort. And sometimes I would stop and listen for any faint sounds around me, to try to get some notion of my bearings.

Stopping now, listening and hearing back only the immensity of silence, I had almost given up when somewhere ahead of me, muffled but there nonetheless, came a sudden deep-throated mournful hooting, like the cry of a ghostly owl. I listened intently. It came again. The hooting of a tug boat on the river. I began to walk towards it, quickening my pace. Soon I could see small pinpricks of light that grew into the muzzy glow of lamps, and I fancied I could hear the lapping of water. The Embankment. I stumbled across a road, jarring my foot against an invisible kerb. My hands touched the clamminess of a stone parapet. I leant over, looking for the river and finding only that same blank darkness, but hearing it distinctly now, the eerie lap-lapping of water breaking gently upon stone. It must be high tide. I looked out into the darkness and my teeth chattered.

Then suddenly there was a noise somewhere to the left of me, in the shadow, beyond the feeble pool shed by the street lamp. And there rose out of the shadow, as if it were formed from it, a figure neither male nor female, matted, toothless, its hands clutching, its eyes blank like glass marbles, its crooked face twisted in a sickly, slobbering smile.

'Come here, dearie,' croaked a monstrous voice. 'Come here and let me feel who you are.'

I screamed. And then I was running, running, until my lungs ached and my numbed legs could no longer keep up with the impetus of my body. And all around me I could hear now the sounds of the night creatures, coaxing, careening, their gnarled hands, stubby and misshapen as lepers', clutching out of the darkness at me, catching my hair, pulling at my coat, brushing like clammy tentacles across my mouth and eyes, clutching, groping, fumbling.

I was crying too much to go on running. I stopped beneath a street lamp. As I wept the tears were freezing on my cheeks. I must pull myself together. I had little enough energy to continue walking, let alone running, and yet I was too frightened to stop, afraid of the cold, of the darkness, of the unmentionable horrors the fog now conjured up. I must find somewhere to go until dawn. But where? The Mountalbans, even supposing I had dared to trespass on their hospitality at this hour of the night, were at Critchley, the Cunningham-Cowpers still in Gloucestershire. And Dilly, who would have welcomed me unquestioningly at any hour, was in St Moritz on her honeymoon. That left only one place where there was any possibility that I might be taken in. And going there meant admitting my failure, surrendering myself to humiliation and to the inevitability of my being despatched to Aunt Jessica in Norfolk by tomorrow's train. I tried to stiffen myself against it by reminding myself of all my resolves, by calling upon what reserves of determination I had left, but try as I might a persistent voice inside me urged me to give in, spoke seductively of hot soup and a warm bed and a fire to toast my numbed fingers, whispered that I would be chilled to death and out of my senses with fear before dawn came. There was nothing for it. I was, after all, somewhere on the Embankment. It should not take so very long to find where my Cousin Felix lived in Cheyne Walk.

In spite of the hour, the house in Cheyne Walk was ablaze with light. My fingers were now so stiff I could barely clasp them round the door knocker, but Felix's manservant answered my feeble tapping almost immediately. He was a small man, dark, foreign, with a face like a child's creased into a patient smile which years of training had obviously fixed there, impervious to surprise or disaster, for his expression scarcely altered when he saw me, or when my carefully prepared speech froze in my throat, leaving me shivering and chattering my teeth at him. He beckoned me in and I followed him across an expanse of chequered marble to a pair of carved and panelled double doors which he silently drew open.

The light within the room hit me like a blast of heat from a furnace. A fire roared in the hearth, candles glittered on the mantelpiece, on low tables, on top of the grand piano. And yet it was not the mere presence of light itself, of flickering, dancing flame, that gave the impression of heat and glowing, but colour where the light fell, vivid scarlets and crimsons, rich blues, brilliant orange and gold, the jewelled colours of the Orient. Kelims hung upon the walls, appliquéed draperies of Persian silk were flung casually across chairs or swathed over a great, deep wicker-backed day bed and piled with cushions opulent with barbaric embroidery; and, at the far end of the room, supported on screens and separated by a heavy fall of dark velvet, two panels of icon painting, mystic echo of those pagan blues and scarlets, took up and refracted the candlelight in the glimmer of their gold-work.

There were seven or eight people in the room, reclining on cushions, lounging in armchairs in attitudes of languor or contemplation. I recognized Tarantin, and Mme Rostova lying back on the day bed with her feet tucked under her, in the act of sprinkling powder from a small enamelled box onto the back of her hand, which she then raised delicately to her nose. There was a strange, pervasive smell in the air too, heavy like incense, which brought with it a pungent sense of a moment interrupted, an atmosphere shattered.

They all looked round when the manservant spoke. Rostova lowered the curve of her hand. Suddenly she caught sight of me standing awkwardly in the hallway, and burst out laughing. Then they were all laughing, their faces split with it, their eyes damp, convulsed with uncontrollable laughter.

I had caught a glimpse of myself in the hall mirror and I suppose I must have looked strange to them, appearing unexpectedly out of the night, my coat and dress torn and mud-spattered, my stockings in holes, my hair falling wildly about my shoulders, one side of my face covered in blood. I wished heartily that I had not come, that I could disappear. Then my Cousin Felix rose. In his evening dress, he looked very tall and black against that brilliant wash of colour. His face was grim. The laughter stopped instantly. He came towards me across the room and through the double doors, pale, grim, as if he were aware of nothing else but my presence in the hallway.

Suddenly I realized that I had forgotten one obvious fact, that he was bound to be very angry with me. I tried to form some words of apology, but again the violence of my shivering prevented me. He stared at me for a moment and there was a strange expression I could not read in his eyes.

'Dear God, little one!' he said quietly.

Then, putting his hands on my shoulders to stop me shivering, he looked me full in the face. 'Do you need a doctor?'

I shook my head.

He took my chin in his hand, turning the left side of my face towards him, where the scratches were, examining them thoughtfully for a moment. Then he dropped his hand abruptly.

'Anatole!' It was like a military command. 'Is there still a fire in the study? And find me some brandy. As quickly as you can.'

The study was a small room, lined with books and lit only with a single lamp standard. Two deep wing chairs were drawn up to the fender. My Cousin Felix made me sit in the one nearest the light, pulling it closer to the heat of the flame. Anatole brought the brandy and, taking the decanter from him, Felix poured a liberal measure and came and placed the glass carefully in the stiffened fingers of my two hands. Then he retired to the other chair.

'I'm sorry – to – cause you – so much – trouble,' I said. 'I know – you're going to say – I told – you so.'

He took a Muratti from the curved silver case. 'My dear little Christie, your teeth are chattering so much I cannot understand a word you say. Sit and drink your brandy and try to get warm. Then you can explain it all to me.'

He lit the cigarette and sat back in his chair. I lifted the brandy to my lips, using both hands because of the shaking in them, and sipped it. After the cold, it seemed to sear my throat. But at the second sip I could begin to feel it warming me within as the fire warmed my extremities, so that after a while I had the sense of it moving through my whole body, expanding and thawing every vein until the blood flowed freely again and I had little pricks and tinglings of sensation even in my fingertips and toes.

And all the time he sat opposite me, his face half in shadow, watching me in that cool, impersonal way of his. Finally, when I had relaxed into the depths of my chair, savouring the relief of that delicious warmth, feeling my cheeks flushed and my head light with it, he threw his cigarette stub into the fire and said: 'Now you will tell me precisely what has happened to you.'

I explained as best I could, omitting nothing except my shameful attack of terror at the appearance of the tramp. He listened without interrupting, his eyes still on my face, and when I came to the end he said only: 'And you're sure that's all?'

'All?' I said indignantly. 'Everything's gone wrong, just as you told me it would. I've made an utter fool of myself. I've been so determined to be independent and I've ended up coming here and begging you for help. And now you'll put me on a train and send me straight back to Norfolk.'

'My dear Christie, it is four in the morning and your eyes are beginning to close. We will talk about all that tomorrow.' He rose and rang a bell. 'Anatole will find you a bed, run you a bath and get you something to put on those cuts. Before you fall asleep in your chair.'

His voice was surprisingly gentle, but I knew that promised nothing. Later, my face still smarting with iodine, I lay in a deep marble tub of steaming frangipane-scented water, feeling the fog and the grimy little hostel room and the terrors of the night wash away from me, dissolving into the steam as if they had never existed, and tried to think what I could say to him next morning that would persuade him to give me another chance. But my mind drifted and my eyelids were heavy. And when I found a vast bed waiting for me, the coverlet turned back on starched linen sheets, and a pair of pyjamas, a man's, of midnight-blue silk, laid out upon it, I could think of nothing but climbing into both. And, feeling the silk cool and the sheets crisp upon my skin, I fell asleep.

CHAPTER FIFTEEN

Diary of Adele Ward.
Monks Last, Norfolk.

2nd May, 1894.

How peaceful it is here! I came upstairs with the intention of reading to poor Mamma, but since she has fallen asleep I now sit in her window lazily basking in the sun, while on the lawn Papa frolics with Baby Meredith and J, Sir Arthur and M are all engaged in a croquet match with the Misses F from Downham. Oh, what could be more delightful, after the miseries of our life in London, than this drowsy country afternoon?

I truly believe Sir Arthur's invitation has been the saving of us – though I should not be grateful for anything whose occasion is the indisposition of poor Mamma. Yet, had we not been able to shut up the house in Albemarle Street and let the servants go, I cannot doubt but that, despite my signing several more of M's papers, we should have seen another visit from the bailiff's men. On occasion I wonder if Sir Arthur were moved to invite us here from some inkling of our precarious circumstances, though I pray not, as I should never be able to hold up my head again. At any rate, on the pretext that Mamma's sudden indisposition will benefit from a change of air and the attentions of both her daughters, and with the added advantage that we shall all be company for J when Sir Arthur leaves for Ireland tomorrow to negotiate the sale of his Wexford estate, here we are. Even M seems not displeased with it. Only J seems out of joint, having apparently formed a positive antipathy to M and not seeking to disguise it, which is very wearisome for the rest of us.

Poor dear Mamma. Dr B says it is only a trifling weakness of the heart brought on by rheumatic fever, but as I look at her now sleeping with the little china doll beside her on her pillow, the bride doll Papa brought her from Paris when they were first betrothed, from which she will never be parted, she seems so frail and small to me, almost a child again.

3rd May, 1894.

Sir Arthur departed for Ireland today and to my mind something of the warm spirit of the house has gone with him. While he is portly and has freckled hands and is not at all romantic-looking, yet he is kind and always good-natured. Although he will be gone some months, J seems to accept his absence with the greatest equanimity: indeed, when dear Baby was brought down after tea and asked most plaintively for his Papa, she merely yawned and pronounced that she despaired of the child's stupidity.

M, on the other hand, seems in high spirits and unexpectedly <u>attentive</u> towards me. This morning, as we were walking amongst the rose beds, he reached out, plucked a great crimson bloom and solemnly presented it to me – which will surely further endear him to J, for her roses are her favourite preoccupation!!! Regarding him thus, I was reminded so forcibly of the old M, my proud and gallant hero, the M who tried to steal a kiss in Mamma's rose garden two days before our wedding: and seeing, as if with new eyes, his noble features and graceful bearing, observing the firm lines of his mouth curved in such a tender expression, I could once again scarcely believe him capable of any immorality, let alone the great weaknesses I know him to possess, so that I felt my heart for an instant give a tremulous flutter of hope. Perhaps the suffering of this past year has been no more than the trial of pain and expiation which love is sometimes compelled to undergo before it can emerge purified from the <u>chastening</u> flame. Perhaps, M truly struggles with the low side of his nature and the fault is in me that I have not the generosity to forgive him. After all, Papa, whose *judgement is in all respects superior to mine, likes him well enough and laughs at his wild stories and spends hours after dinner smoking with him and playing billiards; and dear Papa, whose own sense of honour is so fastidious, could never be comfortable in the company of one whose character had no admirable or redeeming features.*

4th May, 1894.

Another balmy day, shadowed only by two clouds: Mamma's continued indisposition and J's constant warring with M. Papa intends to make a brief visit to London tomorrow to pursue his studies in astronomy and to attend the giving of a paper at the Royal Society, leaving Mamma and myself as sole mediators. I wish they could be persuaded to make a truce, but J is so unreasonable, as prickly as her roses. While I, of course, have heard all M's stories many times before and know them mostly to be empty bragging, she must needs challenge him on every point, whereupon he weighs in against her, feeling his manly honour has been slighted. I know I resolved yesterday, in the matter of M's faults, not always to be so hasty to condemn, but I cannot avoid relating a most disagreeable incident which occurred this evening at dinner.

M was holding the floor as usual and after a while the conversation turned to hunting. There was much discussion of dangerous hedges and dykes in this part of the country, with M, of course, boasting he could take the most spirited horse over anything and backing up his claim with a number of most improbable yarns from his time in Ireland. Whereat all of a sudden J rounded on him, declaring that he was nothing but a sham, that he would not dare even what she would dare and that all his professions of courage were as insubstantial as the wind, blowing very strong while they lasted but gone in a moment once they were out of his mouth. A dreadful silence fell, during which his face flushed and his eyes seemed to glitter in the candlelight. Then he said, very quietly, that he was not a coward and if she liked he would prove it to her. He would put his hand into the candle flame and hold it there until she ordered him to take it out. Which, to our dismay, he then did.

We watched in shocked silence for a moment, expecting, of course, that J would make him desist instantly. But she did not. She sat completely still, watching his fingers in the flame. Though the pain must have been intolerable there was nothing of it in his face, only an insane intensity which was reflected, flickering and dancing like the candlelight, in hers, as if they would both allow themselves to be devoured before either would give way. Suddenly the room seemed to fill with an unspeakable, sickly stench which I realized, in horror, was the smell of burning flesh. Choking, I turned my head away, while Papa cried out: 'In G—'s name, Jessica! In G—'s name, have done!' Then I heard her say, almost in a whisper: 'That is enough. For now.'

He took some butter with his other hand and made a bandage with his napkin; but all the while his eyes seemed to glitter with that same mad triumph, and when I glanced at her it was still there in her eyes too, as if she had proved something and was proud of it.

CHAPTER SIXTEEN

I awoke to the disorientation of a strange bed and a tapping on the door. The dark figure of a maid glided over to the curtains and daylight flooded in.

'If you please, madam, Mr de Lisle says if you are awake would you be so good as to go down and see him in his studio.'

I yawned, blinking at the light. 'What time is it?'

'Three o'clock, madam.'

'In the afternoon?'

'Yes, madam.'

I struggled to a sitting position, trying to shrug off sleep. If Felix wanted to see me it could only be for one reason. I must clear my head.

I looked across at the chair on which I had thrown my clothes the night before and saw with alarm that they were no longer there.

'If you please, madam, Mr Anatole gave me your dress to have it cleaned and mended. It won't be back till this evening. Mr de Lisle knows, but he says he must see you immediately. He said it would be all right.'

Did he indeed? Surveying myself in the cheval glass, I thought he could not have constructed the situation more perfectly to put me at a disadvantage. Even with the arms and legs turned up, his pyjamas swamped me, drooping from my shoulders, rendering my wrists and ankles unnaturally thin and frail and giving me overall a pathetically gamine appearance. My face was alabaster-pale, throwing into relief the three crimson gashes below the left cheekbone. My hair, too, despite vigorous brushing, had taken its usual rebellious way and tumbled in an unruly copper mass about my shoulders. In every particular, I thought, the mocking image in the cheval glass precluded dignity and seriousness. Yet dignified and serious I should have to be.

I made a couple of futile little sallies at my hair and bit my lips to try to bring some colour to them. Then, trailing midnight-blue silk, I went downstairs to confront my adversary.

My Cousin Felix's studio was on the first floor of the house, overlooking the river. It was a long, lofty-ceilinged room with tall Palladian windows which flooded it with light. A cushioned seat ran across both window embrasures, affording a view of the Thames, sluggish in the wintry grey of the afternoon, of the fantastic arches of the Albert Bridge and of the trees on the opposing bank. But beyond that the studio was sparsely furnished; a mahogany desk, a tall, high-backed stool, two battered armchairs, in one corner a Georgian screen with a couple of fringed shawls hanging haphazardly from it, in another a couch draped with crimson chenille and randomly strewn with cushions. Yet, despite the spartan simplicity of its furnishings, my first impression of the room was of its being crammed full so that, notwithstanding the feeling of light and space, there was no surface, no cranny or corner in which the eye did not find something to catch and hold it.

On an easel stood a huge unfinished canvas of two dancers captured in mid-movement, the echo of their images endlessly repeated like pictures in a stroboscope, as if to catch for each split-second of motion its juxtaposition with its successors in time and space. There were canvases piled against the walls too, canvases small and large, painted or virgin, and abandoned easels, and sheaves of sketches, pinned up here, discarded on a chair there, or scattered contemptuously across the floor. Brushes of every kind and size stood clean in jars or soaking neglectfully in turpentine at the foot of a large bronze of Leda submitting to the Swan; a length of embroidered silk half hid another bronze of a stallion's head and trailed indolently across a paint-encrusted palette and pots of water colour; an ivory brisé fan lay amongst a jumble of yellowing photographs and paint rags and sketching pads and, in a tray of palette knives, a jewelled Moorish dagger suddenly glittered; on the desk stood the porcelain cast of a man's head, of the sort used to teach medical students physiognomy, and on the marble mantelpiece, from a confusion of twisted paint tubes, brushes and bottles, gleamed the whiteness of a human skull.

Unlike the opulence of the drawing room, where everything seemed to have been designed with a deliberate eye to luxury and indulgence, this room appeared to have grown organically, of itself, from projects taken up and abandoned, from objects needed once and then discarded, from the exigencies of work. A fire blazed fiercely in the grate. There was a smell of woodsmoke and turpentine and linseed oil. My Cousin Felix, in a soft-collared white shirt open at the neck, sat at the desk working at something with a pencil. Without looking up, he motioned me to sit down too.

I found the couch and, pushing aside a scattering of books, sat on the edge of it. I was glad to be seated for after my exertions of the previous night I seemed to be stiff in every limb. And, besides, the pause gave me time to muster my forces.

There was a silence in which I could hear the scraping of his pencil upon the paper. I fiddled nervously with my sleeves. All at once he put the pencil down and looked up and I thought, as he caught sight of me in my strange attire, there flickered for a moment about his lips an amused smile.

I was suddenly angry. 'You can't send me to Norfolk without my clothes,' I said.

He rose and, going over to the mantelpiece, took a cigarette from a jade box.

'My dear Christabel, today we are not going to argue. As soon as Anatole has recovered your possessions you will set out for Monks Last. I should have thought your escapades last night would have shown you that you have no other choice.'

'Anyone can make one mistake. I'll prove I can learn from it.'

'Perhaps.' He went back to his desk and picked up the pencil. 'But it's not a subject it is any longer sensible for us to discuss.'

I felt my anger rising. He had returned, dismissively, to his work.

'Not sensible? But it's my whole life!'

He did not look up. 'My dear child, it's precisely this tendency of yours to overdramatize that makes discussion pointless.'

I was angry in earnest now. 'It's not overdramatizing. If I go back to Norfolk Aunt Jessica will find some way of forcing me to marry Archie, I know she will. And while that's nothing to you, it has some slight importance to me.'

He put down his pencil with a sigh. 'I will admit,' he said, slowly and carefully, like someone turning over a point of jurisprudence, 'that my mother has perhaps been unnecessarily harsh with you. I do not believe she was within her rights to cut off your allowance—'

'I don't care about my allowance!'

'Nor do I think it was fair to turn down the idea of your studying music out of hand.'

'Then you must see—'

He ignored my interruptions. 'But my mother is your guardian, Christabel, until you are twenty-one. While she is responsible for you, she cannot just allow you to run off and live God knows where. I'm sure that if, instead of defying her and resorting to melodrama, you were to go back to Norfolk and talk to her calmly, she would see the sense of all your plans and restore your allowance. I shall talk to her too, as I promised – although I know you think my promise worthless. And I'm certain that if you can bring yourself to be calm and reasonable with her she won't put any more obstacles in your way.'

I stared at him. 'But you surely can't believe that?'

'I see no reason not to believe it.'

'Even though it wasn't the slightest use for you?'

He raised his eyebrows.

'Oh, you were calm and reasonable enough. But Aunt Jessica wouldn't listen. She had her own plans for you, just as she has for me.'

A look of sudden comprehension crossed his face, followed by a frown of displeasure. 'That is better forgotten,' he said.

I was shaking with anger now. 'You are able to forget it. You have your freedom.'

'It was very different.'

'Different? You wanted your freedom so you took it. Why shouldn't I?'

'My dear Christabel, you must see that our two situations simply don't compare.'

I laughed bitterly. 'Oh yes, I see! Of course I see! You are a man. So when you decided you wanted to be a painter and ran away to Paris – oh, and you did run away, whatever grand name you prefer to call it – no one tried to force you into going back. No one spied on you and followed you and tried to bundle you into cars and trains. No one treated you as if you were a piece of property to be disposed of at will. You're a man and you did exactly what you wanted. But I've got to be calm and reasonable and let your mother marry me off to Archie Cadwallander.'

He sighed. 'My dear child, this obsession of yours – '

'It's not an obsession. And it isn't just Archie. I don't want to marry anyone. I just want to study music. And if I end up a grizzled old spinster with one room in Bloomsbury and nothing but a cat for company, I couldn't care less!'

'Oh Christie, Christie!' His exasperation had gone, he was suddenly laughing.

It maddened me beyond endurance. 'No, it wouldn't do to take me seriously, would it? I'm only a child – or so you keep telling me – and a girl child at that. Why should you understand that it matters to me, that I want to be a pianist every bit as much as you wanted to be a painter, that I care about my independence just as much as you do? You thought what you did with your life was something you should decide, and you alone. You wanted your independence and when Aunt Jessica opposed you you simply took it anyway. Just because I'm a woman doesn't mean I want it any the less. If it was right for you to go your own way, how can it not be right for me?'

His laughter had stopped. There was a small pause in which he rose and went over to the mantelpiece.

'Right?' he said, taking another cigarette from the jade box and turning upon me with a sardonic smile. 'My dear Christabel, it was one of the most cruelly selfish things I have ever done.'

For such an impersonal man it was all at once such a personal admission, as if I had somehow trespassed on some inner recess of pain, as if by touching a nerve I had uncovered the whole reason for his reconciliation with Aunt Jessica, even for his returning to England, that I was momentarily taken aback.

'So you see,' he said, lighting the cigarette, still with that same mocking curve of his lips, 'I expect you to follow my advice, child, not my example.'

The anger welled up in me again. 'But that's arrogant. And unfair. What Aunt Jessica asked of you from love she demands of me only from obedience.'

'To my mother, love and obedience are the same word.'

'But if either word should demand so much? . . . What you did wasn't wrong. Not for you.'

'It could have been done a better way.'

'But she wouldn't have left you one, you know that. What was right for you, what you needed – she was set against all of it. So you went. And you are a painter now, a good painter. And you have your life. On your terms. And I don't believe you regret it, I can't believe it. Oh, you may regret the way it was done, but you don't regret the rest of it, not one jot, one iota of it – '

'Enough, Christabel. Let's finish with this now.' His voice was sharp, and I knew then that I had stepped in too far, that he was irritated by my invasion and would cease to listen to me.

I felt a sudden deep despair.

We stood facing each other in silence for a moment and as I looked at him my eyes began to burn, diffusing his image in a haze of tears.

'Yes,' I said. 'Let's finish with it. I understand that I can't persuade you, that whatever I say you won't listen to me. And I know you think I'm a nuisance and silly and hysterical and – what's Meredith's word for it? – wild. And you probably think I'm ungrateful too, after all your family's done for me. But I'm not, really I'm not. And I want, just as much as anyone, to stop being tiresome to you all. I don't want Aunt Jessica to feel she's responsible for me. I don't want Meredith to worry about me or you to go chasing after me when you've got a hundred and one better things to do. I don't want you all to feel some dreadful sense of family duty towards me. And I don't want my allowance any more. It's been very kind of Aunt Jessica to give it to me all these years, but I don't want charity. All I want is what is mine, the only thing I have – my right to make what I can of my life. Oh, I won't make the same mistakes again, I'll get a better job, I'll get proper digs. But I will have it, my life, my freedom. And no one can stop me!'

His image was a blur now, rippling, wavering, beyond a brimming pool of tears I was determined not to shed. I turned and made my way blindly to the door.

'So if you send me back to Norfolk I'll simply run away again. And this time, I promise you, I won't be so easy to find!'

The tears fell as my hand found contact with the door handle. And I was turning it, escaping before I had to brush them away, when his voice came sharply from behind me.

'Christabel! Come back and sit down.'

I hesitated. Two fresh pools welled up, brimmed over and trickled humiliatingly down my cheeks.

'Sit down,' he said again, more gently.

I drew the back of my hand across each cheekbone. 'I'm only crying because I'm angry,' I said.

'Yes,' he said, 'angry. And also under a misapprehension.' He surveyed me sternly for a moment. 'My mother does not give you your allowance. You inherited the money under the terms of my father's will, just as my brother and I inherited ours. It is your money. It has most certainly never been charity, and I am profoundly sorry that you should ever have been given the impression that it was.'

'It doesn't matter,' I said.

'It matters very much. You will not demean my father's generosity by ever referring to it as charity again.'

The tears, once started, refused to stop. 'I'm sorry,' I said.

'And since it is your money I suppose it could be argued that you should choose how to spend it.'

In the act of wiping my eyes with my hand again, I looked up at him, surprised. His face, though still impenetrable, seemed to have softened a little.

'I have listened to what you have said, and I should like to think about it. I shall let you know this evening what I have decided. Now you had better go and persuade Anatole to give you something to eat.'

I stared at him, opened my mouth to say something, but he had picked up his pencil and gone back to his work. I wondered if this were yet another ploy of his to manipulate me into obedience. I stood for a few seconds struggling with my distrust. But then I thought I should not resist my dismissal lest he really were serious and I should make him change his mind.

I was almost at the door when he looked up again, and there was once more upon his lips that faint sardonic smile. 'And, as for the rest, little Christie, of course you are right. I regret only the cruelty. Nothing else.'

The evening seemed an interminable time in coming. My dress returned, cleaned and patched, but still, when I put it on, a poor thing, as if the mere act of refurbishing had beaten out of it any shape and body that Mme Raoul's strict eye for economy had first allowed. I made of it what I could, and put my hair up with combs, and tried ineffectually to cover the scratches on my face with generous layers of powder. But when Anatole came at eight to summon me to dinner and I found my Cousin Felix in dinner jacket and soft silk shirt waiting for me beside a table that glowed with candlelight and sparkled with glass and silver, my keen sense of being out of place in my bedraggled shop girl's uniform only served to increase my nervousness.

The very idea of the two of us sitting down to eat together with every appearance of domestic tranquillity, after all that had transpired and with so much still hanging unresolved between us, seemed somehow absurd. And besides, remembering from my coming-out dance his reticence, his positive unwillingness to be drawn on the subject of himself, I was struck by a fear that where the normal inconsequences of conversation were required he would prove quite impossible to talk to. And I was on tenterhooks, distrust still battling with a desperate desire for hope. Yet, despite my anxiety, despite the voice within me that cried out against that curious male belief that it is somehow offensive to talk about anything important until one has got all the way through the *oeufs truffés*, the *truite fumée* and the *côte de boeuf en croute*, I found myself chattering on quite easily, about Deauville and Dilly's wedding and the horrors of the hostel and Mme Raoul's floral method of selling hats. He had a natural capacity for listening which even my narrow experience of the ways of Society had taught me was rare, and for asking the right questions, so that when I glanced up and saw his face, half-shadowed in the candlelight, amused, attentive, I could flatter myself he was interested even though, as I thought most likely, he was really not.

Nevertheless, I was immensely relieved when, after the sorbet, he lit a cigarette, looked at his wristwatch as if he were expected somewhere and would already arrive late and, assuming an expression of sudden seriousness, scrutinized me thoughtfully for a moment.

'So,' he said, flicking ash indolently from the Muratti, 'you will want to know what I have decided. Well, it is this. I am going to give you a temporary stay of execution. I shall not send you back to Norfolk for three weeks. During that time, I shall find you a music teacher and you will work with him. If, when the three weeks are up, it is his opinion that you should continue to study the piano, then we shall have to decide what we do about it. If it is not, then you will return to Norfolk.'

I stared at him. There must, like the last time, be some catch.

'I have written to my mother asking her to restore your allowance and undertaking responsibility for you for the next three weeks. I do not expect her to raise any objections.'

Still I scanned his face, disbelieving, waiting for the inevitable conditions that would make it all impossible. But none came.

Seeing that I said nothing, he glanced at me questioningly. 'You understand, Christabel? If you cannot succeed in convincing me of the justice of your cause in three weeks, I shall send you back to Norfolk. And this time I will have no resistance. And no running away.'

I felt suddenly such an enormous sense of relief and joy that I was almost dizzy with it. 'Oh, I understand, Felix. And I'll work and work, I promise you that. I'll work till my fingers bleed.'

He was smiling at me quizzically. 'I think,' he said, looking at the scratches on my cheek, 'I should prefer you to be a little less prodigal when it comes to shedding blood.'

'And if I succeed, can I really go to the Royal College?'

'We should see whether it's possible, yes.'

'Oh Felix! If it's possible, I'll do anything. If my allowance isn't enough to pay the fees, I really will get a job. I don't care what I do – I'll even go back to Chez Raoul. And I'm sure if I found a decent place to live, Maisie Cunningham-Cowper or Venetia Mainwaring might come in with me, go halves with the rent—'

'No,' he said, firmly. 'For the moment, there is another condition. As long as I am responsible for you I want you under my eye. I have absolutely no intention of chasing all over London looking for you again. So, for the next three weeks, I have come to the reluctant conclusion that you will have to stay here. It won't be particularly satisfactory for either of us, but we will both have to make the best of it. I shall, of course, expect you to treat this house as if it were your home. Is that understood?'

I was now riding such an overpowering wave of euphoria that nothing seemed an obstacle to it. 'Oh yes,' I said, laughing. 'So long as I can stay in London, so long as you'll give me a chance. I won't get in the way, I promise. I'll be so quiet you'll scarcely notice I'm here. I'll even make myself useful, if you want. I'll – I'll tidy up for you and clean your brushes, I'll stand in if you need a model. Unless – ' I suddenly remembered Lady Dolly – 'unless you think I haven't got a face.'

He took the reference instantly and a slow, satirical smile spread across his lips. 'Oh no, my dear Christie. You have a face.'

And, meeting his eyes for a moment, I was disconcerted by an expression in them I did not understand.

He looked away, at his watch again. I wondered suddenly for whom I was making him late, whether somewhere Mme Rostova was impatiently waiting.

'There is one other thing,' he said, withdrawing a crisp white envelope from his pocket. 'Anatole went to the address you gave him to try and retrieve the rest of your belongings but he could find no trace of your ever having existed anywhere in the hostel. And since you've also lost the ticket for your trunk, he hasn't met with any success at Paddington either. So tomorrow you will take this money and buy yourself some clothes. And in case – ' and here his voice became dry and his eyes mocking – 'you should take it into your head, my child, to reject it as another piece of de Lisle charity, let us agree this. So long as you are in my house I shall require you to be an ornament to it – something you will singularly fail to do in that execrable dress. I think I prefer you in my pyjamas.'

And before I could say one word in reply, he had swept out.

CHAPTER SEVENTEEN

The challenge of proving myself during my three weeks' term of trial exhilarated rather than frightened me; I had not exaggerated when I had told Felix that I would work until I dropped. But that I should be so constantly under his eye was daunting. It annoyed me that his mockery and his criticism still had the power to disconcert me, and I resolved to harden myself against it. It was almost as if I had found myself suddenly back at Monks Last after all and would have need of my strongest defences. But, in the event, my weeks at Cheyne Walk were not as I expected.

I soon discovered that my Cousin Felix's unorthodoxy extended well beyond the wearing of soft shirts with his evening dress and choosing to live in Bohemian Chelsea rather than fashionable Mayfair. I had spent so much of my life in other people's houses since my mother died that I was a past master at fitting in tactfully with all the rules of domestic routine, which invariably sprang from the belief that the foundations of order would disintegrate without the observance of clockwork punctuality for meals. But the house in Cheyne Walk seemed to have no rules, nor for that matter any mealtimes (the dinner at which I had been given my amnesty was the only occasion I was to sit down to eat formally with my host for days) although Anatole, with his perennial smile, at once childlike and supremely worldly-wise, could be prevailed upon to supply food if it was required, apparently at any time of the day or night.

No, Cheyne Walk ran with a different momentum, the momentum of my Cousin Felix's work. For, despite the impression he liked to give of being very much the elegant dilettante, with no greater preoccupation than the usual round of cocktail parties and nightclubs, the private Felix de Lisle worked with a dedication that would have shamed my Cousin Meredith or anyone else I knew who made any pretence at having an occupation, so that it was not unusual for him to be out till dawn, sleep for four hours and then spend the rest of the day until eight or nine shut up in his studio, only to appear fleetingly, in immaculate evening dress, off to the Ritz or the Café Royal to begin his gruelling schedule all over again.

Yet, despite the prolonged absences of its master, the house, like some eighteenth-century court in which the fact of the monarch being in residence seemed on its own to impel attendance, was always full of people. I became used to passing strangers on the stairs or finding them reading newspapers in the study, apparently more at home there than I was myself. There was a curious attenuated pair, the Fortunins, Ambrose and Yseult – whether husband and wife or brother and sister I never did discover – whom I would surprise from time to time giving impromptu poetry recitals in the dining room, he in a crumpled suit and an earnest expression, she tall, pale, beaky, in flowing batik and a jewelled cardinal's cap, with an emerald cockatoo perched on her shoulder. There were several artists, and a quiet, gentle poet who had been gassed in the war, and a large, jolly woman who printed a left-wing magazine and arrived occasionally with a solemn man who was trying to commission Felix to make lithograph portraits of the Tarantin Ballet's principal dancers. And once I walked into the study to find Vladimir Tarantin himself, complete with his gilded retinue drinking lemon tea out of glasses; but the interest my existence had first aroused in him seemed to have been extinguished by his investigation of me at the private view, for he gave me such a malevolent glare, as if I had trespassed unforgivably upon his privacy, that I shut the door and went away at once.

Only the presence of Rostova, amongst this constant traffic, was missing. And yet not so, for the very fact of her absence and of my Cousin Felix's mysterious nocturnal life seemed to fill the house with a constant reminder of her, like the lingering of heavy perfume in an empty room.

But, with all the strangeness of it, I was not unhappy. The itinerant presences came and went with no indication that I was obliged to entertain them or even introduce myself if I did not wish to, and I was able to spend hours at the Steinway in the drawing room, working undisturbed, with greater concentration and energy than I had been able to achieve for years. The feeling of having worked hard and well and of not having to apologize to anyone for taking up time in doing so gave me an unaccustomed sense of freedom. True, I was alone much of the time, but there was freedom in that too. My only obligation was to appease the largely invisible presence of my Cousin Felix: and since the hard work he required of me was the very thing that gave me most pleasure, there seemed little difficulty in that.

Not, though, that his superciliousness towards me had in any way diminished. I had gone out, as he had insisted, and bought myself clothes to wear until my trunk was found, some sensible frocks for the day and, as an afterthought, in case it was needed, an evening dress. I was rather proud of the latter, particularly as I had never bought clothes 'ready-made' before and had been in some doubt about it at first, until the manageress of the shop had encouraged me. It was very imposing, my new evening frock, a confection of dark green satin and crêpe marocain, so dark that it was almost black, with a silver underskirt and silver and green bows at the neck, shoulders and at its dropped waistline upon both hips. Turning before the glass in it, and observing how much older it made me, how much more worldly and sophisticated, I could not understand why I had ever doubted its suitability. And, on the strength of the new, indisputably grown-up, me, I went straight into the nearest salon de coiffeur and had my hair shingled.

It was, I admit, despite the hatred I had always had for my mass of ungovernable hair, a wrench to see so much of it falling upon the salon floor. And I felt oddly cold in the January wind, even underneath my hat, as if I had been scalped. But there it was: I had done it and I was proud of it. And I secretly hoped my

Cousin Felix, on noticing it, would take it as a sign of the sophisticated, mature person I had become.

So it was a setback when I did not catch sight of him for two days and then only when I was crossing the hall in search of Anatole and breakfast and he, back no doubt from the Kit-Kat or the '43', was sweeping through in a swish of black opera cloak on his way upstairs. I watched his retreating back as he shed gloves, scarf and cloak for Anatole hovering in his wake, without apparently noticing me. But just as he reached the top of the first flight of stairs, he turned and fixed me with his eye.

'I shall never understand,' he said, 'what it is about fashion that makes perfectly intelligent young women fall over one another to disfigure themselves.'

Then, without another word, he swept on upstairs.

For the rest, as I say, I scarcely saw him; though I would sometimes come across him padding barefoot in the corridor outside his studio, or in the study with a half-smoked Muratti searching for a book, in an eccentric black silk dressing gown he had which, swirling about his ankles, gave him a wild Cossack air. And then, getting a sudden measure of his height, of the tallness and leanness of him, I would also have a threatening sense of his being naked under the silk which would make me doubly uncomfortable in his presence.

But, as the days wore on, he took to dropping in while I was practising or working with my music teacher, not interrupting or commenting, but simply stretching himself out upon the day bed and listening. And, once again, as at Monks Last, I had such a clear, abstract perception of it, of the notes existing beyond me, of their clear pure embodiment in his listening, that I felt, despite his mockery and his arrogance, despite his refusal to acknowledge me as anything other than a wayward child who was apt, if left unchecked, to be a nuisance, that I was doing what was required of me and he was not displeased with it.

My music teacher, Stepan Sergeyevitch Sokolov, was prone to moods of deep Slavonic melancholy. He was a gangling man of about twenty-five with a shock of blond hair which stood up in tufts as if he had absentmindedly parted it on the wrong side, and steel-rimmed, pebble-glass spectacles that gave him a bewildered, owlish look. He played the rehearsal piano for the Tarantin Ballet and he was at first so shy of me that his fluent but heavily-accented English was lost beneath a paralysing stutter which jumped and rattled like volleys of machine-gun fire. But his command of the language of music was unfaltering and, although I think he would no more have dreamed of getting angry with my shortcomings than he would have contemplated shouting at Tarantin, of whom he was much in awe, he proved a hard taskmaster simply because of his enthusiasm, which drove him to make me repeat faulty passages time after time and spurred him to go on working with me long after the appointed hour for him to stop. In music almost solely, therefore, he and I communicated for the first few days. But, after a while, watching him deep in gloom as he worried over some technical problem then suddenly, jumping up, thrusting his hands through his intractable hair, illuminated with a mercurial gaiety to think he had solved it, I found myself so much imagining him, with his flapping suit, his straight, ungainly frame and his long thin spike of a face, as an umbrella, spreading blackly against the thundery burden of a February sky, then snapping together just as abruptly at the first shaft of sunlight, that I could not resist laughing. And he, after a moment's disconcerted pause, began laughing too.

From then on we became firm friends, I was instructed to call him by his diminutive, Stenko, and the umbrella, when it spread, unfurled more gently, so that sometimes you might have almost mistaken it for a parasol. Although he played the piano for the Tarantin Ballet, would have willingly swept the floor for them, done anything at all to be considered part of the company, he was, he confided, a composer – one day, he hoped, a great Russian composer like Stravinsky or Prokofiev. He would talk to me for hours of modern composers, Satie, Ravel, Poulenc, Milhaud, whose music I, with my conventional English nineteenth-century education, had never heard, even bringing me cherished hand-copied scores of piano pieces to play. He would also, if pressed, become more forthcoming about Tarantin and his company, how Tarantin's word was the rule of law, what it was like backstage, who quarrelled with whom, and so on. The ballet my Cousin Felix was designing was based on the myth of Icarus – 'all fire and burning', as Tarantin had said – and the Master was pleased with its progress so far, although there had been some disagreements; but that was only to be expected when Tarantin became deeply involved in any work.

One afternoon, when we were at the piano together, the sound of Tarantin's voice in rolling, raging Russian flood, apparently concluding one of these only-to-be-expected working arguments, burst without warning from the hall, with my Cousin Felix's quieter, drier voice punctuating it coolly at intervals. They were arguing in French, which Stenko understood well, though I did not, and his face suddenly took on the embarrassed expression of someone forced to overhear something he would prefer not to. Eventually, not realizing that I had understood only the merest snatches of the conversation, he seemed to feel himself obliged to offer some explanation for it and, shrugging his shoulders, said that it was a peculiar characteristic of Tarantin's always to desire most what he could not have. But when I asked in what way my Cousin Felix had balked him, thinking of Tarantin's godlike compulsion to 'create' and Felix's evident unwillingness to be 'created', Stenko began to stutter so much in his anxiety to change the subject that I found myself wondering whether the argument had been about the designs for the ballet *Icarus* at all.

Since Stenko was not needed by the company during performances in the evening we took, as a natural extension of our days' conversations, to going to concerts together. And, of course, we went, through the Moorish arches of the Alhambra in Leicester Square, to see the Tarantin Ballet.

It was a night Rostova was dancing and, although the company had nearly come to the end of its London season, the house was packed, a sight which seemed to gratify Stenko, since, he confided, Tarantin, with the prodigious expense of his spectacular productions, was always on the brink of financial disaster and had debts to repay the London management from a past quarrel over contracts.

Rostova was to dance *Les Sylphides* and *The Firebird*. But first there was an ensemble piece, *The Polovtsian Dances*. I had never been to a ballet before and was dazzled by its energy and colour, by the sheer spectacle of it; and Stenko, unusually dignified in his evening dress and definitely tonight a closed and neatly rolled umbrella, delighted by my excitement, suggested in the interval that we go backstage.

The greenroom of the Alhambra lay between the stage and the dressing rooms down a short flight of steps from the pass door to the auditorium. I tiptoed after Stenko, suddenly assailed by an admixture of size, greasepaint, stale perfume and Havana cigars, plunged into the strange world backstage, at once exotic and blowzy, where glittering jewels became paste and cardboard and elfin faces sweat-runnelled masks of orange panstick, instantly feeling an intruder. The room was small, low-ceilinged and rectangular, with a large mirror and two small tables at the far end of it, a props skip and a treadle sewing machine in one corner, an assortment of rickety chairs and a larger table at its centre. From the corridor off which the dressing rooms led came a babel of swearing and laughter as the company changed out of its ensemble costumes. At one of the small tables Tarantin's *régisseur*, Gavrilovitch, was counting out a wad of pound notes, and at the other the conductor, Likhachev, totally absorbed, beating time and singing to himself, was studying his score. Members of the corps de ballet in their long white dresses drifted through on their way to take up their opening positions for *Les Sylphides*, and, in the midst of all this bustle, apparently oblivious of it, sat Tarantin in an astrakhan coat and my Cousin Felix in his opera cloak, examining a cardboard model stage, presumably the projected set for *Icarus*, which was placed between them in the centre of the large table. The cigar was Tarantin's and he was making a sweeping gesture with it while his other hand was placed upon my Cousin Felix's shoulder; Felix, draped languidly sideways in his chair, had his head thrown back in laughter; and there was, in the laughter, in the pressure of Tarantin's hand, in the expression on their faces, so much of the private language of a long-established friendship, an intimacy which, within all that noise and activity, held and enclosed them like a territorial boundary, that I felt awkward, even more of an intruder, at our invasion of it.

They stopped laughing when they saw us and my Cousin Felix assumed an expression of mild surprise. But Tarantin, as if his eyes bored through Stenko and past him to me, creased his simian features into that smile I had once seen him give Rostova, at the same time gleaming and vindictive. My Cousin Felix half rose to present me but Tarantin, the smile never wavering, cut him short: '*Mon cher*, already I have met your little cousin. But if I had not then I think I imagine it anyway – you and Stepan Sergeyevitch are so often talking about her.'

Surprised and feeling certain I was mocked, I blushed, and Stenko began to stutter violently. But at that moment the small room seemed suddenly filled with a scented cloud of white muslin. And Rostova herself, her black hair wreathed in white flowers, her lips vermilion, her slanting eyes attenuated with kohl till they glittered like jet, made her entrance, followed by a dumpy grey-haired dresser who carried her shoes, a powder puff and a large bottle of eau de cologne.

The jet eyes gleamed, the vermilion mouth broadened to a gash and, with a sinuous gesture that uncoiled so slowly and expansively that it seemed to take up and diminish everything in the room, she wound herself round my Cousin Felix's neck and kissed him on the cheek; while he, without looking back at her or changing his expression, lifted one of her hands and pressed it for a second to his lips. And, in that instant, as her eyes seemed to glitter defiantly at all of us around the table, in the expansive sensuousness of her gesture and the casualness of his response, as if the touch of her, the smell of her skin, had taken on the familiarity of habit, I had suddenly, sharp as pain, no longer as an idea but as the vivid physical embodiment of its reality, a clear perception of what, after all, I must have assumed, must have known all along, that Anna Rostova was indeed my Cousin Felix's mistress.

The words rushed echoing through my head like a train through a tunnel, their sibilants hissing like steam. And I heard Tarantin, to whom this challenge of hers, like a counter declaration to the laughter Stenko and I had interrupted, must presumably be addressed, bark suddenly: 'All very well, my dear Anna Nikolayevna. But tonight you will please to remember that you are too tall to be a dancer and that in the days before the Bolsheviks you would have been fortunate to grace even the corps de ballet of the great Mariinsky. Tonight you will please to give us a passable rendering of the choreography of Fokine, not an imitation of a Tartar peasant humping potatoes.'

Rostova had seated herself on one of the chairs while the little dresser, spitting carefully inside the first one to make sure it would not slip, fitted her into her shoes. She gave Tarantin a broad exposure of her sharp, white teeth. Then she took the second shoe from the dresser and, pointedly and very precisely, spat into the depths of it. A moment later she was gone, with the dresser rushing along beside her, reaching up on tiptoe to pat her forehead with the powder puff and cool her with eau de cologne.

After that, it was strange to return to the auditorium and watch her dance, no longer, it seemed, flesh and blood but, distanced by the gulf of the footlights, cool, ethereal, a chimera created by a clever conjunction of light and shade. And, although, despite Tarantin's insults, she danced with indisputable magic, I somehow could not take pleasure in it. It was as though I could not reconcile the two images of her, the one so impalpable, the other so tangible and passionate. For I kept seeing, as she moved in fluid harmony in her *pas de deux*, her limbs a perfect counterpoint to her partner's, a vision, no matter how I tried to drive it away, of the real Rostova and my Cousin Felix, secretly, languidly entwined in some mysterious, intimate ballet of their own. And although her second appearance, as the Firebird, showed a different Rostova again, half-woman half-bird, luminous as flame and palpitating in the imprisoning arms of the Prince, yet imbued with all the passionate earthiness of the woman who had so eloquently spat her disapproval of Tarantin, I felt there was something so unaccountably disagreeable, repellent even, in all these sea-changes of hers that, when the bouquets had been presented, the cheering and stamping had died away, and Stenko again suggested we go backstage, I was filled with reluctance to follow him.

But Tarantin seemed to draw Stenko like a magnet and there was no question of disappointing him. And so we found ourselves crushed against the wall of the corridor outside Rostova's dressing room, waiting until her dresser came out to tell us she had finished changing and was ready to receive our congratulations. And, when the door was finally opened to us, it was no longer a shock to find my Cousin Felix already there, stretched out upon the cretonne-covered sofa, smoking a Muratti and following her with his dispassionate gaze as with lipstick and powder puff she put the finishing touches to her toilette.

'*Ah! Come c'est charmant! La petite cousine!*'

I was all at once drained, I wanted more than anything else in the world to go home and sleep. But Rostova, appearing to register my presence for the first time that evening, seemed as inexplicably and excessively friendly as Tarantin had been hostile. Drawing me to her, suffocating me in a heavy pall of Mitsouko, she insisted on my kissing her on both cheeks.

'*Tiens!* But how brave of you to cut off all your so-beautiful hair! Félix does not like it? But a woman must have a change, *mon ami*. After all, it is so dreadfully *ennuyant* for a plain girl always to have people make it up to her by saying she has beautiful hair.'

Tarantin put his head round the door in search of Felix: 'Ah, Anna Nikolayevna, Gavrilovitch tells me you are feeling your age tonight. Well, how else do you explain your last pose in the *Danse Infernale*? It seems you are so tired you must finish your part three beats before the orchestra finishes it.'

Rostova let out a laugh that enabled me to see right to the back of her pink throat. 'The Great God Tarantin! *Merde!*

'And now,' she said, twisting a curl of my hair in her fingers, petting me like a doll, '*cher Félix* says Stenko will make a musician of you. You must tell me everything about it.' And she began, before I could open my mouth, to expand in her purring, silken voice upon the ridiculousness of Gavrilovitch's early-morning calls to class, the incompetence of Likhachev and the sheer impossibility, with such a company as Tarantin's, of giving even a half-respectable performance.

It was a game to them, I decided, their viciousness and backbiting, their sudden likes and dislikes, a venomous, enjoyable game. Even Stenko, sitting nervously on the edge of the sofa, afraid to speak in case he stuttered, was, with his dog-like devotion to Tarantin, part of it. When Tarantin and Felix returned, someone suggested dinner at the Troika, and I found myself swept up with the rest of the party to continue to play over bortsch and shashlik and red-caviar omelettes.

Or perhaps it was not a game, but a dance; an intricate ritual dance in which everyone had their allotted parts to perform. And at the still centre of it – impresario, choreographer or simply the audience? – was my Cousin Felix.

From the walls of the restaurant on all sides paintings of Mother Russia loomed, a stage set dressed darkly for melodrama. Our faces seemed distorted as we twisted in our fanciful contortions, like masks. I thought again how strange Rostova's eyes were, with their pinprick pupils, as if they had somehow drunk the light and were crazed with it. Beside me, Stenko had replaced his glasses and was spread for thunder. I was dizzy with the wine, my head ached, I wanted it, oh how I wanted it all to stop. And suddenly, looking up, I caught the eye of my Cousin Felix across the table and saw that he wanted an end to it too.

He said something very quiet in French I did not understand. There was silence for a moment. Then Tarantin, clearly in a huff, rose, saying he must be getting back to his suite at the Savoy. And, moments after he had gone, Rostova exclaimed that she was sick to death of stupid class-calls, that there was a new nightclub opening tonight which promised to be absolutely *le dernier cri* and that she would never forgive my Cousin Felix if he did not take her there this instant. So Stenko and I, like children who are suddenly discovered to have stayed up long past their bedtime, were packed into a cab that would drop me off at Cheyne Walk and then take him on to his digs.

It had been drizzling as we had come out into the Piccadilly night. But Rostova, stretching her ermine-clad arms up towards the sky, had cried: 'Snow, Félix! We shall have such a snowstorm tonight!'

And I, feeling only the bleak damp of English rain upon my face, thought that I was waking from a dream in which there had been no sense or logic anywhere.

My three weeks sped by and began, without anyone apparently noticing it, to creep into four. The scars had gone from my face, my trunk had at last been recovered from Paddington. And Stenko had confided in me, as much almost it seemed to his joy as to mine, that he had told my Cousin Felix he was well satisfied with my progress and that while he was delighted to go on teaching me as long as the Tarantin Ballet was in London, some more permanent arrangement should now be considered.

I waited on tenterhooks for my Cousin Felix to broach the subject. But, to my surprise, he said nothing. I saw him more often now, usually in the mornings when Stenko was at rehearsal. He would drift in, ostensibly as he had always done, to listen to me practise. But he seemed unaccountably restless and preoccupied these days, getting up and wandering round the room or taking out cigarettes and then putting them back in his case without lighting them. I sometimes began to wonder if Stenko had simply invented his conversation with him, so complete was his silence about it. I longed to bring it up myself. But the undercurrent of tension in his manner prevented me.

Towards the end of my fourth week, he suddenly announced he had decided to give a dinner party. To my considerable relief, neither Tarantin nor Rostova was present since they were both dancing that night. It was an unexpectedly enjoyable evening. My Cousin Felix, with his natural talent for encouraging conversation in other people, was an excellent host so that, by the end of dinner, even the painfully gauche Yseult Fortunin had revealed herself as a sharp and entertaining raconteur. And I, to my surprise, found myself designated hostess for the evening, sitting opposite Felix at the other end of the table, with Stenko and the publisher and the war poet, Pascoe, whom I had always instinctively liked. Felix, too, seemed to have temporarily thrown off his restlessness: once or twice, catching his eye down the long expanse of table with its tall silver candlesticks, its flowers and its crystal, I found him smiling at me, as if together we had stage-managed the whole proceedings and were secretly sharing our enjoyment at its effect.

In my Cousin Felix's house the women were not required to follow the tedious custom of retiring with the port. Instead, the whole company returned to the drawing room, where Felix, who had heard Stenko and me playing the fool one afternoon with a Ragtime duet, asked us if we would entertain everyone now. We gave them the Ragtime and then improvised a selection of other numbers, 'After You've Gone', 'Way Down Yonder in New Orleans', three or four blues melodies. We even cobbled together a couple of encores. When we had finally been allowed to stop and everyone was laughing and clapping, Stenko, who had by now completely forgotten the possibility of thunderstorms, took my hand and, bringing me forward to our audience for all the world as if we were on a concert platform, bowed to me solemnly. And then even he was laughing too, and I kissed him on the cheek and he led me back to my chair, and I looked up and saw my Cousin Felix smiling at me, not mockingly as he usually did, but openly, affectionately, as if he were almost a little proud of me. I sat back, feeling flushed and all at once very happy, obscurely glad to have pleased him, no longer just because he had championed me against Aunt Jessica, but because of pleasing him for its own sake.

Then a curious thing happened. He rose with the port decanter and, as he passed behind my chair, his fingers brushed against the bare skin of my shoulder just below my neck, lingering for a moment with a gentle pressure which, though his hand was gone in an instant, was too prolonged to be accidental. I felt suddenly as if my skin were burning and, aware that I must have blushed scarlet, did not know where to put my eyes. But when I could bring myself to look up, no one seemed to have noticed, and he himself was absorbed in conversation with Ambrose Fortunin and the Pascoes, so that I might have imagined the incident.

Later, when his guests had gone, I became almost certain that I had imagined it. While he was in the hall with Stenko and the publisher, the last two to leave, I had gone back to the piano to tidy the scattered sheets of music. I sat for a moment at the keyboard, not playing but just resting my fingertips on the cool ivory, thinking how much I had enjoyed the evening, feeling warm and light-headed with it as if I had drunk too much wine. And when I looked round he was standing in the doorway, his hand upon the door knob, watching me. I had no idea how long he had been there. His face wore a taut, concentrated look like someone willing themselves to ignore pain. I started to smile, to say something, but his expression changed instantly, he was all at once as cold as if I were a perfect stranger.

'It's late, Christabel,' he said abruptly. 'And time you went to bed.'

My mood of elation evaporated in a moment. I climbed the stairs slowly and heavily. When I was on the first landing I heard the sound of the front door knocker. Looking down the stair-well, I saw Anatole cross the hall to answer it. Then I saw Rostova glittering with diamonds and swathed in ermine. My Cousin Felix walked towards her across the chequered marble. She threw out her arms to embrace him.

'I had to come, my darling. I could not go home and sit all alone.'

I did not want to see him return her embrace. I found myself running up the next flight of stairs. And, by the time I had reached the top, the last embers of my pleasure in the evening had flickered and died.

CHAPTER EIGHTEEN

My Cousin Felix remained shut in his studio the next day and I did not see him. But the following morning he appeared as usual while I was practising. This time, however, he did not sit down or make any pretence of listening but, having circled the room once, went over to the mantelpiece, lit a cigarette, picked up first an ivory figurine, then a soapstone snuff bottle, then turned abruptly towards me as if he were impatient for me to stop playing. I was only too glad to, for my hands had suddenly begun to shake uncontrollably, so convinced was I that he had finally come to talk about my future.

But instead he said: 'It's Lady Ambleside's birthday ball to-night. When she discovered you were staying with me she asked me if I would bring you. Will you come?'

I said I should be pleased to. He told me when to be ready and then, replacing the snuff bottle on the mantelpiece, left the room with the air of someone who is relieved to have concluded speedily a necessary but tiresome piece of business.

The thought that I was going to the Amblesides' ball with him seemed curiously to preoccupy my day. So when, after luncheon, the telephone began ringing, I did not pay much attention to it, even when it continued to ring incessantly throughout the afternoon and I several times heard Felix snap at Anatole that he was not in to anyone and did not wish to be disturbed. I was surprised when Stenko did not appear for my music lesson, but a little relieved too because it left me more time to dress for the evening.

I had allowed myself two hours to complete my metamorphosis into the very image of sophistication – two hours to pluck my eyebrows to a razor-thin line, to rouge and powder my face to a flawless mask, to flatten my impossible hair until it was as straight and sleek as everyone else's, to climb finally into the dress, the dark green satin and crêpe-marocain dress with the silver and green bows, the grown-up dress that my Cousin Felix had never seen before. And it was as well I had taken such generous precautions, for I was still applying lipstick when there was a knock at my door and a maid appeared to tell me that Mr de Lisle apologized, but he required me to be ready earlier than he had planned.

I duly presented myself at the studio. I had not entered the room since my argument with Felix on my first day at Cheyne Walk. There was a different canvas on the easel, a dense abstraction of a painting in which colour seemed to riot in anarchy. Anatole was at the telephone just replacing the receiver in its stand. My Cousin Felix, already dressed, stood before the fire smoking.

'Something irritating has happened,' he said. 'I'm afraid I shall have to call in at the Alhambra before we go on to the Amblesides'. It means we shall miss dinner, but their buffet suppers are always overgenerous.' He threw the cigarette on the fire. 'Now, let me look at you.'

I flushed beneath his critical eye, both unnerved and irritated by the sharpness of his scrutiny.

At length he asked: 'Where did you get that frock?'

'You bought it for me,' I said.

'Did I really? It looks like a tea cosy in mourning.' A flash of devilish amusement gleamed in his eyes. 'Anatole, scissors!'

There was a pair on the desk. Anatole presented them to him like a nurse offering a scalpel to a surgeon. And, before I could protest, almost before I was aware of his intentions, my Cousin

Felix was standing over me, snipping off, one after the other, my precious green and silver bows.

'How dare you!' I said, choking with anger.

'Shhh, child!' he said, snipping meticulously, his face bent close to mine, absorbed, concentrating. 'You'll find it's a considerable improvement.'

The bows at my shoulders fell first, then the two at my hips. I stood, speechless with fury, as he stepped back to consider his handiwork.

'Hmm. Better. But still with much to be desired. The fuss at the neck is the worst. And that requires more drastic surgery.'

'No!' I said, almost in tears. 'It's the newest thing. You're ruining it!'

'Better that I should ruin it than that it should ruin you. You have the most beautiful swan-like neck. I can't imagine why you should want to cover it up with all this tasteless frippery.'

And he was upon me again with the scissors, this time not content with removing my last and most despised bow, but cutting down into the fabric of the dress itself, reshaping the neckline into a careful V. His hands moved efficiently, precisely, somehow never once touching my flesh, as if he were deliberately avoiding doing so. His face was now so close to mine that I could smell the faint aroma of his eau de cologne and the scent of his skin, could see the tiny muscles at the corner of his mouth contracting as he concentrated on the slash of the scissor blades, could have put out a hand and touched the clean hard line of his jaw. I hated that aloof, absorbed, good-looking face; for two pins I would have slapped it. I could not think why I did not.

He laughed. 'Keep still, little Christie. These are very sharp scissors and I find the sight of your blood curiously distressing.' Then, with one final, decisive snip, he stood back again to examine me.

'A shawl, Anatole, from the screen. No, the other one! That's it.'

It was of ivory silk, heavily fringed and embroidered with birds and flowers in silver thread. He arranged it in soft folds about my shoulders to cover the scissor cuts, carefully adjusting the drape of it here, the fall of the fringe there. He seemed infuriatingly pleased with the result.

'Now, there is one last thing. Your hair. I can understand that you should be ashamed of what you have done to it, but I can't see that you need pretend not to have hair at all. Would you please run your fingers through it.'

'You're hateful,' I said. 'Utterly hateful!'

'Very possibly. But will you please do as I ask. That's right. More. Harder!'

I tore at my hair in rage, feeling my carefully-flattened curls spring back, reasserting themselves in all their maddeningly unfashionable perversity.

'My dear child, there is no need to scalp yourself. That's perfect. You may stop now.'

He came and gave my abominable handiwork one final ruffle. Then, not ungently, he took my chin between his fingers and thumb and tilted my face towards his. For a moment his lips were inches from mine, his eyes looking down directly into my eyes. I met them squarely, rebelliously, and saw in them again, to my amazement, the intense, almost frightening, concentrated look he had worn the night of the dinner party. I could feel myself beginning to tremble uncontrollably. I jerked my head away.

He let his hand fall with a small exhalation of breath that might have been a sigh.

'If you can bring yourself to wipe that disagreeable expression from your face, you will find you are now astonishingly beautiful. There is a glass in the hall. Go downstairs and look at yourself.'

Angry as I was, there seemed nothing to do any more but obey him. The vision that confronted me was so extraordinary I scarcely recognized it. My face was a clear, pale oval a out which my hair seemed to float in a burning copper aureole. My neck arched from the silken folds of the shawl, ivory upon ivory, a graceful, fluid curve. I looked like a strange, pale, moonlit flower on a long fragile stem. Only my hair and lips gave me colour. I stared at the unfamiliar image for some moments, in spite of myself transfixed.

My Cousin Felix came down the stairs, with Anatole behind him carrying my chinchilla coat. He raised his eyebrows questioningly.

'It's most peculiar,' I said. 'And not at all fashionable.'

'If you mean,' he said, 'that you will not look like every other woman at the Amblesides', I would most certainly agree with you. Now, I am late. We must go.'

At the Alhambra my Cousin Felix, glancing with irritation at his watch, hestitated between the stage door and front of house. Eventually, as we were ushered into two empty seats next to the aisle – seats which Stenko later told me were reserved for Tarantin himself – I understood why. The curtain had already risen and Tarantin was on stage, dancing. He was giving his own newly-choreographed version of Nijinsky's *L'Après-midi d'un faune*. Despite his disconcertingly ageless face, the Russian had always, to my seventeen-year-old eyes, seemed, with his autocratic manner, an old man, and I suppose I had expected him to dance an old man's *comédie bouffon* roles. Seeing him now, his body muscular as a Donatello statue, his proud head set upon a column of neck in which you could almost see the corded sinews quiver, his torso and thighs, splotched to resemble calfskin, suggestive of a nakedness at once human and bestial, I sat, my eyes fixed in an involuntary but overwhelming fascination. Rostova had appeared to emanate from the music like a vapour, but the presence of Tarantin seemed rather to command it, filling the stage, the auditorium, with a mesmeric sense of physical power. With his head thrown back, languid, sybaritic, crushing grapes, his body at first indolent, rippling, fluid, then awkward with arousal confronting the nymphs, he seemed at the same time youthful and ageless, sexual and epicene, innocent and all-knowing. The golden horns upon his head made him both god and devil. And when at last he came slowly, slowly down upon the nymph's veil and, with a final thrust of his pelvis which would have set every cherry on the Duchess of Rosslair's hat aquiver, lay still upon it, I wanted suddenly to tell him that I did not care however much he disliked me, so long as he would let me show him that in this one thing alone I gave him absolute right to his presumption of divinity. I wanted to tell my Cousin Felix as well but he, assumedly long familiar with all of it, had sat beside me unmoved throughout, smoking and restlessly consulting his wristwatch; and even before the curtain had fallen, a figure in the aisle was bending over him, thrusting into his hand a slip of paper.

The house lights went up and I saw that the figure was Stenko. My Cousin Felix read what was on the paper and, crumpling it impatiently, rose to his feet.

'Look after Christie, will you,' he said to Stenko, and began to walk quickly in the direction of the pass door backstage.

We followed him automatically.

'It's R–r–r–ostova,' Stenko stuttered excitedly. 'She did not come for the m–m–m–atinée. She is n–n–n–ot here now for *Firebird*. She has d–d–d–isappeared!'

The greenroom, when we reached it, was in turmoil. Rostova's dresser was crying in a corner, Gavrilovitch was tearing his hair, Yermilova, the company's other principal ballerina, dressed in Rostova's Firebird costume, was screaming angrily at him, Tarantin's whole retinue seemed to be there, shouting and tripping over one another. And at the centre of the whirlwind Tarantin, still in his faun's costume, sweat dripping from his face and chest, was biting into a slice of orange, talking and gesturing violently, all at the same time.

Then he saw my Cousin Felix and the room went still.

He spat out the orange. His face with its painted eyes and overdrawn lips creased into an expression of ungovernable rage. Beneath the gilded horns, he looked more than ever half-beast, half-devil. The words I had wanted to say to him died within me and I suddenly wished I were not in the room.

'So! At last, my friend, you have deigned to show yourself! Perhaps if you now can bear to take the trouble, you will explain to us our little mystery. Perhaps you will tell me what you have done with her!'

My Cousin Felix's voice, though it was quiet and controlled, was also on the verge of anger. 'Teddy, I have told Gavrilovitch on the telephone; I have told your secretary, I have even told you three times, I do not know where Anna is.'

'You do not know? Or is it that you do not care?'

'Teddy, I have not seen Anna for two days.'

'You do not care. You do not care that I have an audience who have paid only to see Rostova. Rostova, who dances like a mule, Rostova who will not attend class, Rostova who has broken her contract and who I will sue through every court in Europe, Rostova who is now making this company bankrupt! And you, my friend, do not care. Why did you come here?'

'I came, Teddy, because nothing else would satisfy you.'

Tarantin's black eyes rolled. Then, as they spun round, they suddenly lighted upon me. It was as if the sight of someone he disliked brought him to breaking point. His face contorted, he let out an animal roar of fury. 'Now I see why you come! You come to mock me!'

Felix seemed for the first time aware of me behind him. 'Stenko,' he snapped, over his shoulder, 'I asked you to look after her. Why did you bring her in here?'

'You come to mock me!' screamed Tarantin, his lips drawn back, his teeth bared. 'You, with your womanizing and your whoring, you want to destroy my company. My company, which I, Vladimir Tarantin, have created out of my own sweat, my own blood! My company, which keeps alive the sacred Russian traditions of the Mariinsky, my company which exists only for art, which is the greatest ballet company in the world! You destroy Rostova, you destroy me, you destroy the company I love like a child. And you do not care. Because love for you is only a dirty act in a dark room. You care for nothing, not love, not loyalty, not friendship, not art, not even for God. So long as you can satisfy your disgusting appetites, you do not care if you break me in two!'

He paused for breath. His glistening pectoral muscles heaved. Sweat and kohl ran down his face like black tears and a froth of saliva bubbled at the corners of his mouth.

Suddenly he bent and picked up a wad of notes that Gavrilovitch had left upon the table.

'Here, my friend. You think my company should run according to the demands of your ever-ready priapus? Take its money then, take everything I make at the box office for tonight. Take it all! And buy yourself a whore!'

With great force he flung the money at my Cousin Felix. It hung in the air for a moment, fluttering, then it fell like snow upon the table, and the rickety chairs, and on the hair and shoulders of his retinue and upon the floor to within a few inches of my Cousin Felix's feet; and with it fell upon the whole room the hush of a snowfall, a soft, dead, blank silence.

My Cousin Felix did not move. After the violence of Tarantin's words and gestures, his very stillness had a quiet, cold power.

When he spoke, his voice was not much louder than a whisper but in the absoluteness of that silence it was in every word precisely clear and audible.

'Teddy, you stretch the limits of our friendship beyond endurance.'

Then he left and Stenko and I followed him.

My Cousin Felix was not given to explaining or apologizing or to any of the gestures most people would find natural to make in the aftermath of such a scene. In the car on the way to the Amblesides' house in Park Lane he said not a word to me, except once, giving me his matches and his silver case, to ask me to light him a cigarette. I was left to speculate unproductively as to why Tarantin should blame Felix for Rostova's disappearance and as to where she could have gone.

On the second point I was answered almost immediately. For, as we entered the Amblesides' spacious marble and stucco ballroom, Rostova was the first person we saw.

'*Félix! Mon cher!* My darling! How I have missed you these two days!'

In jade sequins and silver tissue she seemed more shimmering and serpentine than ever. A cluster of emeralds and diamonds gleamed at her throat, two cascades of diamonds swung like miniature chandeliers from her ears. She appeared not in the least aware that there was anything unlooked-for about her being at Lady Ambleside's ball when she should, at this minute, be helping Prince Ivan free the maidens from Kotschei's enchantment at the Alhambra. Yet there was about her, nonetheless, not a change precisely, but a strangeness, an exaggeration of every element of her presence, so that her voice was even silkier, her gestures even more studiedly sinuous, her green eyes with their tiny pupils even shinier, glazed over, hard with the brightness of the emeralds about her neck. The effect was overpowering, like clouds of incense in a small room.

She did not see me at all, having only eyes for my Cousin Felix. Though we were surrounded by people, her arms went up to embrace him as if she were alone with him again in the hall at Cheyne Walk.

To my surprise, he caught her sharply by the wrists, bringing her hands down to her sides and holding them there.

'I've just seen Teddy.'

'Ah! The Great God Tarantin. *Merde!* Who wants to be one of his drab little creations? Tonight I am not Firebird, I am the Snow Queen. Come into the blizzard with me, Félix.'

'No, Anna. Not here! The foolishness has gone far enough already.'

Her neck seemed to arch and swoop, her tongue flickered. 'But the snow is deep, Félix. I feel every crystal of it falling on my face. Come into the snow with me.'

Her hands went to the clasp of her little silver mesh bag. Her fingers fumbled, the bag fell to the floor and out of it rolled a tiny enamelled box I had once seen somewhere before. She stooped but my Cousin Felix was there ahead of her. He handed her back the bag, but the box he slipped into his breast pocket.

'No!' Suddenly her voice was shrill. 'I must have it! All these so-stiff English gentlemen and their braying English wives. I must have help. Otherwise I shall die of boredom.'

Several people were looking round. But she was only aware of my Cousin Felix. His face was emotionless but in his right cheek, just above the jaw, a small muscle contracted.

All at once she threw back her head in laughter. '*Ah, merde!* I shall dance for you. Lady Ambleside has invited me so that I will dance. But I shall not dance for any Lady Ambleside or for all these English *ânes bâtés*. I shall dance for you.'

And in an instant she had disappeared into the crowd. In that moment too I suddenly heard my name being called from behind me and, turning, I saw Dilly.

We fell upon each other ecstatically.

'Oh, Dillo, I didn't know you were back!'

'But, Christie, darling, you'd vanished off the face of the earth. We've been home three days and no one in London knew where to find you. Oh, and you look too wonderful, and I've got oodles of things to tell you – but goodness, what's everyone going shush for? Why are they suddenly clearing the dance floor?'

Rostova seemed to have taken up her impulse immediately. She had not changed into a costume but had simply kicked off her shoes and, after a hurried dialogue with the band leader, had run barefoot into the centre of the dance floor, spun round once and sunk into a deep curtsey. Then she began, to the saxophone instead of the cello, upon a rendering of 'The Dying Swan'. But Rostova's swan seemed to swoop not so much with the lingering poignancy of departing life as with a sustained, expanding sensuality, as though with every movement she were unfurling more and more of her body, laying it open for us all to see in every white silken curve, offering up her breasts, her thighs, the thrust of her loins, with an infinitely slow and calculated defiance. She seemed to me to teeter on the edge of control, as if she no longer knew or cared what steps she danced. The throaty wail of the saxophone seemed to emphasize her abandonment. She was, I thought, no longer the ethereal Rostova of *Les Sylphides*, no longer the great Rostova at all, but a woman dancing for custom in some cheap Oriental bordello.

I looked round at my Cousin Felix. The small muscle continued to move above his jaw and, though he was a foot away from me and perfectly still, I could feel his anger, cold, rigid, like a barrier between us. His eyes watched Rostova with a chilling intensity as she reached out towards him, until it seemed to me there was no longer anything else in the room, that we had all been obliterated, that nothing more existed beyond his anger and her desire.

It was an eternity before the music ended and everyone was clapping and Rostova was standing to receive her acclaim, arms extended, head thrown back, teeth bared in a triumphant smile.

'Oh, goodness!' said Dilly. 'Wouldn't it be just too divine to be on such good terms with one's feet!'

I looked round for my Cousin Felix as Rostova plunged into the parting waves of the crowd, but he had vanished.

'But, darling, tell me about yourself!' Dilly said. 'Here I am, an old married woman – positively antediluvian – and here are you, looking – well, absolutely divinely ravishing. And with *him*!'

'Him?' I said.

'Your Cousin Felix, of course. I saw you both come in and you were quite extraordinary together, both of you so tall and so good-looking, positively unearthly and Olympian. And do you know, I'd never realized how alike you are. Oh, your colouring's different, of course. But the resemblance is striking, all the same.'

'It's the Cavendish face,' I said.

'I simply must hear all about the two of you. Don't spare me the slightest detail. Oh, Christie, are you dreadfully in love with him?'

I flushed. 'Of course not,' I said irritably.

'Oh, dear,' sighed Dilly. 'Is he still being horrid?'

I thought of my beautiful green and silver bows. 'Yes,' I said. 'Entirely horrid.' Then, remembering that this was perhaps not altogether just, since he had after all defended me against Aunt Jessica and found me Stenko, I flushed again. 'We only came here together because Lady Ambleside asked him to bring me. And anyway he seems to have disappeared.'

'He's over there,' said Dilly, 'talking to his Russian ballerina.'

I followed Dilly's eyes to where Rostova and Felix stood. Though they might, from a distance, have been having a perfectly ordinary conversation, something in the way her body bent towards him and in the set of his face made me certain they were arguing.

I tried not to look. Robbie appeared, and he and Dilly fell into an account of their honeymoon trip. Maisie Cunningham-Cowper drifted by with Crikey in tow. Miles

Millington came and asked me to dance. And when I arrived back from the dance floor Rostova and my Cousin Felix had vanished.

I danced some more. Dora Chantry spent an age telling me what a shame it was that Archie couldn't be there because of his father's being ill and his having to go up North to be with him, as if this were information I should not dare to ask for but must all the same be burning to know. Lady Dolly appeared on the arm of Charlie Devereux, sporting a spectacular sapphire and diamond engagement ring. Everyone asked me where I had been until I grew quite exhausted with explaining. And I was just beginning to think it was not impossible for my Cousin Felix to have forgotten all about me and gone off to some nightclub with Rostova, and was wondering if I could prevail upon Robbie and Dilly to take me home, when the two of them reappeared.

Rostova was wearing her ermine. She held the collar up to her cheek as if she were suddenly cold and all the brightness had gone from her now, as though someone had taken her by the shoulders and shaken her very hard to sober her. My Cousin Felix's hand rested lightly on her elbow but she detached herself from it impatiently.

'No, no. My car is waiting. There is no need for you to come.'

Then she seemed to catch sight of me, and for a second the brightness flooded back as she extended towards me a long, knife-sharp look that appeared to take in every last detail of my person, as if she were somehow reassessing it.

'Ah! *La petite cousine*,' she drawled, in her most serpentine voice. 'You know, one day when you grow up men may even find you quite attractive.'

Then she was gone in a waft of Mitsouko and my Cousin Felix was telling me peremptorily that it was time for us to leave.

Felix was an excellent driver, but that night he drove his great grey bird of a car like a weapon, not absolutely courting danger but nonetheless running it close, pushing the Hispano Suiza to its very limits. I wished I could think of something to say to him, anything to break through his impenetrable anger. But his eyes were fixed on the road, his face white and set. And, seeing the tiny muscle still twitching near his jaw, I suddenly felt he was not just angry because of Tarantin and Rostova, but obscurely, unjustly, angry with me as well. I sank back into the depths of my seat, worn out and miserable, thinking at least, now the whole disaster of an evening was over, I could avoid the cruelty of his coldness by slinking off to bed the moment we were home.

But the evening was not over, nor the wretchedness of it. For when we arrived at Cheyne Walk Anatole was waiting for us in the hall with a silver salver and a telegram upon it.

My Cousin Felix tore open the envelope and read its contents without a flicker of expression. But I knew, even before his hand had gone out to pick it up, who it was from and what it said. I felt a sudden mixture of despair and fear.

'It's from Aunt Jessica, isn't it? She's put her foot down.'

With one movement of his hand he crushed both paper and envelope and dropped them back onto the silver tray. 'It's late, Christabel,' he said, turning towards the stairs. 'We will talk about it in the morning.'

'But I need to talk now, Felix. I can't bear to lie there all night thinking about it.'

He turned towards me for a moment. His eyes were cold and his lips a thin, hard line. 'We will talk in the morning. Please go to bed.'

And I knew then from the unyielding set of his shoulders as he disappeared up the stairs, knew with certainty what I had half-known while I had watched him read the telegram, that it was not by accident that he had avoided mentioning the conversation with Stenko, that he would, despite all his promises, betray me.

CHAPTER NINETEEN

Diary of Adele Ward.
Monks Last, Norfolk.

24th May, 1894.

Mamma has taken such a turn for the worse! She moans so piteously whenever I turn her in bed, and asks often for dear Papa. Oh, how I wish he were not so frequently obliged to be away in London, although perhaps it is a mercy that he, to whom above all the spectacle of her suffering must be insupportable, is spared prolonged exposure to it. I am with her constantly, the main offices of the sick room devolving upon me since J has not the inclination nor the disposition for nursing. I do not reproach her with it, for I am happy to give poor Mamma what comfort I can, and at least it spares me J's and M's perpetual bickering.

25th May, 1894.

Storm brewing. Mamma no better, but at least no worse which is some comfort. Sat up very late with her tonight and when at last I reached my bedroom could not find sleep myself. I had dropped off, perhaps for no more than minutes, when I was woken again by a strange noise. At first I thought it must be the beech tree outside my window which, when there is a high wind, rattles and scrapes its branches upon the glass. But no, when I lit my candle I saw that while the air is heavy with thunder the night is calm and windless. Then it came again, a strange echoing, creaking sound, as if from the fabric of the house itself.

I began suddenly to be afraid, imagining intruders prowling the house under cover of darkness. I could not think what I should do, whether I should wake M who was asleep in our dressing room. Above all, I was fearful for Mamma. For a moment there was an eerie stillness. And then it came again – a ghostly creaking and all at once, apparently from far off down the passage, but quite distinct, a hollow, unearthly laugh. The hair prickled on my scalp. It had seemed like a woman's laughter, yet none of us could be laughing in this house of grief. Taking my night light and summoning up a courage I did not possess, thinking only of Mamma, I opened my door and looked out into the passage.

At first there seemed only darkness. Then, as if from a door closing stealthily elsewhere, a sudden draught blew my candle out. For a moment my eyes struggled to accustom themselves to the utter blackness. Then, to my horror, at the very end of the passage, materializing soundlessly as if from the substance of the wall itself, I beheld a figure, very tall and in a long white robe, moving towards me, nay not moving, gliding, noiseless as though its feet never touched the boards. The last vestiges of my courage deserting me, I stood paralysed as it came softly on. Shutting my eyes, I let out a scream. A voice said: 'Tush, Adele! Will you wake the house?' And, on once again daring to look, I saw that it was only M, in his nightshirt and without a candle.

'Oh, M!' I cried, almost fainting into his arms. 'I thought – for a moment I imagined you were a ghost!'

Instantly I regretted my admission, for I felt him stiffen as, grasping me by the elbow, he began to guide me back to my room.

'My dearest, you must take a hold upon your imagination. I know you are of a nervous disposition and have overtaxed your strength in nursing your Mamma –'

'But there were noises. And laughter. You must have heard them, they wakened you too.'

'Rats in the wainscotting, I shouldn't wonder. Every noise echoes in this d——d barn of a house.'

'But—'

'Shush, my dearest! You're overwrought,' he said, lighting my candle. 'I fear with your delicate constitution we shall soon have two invalids to nurse. Try to sleep now. I'll be next door in the dressing room, and you know you have only to tap on my door if you suffer another attack.'

Feeling all at once mortified and wondering whether perhaps, owing to my exhaustion and my anxiety for poor Mamma, I have indeed become neurasthenic, I thanked him humbly, promising to do as he advised. But I still could not sleep, so have sat up with the candle writing this.

26th May, 1894.

When Dr B called upon Mamma this morning M insisted on his also examining me. I was surprised to discover, too, that J and M, momentarily setting aside their differences, have been conspiring in my favour. The upshot is that a nurse is to be sent for from King's Lynn to lessen my burden (though truly to tend poor Mamma is no burden to me). However, I was grateful for M's concern and told him so. 'Though you worry needlessly,' I said. 'I am a great deal stronger than you imagine.'

Whereupon he threw his arms around me and, kissing my forehead, crushed me to his chest with such passionate fervour that I was for an instant taken aback. 'How like my dear, brave, sweet little wife! But we shall take no risks with you, my dearest. How often must I remind you that you are very precious to me?'

The tenderness in his eyes was undeniable, so that, momentarily dazzled, I again bethought myself of how he has seemed over these past few weeks so earnestly to be striving to change. But then, even as I had begun upon my old dream, in which that delicious tenderness between us is constant, the wordless language of a pure and ineffable love, I confess there stole upon me the most unworthy doubt. Does not M's excess of concern more probably signify that he is up to something?

CHAPTER TWENTY

I had never dared go to the studio before without being summoned. But, though I was afraid of Felix's anger and though I knew my action could only exacerbate it, I could not spend the night futilely pacing my bedroom floor. For, despite my exhaustion, sleep seemed an impossibility; I had not even the heart to undress.

Though there was light seeping from under the studio door there was no sound within. I knocked, once timidly and then again, louder. There was no reply. I took my courage in both hands, pushed open the door and walked in.

He was standing before the easel in his long silk dressing gown, scraping paint from a corner of the canvas with a knife. When he saw me he paused, knife in one hand, cigarette in the other.

'Christabel, I asked you to go to bed.'

'I must talk to you,' I said. 'I have at least the right to know why you are going to break your word.'

He moved towards the smouldering embers of the fire to throw away his cigarette. There was a sharp impatience in the movement, a swish of black silk. And once more I had an uneasy sense of his body naked beneath the dressing gown.

'Stenko told me about his conversation with you,' I said. 'I couldn't think why you never mentioned it. I could only suppose you had just forgotten, I never imagined that – that you had changed your mind.'

He stood before the fire looking at me, the haft of the knife in his right hand, the fingers of his left resting on the blade. 'It has been a long evening, Christabel. And it is now two in the morning and I need to work. Would you please do as I say and go back upstairs.'

'But I don't understand. I've kept my side of our bargain. Is there some fault in me that has made you decide you can't keep yours?'

He was still looking at me, tapping the knife blade impatiently upon his knuckles.

Eventually he gave an exasperated sigh. 'Very well. I have listened to Stenko and I have no intention of breaking my promise. But we agreed you should stay here three weeks and that has now become four. It simply isn't possible for you to continue living in this house indefinitely.'

I felt a sudden chill. 'So you will send me back?'

'Only as a temporary measure. Until we find somewhere else for you in London.'

'But you know, I've explained to you, what will happen.'

He had returned to the canvas and was working away at the paint again. He spoke without looking up. 'We'll have to put it to the test, Christabel. You can't continue to stay here, and there's nowhere else for you to go.'

I stared at him as he worked with the knife, intent, concentrating, the very attitude of his body signalling my dismissal. I took three steps towards him, until I was level with the desk.

'I don't understand why. I don't know why you're so angry with me. It isn't my fault that you've fallen out with Tarantin and quarrelled with your mistress – '

'Anna is no longer my mistress.'

Though he said it without expression, without lifting his eyes from the canvas, it was once again so unexpectedly personal, such an unlooked-for crack in his cool façade, that I found myself disconcerted. Then suddenly I thought I understood. And I began to burn with anger.

'So you do blame me! You think that my being here gets in the way of your – of your enjoying yourself.'

'Don't be ridiculous, Christabel.'

'You decided to help me on a whim and now it's turned out to be inconvenient you've changed your mind.'

'Please stop talking like a silly child.'

'And I thought, underneath all your indifference, you were really rather kind. I thought even if I was only your silly little girl cousin you cared about the music, at least you saw some point in that. But it was all just a diversion for you, wasn't it? Your protégée, someone to patronize, someone to take up and put down as Tarantin does, something to amuse you. And now it's getting in the way and you're bored with it—'

'Stop it, Christabel!' He had looked up and was facing me now, the knife, raised halfway from the canvas, still in his hand.

'Perhaps Tarantin is right. When all's said and done, you don't really care. You're incapable of caring about anything or anybody – '

'Christabel, will you please stop!'

There was an edge to his voice now that suddenly suggested he was struggling to keep control. But I was beside myself.

'Yes, I will stop. Because now I realize I am to blame after all. I'm to blame for having so much lost my pride as to take anything from you, ask you for anything. I'm to blame for having put up with all your mockery and arrogance, for being so stupid as to think there was something underneath. How dare you treat me like a parcel to be shuttled around! How dare you keep calling me a child! How dare you, how dare you cut up my dress! I suppose you thought it was very clever to humiliate me. And to think I stood by and let you do it. Well, I'm not standing by now and letting you send me to Norfolk just because it's convenient for you. I'm leaving this house tonight and you won't stop me. I don't recognize any right of yours to tell me what to do. I don't want your shoddy promises and your patronage. You're a sarcastic, bullying, arrogant, self-centred, shallow, supercilious pig, Felix de Lisle! And I don't want anything from you! Starting with your rotten shawl! And your beastly, beastly dress!'

And, tearing off the shawl and flinging it at him, I grasped the front of the green and silver dress where he had cut it and with all my strength ripped it apart as far as it would go, right down to the low satin band at the waist.

An immense silence fell.

The shawl had gone far wide of its mark and, landing across the desk, had knocked over a pot of scarlet ink which spread in a bright stain. Looking down, I saw that apart from my chemise I was undressed to the waist and, suddenly feeling very foolish, suddenly thinking that perhaps I had behaved like a silly, spoilt child after all, I put up my hands to cover myself.

But at that point something inside my Cousin Felix, all his steel-cool control, seemed to snap. There was a sound like a scream as the knife in his hand came down upon the canvas. Then a clatter as, sliding away from the great rent it had made, it fell to the floor. Then he was bearing down upon me, his eyes no longer cold but blazing, his face white, the whole dark presence of him frighteningly tall, savagely naked under the silk.

'Dear God!' he shouted. 'Tarantin can see it, Anna can see it! Are you so innocent or so stupid that you are really unable to understand why you can no longer stay in this house?'

I thought he was going to hit me, and turned my head aside. But his hand fastened upon my chin, wrenching it towards him. And suddenly he was kissing me, full upon the lips.

I knew what to do. I had, after all, been kissed before, by Archie Cadwallander. I began to fight. But though his lips were crushing mine, my Cousin Felix did not kiss like Archie. His tongue, invading my mouth, seemed to possess it. And mine, all against my will, seemed to surrender to that possession, moving darkly, mysteriously with his.

I stopped struggling and his lips became more gentle. Now they drank from mine, sometimes in slow, languorous draughts, sometimes in playful sips. And all the time his tongue, probing the realms of its possession, danced upon mine, danced slower, deeper. A heaviness grew in my body till it seemed my being was concentrated on that one point, that the rest of me was dispersing, melting against him, melting into the hardness of him, that insistent hardness I could now feel thrusting against my belly. His fingers slid down and gently closed in turn upon each of my nipples and I felt them grow tight and pert under my chemise. Then he took my hand and passed it beneath the black silk above his waist and, kissing, exploring, I drank in the sweetness of his skin and felt the contrasts of it, hard with muscle and dark with hair across his chest, soft beneath his arms, taut and sinewy at his back. And the heaviness grew, my body seemed to open with it, opening to him, soft and deep and wet, and little muscles I had not known I had, contracting and expanding, sent up such sweet darts of pain that my stomach was filled with them and all of me was aching, heavy, aching for him.

We seemed to go on in this way for a long, long while: until, putting his hands in my hair, he gave me one slow and infinitely gentle kiss, then stood me away from him with something between a shudder and a sigh.

'Don't stop,' I said.

His hands, I noticed, were trembling and his voice, when he spoke, was not quite distinct.

'My dear little Christie, you are too innocent and too sweet. Go to bed now, and we will talk properly in the morning.'

'You're always sending me off to bed,' I said.

He laughed and, very lightly, touched my cheek. 'Little one, if I don't stop now, I shall not be able to stop at all.'

I looked up at him and saw again in his eyes that look of suppressed pain, and felt the ache in my own body answer it. My voice rose with difficulty from my throat. 'I don't want you to stop,' I said.

He seemed to struggle with himself. Then, taking my chin in the hollow of his hand so that my face was tilted directly towards his, he looked at me for a long time with a concentrated intensity which, examining what was in my eyes, seemed inwardly to examine himself too; and in the look was a question which my head, only half-understanding and being all at once, like someone planning to jump into deep water who cannot swim, a little frightened, could not answer, but to which my body cried out an unreserved, instinctive yes.

He let his hand drop and his eyes became suddenly hard. He kissed me again, almost perfunctorily, as if he were now deliberately holding himself back. Then, very slowly and carefully, he began to ease the tattered remains of the dress from my shoulders.

I watched it fall, and after it my chemise, my belt, my stockings, fall like discarded veiling about my feet, all the time feeling his hands and mouth explore my body, kissing my neck and breasts, stroking, caressing my thighs; and in his touch, in all his movements now, was that fine deliberate control, like the stretching of an infinitesimally thin thread which brought too soon to its ultimate point of tension will snap. I stood, stock-still, as he knelt before me, my hands upon the nape of his neck, sensing the tension, suddenly frightened by it, feeling no longer the ache of desire but a growing, paralysing fear.

He rose and with his hands upon my shoulders looked at me, his eyes still hard, almost dispassionate. I felt myself quiver before that look, felt in my white nakedness infinitely vulnerable.

'Dear God, little Christie,' he said very softly, 'I think I have wanted you so badly for so long.'

Then, kissing me, he lifted me up and laid me among the cushions on the couch.

I turned away as he untied the belt of his dressing gown. I had never seen any man naked before. Then I felt him kneeling over me and I was afraid in earnest now, afraid to open my eyes and see him towering over me, afraid of the proud, dispassionate hardness of him, afraid, afraid. And then he was moving my legs apart very gently and I wanted to cry out, my body was rigid with it, and I knew, did not know what would happen, wanted to struggle free before it was too late, wanted to scream that it was impossible, he would hurt me; and it was too late, and I screamed, screamed at the pain and began to fight him, thrashing with my legs, clawing his back with my fingers, heaving up my loins to thrust him out of me and I heard him cry 'Oh God, little one, don't fight me now, don't make me hurt you!' and his hands were down on my shoulders forcing me back and his pelvis was down on mine crushing me and he cried out again: 'Dear God, no. No, no, no, no, no!' and then there was nothing but the brutal force of him, as if I had ceased to exist, as if I were obliterated in the act of possession, as if there were nothing now but his need.

And then there was silence. A long, blank, bleak silence. He came off me in a moment and I lay quite still, my lower lip caught between my teeth where I had bitten it, my head thrust back, my arms rigid by my sides. The space between my legs was seared with pain, my stomach felt as if, deep inside, someone had kicked me. I sat up stiffly. And saw to my horror that I was bleeding.

I began to cry. I cried as if I would never stop, for the pain and the blood and for no longer existing, for the loss of my virginity, for the utter humiliating emptiness of me and for all the other emptinesses in my life, for the death of my mother and the joyless years at Monks Last, for having to struggle so hard to keep my head above water and having no one any more to comfort me or talk to, and for wanting him so much and losing him, and above all for knowing, for knowing now that was all anyone meant by love, that emptiness was what love was.

My Cousin Felix raised himself quietly from the couch, went to his dressing-gown pocket and came back with a very white linen handkerchief. With the utmost tenderness, so that I scarcely felt him touching me, he wiped away the blood from between my thighs and kissed them. Then he lifted me up and held me to him, with my face in the crook of his shoulder and my arms about his neck, rocking me softly against his body, stroking my back and the cleft between my shoulder blades and pressing his lips to my hair.

After a while, lulled by the warmth of his body and the sweetness of his skin, I stopped sobbing and began to issue only a trickle of tears.

'I'm sorry,' I said.

'Dear little one, you have nothing to be sorry for. You must forgive me for being so selfish. When you began to fight me you brought me suddenly to the point of no return.'

I looked up and met his eyes and saw in them tenderness and concern. Then all at once, beyond him, I glimpsed the easel and the ruined canvas and began absurdly to cry again.

'And it's all my fault you've destroyed your painting. Everything's destroyed. And it's all my fault.'

He laughed. 'My dear Christie, if you keep apologizing to me I shall become extremely angry. And anyway it was an appalling painting. My concentration's been rather to pieces these last few weeks.'

I found myself suddenly laughing too. I wiped my eyes on the back of my hand, trying not to sniff. 'Oh, how I hate crying. I must look absolutely awful.'

He kissed the tip of my nose. 'You look at least thirteen. And very, very beautiful. And now I'm going to take you to bed.'

I stood by and watched while he found me another handkerchief from the drawer of his desk and, casting aside the cushions, drew back the crimson chenille from the couch to reveal pillows and starched white sheets. Then, making me climb between them and getting in beside me, he drew me towards him and enfolded me in his arms.

We did not speak. I felt myself begin to quiver, suddenly nervous of him again. But he stroked my hair and my face, very softly and gently, as if I were a small, frightened animal to be soothed and reassured. Then, after some time, he began, tenderly, to kiss me.

There was in that tenderness such an unhurried calm, as if, freed from the urgency of need, he were negligently luxuriating in my hair, my throat, my lips, that I felt myself begin to bend to it, felt my body unfold against his, responding generously to his touch, like a piano giving out a long, lazy ripple of notes. And now his hands were playing indolently over the whole length of me, caressing the curve of my belly and the soft skin inside my thighs, tracing a leisurely line from the hollow at the base of my throat to between my breasts, lifting them, cupping them, softly, softly touching my nipples, exploring in careless runs and trills the pitch and tuning of me. And I found myself responding louder, kissing him harder, wanting to draw his head down and press my nipples to his lips, wanting to follow where his hand guided me. And suddenly I was flooding out with my need of him, moaning with it, my head thrown back, my breasts exposed nakedly to him, and I wanted him, wanted him inside me, could not bear that he was not, cried out to him, spread myself wide for him: and he slid into me, slowly, deliberately, up to the hilt in me and I felt how he filled me moving, deeper and deeper with a measured, unbearable slowness.

When eventually I opened my eyes he was still inside me, lying across me with his head on my breast. I put out my hand and touched his hair. He raised his head and then, working his arm underneath me, manipulating me with great care so that we moved in unison, turned us both sideways so that we were lying face to face with our arms about each other and our legs entwined. Our bodies seemed to fit together thus as if they had been precisely designed for it.

I could feel him still, diminishing slowly, so that my muscles continued to give out little involuntary squeezes as if to hold fast to him. I looked into his face and saw the movements of my body reflected there like tiny twinges of exquisite pain. I watched his eyes grow cloudy with tenderness and his mouth broaden into a lazy smile. I wanted to put out my hand and touch his lips, but almost did not dare to.

He was laughing. 'My dear little Christie, you have such a crazy wondering look about you, as if you did not believe in the existence of either of us.'

'It's not disbelief,' I said. And suddenly, because he was laughing, I was laughing too.

He shifted slightly, drawing me closer to him. 'Don't laugh too much, little one, or we shall lose each other.'

Then he kissed me on the lips and began softly to stroke my cheek. 'Well, I am not sure I believe it,' he said. 'I seem to have been in such an agony of wanting you for so long that I'm not even sure when I began upon it. Whether it was watching you always so angry with me, eyes blazing, determined little chin thrust out, or whether it was finding you tattered and bleeding on my doorstep and feeling a desperate but, thank God, quite erroneous certainty that you'd been raped. Or whether it began much earlier still, with the strange hoydenish little creature I kept seeing turn suddenly pale and run away from me at parties. My funny little skinny cousin. So completely beautiful and so utterly unconscious of it. And always in the most appalling frocks as if, being so beautiful, she had to expiate the fact in a positive penance of mauves and sickly greens and, heaven forfend, heliotrope – '

'Cyclamen,' I said.

He laughed. 'Whatever it was, it was abominable. You will grow your hair, you will acquire some proper clothes. You will endeavour always to look as beautiful dressed as you do lying in my arms naked.'

'I see,' I said, smiling. 'You're taking me over.'

To my surprise he was suddenly serious. 'No, my dear, sweet, virginal little Christie. I think I have no right to take any part of you.' And in his eyes there was all at once a curious sadness.

I reached up and kissed him. We kissed for some time, tenderly at first and then with increasing passion.

'So this is what it's like,' I said softly, feeling him moving, growing inside me and my body beginning to echo the movement. 'This is what it's like, the act of love.'

He smiled. 'Good heavens, you make it sound like some dreary document concocted by Meredith and his Parliamentary colleagues. But no, this is not always what it's like. Only, for some mysterious and quite remarkable reason, it is like this for us.'

I opened my mouth to say something else but his lips were nuzzling at my breast and, finding myself now filled with the hugeness of him, I let the words expire in a sigh.

Much later, I awoke, stretched luxuriantly and, discovering that the other half of the bed was empty, struggled up onto my elbows, looking round me with desolation.

He was sitting in his dressing gown in the window, smoking a Muratti and sipping a glass of champagne. Outside, a murky daylight glowered. Seeing that I was awake he rose and kissed me, then brought from the desk to the bed a linen-covered tray.

'Smoked salmon, lemons, brown bread and butter, cream and some out-of-season strawberries Anatole managed to get sent from Harrods. Oh, and a bottle of 1911 Bollinger.'

'Breakfast?' I enquired. 'Or is it luncheon?'

He was propping me up with cushions and straightening my sheets as if I were an invalid. 'I should think, by this time, probably tea. But vintage champagne is not unacceptable at any hour of the day.'

I discovered I was ravenously hungry. He sat smoking and watching me eat, occasionally filching the odd strawberry. It seemed to me suddenly an immense absurdity to be sitting up in bed stark naked working my way as decorously as possible through a huge plate of the finest Scotch smoked salmon. Beginning to laugh, I spilt my champagne so that a cold trickle of it ran down between my breasts. I stopped it with my finger, which I then licked. And, looking up again, I saw his eyes go dark with the now-familiar indications of burgeoning desire.

He was, I thought all at once, so beautiful, my Cousin Felix, with his proud patrician face, and his eyes clouded with the need of me, and his half-mocking, half-tender smile, that I began to laugh in earnest from the sheer joy of it.

'My dear child, first you put me in pain, then you start laughing at me. Whatever is it?'

'Oh, Felix,' I said, lying back on the pillows, 'my dear, wicked Cousin Felix. Evil seducer of innocent young virgins with champagne and out-of-season strawberries.'

He rose to remove the tray. 'Your wicked Cousin Felix,' he said wryly, 'more usually seducer of impervious, cynical people like himself. People he can't hurt. Though which of us,' he added, taking the champagne glass from my hand and kissing the place where I had spilled it, 'is now in more danger I begin seriously to question.'

CHAPTER TWENTY-ONE

The world, when we returned to it two days later, seemed quite improbably to have remained unchanged; and yet perhaps it had shifted imperceptibly on its axis after all, for the winter sun upon the river seemed to glint more sharply, the kiss of towels upon newly-bathed skin to linger more chasteningly, the aroma of Anatole's coffee, freshly brewing in the kitchen, to speak with an even more eloquent and seductive voice. I could not imagine how I had thought my Cousin Felix's face unfathomable, or even that it had but one perspective to it. Watching him talk to the young man who made the models of his set designs, by turns thoughtful, decisive, then, throwing back his head in laughter at some chance remark, almost boyish; searching out his eyes at parties and finding him, trapped by Phoebe Millington, unfailingly charming yet sending out signals of amused despair; seeing his expression in the preliminaries of our lovemaking, gentle, absorbed, infinitely tender, I felt gradually most of the barriers which rose one upon another to build up his façade of studied indifference fall away. I knew now, watching him work, catching him shifting uncomfortably on the high-backed stool, that his self-discipline was still often bought at the price of physical pain, and knew too that sympathy would anger him, that it was a courtesy never to refer to it. I heard now the affectionate undertones in his mockery and had learnt to mock him back.

But, for all that, I sensed that there was still some part of my Cousin Felix that I might never know, still deep within him doors that held fast, which I could not without his consent force and which might never be unlocked to me; and sometimes running my hands softly over his long lean body as he lay beside me, I would gingerly finger the harsh white scar at the base of his spine and think that he had other scars I could not see, scars not only the war had given him. One morning, waking up to find him still asleep beside me – a rare occurrence since the pain in his back and his natural disinclination to sleep always meant he had risen long before me – I was so struck by the sight of his face as it never was awake, completely peaceful and unguarded, that I found myself aching with a poignant sadness for it.

I lived now in a whirlwind, caught up in the reckless impetus of Felix's life. The war, he explained, had taught him to value impulse, to snatch the utmost from every moment that was given to him. I became very soon used to lying in bed lazily beside him one minute, then the next being told I must dress, that we were going to dinner at the Berkeley or to a party at the Chantrys'. It was yet another part of his complexity, that whirling energy which spun, as in his paintings, in fine balance with his cool control, and willingly, joyously I became infected with it, so that sometimes I would catch my breath and think we had even made time run before us in our dizzy pursuit of our happiness in each other.

We went everywhere together. At Lucile where, characteristically dictatorial, he insisted on my choosing only what was understated and simple in greys and creams and soft browns, colours he said I would wear without their wearing me, we scandalized the hushed dignity of the salon with our laughter. At parties we sought endless secret ways of touching each other, as if the contact of our bodies were an addiction we knew it was hopeless to fight. We seemed to emit our happiness like an aura so that, in restaurants or stopping to buy a paper from a street corner stand, we would find ourselves smiled at and treated with a protective generosity. We made love with an appetite that grew insatiably as we indulged it. We talked and talked, about music, about painting, I of my childhood in Weymouth and my soft, sweet mother and my father who, since he had died two years after I was born, I had never known; he of Paris and sometimes with regret of his own father to whom he wished he had been closer – though never of the war and only tangentially of Aunt Jessica, as if again there were areas of his life he closed off even to himself, which he could not, would not examine. And in the midst of it all, Stenko reappearing in the afternoons and Tarantin still demanding refinements to the *Icarus* designs, we worked, hard and with satisfaction.

I did not doubt that I loved him, nor did I seek to analyse the feeling as I should now, to differentiate between loving and being in love. I was consumed with wonder at the mysteries of my intimacy with him, so that even the most trivial testimonies to his existence, his stud box or his tortoiseshell-backed brushes, had a capacity to fill me with tenderness. I felt no longer any trace of regret at having given myself to him – perhaps, after all, Meredith was right and I was 'wild'. When my period was two days late I was for a moment frightened, but when it came I was stricken with a sense of loss, as if the natural consequences of my love for him had been most unnaturally frustrated. For I trusted his strength and his certainty. And although he had never said he loved me, I felt loved, wrapped round with it, safe in its all-encompassing warmth.

I, too, did not tell him that I loved him, for it was part of my understanding of the shut-away areas of him, part of my not forcing him, that I should be prepared to take only what was given, when he was able to give it. But I was glad when, seeing Dilly and Robbie off on the start of their voyage to India, she asked me if I were sure I didn't care for him a little and I was able to put it into words at last, to tell her secretly, on pain of death, how much, oh how very much I did. And I was glad, also, when she giggled delightedly and said: 'Well, he's obviously dotty about you. He can't bear to take his eyes off you, even for a minute.'

Altogether, there was only one obstacle to my complete happiness. And that was an uneasy consciousness of Aunt Jessica, waiting, wondering in Norfolk. At Felix's suggestion, I had left all explanations of my continued absence to him. But I knew even he could not hold her for long. And I realized too that once she caught the slightest whisper that there was anything more than the accepted familial relationship between us, her fury would know no bounds. As to how he had up to now parried her questions, he remained noncommittal. But, catching him one day at the tail end of an acrimonious telephone conversation with Meredith who, now the House was in session, had returned to London, I felt certain that she was increasing her pressure. It seemed inevitable that sooner or later there should be gossip, if it had not already started. And one day, after we had been lovers for just over five weeks, I saw with a sinking heart that it had.

He had taken me for luncheon at the Ritz. We were sitting at a table by the window, bathed in the pale spring light that filtered in from Green Park, drinking champagne. Suddenly serious, he took my hand, interlacing my fingers with his, gently touching my fingertips, then raising them to his lips. And as he did so, looking up to meet his eyes, I saw beyond him, at the very next table, the Dowager Duchess of Rosslair quizzing us with her lorgnette.

'Christie – ' he said softly.

The Duchess's pearl-festooned *embonpoint* heaved impressively. She turned to say something to her companion.

'Oh damn!' I said.

He stopped, my fingers halfway from his lips, raising his eyebrows in surprise.

'Don't turn round,' I said. 'But it's Bunty Rosslair. Looking as if she had just come upon the Clapham Branch of the Naturists' Club having their AGM in her drawing room.'

He laughed. 'Well, you can be perfectly sure it's me she disapproves of. She's never quite recovered from the private view.'

'Oh, Felix,' I said, 'you don't understand. She'll tell Phoebe Millington she's seen you kissing me. And Phoebe'll tell Miles and Miles will tell Archie and Archie will tell Meredith and Meredith—'

'Will tell my mother?' His serious expression returned. Despite my attempts to release my hand he held it fast. 'Little one, has it not occurred to you that there is a simple answer to all this?'

The Duchess's lorgnette, catching the light, sent out shivers of disapproval like rays. 'There isn't an answer,' I said hopelessly. 'Aunt Jessica will insist you send me back after this. And I don't want to marry Archie. I don't,' I said defiantly, 'want to marry anyone.'

I knew these last words were now untrue even as I uttered them. Flushing, I all at once felt profoundly miserable. Felix, seeming to catch my mood, released my hand and changed the subject, so that I never found out what his answer might be. But that there was need of one became only too apparent a couple of days later.

I had, for the same reason that I was silent about my love for him, always scrupulously avoided interrupting Felix while he worked, or indeed ever again entering the studio uninvited. But recently, if we were alone in the house – its itinerant population had gradually drifted back but did not now stay as often or as long as it had been wont to – he would, if I were not practising or having a music lesson, come in search of me.

'My dear little Christie, I cannot bear to be without you for so long. Come and sit with me in the studio where I can see you.'

And it was on one of these occasions, when I had taken my book and curled up with it in the window seat, that our peace was so suddenly shattered.

I must have gone to sleep over the book. When I awoke, rubbing my eyes and stretching from stiffness, he was sitting at his desk, pencil in one hand, cigarette in the other, but turned towards me, watching me, smiling. Going over to him, I saw his drawing pad that was filled with sketches of me, like studies for a portrait; full drawings of my body curled up sleeping, closer sketches of my face, the angle of my shoulders, minute details of my hand upon the book, of the folds of my skirt as it fell about my ankles, of my eyes, my lips, even of the way my hair wreathed my forehead.

'Gosh,' I said. 'I must have been asleep for ages and ages.'

He put his arm around my waist. 'And now you are awake I await your judgement.'

Staring at the sketches, I found myself disconcerted. They were different from most of his work, simpler, more contemplative, perhaps because they were in pencil, softer. And there was, in the strangeness of looking at myself through his eyes, another strangeness too that I could not put my finger on. But I could not deny they were decidedly flattering.

'Do I really look like that?'

He tightened his arm, folding me towards him. 'Alas, a great deal more beautiful.' And he was just about to kiss me when there was a knock at the door. His arm fell away, he gave a small sigh of irritation. Anatole appeared.

'Mademoiselle, there is a Mr Cadwallander downstairs asking to see you.'

I felt Felix stiffen.

'Oh, Anatole, tell him I'm not here. Tell him I've gone away – to the country.'

'No.' Felix had moved over to the mantelpiece. His face, as he took a cigarette from the jade box, was once again as it used to be, closed, impenetrable. 'No, little one. If he has taken the trouble to come, you must see him. No, don't protest. To send him away would be gratuitously rude. I insist you go downstairs and see him.'

Archie was sitting on the edge of one of the drawing-room armchairs, rotating the brim of his hat in his hands. Against the Oriental opulence of the room he looked, in his grey suit and with his light hair, washed out, inappropriate, like an actor who has strayed from another play onto the wrong set.

'Oh, Archie,' I said, 'you shouldn't have come here.'

'Had to come, old girl. You know why.'

Seeing the familiar redness spread from his ears, I thought I knew only too well. 'Archie,' I said, as gently as I could, 'I am very grateful you should think fondly of me. But I am afraid nothing has changed.'

He gulped. 'Ah! But that's where you're wrong, don't y'know. All sorts of changes since I saw you last, old thing. My guv'nor for a start. Got a dicky heart, quacks say he may peg out any minute.'

'Oh Archie,' I said, 'I am sorry.'

'Well, got to take the rough with the smooth, what? Thing is, got to look after the business – only son and all that. Run things, up North. Won't be able to see you.'

'I'm sure you'll come to London every so often.'

His shoulders heaved, his Adam's apple bobbed. His hands mashed the brim of his hat. 'Not exactly the point, old girl.' He took a great gulp, like a fish coming up for air. 'Chap on his own needs support. Not very jolly, fighting the blighters on the Board, not having the foggiest about the company. Need some encouragement, someone to put a bit of iron into the old soul – '

He had begun fumbling in his breast pocket. Finally he produced something that looked, to my horror, suspiciously like a jeweller's box.

'Need the help of a decent girl, don't y'know. Other half, as the saying goes.'

Suddenly I was angry, angry that he was always forcing me to hurt him, that he would make me hurt him now when his father was dying, that he should at once be so absurd and so lost, so pathetic. 'No, Archie,' I said.

'Solitaire diamond, old girl. Asprey's. The pukka stuff. Cost me a monkey.'

'No, Archie.'

'Must have had a slate loose to propose in that bally hat shop. This time, going to make sure I do the proper thing.'

'No, Archie!'

'Go through the whole caboodle for you, old girl. Even go down on bended knee.'

'No, Archie!' I said, seeing that he was about to suit his actions to his words. 'No, Archie, no, no!'

He staggered for a second, as if thrown off balance by the violence of my response, then clumsily righted himself. He looked at me, then at the solitaire diamond in its box, then back at me again. Suddenly he was crimson, no longer with throttled emotion but with rage. He snapped the box shut. 'It's him, isn't it?'

'Archie, I—'

'It's that bounder de Lisle!'

'Archie—'

'Oh, don't deny it, old girl. Not cuckoo, don't y'know. Been seen, the two of you, seen everywhere, making sheep's eyes at each other, dancing together, canoodling, thick as thieves.'

'Archie, that's none of your business.'

'Make it my business, old girl. Blighter like that! Bally poodle-faker, goes about with a bunch of ticks and sissy Bohemians and dope fiends! Even his bally brother says he's a cad of the first water – '

'Archie, how dare you!'

'A rotter like that only wants one thing. And once he's got it he'll leave you in the cart, you'll see. Got to protect you from yourself, open your eyes before it's too late—'

'Archie!' I was shaking with rage. 'You wouldn't dare say any of those things to Felix's face. How dare you say them behind his back! How dare you stand here in his house and slander him with such contemptible, wicked lies! I'm sorry about your father, I'm sorry you're wretched, but I want you to pick up your hat and your ring and go. And I don't ever, ever want to see you again!'

* * *

The moment he had left I ran upstairs to the studio. But I knew, even before I had opened the door, what I should find. Felix had gone, was no longer anywhere in the house and, according to Anatole, had left no message about where he had intended going or what time he could be expected back.

I sat for a long while at his desk, looking absently at his sketches of me, until I had finished trembling. It was all up now, I knew. Archie could not fail to report back to Meredith, that I loved his brother. Aunt Jessica, in her anger, would use her power as my legal guardian to take steps to separate us which even Felix could not resist. And did he, in any case, want to resist them? Had everything now, for some reason I did not understand, suddenly changed between us? Why had he gone like that, without saying anything? Why had he gone and where?

I looked down mournfully at the sheet of sketches. Again it came back to me, that haunting strangeness; and suddenly, with a shock, I knew what it was. 'You look so alike,' Dilly had said, and I had replied without thinking that it must be the Cavendish face. Now here it was, the Cavendish face, staring back at me from Felix's drawing pad, stripped, by the natural tendency of the artist to imprint upon everything he draws a little of his own image, of all the variations of detail and proportion that rendered it different in both of us, so that in looking at Felix's drawings of me I received back not only my own likeness, but his, two faces, subtly superimposed upon each other, blending into one. I stared, fascinated; and as I did so, seeing now in my face only his, I felt such a distracted longing for him that I was almost beside myself with it. Where had he gone? To Tarantin? Or, I thought bitterly, remembering his previous disappearances, to Rostova? To shimmering, serpentine Rostova who would be waiting for him, waiting for him to tire of me, waiting to wind him once more in the coils of her undulating sensuality. I tried to put the thought from my mind, but the more I fought it the more its focus sharpened.

I dined alone, scantily and miserably. And at about nine o'clock Anatole announced that Mme Rostova had arrived and had been shown into the drawing room.

CHAPTER TWENTY-TWO

'So you do not know where he is or when he will return?' purred Anna Rostova, kissing me on the cheek, fondling my hair. 'So you have had, *ma petite,* a lovers' quarrel!'

I drew away from her. I did not want her to touch me, I did not want her here, filling the room with her shimmering, snaky presence. 'No,' I said. 'I wasn't there when he went out. I'm sure he'll be back soon.'

She divested herself of her ermine, began to draw off her gloves. '*Alors, bien.* I need to see him, you understand. On a matter of urgency.'

And, coiling herself up languorously upon the day bed, she gave at once the impression of being completely in command, of being more at home there than I was.

'Come, *ma petite,*' she said, patting the seat beside her, 'we shall take the chance to talk while he is away. We shall talk together as only two women can when they are alone, without a man.'

Still I held back, knowing that politeness decreed I should submit, but fighting it, wondering whether I dared to demand of her, as I had of Archie, that she leave Felix's house.

She reclined upon the cushions, watching me, smiling. 'Some refreshment would be delightful. It is too late for cocktails, but perhaps a little wine . . .'

Politeness and fear of displeasing Felix won. Anatole brought claret and I sat beside her in the place she had allotted me. Her eyes were hard as malachite, her hand, as it curled about the blood-red bowl of her wine glass, ivory-white with nails like talons. There was something in her smile, in the very gush of her friendliness that frightened and yet mesmerized me – the snake, I thought, immobilizing its prey.

'But, my dear,' she said, pinching my cheek between her cold, dry fingers, 'you are so pale. You are certain you and Félix have not quarrelled? He is, of course, so charming, so handsome. But when he falls into one of his black moods he can be also – shall we put it kindly since he is not here to defend himself? – he can, *ma petite,* be *fâcheusement difficile.*'

I shook my head, knowing as I did so that my very vehemence lent doubt to it.

She laughed, stretching herself out upon the cushions. 'Oh, the pain of first love! How I remember it, even now. Believing he would always be faithful, believing I should always be faithful to him. Ah, *comme la jeunesse fait du sentiment*! But you will learn, *ma petite innocente*. Perhaps – ' and here she stroked my hand – 'you are already learning.'

I withdrew abruptly from her touch. 'Felix and I have not quarrelled. He has simply gone out.'

'Oh come, *chérie*. Do not be angry with me. I want only to be your friend. Do not forget that I am – *hélas* – older than you and know the world. And, *tiens*, I know *cher Félix*!'

'I think I also know him,' I said; and wished as I said it I had more faith that it was true.

She overrode me. 'Ah, but now I see! You imagine I am jealous.' Her head went back in a peal of laughter that showed all her sharp white teeth. 'But, *ma petite,* you must not believe that I loved Félix. Oh, one admires, one takes pleasure in such a man. But one does not love him. One plays him, finesses him, as one does cards at bridge—'

'I ask of Felix nothing he is unprepared to give.'

'But it is what you give, *ma petite,* that counts. Give him everything and he will soon be bored to distraction. But keep always a little back, tease him a little, and you will have him in the palm of your hand to hold, like so!'

'Mme Rostova, I hardly think—'

'Oh, but you must listen. It is good advice.'

'Thank you. But I don't need—'

Laughing, she pinched my cheek again. 'Oh but, *ma chérie,* you do. I want you to think of me as your friend, your confidante. Let us have no more secrets from each other. And now you may start telling me about your silly quarrel.'

Shaking her off, I stood up. 'Mme Rostova,' I said, summoning all my courage, 'I don't wish to seem ungrateful or disagreeable, but I must ask you to—'

But the words that would free me from her were abruptly cut off by the entrance of Anatole.

'Mademoiselle, Monsieur de Tarantin is here asking for Monsieur de Lisle.'

Anna Rostova clapped her hands together in delight. 'Ah, Le Bon Dieu! Le Grand Tarantin! Oh, *ma petite,* now we are in luck. Now we shall have great sport this evening.'

And while my heart quailed, Vladimir Tarantin was shown in.

He seemed, in evening dress with his hair freshly pomaded, with his dandified air and his lithe, quick movements, more sinister, more simian than ever. His glittering black eyes flashed round the room, firing first a poisoned dart at me, then a great shaft of venom at Rostova.

'So, Anna Nikolayevna! You cannot resist it, you must still come here.'

She lay back on the cushions, sipping her wine. 'My dear Vladimir Andreyevitch, I am no longer a member of your company, you do not own me. You may be suing me for breach of contract, but at least I may do as I please.'

He bared his teeth at her in a snarl of displeasure.

'For that matter,' she purred, not a whit disconcerted, 'why have you come? Is the Great Vladimir Tarantin, now that his creation is stolen away, suffering like a rejected lover?'

'I have business with Felix. He has not made the alterations I asked to the *Icarus* designs. I must see him immediately.'

She was laughing, holding her hand out to me. 'Oh, you must tell him, *ma petite*. You must not be ashamed.' And then, as I opened my mouth to protest, she continued to talk over me. '*Félix, comme d'habitude fait la bête.* He has quarrelled with this poor child and stormed out of the house. And no one knows when he will return. If he intends to return at all.'

Was it my imagination, or did Tarantin's eyes, beneath their hostility, glitter for a moment with sudden pleasure? 'So, Anna Nikolayevna, whose doing was it? No doubt it was some wicked game of yours.'

'Ah, *ma chérie*, see how he distrusts me. See how he will never have a good word for me when a bad one will do.' Her arms were thrown wide to me in theatrical appeal. '*Merde*, Vladimir Andreyevitch! I am sitting here simply to keep *la petite* company, to dry her tears.'

The thought seemed to afford him amusement. He snorted derisively. 'Dear Anna Nikolayevna, I trust the day I need consolation you will spare me. I think I am more comfortable with Lucrezia Borgia.'

She lowered her glass in mock outrage. 'Oh, *mon ami*, very fine, *très amusante*. I at least feel only what is natural, I at least am not—'

He whirled round upon her suddenly with a savage volley of Russian. She met his eyes, held her ground, but nevertheless she did not finish her sentence. In the wake of its unspoken accusation, a silence fell.

Watching them, he before the mantelpiece, his legs apart, his neck arched, his finger playing upon his waistcoat lapel, his whole muscular body alert, flexed, ready to spring, she reclining on the day bed, her head back, her lips slightly apart, her tongue flickering softly over them, as if, conscious of the possession of superior force, she were daring him, I felt again that there was something in their mutual hostility, in the time-honoured ritual of their loathing, that united them against me, so that as they let fly their poisoned barbs, knowing they would glance wide of their mark, it was I and not they who was most in danger. I wished Felix would come back, I listened for the sound of the front door, for his footsteps in the hall, but in vain. I found myself wondering, if he were not with either of them, where he could have gone for so long. And a voice inside me whispered, no matter how I tried to shut it out, that since I could not know him completely perhaps I did not know him at all, that it was foolish to assume the narrow space of our five-week idyll had laid open every area of his life in London to me, that perhaps there had been other women besides Rostova.

As if suddenly bored with the business of outfacing her, Tarantin disengaged his eyes and, moving restlessly from the mantelpiece, lit a cigar and poured himself a glass of wine.

Again Anna was laughing, throwing out an arm in appeal to me. 'So you see, *ma petite,* though he finds our company disagreeable he has nevertheless decided to stay. Can it be the Great Tarantin is afraid to go now, frightened of what we will say behind his back?'

Tarantin let out another derisive snort. Moving to the piano, he lifted the lid and, cigar between his teeth, essayed a few desultory notes. Then, closing it again as if the dislocated sounds only served to increase his impatience, he wandered back to the mantelpiece and began to pace to and fro in front of it, emitting little peremptory puffs of cigar smoke, like signals of war.

'Oh come, Vladimir Andreyevitch,' purred Rostova, 'you will make us nervous with all this activity. You are supposed to be helping me calm the child, not bring on a fit of the vapours. If you cannot sit down at least think of something to amuse us. You are making my head ache.'

Tarantin issued a cloud of smoke through bared teeth. 'My dear Anna Nikolayevna, I assure you it is not my intention to break in upon your *tête-à-tête* with the so-charming Miss Ward for one second longer than is necessary. The moment Felix arrives, I shall leave you.'

'*Ah, comme tu es ennuyant!* And we were depending upon you to entertain us, were we not, *ma petite*? We must do something to help us with this unbearable waiting. I know – ' and here she sat up, no longer languid, eyes suddenly glittering with excitement – 'we shall play a game!'

'I have seen so many of your games, Anna Nikolayevna. I think perhaps I prefer to play when there is a possibility I may win.'

She had risen, had taken my hand, was squeezing it excitedly. There was in her sudden animation, I thought, more menace than in her languor, as if there would now be no deflecting her, as if she would catch us up and bend us to her will, whether we consented or not.

'*Merde,* he is so selfish, so impossibly dull! But you would like to play a game, would you not, *ma petite*? Come, we must do something to distract you. Now, let me see . . .'

She sat for a moment, chin upon hand, in a dramatic exaggeration of thought. Then all at once her head was thrown back in laughter, throaty, triumphant, mocking laughter, as if at some secret joke of her own. 'Oh, *ravissant*! *Tout à fait parfait!* This will be a game to end all games!' And she leapt up and went to her handbag.

Tarantin had been watching her narrowly. Now, to my amazement, as she moved so, seeming to read that laughter, did he, as her arm went down so did his hand, closing about her wrist until even from a distance I could see how his fingers bit into her flesh. She spat at him in Russian, he snarled back, every crease in his face writhing with an ugly, brutish anger. Eventually, giving a little laugh, she jerked her hand free and turned away, pouting, full of theatrical disappointment.

'*Pourquoi pas? Les petites boules de neige. Enfin, si elle connait cher Félix, elle devrait connaitre ceci.*'

Tarantin spun round, hurling his cigar butt into the grate with a violence that suggested disgust with himself, a sudden regret for his part in what had just passed. Then, levelling his mica-bright eyes at me with a look of undisguised loathing, he spat: '*Je m'en fiche d'elle! C'est pour lui!*'

I had backed away from them to the door. I wanted to tear it open and run, fearing them in earnest now, fearing even more than her pretence of friendship the nakedness of his hatred for me. Yet at the same time, trickling in my veins like poison was the sense that there was nowhere I could escape, that Felix would not come back and save me, that he had in some way gone irrevocably and this, this ugliness was all that was left.

I drew myself up determinedly. 'It's late,' I said. 'There seems little point in your waiting any longer. I think you had both better go.'

'Oh, Vladimir Andreyevitch, now see what you have done! You have frightened the child.' And, before I could prevent her, Rostova had thrown her arms around me, was smothering me with her scented presence, pressing her lips to my cheek.

'You must pay no attention to him, *ma petite.* He is always like this, a great bear with us poor women. Come, sit by me again. *Alors, bien.* And now we shall put our heads together and think of a real game we can play, something *tout à fait amusante.'*

'It's late,' I said. 'Forgive me, Madame Rostova, but I am too tired for games.'

Tarantin laughed. 'You see, Anna Nikolayevna. We are all bored with your charades.'

Rostova brushed aside our objections with one queenly sweep of her hand. 'We must do something while we wait, we must not let *la pauvre petite* go to bed alone and cry herself to sleep. Ah! Now! Suddenly I have a brilliant idea. We shall hold a *séance.'*

Tarantin let out a groan. 'My dear Anna, I will allow you this – you not only dance like a mule, you have the obstinacy of one.'

'*Merde! Tais-toi!* Has *cher Félix* a ouija board?'

'Now you are ridiculous!'

'Well, no matter. We shall make our own. Ring for Anatole. Ask him to bring pen and paper and a water glass. Oh, and incense sticks for atmosphere. We must have atmosphere *pour évoquer des ésprits.'*

'Spirits!' snorted Tarantin disgustedly, biting the end off another cigar. 'I shall have no part in it.'

'But you must, Vladimir Andreyevitch. I insist. We cannot have a *séance* with only two.'

'*Domage!*'

'But my dear Vladimir Andreyevitch,' she purred, fastening upon him her silkiest smile, 'it is to amuse *la petite.* And you would not care for *cher Félix* to return and find you have been frightening and upsetting her.'

He returned the smile for a moment with a hard bright look of his own. And was it my imagination that again in the very hostility of the exchange there was a complicity, so that when, a second later, he unexpectedly gave way, shrugging his shoulders, there was in his eyes a gleam of understanding, even of relish?

'I don't think I care for seances,' I said. 'I don't believe in spirits.'

Her hand went on mine again, her arm around me, compelling me. 'Ah, but, *ma chérie,* you will. With me as your medium you will be converted. When I was a child I was touched by the great Madame Blavatsky. I can feel them already, those waking spirits. You will have faith. You will see.'

Fixed by the sharp pinpoints of her pupils, I found myself drained of any further power to resist. My misery at Felix's desertion welled up within me, crushing me. She would have her way now, they could both do what they would. In my desolation I no longer had the will to struggle.

Having made us submit, she took command of us, organizing us, chivying us, making us turn out lights, move candles, draw up in vases and wine bottles a pentagram of burning incense, while she, in the midst of it, wrote the letters of the alphabet one by one on squares of torn-up paper and arranged them in sequence round a low circular table. Then it was dark, shadowy except for the guttering of a single candle, and she sat us on cushions around the table and ordered us to close our eyes, place our index fingers on the glass and concentrate our whole being into conjuring up the spirits.

The incense scorched my nostrils, filled my lungs until they were heavy. With my eyes closed I seemed to feel the darkness not around me but inside me, a great, blanketing, suffocating darkness of despair. And into it, little by little, welling up and brimming over, poured not the presence of spirits but all the evening's poison, the poison of Archie's words and of Rostova's and Tarantin's hatred.

The glass began suddenly to move, shooting precipitately across the table, carrying our fingers, our arms, our bodies with it.

'Tush, Vladimir Andreyevitch, you are pushing it! Now let us concentrate and try again.'

Why had he left me like this? And why did I so suddenly doubt him, why did I let this poison invade me? Because he had not told me he loved me? But he had shown me in so many ways, he had made me feel loved. Because I did not know him? But I knew him well enough to be certain of him, well enough to trust him better. Because he would have to fight Aunt Jessica, because she would do everything in her power to turn him against me? But he had fought her before and won. Why could I not be content with what I had, loving him freely, demanding nothing? Why did I want all at once to possess him, fetter him, force assurances from him? Why, why?

The glass was moving again, regularly, rhythmically this time.

'The spirits, *ma petite*! The spirits have heard us. You may open your eyes.'

Oh why when I opened them would I still see those pictures, Felix's face bending close to Lady Dolly's, close to Rostova's, close to some woman I did not know, closer, closer in some dark nightclub? . . .

'Speak, O Spirit! Tell us your name.'

'K-O-T-S-C-H-E-I-'

Kotschei. The demon of the Firebird. A made-up name, a name no spirit could possibly possess. It was true – it was a cruel game they were playing with me, one of them contriving it, deliberately pushing the glass. Tarantin or Rostova, which one?

Tarantin let out a gust of sarcastic laughter.

'*Tais-toi,* Vladimir Andreyevitch! You will frighten the spirit. Tell us, O Spirit, if you have a message. A message for one of us?'

'Y-E-S-'

I could feel them now, feel the power of their wills, like electricity conducted through their fingers to the glass. I set my will against theirs, pushing against them with all the power I could summon. But I could not prevent the relentless movement of the glass, backward and forward, inevitably spelling out my name.

'And who is the message from, O Spirit, O great Kotschei?'

'M-O-T-H-'

It was Tarantin, I was sure of it. I could feel it in my finger, sense his will, the power of his hate moving, pushing, dominating the glass. Beneath the heaviness of the incense, beneath the cloying warmth of Rostova's perfume, came like the manifestation of an aura the almond scent of his brilliantine, bitter almonds.

'M-O-T-H-E-R. And what is the message, O great Kotschei? What is the message of Christie's mother? Tell us, tell us what only the spirit world can speak.'

Suddenly the glass was juddering. The candle flickered and almost went out. I saw the pinprick pupils of Rostova, the black inimical eyes of Tarantin, the shadows of us dancing on the wall in the grotesques of *Grand Guignol.* My head was reeling with the incense, my throat burning with it, the taste of almonds bitter in my mouth. The glass was moving regularly now, moving, spelling, regularly, mesmerically, back and forth.

'B-L-O-O-D-'

I loved Felix, I would not listen, I would not let them.

'W-I-L-L-'

I pushed against the glass, pushed with all my power.

'B-L-O-O-D- W-I-L-L- B-E-T-R-'

The candle flickered. The pungent scent of almonds seemed to fill the air. The glass gave suddenly under my pressure, flew across the table and dashed to pieces on the floor. And simultaneously, as Rostova shouted out her protest and Tarantin began a burst of laughter, the light was snapped on, flooding the room with its harsh, impartial glare.

My Cousin Felix stood in the doorway. His face was white, his lips a thin, set line. His voice was like a knife.

'So! I leave my house for one evening. And when I come back I find it given over to a Witches' Sabbath.'

Rostova stopped in mid-sentence, Tarantin's laughter died. I stared at Felix, blinking, as if I were suddenly emerging from a dream.

'Christie, come over here to me.' He held out his hand and I rose, stumbling, and took it. His fingers grasped mine for a moment so tightly that it hurt. Then he said, without looking at me, his eyes still fixed in cold fury upon the other two:

'Go upstairs to the studio and wait for me. I shall be with you as soon as I can.'

As I was mounting the stairs I heard Rostova's voice burst out and then cut off again as if it had been peremptorily silenced. I saw her, from the window seat, soon after, the great ermine collar pulled up to conceal her face, climb into her car and drive away. Tarantin was longer and only the slamming of a cab door told me he was finally gone.

I sat in miserable loneliness, waiting. I felt tainted by the evening, not just by the cruelty of their games but by my own complicity in them, by the jealousy and distrust I had discovered in me. It was, I thought, easy to make claims, set up obligations, turn the free giving of two people into a tangling net of suspicion and deceit, but not easy to love. I felt that he would see my failure like an ugly mark imprinted on my face, and when he came up the stairs at last and into the room I went almost unwillingly towards him as if I dreaded the scrutiny of those keen grey eyes.

'My dear little one, are you all right? I shouldn't have left you for so long.'

I nodded.

'I wanted to give you time, I wanted you to be free to think.'

It was with an effort that I realized he was referring to Archie. 'There was nothing to think about,' I said.

He gathered me to him, not kissing me but just holding me for some moments, so tightly that I could scarcely breathe.

'You must know there was nothing,' I said.

He turned my face towards him, his eyes exploring it as if he were searching for something. His expression was gentle, his lips very close to mine. 'Christie, if you're certain – '

'Of course I'm certain. But Felix, he's bound to tell Aunt Jessica. And – '

His expression changed instantly. 'And she will make you marry him. And you don't want to marry Archie. You don't want to marry anyone.'

His tone was ironic, he had moved away from me. Taking out his cigarette case, he lit a Muratti, then stood for a moment, drawing deeply on it, slowly, thoughtfully expelling the smoke.

'You mustn't be too hard on Teddy,' he said eventually. 'Perhaps, in the end, you should blame me. Oh yes, he is sometimes impossible. But he's always, up to now, been a good friend. Did he ever tell you that when I met him in Paris I was in pretty bad shape, still constantly in pain?'

'Yes,' I said.

'But what I don't suppose he told you was that he found me the man who put me back together again, wanted to pay for everything until I convinced him I wasn't starving, kept me going when I was down, wouldn't let me give up and crawl away into a hole somewhere and die, which occasionally I very much wanted to. And in return he asked nothing. Most particularly he did not ask of me what he knew I was unable to give.'

He drew upon his cigarette again.

'So I suppose,' he said, 'I didn't think there was much harm in the closeness of our friendship over the years. I had never before realized, on my part, the cruelty of it.'

He was silent for a while. Then, throwing away the cigarette, he came and kissed me on the forehead. 'Jealousy, my little one, is a bitterly demeaning thing.'

And which of the four of us he was talking about I was suddenly not perfectly certain.

There seemed, in my mind at least, still a barrier between us, as if the events of the evening could not be undone in an instant but must be left of their own accord to unravel themselves. He too appeared preoccupied. When he shut himself in the studio to begin writing a letter I went up to bed without him. Some scruple, the last traces of my distaste for myself, made me forbear to go to his bedroom. Instead I settled in my own bed and attempted, unsuccessfully, to read a book.

After a while there was a soft tap at my door and he appeared, still fully dressed, and came and sat down beside me.

'My dear little one, why are you hiding from me?'

I threw my arms around his shoulders and buried my face in his neck. He held me for a little, stroking my hair, then he laid me gently back upon the pillows. His face was serious.

'Christie, I have had time to think too. And I've decided I'm bored with London. My work for Teddy is virtually finished and I want to go back to France.'

I stared at him, feeling suddenly all the pain, the loss, the emptiness flood back. I willed myself not to show it. 'Oh,' I said. 'But if you want to, you must.'

'You don't approve?'

'Yes, of course I do.' I prayed my face did not look as pale and stiff as it felt.

'You hardly seem overwhelmed with enthusiasm!'

'Well, I shall miss you a bit at first. But it'll be all right, I'll – '

His seriousness suddenly collapsed into laughter. 'Oh, my dear, sweet, lunatic child! I thought you were worrying about leaving Stenko and the fact that it would delay our settling something more permanent about your piano studies. You don't imagine for one instant that I would go to France without taking you with me?'

I began to smile. I felt all at once light-headed, as if a great weight had dropped away from me.

He bent over and kissed me. 'I arranged it all with Ambrose Fortunin this evening. They have a villa we can borrow in the South, above Cannes, near Mougins. We take the Golden Arrow and then the Blue Train. Ambrose has wired the couple who look after the place. Anatole can stay behind here to hold the fort and forward any urgent post. And if the Riviera bores us we can always move on to my apartment in Paris – '

'Oh, Felix,' I said, returning his kiss. 'It sounds glorious. When can we leave? You make it seem as if we were going now.'

Smiling, he kissed the tip of my nose. 'I can't quite manage that, little one. But Anatole has instructions to send a maid to pack for you at first light tomorrow.'

CHAPTER TWENTY-THREE

Diary of Adele Ward.
Monks Last, Norfolk.

19th July, 1894.

The loss of Mamma has left me for three days quite unable to lift my pen. This morning we laid her to her last rest in the village churchyard, in the family plot of the de Lisles. The vicar gave a most moving address and poor Papa is bearing up bravely. Sir Arthur's gentle kindness is sorely missed at this time of bitter trial but, though I entreated her otherwise, J wrote dissuading him from returning for the funeral, for, as she pointed out with a somewhat callous practicality, he would waste his journey since Mamma would already be buried when he reached us. Now that the mourners have taken cake and sherry and departed we are all very low-spirited and have not the heart for anything. J has gone for a walk about the grounds, M is off somewhere by himself, and Papa and I sit in the drawing room, too oppressed to speak.

Oh merciful Heaven, how can I write this? On this day of all days! When the dressmaker's pins are scarcely out of the black we wear to pay poor Mamma our final respects! Animals!

But I must set this down calmly so that it may assume reality and not the horror of a vile dream!

Feeling that I could no longer endure the oppression of the house, for there is thunder in the air again and the atmosphere is stifling, as if we should suffocate in our grief, I too decided to walk a little. Scarcely heeding where I trod, making my way over the west lawn towards the lake, I found myself crossing the little bridge that reaches the folly. There, pausing to dry the tears which were coursing silently down my cheeks and pressing my forehead against the cool stone of a pillar, I thought to calm myself before I returned to poor Papa; when suddenly I heard voices and muffled laughter. The sounds appeared to come from the long grass behind me, which the folly obscures to all view from the house. Though I could see no one, the voices were borne to me through the still air so that from time to time I could make them out quite distinctly, one a man's, the other a woman's.

'— so long to make your escape, my darling! I began to believe you had stopped wanting me.' This the woman's voice, vibrating with a curious, pent-up, teasing note.

'Wickedness!' This the man's. 'How could you believe such a thing when you know I want you so much I'm in a fever with it, when you know just to look at you and not be able to touch you is excruciating torment? Want you?' Here there was an interruption followed by a muffled upheaval of breath. 'By G–d, I've never wanted any woman so badly –'

She laughed. And when she spoke it was again in that low, vibrant tone so different from her customary terseness. 'Prove it to me.'

'Haven't I proved it, my love, till we are both weak and fainting with it, these past months?'

The woman seemed to catch her breath. 'Then prove it to me again.'

There was a sudden sharp gasp, a little cry, and then a low, shuddering moan. 'Now, my love,' came the man's voice hoarsely, 'do you feel the proof?'

I had stood where I was, transfixed. But, as the moaning swelled in crescendo to an animal howl, my head seemed to fill with the sound, and with the dreadful, harsh, rhythmic grunts that answered it. Clasping my hand to my mouth, I picked up my skirts and ran, ran until, choking, sobbing, I had no more breath to continue. But the terrible sounds still rang in my ears, and those two voices, which until that moment I had never heard but levelled in sharp opposition to each other.

CHAPTER TWENTY-FOUR

We had both fallen asleep in the bottom bunk of our *wagon-lit* compartment with the blue light on; and when I awoke he was screaming.

He had become strangely silent after Calais on our way to the Gare du Nord, when we had exchanged the Golden Arrow for the blue and gold splendours of the Calais-Mediterranée Express. Yet later, as we sat in the dining car at a table decked with flowers and gold-emblazoned china, held in a soft glow of light that isolated us like impartial spectators, with Avignon slipping past mysteriously in the darkness and making northern France seem far behind, his mood had lifted again.

But now he was bathed in sweat, muttering, shouting, screaming, pitching so violently in the narrow confines of the bunk that my arms could not hold him. I climbed out and, drawing my peignoir about me, knelt beside him. His forehead was soaking-wet and ice-cold. He could not feel my hand upon it. I could not think what to do, how to help him. He seemed to be shouting orders at someone in a voice so hoarse it was almost unrecognizable. The words were garbled, I could make out none of them distinctly. Then after a while his voice changed, there was a rhythm to it, a pattern that was familiar. It took me some moments to realize that crazed, broken voice was, with a chilling absurdity, tunelessly chanting out 'It's a Long Way to Tipperary'.

There was a hammering on the compartment door, a French voice shouting, the sleeping-car attendant woken by the noise and come from his armchair at the end of the corridor to find out what was happening. The banging seemed to work with the violence of his own delirium to jerk Felix out of the nightmare. He sat up abruptly, looked for a moment bewildered, then, realizing where he was, seeing me, he grasped my hand.

'Don't worry, little one.' The reassurance was automatic, like a reflex. 'Don't be frightened, it's not serious, nothing to worry about.'

The voice of the sleeping-car attendant came again. He shouted a reply to it in French and there was a grunt of comprehension from the other side of the door, followed by the sound of retreating footsteps. Then he lay back on the pillows, exhausted, shivering.

Finding his cigarettes, I lit him one and put it between his lips, and he lay in silence for a while smoking it, his hand on mine. We rocked gently to the regular motion of the train as it sped on through the night, eating up the miles of the Rhône delta, putting every second a greater distance between us and the bleak, flat planes of the North.

'Forgive me for frightening you, little one. It was bad for about a year after I came back from the front, but it doesn't happen so often now.'

'Is it always the same?' I said.

'Yes,' he said. 'Always.'

'I couldn't make out most of it. But you seemed to be singing.'

He gave an odd, tight laugh. Then getting up and pulling on his dressing gown he went to the washbasin and splashed his face with cold water. When he came back he was still shivering.

'Corporal Routledge,' he said.

'The blacksmith's son from the village?'

He nodded. And, lying upon the bunk again, he drew me down beside him so that my head was on his chest, nestling in the crook of his neck beneath his chin. Though his hand was gently stroking my hair I could still feel the shivering, the tension in him. I hesitated. It seemed to me that one of the closed doors had been left very slightly ajar, but even now I could not judge his response if I were to push it open.

Eventually I said: 'Do you think you can talk about it?'

'I don't know, little one. I never have before.'

He moved his arm and I felt him reach out, find another cigarette and light it. Then he resumed stroking my hair and, though I could not see his face, I could sense in the motion of his hand, in the rise and fall of his breathing, that he was turning it over, thinking.

'It was a night raid,' he said at last. 'Volunteers. There wasn't a great deal of my company left to volunteer. But anyway, we found the place where the wire was cut and crawled through all right, even got hold of a couple of Jerry shoulder flashes with two live Jerries attached to them. Then some bloody idiot gave the order for covering fire too soon and the enemy opened up on us with everything, shells, mortars, machine guns. We didn't stand a chance. I remember being hit. Not pain exactly, but a tremendous sensation of impact, like being kicked by a cart horse. And when I came to I was lying twisted up in a shell hole in about six inches of muddy water.

'I wasn't, I recall, much concerned about it. My tunic seemed to be covered in blood, there was blood on my face, but I didn't have any pain, couldn't tell where I'd been hit. Far away I could hear someone screaming. I supposed at first that it must be me, that some part of me more interested in the fate of my body was in pain after all and shouting about it. But after a while I realized there was a pressure against my shoulder, a foul stench, that there was someone else in the shell hole with me and that dreadful, ungodly howling was coming from him.

'If I turned my head I could see his face. A Verrey flare went up and in the light, despite his being blacked-up for the raid, I recognized Routledge. His mouth was open and the noise was coming from it but his eyes seemed to be elsewhere, so that I couldn't tell whether he knew me or not.'

Felix paused to stub out his cigarette.

'He was their third son, about my age, twenty-one. He'd been in my company ever since I'd had the command. A good soldier, always cheerful. Not imaginative, but with a straightforwardness you could see shining out of his face. He was lying sideways, half on top of me. I realized then that the blood I was drenched in was not mine but his. I thought by putting out my hand I might be able to find out where he'd been hit. I—'

He made a sudden movement with his head, as if averting his face from something he could still see. 'I should have known what the stench was. But I'd seen enough men with stomach wounds to know that even when the injuries were terrible they could still take a long time to die. I thought if I could find my pistol I had the strength left to shoot him. But it must have lodged under me as I fell and I discovered I couldn't move to reach it, in fact – and I remember it irritated rather than concerned me – I had no sensation in the lower part of my body at all. I could do nothing for him except lie there listening to his screams and pray that if there was any superior power controlling the whole obscene mess it would have the decency to let him die.

'Then another flare went over and I could see his face again and knew this time he recognized me. I said something to him. He stopped that dreadful wordless screaming and began to cry out, asking if he was badly hit, if he was a gonner. I told him all the usual lies about how the stretcher bearers would be along for us any minute, how it was a piece of luck to be wounded since we'd both be back in Blighty in a couple of days. I saw from his eyes that he understood me, that the words reassured him. I went on talking to him. I talked about leave and England and Norfolk, about his family and the people he knew in the village. I went through all the seasons of the year and how the countryside changed with them. I talked about the sea fishing and digging for molluscs in the sand around the samphire beds and shooting in Kite's Wood and all the things I could recall from going out with the head keeper when Meredith and I were boys. He'd been a stable lad at Monks Last and I catalogued every horse I could remember us keeping there. I think I hoped if I could make him concentrate on my voice he would feel the pain less, be less afraid, that somehow my words would carry him into unconsciousness. But every time there was a bright light, a flare, or a star gun, I could see his eyes wide open, fixed on me and his mouth twisted into that endless animal howl.

'After a while my voice was cracked and I'd run out of words. The only thing I could think of now was to sing – "Keep the Home Fires Burning", "Goodbye–ee", "Tipperary", "Roses of Picardy", anything I could remember. I ordered him to sing with me. He tried very hard, I could see his eyes fighting to follow me, I prayed the exhaustion of it would push him under at last. But he carried on, perfectly conscious and screaming. So I went on singing, the same songs over and over again, sometimes the words, sometimes only the tune. I don't know whether he knew me any more or understood. I just knew that his eyes were still there, struggling, terrified, and yet all the time filled with a vain hope.

'We were in that shell hole for eight hours. I was still gibbering and singing apparently when they dragged me out. They thought I was delirious with pain and pumped me full of morphia.'

Felix paused. I looked up at him. His eyes were fixed on the overhang of the top bunk and in the dim blue light I could not read their expression.

'It was brave of you,' I said softly.

His lips twisted sardonically. 'Oh, no, little Christie. Not brave. Damnably, undeservedly lucky. I don't suppose my ravings were of any help to Ted Routledge. But the effort of concentrating on them stopped me slipping under myself. Routledge's death agony kept me alive.'

I stared at him. He lit another cigarette. His hand, as he struck the match, still shook just perceptibly.

'For three weeks afterwards I couldn't speak. I couldn't speak, I didn't feel pain, I seemed to have no physical sensation of any kind. But my mind was working and I had plenty of time to think. And it occurred to me it had always been so, that the Routledges of this world were always sacrificed so that people like me could live. Routledge hadn't wanted war, it was my people, the landowners, the politicians, people with power and interests to protect who'd wanted it. It was they who'd put him in a uniform and filled his head with trumpery notions of honour and glory and love of King and Country and sent him off with thousands like him to be killed for a quarrel he didn't understand. And those who came back, would it be any different afterwards for them? Would there be more jobs, decent wages, Homes for Heroes? The village would go on standing in the shadow of the big house, working to keep us in claret and game and full stables and more time and space than we knew what to do with. God, I'd hated that house as a boy! I used to imagine there were ghosts there, something misbegotten that had never been properly buried. And I, the child of that house, wasn't I a part of that corruption? Ted Routledge would have lived a useful life, but I? I had been brought up to be perfectly useless. Oh, I had captained the first eleven at Eton, got a blue, had a modest talent for painting and drawing which it was incumbent on me, as a gentleman, to keep as well concealed as possible. But I wasn't expected to work, to give anything, only to take. Was that worth Routledge throwing away his life for?

'I was glad when after a while I began to feel pain. I was determined to prove the medicos wrong, to use the pain to make my dead nerves work again, to force myself to walk so that I could take the only honourable course available to me, to go back to the front and die there. But they defeated me in the end, discharged me and sent me home, and I was left to find some other way to expiate Corporal Routledge.'

He laughed suddenly, I still could not read his eyes. 'Only there wasn't a way, little Christie. I had some vague idea at first of helping the family, with money, with work, I wasn't sure what. But they accepted their son's death much more readily than I, and in the end John, the father, was far more help to me than I ever could be to him. I remember I became almost unable to bear the sight of him, his kindness seemed such a reproach for my guilt. But it passed after a while. I learnt I was powerless, on my own, to change anything. I've come to terms with what I am.

And one day I may even exorcize the ghost of Corporal Routledge.'

I put out my hand and touched his face. I wanted to argue against the harshness of his judgement but did not know what to say, wanted to tell him how much I loved him and was afraid to.

Eventually I said only: 'And do you still believe you have no right to live?'

He smiled and the bitterness left him. And, kissing me on the forehead, he drew me closer to him. 'My dear little one. I think in the last few weeks I've begun to cling to life most selfishly.'

But I, in my mind's eye, seeing out there in the darkness the fields of neat white crosses I had been told about, stretching farther than vision beyond the horizons of distant hills, held tightly to him all the same, as if I were in mortal fear of losing him.

We were met at Cannes by M. Jouvet who, with his wife, would look after us, and driven up into the hills in an open-topped Isotta Fraschini. The villa was low, white, built in the Spanish style, with a garden dark with cypresses and golden with mimosa. Our days there I remember still, frozen into split seconds of time like images caught in a camera shutter: the moment I came down next morning to find two French workmen stuck half-in, half-out of the drawing room with a grand piano specially delivered from Cannes, Felix in white flannels in the garden trying to finish a watercolour of a sky spectacular with thunder before the heavens fulfilled their threat and opened upon him, both of us arm in arm on the Promenade des Anglais, blown by the wind from a grey spring sea; warm brioches and the smell of chicory, and honey in the comb from Gourdun, and the peasant woman who sold crimson roses on the quayside and the man who rode a bicycle with a monkey on his back, and a restaurant we found in the mountains at Valbonne where we drank coarse red wine and ate salami in a low room fragrant with pork fried over an open fire; and the two of us perched on high stools in the dark bar at the Carlton, sipping champagne, saying nothing, just looking at each other and smiling.

One afternoon of March rain, when we had been away a week, we were lying in each other's arms in the dazed aftermath of making love. The rain had stopped and a shaft of sunlight in which the droplets on the window pane glittered like jewels slanted beneath the half-drawn blind, across the bed; and stretching in it, luxuriant, cat-like, replete with love, without thinking I said:

'Oh Felix, I want so much —'

I stopped myself in time. But out of the silence his voice came back very quietly:

'Say it, little one.'

I hesitated. Gently, he drew me towards him so that my eyes were level with his.

'Please, Christie. Say what you were going to say.'

His eyes, though they were tender, were insistent too, admitting of no escape. 'I want so much,' I said softly, 'to have your child.'

I had been afraid he would withdraw, that I should feel all the doors that had so gradually opened suddenly shut fast against me. But instead his expression deepened into thought, his hand explored the shallow curve of my belly.

'And what about the music, little one?'

'Oh, I want that too.' I laughed uncertainly. 'I want everything.'

He smiled. 'And I also want everything. And I want very much to make you pregnant. But I don't see how I can let you have my children while you keep refusing to marry me.'

I stared at him in amazement. 'But you've never asked me.'

'You haven't exactly given me the chance.'

Suddenly my arms were about his neck and we were both laughing. Then his mouth found mine, stopping my laughter.

When our lips parted, his eyes were serious again. 'Love is a word I've always feared. I've heard it used to wound and blackmail and dominate but never in any sense that was good. But if it has any meaning, my darling little Christie, I do love you, I love you so much I am consumed with it.'

'And I love you,' I said. 'Oh Felix, I love you, I love you.'

Reaching up, I kissed his eyelids, very gently, one after the other. His arms tightened about me.

'My darling Christie. Then you will renounce your grizzled spinsterhood in Bloomsbury and marry me?'

Suddenly, as if I were coming out of a dream, the reality of our situation hit me like cold water dashed in my face. I struggled free from his embrace.

'It's no good,' I said. 'She'll never let us.'

'My mother? But you say she's desperate to marry you off.'

'Not to you. She wouldn't like anyone who married you, and you know how she feels about me. She'll go mad with rage when she finds out.'

'My dear child, she already knows. Before we came away I wrote to her telling her that I intended to marry you and that the only obstacle I would accept was your refusal.'

I stared at him. 'But she's my guardian until I'm twenty-one. I can't marry without her permission.'

He kissed the tip of my nose. 'In England, yes, that's true. But not here.'

I continued to stare at him. He was smiling a sphinx-like smile.

'Do you mean,' I said, 'that I've eloped without even knowing it? Oh Felix, my wicked Cousin Felix, I do so love you!' My arms were about him again, hugging him with joy. 'Oh, when? When can we be married?'

He held me for a moment away from him. 'I want you to be absolutely certain, little one.'

'I am,' I said, 'if you are.'

He laughed. 'I was never more certain of anything in my life. I've been bewildered by it, terrified of it sometimes. But I've always been certain. In every true sense you've been my wife from that first night in Cheyne Walk. Oh God, darling Christie! Damn laws and ceremonies! Marry me now.'

'Now?'

'Tomorrow first thing we'll find someone in Cannes to go through the formalities. But until then – ' He was loosening the signet ring he wore on his little finger. It was gold, set with a cornelian and engraved with an armorial crest. He kissed me lightly on the lips then, taking my left hand in his, slid the ring slowly onto my third finger.

'Until then, my dear, dear little Christie, with this ring I thee wed, with my body I thee worship, with all my worldly goods I thee endow – '

I shivered. It seemed suddenly like a blasphemy, a bad omen. 'No, don't,' I said. 'Let's wait till tomorrow.'

He paused for a moment, my hand still in his. Then he smiled and, kissing the tips of my fingers, let it fall. I moved to take off the ring but he shook his head.

'No, little one. It was my father's, the only personal thing I have of his. Wear it until tomorrow when I can buy you a proper wedding ring. Wear it and know how very much I love you.'

He gathered me up then and kissed me long and deep, and I felt him wanting me, felt my body answer his.

'Oh God, little Christie,' he said, kissing my throat, burying his face in my hair. 'Amongst all the strange emotions you arouse in me is a monstrous jealousy. If you had decided to marry Cadwallander I like to think I would not have tried to stop you. But I should have wanted to tear you both apart with my bare hands.'

We dined in the village that night, at the local café, where Felix knew the *patron*. The walls of the dining room were lined with paintings and sketches, gifts made by artists, from the renowned to the amateur, who had at one time or another eaten there, and Felix had promised the thunder-cloud watercolour to add to the collection. Our happiness, like an incandescence, seemed to touch everything about us, from the old men playing cards at their corner table to the bottles and glasses sparkling behind the zinc-topped bar. Everyone smiled, the *patron*'s wife presented me with a huge bouquet of mimosa, the village band, coming away from rehearsal, drifted into the bar halfway through our meal and seemed to be playing especially for us. We made endless excited plans about the future, whether we should live in London or Paris, whether I should go to the Conservatoire, whether we would travel, how many children we would have. At intervals, as if once the dam was broken there was no restraining the flood, we told each other again and again how much we were in love. We were intoxicated with it, crazy, dazzled. And we were just finishing the last of our wine when we were suddenly aware of the *patron* standing beside our table, no longer smiling but holding out an envelope to Felix.

'An urgent telegram from England, monsieur. Your servant brought it from the villa.'

I watched Felix tear it open, watched his face change as he read it. He read it twice. Then he handed it silently to me.

'MOTHER COLLAPSED STROKE TUESDAY STOP ASKING FOR YOU CONTINUALLY STOP DOCTOR HOLDS OUT NO HOPE STOP WHERE THE DEVIL ARE YOU STOP MEREDITH'

Even as I read it, Felix was settling the bill so that we could return and ask the Jouvets to begin packing.

CHAPTER TWENTY-FIVE

As we rounded the bend in the drive the chimneys and gables of Monks Last came sharply upon us, etched in harsh relief against the moonlit sky. Despite the travelling rug about my knees, I shivered. Beside me, Felix, his face expressionless, stared out beyond the croquet lawn towards the hunched and leafless trees.

I had felt the barriers fall again in those two days we had been travelling, felt him gradually move back to where I could not reach him. We had not spoken of it, we had treated one another with a gentle but distant courtesy, as if each were aware of a fragility in the other which any incautious movement might endanger. At night we had lain together, each pretending for the other's sake to sleep, but we had not made love. His face showed nothing, I could only guess what was in his mind – grief, reluctance, guilt? Later I wondered, seeing the drawn lines around his eyes, whether he himself knew. And suddenly, hearing again quite clearly Aunt Jessica's voice crying out in the garden, I thought how cleverly she had arranged it so that there should be no certainty of right for any of us, but only that imperative cry of possession from which even he, for all his proud indifference, would never be free.

The Hispano Suiza, with Anatole at the wheel, jerked to a stop. The great grey pile of the house loomed before us, dark, as if the blinds were already drawn for death. We sat for a moment, not moving, holding back from it. Then Felix turned and took my hand.

'Thank you, little one,' he said. 'Thank you for being so generous and loving these last two days. Trust me now and don't be frightened.' He kissed me softly on the lips. 'I love you, little Christie, so very much.'

He took my arm as we walked into the shadow of the house. The gravel crunched with frost beneath our feet. At the top of the stone steps Grover was already holding open the front door. He murmured condolences as he took our coats. There was a familiar chill of damp in the hall.

From the open drawing-room door light spilled, and the sound of Sybil's voice, peremptory, shrill. I thought, though the timbre was different, how like Aunt Jessica's in expression it had become.

'If you weren't so weak with him, if you stood up to him like a man instead of feeling sorry for yourself – '

Meredith was sitting in one of the deep armchairs, a whisky and soda at his elbow, a newspaper across his knees. His monocle dangled, his body was slumped, his face was red and heavy as if he had been unresistantly sustaining blows. Before him Sybil, the long string of her pearls knotted impatiently around one hand, stood braced with the force of her tirade.

Meredith saw us first. The movement of his eyes made Sybil break off and spin round.

'Well, dash it all,' said Meredith. 'If it isn't my dear brother! I'll be damned if after a week of playing hide and seek across Europe he hasn't actually found the time to come back and discover whether his darling mother is alive or dead – '

Felix's voice cut sharply across him. 'How is she?'

'Obstinate as ever, dear boy. Holding on by her fingernails until she can say goodbye to her favourite son.'

'Then there's been no improvement since your wire?'

'Even that drunken sot Blair agrees she's beyond cold compresses and sal volatile. Says she could have another attack any minute.'

It struck me that Meredith, reaching out clumsily for his whisky and soda, was also the worse for drink, that perhaps both he and Sybil were. She was staring at me, the pearls still knotted, her tiny, perfect features quivering with outrage.

'How dare you!' she hissed at Felix. 'How dare you bring that little trollop back into this house!'

Felix went white. 'Sybil, you will not talk – '

Meredith guffawed, spilling his whisky. 'You try and stop her talking, dear boy. Been trying myself for seven years.'

'I won't stop,' shrilled Sybil. 'If it hadn't been for her, your mother wouldn't be upstairs dying. If she hadn't run away, if Felix hadn't written that letter, if poor Jessica hadn't had all the worry of trying to make the little slut a ward of court, she'd never have had a stroke in the first place – '

The small muscle had contracted above Felix's jaw. 'Sybil, you will apologize to Christie!'

'Apologize?' Sybil laughed. 'To her? After the way she's behaved? After poor Jessica bearing the responsibility for her all these years, after everything this family has done for her!' Her eyes flew to my left hand, taking in Felix's signet ring. 'Anyway, my dear, I see you haven't persuaded him to marry you yet. Despite all your efforts.'

Felix took a step towards her. His voice was like ice. 'I have never yet struck a woman, Sybil. I suggest you don't let me forget you are one.'

I touched his arm. 'Please,' I said softly. 'It doesn't matter.'

He turned and looked at me. There was a pause. Then, from the depths of the armchair, we heard Meredith chuckling to himself.

'Poor Jessica! By God, that's rich! Poor Jessica. So concerned is my dear wife about her mother-in-law that she spent all afternoon measuring the drawing room for new curtains and wondering whether we should build a swimming pool on the croquet lawn. Poor Jessica.' He looked down into his whisky tumbler and suddenly he was no longer laughing, suddenly his face seemed to sag, his breathing become laboured. 'A plague on this house! A plague on the whole bloody lot of you!'

Felix took my hand. 'I must go and see my mother, Christie. Come with me.' And clasping his fingers tightly around mine he led me out of the room and up the stairs.

The sickroom was in darkness except for a pool of light beside the bed in which a white-uniformed nurse sat, reading. There was a faint smell of carbolic and chloroform and urine. From the shadows the great rosewood bed loomed like a ship becalmed on a dark sea. I hesitated to look where the light fell, at the head propped upon the pillows, the arms laid stiffly out over the coverlet.

We moved forward, Felix still holding my hand. The body in the bed seemed to stir jerkily, like a marionette when only half its strings are pulled. The palm of the left hand went up to shield the eyes from light. A voice, weak, querulous, slurred like a drunk's yet still recognizable enough to bring back all my childhood fear, murmured: 'Felix? Felix, my darling, is that you?'

The nurse closed her book, rose and tiptoed out of the room.

Aunt Jessica lay with her grey hair spread out on the pillow like a young girl's. There was about her face a dislocation, as though someone had taken the right side of it in both hands and jerked it fiercely so that no part matched exactly with the left.

The right eye, glassy, shot with blood, stared fixedly at the ceiling, the right side of the mouth was twisted into the parody of a sneer. A gout of spittle hung from her lips. And yet, despite her helplessness, despite her sudden, almost childlike frailty, there was in the side of her face that moved, in the one bright, seeing eye, such an undimmed sense of her old severity, such a will even now to command, that I wanted to draw back beyond her range.

Felix bent and kissed her on the forehead. Her good arm went up, pulling him towards her, clawing at his neck like someone drowning. Letting go of my hand for a moment, he settled her back upon the pillows.

'I knew you'd come. Meredith. Stupid as ever. But I knew.'

'Forgive me, Mother, for not coming sooner.'

'I knew you'd come. I knew you'd leave her. That wretched girl.'

Though I drew away, Felix took my hand once more. 'Mother,' he said softly, 'Christie is here.'

She put her hand up to her forehead again, peering, seeming with difficulty to make me out. The mobile part of her face, in grotesque contrast with its motionless other half, underwent a paroxysm of such violence that I took it to be rage.

'Not married? Not married to her?'

Felix touched her cheek to quiet her. 'You must understand, Mother,' he said gently, 'and give us your blessing. I love Christie very dearly. And she has agreed to be my wife.'

'Not married yet then?' And was it my imagination, or was there suddenly in that one eye, that half a mouth not just relief, but a gleam of triumph? 'Send her away!'

His fingers tightened on mine. 'No, Mother.'

'I want to talk to you. Alone. Send her away.'

'Mother, understand me. No.'

Though I feared her I could not bear that, ill as she was, he should, because of me, be forced to defy her. 'Felix, don't. Let me leave you. She has a right to ask it, the best right in the world.'

He hesitated, looking first at me and then back at the woman in the bed. Reluctantly, he released my hand.

'Don't let the others hurt you. Go to your room and wait for me there. I'll come and find you as soon as I can.'

Although my bags had been unpacked, my room was cheerless, impersonal, as if every trace of the years I had spent in it had been carefully expunged. An hour passed. A maid brought me dinner on a tray but I had no appetite. I tried to read but could not concentrate properly. I lay on my bed, staring at the ceiling. The hour drew into two and then three, without any sign of Felix.

Eventually I could stand my seclusion no longer. Downstairs from the hall I could hear Sybil and Meredith, voices still raised in argument. If Felix were not with them perhaps he had stayed at Aunt Jessica's bedside. There was light coming from under the smoking-room door. I turned the knob and softly pushed it open.

He was sitting in the great leather wing chair, the chair in which his father had died. His cigarette had burnt down almost to his fingers, but he stared straight ahead of him, not moving, oblivious of it. His face was deathly pale, blank, like the face of someone numb with shock. It was some moments before he noticed me. But when he did, an extraordinary expression came into his eyes, almost as if he had never seen me before and were taking me in properly for the first time. He sprang up, moving away from me behind the chair, throwing his cigarette into the fire.

'Christie. What time is it? It must be late.'

I wanted to go to him but the sharpness of his movement and the strangeness of his manner prevented me.

'I'm so sorry, Felix,' I said.

'Sorry?'

'About your mother. I'm so very sorry.' My words sounded even to my ears lame and meaningless. I was not surprised that he looked at me as if he did not understand them. He was pacing restlessly from the bookcase to the chair like someone dispossessed. It stood between us, that great battered chair, as if it were an insurmountable barrier that neither of us could scale. Sometimes as he passed it his fingers brushed its scuffed leather lightly. Finally he came to a stop behind it, his hands resting one on each wing. His face now wore again that numbed, stricken look. When he spoke it was as if he were assembling the words with difficulty.

'Christie, don't wait up for me. I can't sleep. I don't think I shall come to bed tonight.'

'Felix – '

'No, don't, little one. I'll be all right here. Just leave me.'

I hesitated still, wishing that I were not so helpless against his grief. 'If there's anything – '

His lips twisted into a strange, bitter smile. 'Nothing. Nothing.'

There was such a cruel emphasis in the word that I felt my eyes begin to burn. I made to turn away. But suddenly he came out from behind the chair towards me. He came three paces. Then he stopped. As if the effort of stopping, of holding the distance between us, required superhuman strength, he began to tremble. His eyes were fixed upon my face.

'Never forget, little Christie,' he said, 'how desperately I love you.'

I could no longer bear the pain in his voice. 'I love you too,' I said, 'more than life.' And I moved towards him.

But, as I moved, he turned his back on me. 'Go now,' he said. 'For God's sake, go!'

I could not sleep. Despite the stone water bottle in my bed, the sheets felt cold and damp and there was a musty smell, like the creeping of mildew, which seemed to grow when the lights were turned out. Outside the tree pitched and rattled its bare branches against the window. And within the house, like a restless echo, there seemed to be movement too, a subtle, stealthy shifting, as if its mass of stone and mortar were no longer inert, but alive, organic, stirring on its foundations. A door creaked here, a floorboard there, unseen feet seemed to pause upon the stair and voices whisper. I thought perhaps he had changed his mind and would come to me. But it was nothing, nobody. Ghosts, he had said. What room had he slept in as a child, I wondered. Had he too lain still, unbreathing, watching the shadows grow and become palpable?

I overslept. And when I came down, late, for breakfast, I froze in the doorway of the dining room. For there was such a chilling familiarity about the scene it was almost as if history were mocking me.

The serving table groaned with its usual largesse of kidneys and kedgeree under silver covers. Meredith was already seated at the table, vainly trying to arrange *The Times* so that it warded off the conversation that was in progress. But now the figure which paced the room was not the tall, commanding one of Aunt Jessica, but the tiny elegant form of Sybil, and her attitude, as she knotted and unknotted her pearls, signified not so much distress as ungovernable anger.

'And you don't know why? You don't know anything about it?'

'Dash it, m'dear,' said Meredith, shuffling the pages of the paper, 'how often do I have to tell you—'

'Oh yes, I know. You're not your brother's keeper. But how could he? At a time like this. With his mother on her death bed.'

'If you ask me, it's bloody typical of my delightful brother. Never gave a tinker's cuss about anybody. Never has, never will.'

'But what are we to say to Jessica? What are we to tell everyone?' She broke off, suddenly seeing me. Her eyes swooped again to Felix's ring on my third finger. 'Well, here's the one who's supposed to know everything about him. Perhaps she can tell us. Perhaps he's let her into his plans.'

Something icy was impeding my breathing. 'Tell you what?' I said.

'You mean you don't know?'

'Know?'

'That Felix has gone. Packed his bags, took his man, drove away in the middle of the night. Without so much as leaving a message.'

The room began to blur and sway. Then a blackness engulfed me.

I was lying on the chaise longue in the drawing room. The smelling salts still stung my nostrils. I felt weak and queasy and strange. I had never in my life fainted before. A figure was hovering over me. It coalesced into the ample form of Mrs Wix.

She looked uneasy at being discovered in the wrong part of the house. Her big, chapped hands fumbled in the pocket of her apron and drew out an envelope.

'The Captain left this, Miss Christabel. He was waiting for me in the kitchen when I came down this morning. He said he knew I'd always had a soft spot for you. He said I was to give it to you personally and on no account to anyone else.'

She thrust the letter in my hands.

'Thank you, Mrs Wix.'

She shifted uncomfortably. 'Well, I'll be off then, Miss Christabel, back to my kitchen.'

I watched her go, then tore the envelope open.

My dear little one,

I do not know how to write this letter. I cannot leave you without any word of explanation. Yet God knows whether I can bear to put into words what I must tell you.

Last night, after you left us, my mother laughed and said that I would never marry you. And when I replied that she could not stop me she laughed again, saying that if I knew the truth she have to. The truth. Oh God, Christie, this is then the truth she told me.

I am not the son of Sir Arthur de Lisle, but her child by Montague Ward, her sister's husband and your father. You, Christie, are my half-sister.

She was smiling, little one, when she said it, with that dreadful crooked smile the stroke has given her. The repulsive words she used are still ringing in my ears. 'My darling, you are my love child.' Love? With those words she has swept away not just the memory of the only father I have ever known, but also my only hope of loving. For I knew what she told me was true, I felt it as if I had always known it. It explains so much of the past, so many things in my childhood I understood by instinct but could not name. It is as she says it is. And it means I must give you up, give up the only woman I have ever loved.

Oh, little one, I cannot love you like a brother. I cannot look at you or touch you without wanting you. Yet now I must call everything I feel for you an ugly name. So I must go. We must learn to live without each other, little Christie. Oh God, is that to live – without life?

As for the appalling wrong I have done you, I beg your forgiveness and hope that time and my absence, though they cannot wipe it out, will lessen the pain. Beyond the two of us and my mother, no one knows our true relationship, and at least in that there is some protection for you – I shall never speak of it to anyone. Forgive me, too, for not saying goodbye properly. But if I were to see you I think I should lose the strength to go.

You are so sweetly, joyously, generously beautiful. I hope that when the hurt dies away you will be happy. Think of me sometimes. I shall never cease to think of you.

Goodbye, my dear, dear love,

F.

I read the letter through several times, my disbelief growing with every reading. It could not be true. Aunt Jessica knew she had little time, knew he would not listen to any of her commands or persuasions. So she had taken the only way left to her. She had lied to him. Oh, it was a clever lie, to play upon his sense of right and honour, if she could not kill our love to cripple it. But it was a lie, nonetheless, and ill though she was she must be made to retract it.

I was suddenly no longer weak but seized with a frenzy. The letter still in my hand, I ran from the drawing room, through the hall and up the stairs. I flung myself across the landing towards the door of the sickroom.

But my way was barred by Sybil. She was dabbing her eyes with a lace handkerchief. Her chin quivered.

'She's dead,' she said. 'She had another stroke and died five minutes ago. You and Felix, you killed her.'

PART THREE

IN THE DESERT

CHAPTER TWENTY-SIX

Diary of Adele Ward.
Monks Last, Norfolk.

25th July, 1894.

Something has happened between J and M. I believe they are planning to run away together. J has appeared strained these past three days and this morning at breakfast she turned chalk-white and rushed from the room, muttering that she was indisposed. Later, going in search of M at Papa's request, I stumbled upon the two of them deep in conference in the conservatory.

'— or is it that I am now repugnant to you?'

He sighed. 'My love, you know that's not so.' His back was to me but I could see her face beyond him, through the palm fronds, white, as it had been at breakfast. 'It's only that I draw back from sullying you with scandal.'

'There will be scandal in any case.' Suddenly she seized his hands. 'Oh, at least this way we may be together always.'

I stepped forward from behind the palm. They sprang apart and he whirled around towards me. For a moment all three of us appeared dumbstruck. Then J, her countenance registering shock swiftly followed by a cold, implacable fury, swept past me and out of the conservatory, leaving M and myself face to face for an instant of silence which spoke volumes.

I do not care that he will leave me. The thought comes with relief after these two years of misery and wretchedness. My gallant M, my true knight? It is only in novels that suffering is rewarded, that modesty and virtue hold the power to conquer and transform man's baser nature. Love? No perfect communion of twin souls made one, but only this – this monster revealed to me on my wedding night, this animal greed which taints everything it touches.

And yet . . . When I think of poor Mamma and dear Papa and what they have been to each other – so different from this vile thing between J and M – when I remember dear, darling

Papa, so fine and upright, I cannot believe all love is base, all hope is dead. . . .

J is welcome to her lover. I am no longer M's wife, I am absolved from all duty towards him. I see now that my duty lies in another direction, where my heart and inclinations have tended ever since poor Mamma was taken from us. I have turned it over in my mind through these past sleepless nights and have made my decision. I shall put my plan to darling Papa tomorrow.

26th July, 1894.

I found Papa in a leather wing chair in Sir Arthur's smoking room, perusing the newspaper. He is so brave, dear Papa, always keeping a firm and well-regulated countenance and already, with great fortitude, talking of once more picking up his interest in astronomy, so that, were I a perfect stranger, oblivious to the extent of his suffering, I should scarcely credit his having been not a fortnight ago brought low by such a grievous loss. Gently moving his newspaper aside and settling myself on his knee as I used to when I was a little girl, I wound my arms around his neck and buried my face in his shoulder.

'Now, now, little Adele,' he said, disentangling me. 'What's all this?'

'Oh, dear Papa,' I replied, stroking his poor grey hair and the furrows in his brow, 'what shall you do when – when? . . . '

'When the time comes to leave here, m'dear? Well, I shall make the best of things.' Again – how like him! – he contrived a brave smile, so that, did I not know him, I should have believed he counted his desolation not as a burden but a blessing.

'But you will be so lonely without poor Mamma. Papa – oh, dearest Papa, I have made up my mind. I shall come home with you and be your housekeeper.'

Perhaps I had put my idea to him over-suddenly, for he held me away from him with an expression of alarm. 'Now, Adele – '

'Oh Papa, do not have any anxiety for M. He can spare me for a while, he cannot but recognize I answer a higher duty. Oh Papa, it is more than duty and I embrace it gladly. Though I cannot fill Mamma's place, I shall devote myself in every way to your comfort and happiness – '

Removing me from his knee, he stood up and I was horrified to observe a frown of intense displeasure darken his face. 'Adele, you forget yourself! You are no longer a child. There is no higher duty than your duty to your husband.'

'Oh Papa, I – ' I paused, for how could I explain the terrible truth, the truth I know I must keep locked within me, lest those who are innocent should be <u>injured irreparably.</u> 'Oh dear Papa, if you could understand – '

'Understand? My girl, I understand, alas, too well.' His countenance had taken on that dreadful aspect, stern, unbending, which it had worn when as children we had merited the ultimate sanction of his punishment. 'Your husband has informed me of your flightiness, your monstrous extravagance, of how you have brought him nearly to the point of ruin by your selfishness and lack of moral sense. Oh, the poor fellow did not volunteer it, he has far too much honour for that – I had to drag the whole sorry story out of him, bit by bit. I suppose I should have spoken to you long before this, but my fondness for you and the pain I know your Mamma's last illness has caused you prevented me. And, besides, I cannot but feel I bear part of the blame. You were always a pretty little thing over-given to dreams – I should have been harder with you, not indulged you so often, disciplined you more rigidly before it was too late. But I shall be hard now, Adele. You will stay with your husband and learn to be a good wife. You will teach yourself to honour and obey him and subject yourself to him in all things. Every night you will go down on your knees and pray to God in gratitude that, despite your faults and weaknesses of character, he has sent you a husband who is prepared to forgive you and help you to change your ways. And the suggestion you have made to me in this room today will be as if it had never been uttered. For if I ever hear that you have wronged your husband or brought disgrace upon him by your selfishness, I shall cast you aside as if you had never been my daughter. Do I make myself plain, Adele? Do I make myself perfectly plain?'

I stared at him for a moment. Then, giving vent to a great choking sob, I rushed from the room. I had barely crossed the threshold when <u>M</u> stole up behind me from the shadows in the passage and seized me roughly by the wrists.

'So we have been talking to our Papa, have we, dearest? I think it is time we had a little talk as well.'

I tried to struggle, would have broken free from him as he dragged me upstairs, but a maid passed across the landing and we were obliged to assume an air of restraint. When we reached my bedroom door he flung me through it and pell-mell into the room.

'So, dearest, we have been telling tales out of school. We have been undoing all the hard and tedious work I have been compelled to put in with your dear Papa to ensure we do not starve.'

With supreme effort, I drew myself up and faced him squarely. 'I, tell Papa of your vile behaviour with my sister? I, inflict such sorrow upon one who is already heavy laden, whose high moral sense renders him unable to withstand such a blow?'

M's lip curled in a derisive sneer. 'Pshaw! Your darling Papa's a man, like any other.'

'He's noble and upright and you are unfit to share the same roof with him. I would not break his heart by unmasking you in all your baseness. I would not break the heart of poor Sir Arthur, whom you have so wretchedly betrayed, or of poor Baby whose mother you have degraded. You may take that upon your own conscience, if you possess one. And it will fall to you soon enough, if you and J are planning to run away together.'

To my amazement he threw back his head in a great peal of laughter which showed, beneath his handsome whiskers, all his fine and very regular teeth. 'Run away with Jessica? By Jove, what an idea! She is even more of a trouble to me than you are.'

I stared at him. 'Then you do not love her?'

'Love? Oh dearest, you must give up reading those sentimental novels of yours. If I'm to be immured in this mausoleum for lack of money then I must be allowed a small divertissement once in a while. But it has ceased to be diverting now and I must find a way to work my release. Which is how, dearest – sweet, loyal, dutiful little wifie that you are – you may help me.'

Again I stared at him. He went to the writing desk and, taking out pen and paper, motioned me to sit down. 'You will write, to my dictation, a most affecting letter to de Lisle.'

While I could not divine his intention, I knew it could only be <u>evil.</u> 'I will never write to Sir Arthur for you. Never!'

Taking me by the arm, he compelled me over to the desk. 'I am your husband, dearest. Remember you promised to obey me in all things.'

His fingers bruised my flesh, he twisted my arm agonizingly behind my back. 'Never!' I gasped. 'Never!'

Regarding me for a moment thoughtfully, he released his hold and, going over to my bed, took from it Mamma's china bride doll, the one Papa brought her from Paris when he asked for her hand, which has been left to me with some few precious trinkets in her will. Taking the doll to the window, he held it above the wooden frame in such a position that one blow against the jutting edge of the sill would shatter its head.

'Never, dearest?'

'N–never.'

He raised the doll in his hand, I watched his arm flex, saw it all at once drive downwards with sickening force. I screamed. With a swift motion he brought the doll up from within an instant of its fatal impact with the sill. 'Never, dearest, did you say?'

It was, as he had promised, a most affecting letter, in which I explained to Sir Arthur that J had been struck such a heavy blow by the death of Mamma, had become so oppressed by sickness and fainting spells that I seriously feared for her. I expatiated a little on the deleterious effect all this must have on Baby, mourned the inability of the rest of us to supply that consolation which only a husband can provide, and concluded by imploring him to return post-haste. When I had finished, M made me address an envelope, then, sealing the flap with a small, satisfied smile, he concealed the completed document in his pocket.

'I shall divorce you,' I said. 'I shall divorce you for your adultery, if not with my sister, then with my maids, with your music-hall soubrettes, with common prostitutes, with – '

He laughed. 'Brave words, dearest. But, while a man may divorce his wife for her adultery alone, a woman must also prove misconduct.'

'Is it not misconduct to trick me, blackmail me out of the money that is rightfully mine, without which, given your improvidence, we should be destitute?'

'There is not a paper, dearest, relating to your affairs, which has not been scrutinized by you and willingly signed.'

'Then I shall leave you. I shall sue for a legal separation.'

His lips curled contemptuously. 'And who would be disgraced by that? Not I, for all the world would pity me for having such a faithless wife. It is you, dearest one, who would bear the stigma, you who would have broken Society's inviolable code, you who would be cut by your acquaintance and disowned by your dear Papa. I am your husband, your vows bind you to me for life.'

I fought back my tears. 'Why, why when you have such contempt for me, when you have never loved me, will you not set me free?'

He smiled. 'Because I have the greatest respect for your dear Papa's considerable wealth. And because, in the meantime, as you yourself so prettily phrased it, we should be destitute without your thousand a year.'

Now I see how I am precious to him, why I may never be free. I can forgive J because she is foolish. I can forgive Papa for thinking so ill of me, for M is clever, and besides it is his word against mine, the word of a man against a mere woman. I shall try to find it in me, since I am bound to him inextricably for the rest of my life, to forgive M for what I know are not mere weaknesses but ineradicable flaws in his character which must be misfortunes of his birth.

But what I cannot forgive is that, as, with my letter to Sir Arthur in his pocket, he was leaving to bribe one of the footmen to convey it secretly to the post, he took my mother's bride doll and, laughing as he did it, placed it on the floor and shattered it with one blow from his foot.

CHAPTER TWENTY-SEVEN

'Oh,' sighed Maisie Cunningham-Cowper, burying her face in pink and white flowers, 'I do think weddings are just the divinest of the divine!'

There are no flowers in the desert. There is no music. There is no pleasure in the touch of silk.

'Damn shame,' said Crikey. 'Poor Charlie stumped middle wicket. Another good man gone.'

'Well, I thought Dolly looked radiant,' said Maisie. 'And wasn't it sweet of her to throw me her bouquet? Oh gosh, how I wish I were on my way to Cannes!'

In the desert there are names you mustn't mention, places you can no longer go to, tables in restaurants where you can no longer sit. In the desert you must avoid Chopin and Hispano Suizas and the aroma of Murattis because they have absurdly acquired the power to make you cry.

'I must say I'm amazed she married Charlie Devereux,' said Dora Chantry. 'When you think of all the others. And when only last summer she was madly in love with—'

I saw Maisie's eyes dart in my direction with a pointed warning, heard Dora's voice tail lamely away.

My cousin, Felix de Lisle. Wasn't there some rumour of a scandal, an elopement even? Oh, but that's old news now. When they mention him, I say I think he's in Paris with the Tarantin Ballet – it may even be true. But they don't like to mention it, and anyway it'll soon be forgotten. May. Another season starting. Other faces, new gossip. Wish I didn't keep seeing him, though, across the room at parties or in the street, someone with his stride, someone tall and dark, someone who from the back looks just like him so that for a moment until he turns . . . Oh, how I wish the sight of champagne didn't make me feel so sick.

'Had this terrific wheeze about Charlie's Bugatti,' Crikey was saying. 'Stick a couple of firecrackers up the exhaust, send them off with a real bang, what? Only his bally man found them.'

'Damn shame Cadwallander's not here,' said Miles Millington.

'I'll say. He'd have got the fireworks past the eagle eye.'

'Hard cheese his guv'nor popping off like that.'

'Pity Dilly couldn't have come back from India,' said Maisie Cunningham-Cowper. 'She'd have been a divine Matron of Honour.'

'Just a couple of Jumping Jacks. Or some itching powder at the wedding breakfast. Would have made the whole thing really go.'

'So Archie's father never did manage to wangle his peerage,' said Dora Chantry.

'Someone told me Dilly's expecting a baby,' said Maisie.

'Yes,' I said. 'That's what she wrote.'

People marrying, dying, children being born. I had not talked to anyone about Felix. Although I exchanged letters regularly with Dilly I had explained nothing except that it had come to an end. I had not even been able to cry to begin with. Only in that wind-torn churchyard, watching the frost-bitten earth being shovelled onto Aunt Jessica's coffin, had I finally found the tears. I remember Archie, breaking for a moment his averted glance, the stiff politeness of the spurned lover, taking me by the arm.

'Bear up, old thing. Mustn't blame yourself too much, don't y'know.'

Blame? I had looked at him bewildered until I realized he was referring to Sybil's accusations. For, as to the real cause of my misery, what blame was there, on Felix's part or mine? It was a lie, Aunt Jessica's last act of possession. And sooner or later he would realize it was a lie and come back. I half-expected to see him then, his overcoat flapping in the wind, his head bare, a solitary dark figure walking towards us between the gravestones. And so many times after that when the doorbell went, or the telephone rang, or I thought I heard someone call my name in the street, I would imagine that he had understood and come back for me. I wondered if he would write, but he did not. The house in Cheyne Walk was empty, shuttered. Stenko sent me a postcard from Paris but there was no mention of him. He could, I suppose, be anywhere in the world by now. But wherever he was, one day he would see how terribly he had been deceived and come to find me. Despite Sybil's disapproval I still wore his ring, forbore superstitiously ever to take it off, lest I should lose the genie which would, I knew, eventually summon him.

I had, for lack of other alternatives, moved temporarily into South Audley Street. It was not an arrangement that suited any of us, least of all Sybil. She and Meredith rowed about it constantly. But Meredith, who usually yielded after a token struggle to most domestic pressure, remained surprisingly firm on this: with Aunt Jessica dead, he had inherited the responsibility for my guardianship and he would as a solemn duty carry out that responsibility till I was twenty-one.

I felt almost sorry for Sybil. She worked tirelessly sitting on charity committees, arranging lavish dinner parties, drawing on every family connection she could muster to conjure up the Junior Minister's post which would rescue Meredith from the obscurity of the back benches. But, whether he was unlucky or whether he simply longed for it less than she did, her efforts had so far gone unrewarded with anything more than a premature hardening of lines around the mouth and a tendency to sick headaches. Into this precisely-planned social scheme, where not a smile or a caviar patty was squandered for naught, I fitted badly, and it was to everyone's relief when I remained in my room. But though I approached Meredith about it, suggesting a flat with Maisie, raising again the question of my music studies, he was adamant. The house seemed to jangle with Meredith's consideration of his family duties like a box full of knives.

And besides, with the loss of Felix, a lassitude had come over ne, so that even when I tried to direct myself towards a plan of scape my head was too heavy for the effort. I dutifully quirrelled away as much as I could of my allowance but I did ot have the energy for another attempt at running away. With tenko gone, I even became sluggardly about my hours at the iano. The sound of it instantly induced one of Sybil's sick eadaches, and anyway I no longer had the heart for it. ometimes even the opening chords of a familiar piece would e enough to reduce me to tears. I seemed to be compensating or my initial inability by weeping all the time now, at the lightest thing. I slept too, insatiably, waking late and going to ed at nine or ten o'clock, and yet still I grew ever more tired. And around me the desert broadened, so that through it, tricken by the blaze of an invisible but relentless sun, I rawled, sick and weak and fainting.

It was my third fainting spell which brought me at last to ace the fact that my exhaustion was not solely due to grief, that rief alone could not account for the mounting disorganization within my body, my lack of periods, my swollen irritable reasts. It must, I calculated grimly, be just over two months. I ay despairingly upon my bed, immobilized, afraid.

Then suddenly it seemed to me that it would be all right. A aby, Felix's child. That would make it all right, prove Aunt essica had lied. It would change everything, remove his obligation to remain in exile, remove mine not to seek him out. When e knew he would see the lie for what it was and we should be appy again. All I had to do was find him.

He must eventually return to Paris. *Icarus* was planned for he Tarantin Ballet's new season and he would have to return o supervise the making of the costumes and the building of the et. I did not have Stenko's address and the rest of the company ad long ago dispersed after the end of their run at the Alhambra. But Tarantin himself, I had read in a newspaper, was back in London, engaged in a law suit with his English ackers. And Tarantin, more than anyone, was likely to know where Felix was.

I hesitated. I felt so weak and tired. I did not know whether I ould any longer summon the strength to brace myself against Tarantin's malevolence, to risk humiliation and defeat. But Felix must know, he would want to know, it would somehow be he thing that saved us. Oh, how I wished champagne and igarette smoke did not make me feel so sick.

'Another Season,' Maisie Cunningham-Cowper was saying. 'All those fresh-faced girls rehearsing for their first Court. Gosh, doesn't it make you feel positively antediluvian just to think of it!'

The remnants of Lady Dolly's wedding had spilled out over the terrace and across the lawns of Critchley Castle, wilting with the afternoon sun and the sense of anti-climax that always comes after the happy couple have departed. People were already mooting the drive back to London. In the Italian Garden a peacock pecked dyspeptically at a discarded canapé. The grass had grown back where the duckboards and jute matting had imprinted the traces of our coming-out marquees, so that you would never have known they had been there.

'Another season,' said Crikey. 'Let's just hope the Middlesex selectors do their stuff.'

'Oh, not cricket,' said Maisie. 'Dancing, parties. Fun!'

In the desert there is suddenly no one to laugh with, no one to put their arms around you, no one warm to reach out and touch.

'I say, Christie, are you OK? You look a bit groggy.'

I could not go on hesitating. I could not let my fear of Tarantin stand in my way. And after all I was no longer possessed of unlimited time. The imperatives of my disordered body left me really no choice.

'It's nothing,' I said. 'Just the heat.'

And, making my decision, I got up and went to find somewhere I could be sick.

The door of Tarantin's suite at the Savoy was ajar, revealing a room overturned with the chaos of packing. A valet moved noiselessly backwards and forwards with shoes and ties and suits on hangers. Through the open bedroom door I could see, stretched out on the bed, one of the gilded boys picking idly at a box of almond dragées.

It was not how I had imagined it would be. I had thought he would be alone, that I could talk to him privately. The palms of my hands felt suddenly damp. I wished after all I had not come.

He was standing in the window, framed in a great fall of velvet that emphasized his diminutive stature, his simian sharpness. His hair gleamed with brilliantine, his carefully-manicured fingers toyed with a large cigar. He did not trouble to disguise his displeasure at seeing me.

'Miss Ward. You are the last visitor I should expect.'

I hesitated, watching him clip the end of the cigar, praying he would not light it, knowing that if he did I should begin to feel sick again.

'Well,' he said impatiently, 'what can I do for you? I have not much time, you understand. I leave for Paris tonight.'

'I – I need to know where Felix is.'

His reaction was unexpected. He let out a great gust of laughter. 'So, Miss Ward, you need to know!' His gold tooth flashed. 'Why, may I enquire, do you ask me?'

'Because he must be in Paris somewhere. And you know where he lives.'

'Must be in Paris? Paris, New York, Africa – my dear Miss Ward, he may be anywhere. I am afraid I am no wiser than you.'

'But the ballet – '

'Oh, I see. The ballet.' He inserted the cigar into one corner of his thin mouth. 'You think perhaps now he is free of you he will again concentrate on his work.'

I swallowed hard. 'Please,' I said, 'I'm certain you know where he is. And I need – '

'Need?' He lit the cigar and suddenly began to advance upon me with it. 'My dear Miss Ward, you need to know nothing. I do not understand why you come to me. I am his friend. Do you imagine I tell you anything?'

He was pointing the cigar at me, jabbing it towards me. A cloud of smoke billowed into my face. I reeled backwards.

'Do you imagine I tell you anything after the terrible thing you have done to him? Oh, I have seen him on the night he left England. And I am sickened for him, disgusted!'

I stared at him, bewildered, seeing his eyes glitter through the cigar smoke, feeling the queasiness begin. Surely Felix could not have told him, surely Felix could not have repeated to Tarantin Aunt Jessica's lie?

'I will say nothing, Miss Ward, only this. Do not try to find him. Do not pursue him and torture him. After all you have done to him he will not wish to see you, the sight of you will fill him only with revulsion and contempt. He has gone away because he wishes to forget, because he wishes to find again his self-respect. Do not prevent him. He will feel only hate for you. And do not come asking me questions. Because I will tell you nothing. Nothing!'

The creases of his face danced and quivered. I felt the wave of nausea grow, felt the edges of the room close in. I did not understand. Yes, in his letter Felix had talked of ugliness and shame. But I had not known what he had meant. I was an only child, could not feel what it was to have brothers and sisters, a father, I could not understand the force of the taboo, it had no dimension for me. And besides, it was a lie, it must be a lie. But Felix believed it. He believed it and he had been horrified, repelled by it. And now his horror extended to me. He had told Tarantin. He had promised to tell no one but the next night, filled with disgust for me, he had told everything to Tarantin.

'I am sure, Miss Ward, now that it is clear you will gain nothing from your visit here, you will excuse me while I return to my packing.'

My stomach heaved, I turned away blindly, choking, to the door. In the doorway a hand caught my arm to steady me. I looked up. It was Stenko.

He was carrying his hat and an armful of parcels. 'C–C–C–hristie! It is so g–g–g–ood to see you.'

Then, taking in my brimming eyes and greenish hue, he paused, embarrassed, shooting a quick, almost shifty glance over my shoulder at the room beyond.

'I am Vladimir Andreyevitch's p–p–p–rivate secretary now.'

'Oh, Stenko,' I said, 'I need to find Felix. Please help me.'

He paused again, shuffling his feet uncomfortably.

'C–C–C–hristie, you are my f–f–f–riend. I know it is not true, I know you would never h–h–h–urt anyone.'

'Oh Stenko, where is he?'

His eyes, behind the pebble glasses, avoided mine, divided eyes struggling for a second with an impossible conflict of loyalties. He glanced through the door into the room again.

'If Vladimir Andreyevitch cannot t–t–t–ell you, then I c–c–c–annot.'

Farther down the corridor, in a wasteland of closed doors, I pressed my head against the wall and wept.

Towards the end of May I stopped being sick and began almost to feel well again. After my visit to Tarantin I had remained for a while in a state of stunned suspension, unable to do anything, unable even to think, for fear of what my thoughts might conjure up. The loss of Felix had before seemed insupportable, but then I had not known how truly he was lost to me. I had imagined him stricken, suffering, but still full of love. It had never occurred to me that he would begin to work upon his self-disgust till I became the focus of it. But that he had was evident from his betrayal in talking to Tarantin. There was no point in finding him, telling him about the baby. He believed the lie utterly.

But if Felix were lost to me there was now Felix's child. My desert was no longer limitless, inescapable. I had hope. And sometimes, when I lay awake at night unable to believe that he had ceased to love me and know that I loved him, I would think of his face when he saw his son and feel suddenly comforted and safe.

A new inertia fell upon me now as my body regained its equilibrium, a certain calm equilibrium of mind in which I willingly surrendered all concern with exterior things and began to focus my thoughts upon the mysterious invasion within me, as if its nurture required the steadfast concentration of my whole being. I began to avoid parties and dances and the people I knew, to spend my time in quiet contemplation in my room. At night I would lie with my hands upon my naked stomach sensing tiny whisperings and flutterings and feeling all my pent-up love for Felix flooding out towards it, that miraculous secret presence, growing boundlessly as it grew. I had no firm plans. I had heard of girls in my situation who had disappeared for a few months to France or Italy or even to India until it was over. But though I knew I should have to go away I had no intention of a furtive adoption, no thought but that I would keep my child. I had saved a little money, I could work, give music lessons, all I needed was somewhere safe until my confinement was due. As to how I should set about arranging this I was vague. But, even when my waist began perceptibly to thicken, I felt only an unhurried sense of certainty that when the time came it would all work itself out. I took to wearing baggy cardigans despite the heat, and to concentrating on walking very upright to make sure my stomach was not thrust out. I thanked God that I was tall and that the fashion was for loose, low-waisted dresses. I avoided Sybil's eye. I was, in a muted way, almost happy.

That no one in South Audley Street seemed even dimly aware of my condition I had not just my new reclusiveness but also politics to thank. On May 20th the Prime Minister, Bonar Law, had suddenly resigned because of ill-health. Since he had omitted to name a successor this left the two obvious contenders, Lord Curzon and Stanley Baldwin, waiting in the lists for the King to choose his champion. Curzon had established peace in Turkey, Baldwin had achieved only a humiliating capitulation in his negotiations to settle our war debts with America. Curzon was aristocratic, arrogant and commanding, Baldwin was insignificant and middle-class. Sybil's family colours, and therefore Meredith's, were firmly pinned to Curzon's standard. The coveted Junior Ministry seemed at last within Meredith's grasp. But, while Curzon waited all weekend at his Somerset estate for the summons to the Palace, the King sent for Baldwin.

'Can you imagine,' said Sybil, dabbing her forehead with a diminutive lace handkerchief, 'a man who spends his whole day with his nose in *The Strand Magazine*. A man who – ' and here she blenched – 'a man who keeps pigs!' But there was nothing for it. Baldwin became Prime Minister on 21st May and was elected leader of the Conservatives on the 28th. And all Sybil's work, the careful cultivation of friends, the judicious invitations to weekends at Monks Last, the discreet selection of sympathetic ears, had to begin over again. All through June the house was in a flurry with it. My keeping to my room was received with relief rather than comment.

But I could not, of course, go on forever undiscovered. That the time was past for waiting, that I should have to stir myself to action came home to me forcibly one afternoon in the park.

I was sitting by the lake, luxuriating in the July sunlight and watching the ducks, while a middle-aged woman on the bench beside me, a cook or a maid on her afternoon off, tempted them with scatterings of stale bread, when I suddenly felt from deep inside me a hard, determined and astonishingly powerful kick.

My hand went to my belly, I let out a small surprised exclamation.

The woman beside me smiled. 'My first used to kick something terrible, too,' she said. 'I always swore he'd be an inside right. Or a dancer.'

I stared at her.

'Of course he was killed at Wipers in the end. The other one fell at Passchendaele. Killed fighting for their country, both my boys.'

My eyes went down to where my hand was. 'I'm so sorry,' I said. But my eyes were on my belly and the soothing, tell-tale motion of my hand.

That night, before the wardrobe looking glass, examining myself in my chemise, I saw how the material strained to cover my ripe belly, how I was irrevocably, unashamedly big with Felix's child.

I must find somewhere to stay until the birth, but I did not know how to set about it. There was only one person I could think of in London who lived in a world where these things must be common practice and who could tell me how they were done. That this was someone I dreaded almost more than Tarantin could not be helped. I had, quite suddenly, run out of time.

CHAPTER TWENTY-EIGHT

'Forgive me for telephoning you so unexpectedly,' I said.

'*Chérie,* you will think nothing of it. You and I are friends, confidantes. Have I not always said so?'

Rostova, in an embroidered kimono looped about with ropes of pearl and jade, was reclining on a sofa, her eyes covered with a velvet mask. Since her rupture with Tarantin she had taken up permanent residence in an apartment in one of the Nash terraces overlooking Regent's Park. But in the carefully-dimmed light the generosity of the architecture seemed diminished by the oppressive clutter of objects within the room, cushions, trinkets, modish bric-à-brac, but principally pictures in all shapes and sizes of Rostova herself. Ballet posters hung upon the walls, photographs in ornate frames jostled for space on every available surface and above the sofa, I saw, with a now familiar lurch of pain, there towered one of Felix's portraits of her. She herself seemed, in comparison, to have lost some of her brightness, as though it had been overlaid with a languid veil. She removed the eye mask and looked at me, making only the faintest motion of her head. In a corner, half-shrouded, a cage of finches twittered.

'So. We are two women together. You will sit and we shall talk.'

I thought, as if the stirrings of that precious life within me gave me courage, that I was not afraid of her now. 'I've come to ask your advice,' I said.

'My advice?' Her head moved a fraction upon the cushions, then subsided into languor again. 'About *cher Félix*? Well, *ma petite,* you can be sure that I will do my best to give it. I shall not be prejudiced by anything he has said.'

I stared at her. 'You've seen him?'

'Oh yes. Of course I have seen him.'

'Then you know where he is?'

She gave a little, lazy laugh. 'Oh, not now. But that night he left England, then I saw him.'

'He came here?'

'But of course. He may come and go – that is the way of men, is it not? But Félix and I, under the skin, we are two of the same kind. Always he comes back to me in the end.'

I was stung by a sharp jealousy, followed by an immense feeling of betrayal. 'He talked to you?'

Rostova leant over and picked out a macaroon from an alabaster bowl at her elbow. '*Ma chérie,* he was wretched. What else could he do?'

The betrayal grew. 'No,' I said in disbelief. 'No.'

Rostova bit into the macaroon with sharp white teeth. 'He was wretched, beside himself. He told me everything.'

'No! How could he?'

'*Ma petite*, I do not condemn you. I have, of course, only his side of the story. I know only what he believes to be true.'

First Tarantin, now Rostova. The betrayal seemed so complete I was overwhelmed by it. 'But it's not the truth!' I cried. 'It's a lie. Aunt Jessica lied.'

Rostova paused in the selection of a second macaroon. 'He believes it,' she said.

'But I don't. I'll never believe Felix is my brother!'

My vehemence seemed to arrest her, for the macaroon paused halfway to her lips and for an instant her eyes narrowed strangely. 'It is,' she said slowly, 'a terrible thing, a mortal sin, what you have done.'

'No!'

'A vile sin against God.'

'No, no!'

'He understands it. This is why he has gone away.'

'But that's what Aunt Jessica wanted. She lied because he loves me.'

'He cannot love you now.'

'But he must.'

'Such love is what animals do. Dogs in the street.'

'Oh no. He must, he must.'

'Such love will make him sick to his stomach.'

'Oh no, no!'

'You fill him only with disgust!'

'No!' I screamed. 'It's a lie, he mustn't believe it. He can't believe it. I love him so very much. And I'm going to have his baby!'

'*Merde!*' said Rostova. She was sitting up now, all her languor gone. 'You are certain of this?'

'That's why I'm here,' I said. 'I came to ask your help.'

'How far gone are you?'

'About four and a half months.'

She clicked her tongue against her teeth. 'Stand up. Let me see.'

Reluctantly I unbuttoned my cardigan. Her stare humiliated me. As if it too were affronted, the presence in my womb began to kick indignantly.

'And you are sure it is Felix's child?'

The question stunned me. 'Yes. Of course.'

'You are getting big. You have left it very late.'

'I know. I must go away as soon as possible. I have a little money and I'm well enough to work if necessary. But I need somewhere to go for when the time comes, somewhere the baby will be born safely – '

Rostova rose. There was something menacing in the way she walked towards me.

'You are not,' she said, 'intending to give birth to this child?'

I stared at her.

'You cannot bring such a child into the world.'

'I can work,' I said. 'I'm perfectly able to care for it on my own.'

'Care for it? Your brother's child?'

'My child. Felix's and mine.'

'And you are not only brother and sister on your father's side but – correct me if I am mistaken – your mothers are also sisters?'

I recoiled from her, bewildered.

'You cannot have this baby. You must get rid of it.'

I took a step backwards. My hands flew instinctively to protect my belly. 'No. No! That's not why I came.'

'It will be difficult. But it can be arranged.'

'No. I won't contemplate it.'

'But, *mon enfant,* anything else is out of the question.'

'Kill it? Kill Felix's baby?'

'Your brother's child.'

'But I can feel it moving inside me.'

'A child from your own blood.'

'What you're saying is wickedness!'

'More wicked to give birth to it. *Merde!* It will be a monster!'

I stared at her, my hands still held protectively against my womb. Her eyes were hard, her tiny pupils glittered.

'The child of incest. It will be a monster. A drooling idiot.'

'But I don't believe Felix is my brother.'

'He believes it. Only you do not.'

'Because it's not true.'

Her lips twitched impatiently. 'If it is as you say, why is he then so certain? Why did he go away? If he loves you. Why did he go?'

I felt suddenly weak. I sat down with my head in my hands. 'The resemblance is impossible to mistake,' Tarantin had said. And Dilly: 'I'd never realized you were so alike.' Had I not even seen it myself in his sketches of me? 'Your colouring is different, of course. But the resemblance is quite striking.' No. It was the Cavendish face, nothing more. Like the portraits at Monks Last. The Cavendish face.

Rostova stood over me. 'You are the wicked one,' she hissed. 'How can you even consider it?'

'You're wrong,' I said. 'It will be tall and straight and strong. Like him.'

'Your colouring is different. But the resemblance . . .'

'I have seen them,' Rostova said. 'In fairs, in Latvia, in Odessa. Boys with growths like cauliflowers upon their face. Women with humps like a camel. Grown men with the minds of little children. Performing like animals for the people to laugh. Circus animals.'

I covered my eyes. 'No, no! It's normal, it's healthy. I can feel it kicking me.'

Rostova snorted contemptuously. 'That means nothing, *mon enfant*.'

The Cavendish face. Oh God, please let it be the Cavendish face.

'I do not understand,' Rostova hissed, 'how you can even consider such a risk.'

I looked up at her, despite myself almost pleading. 'But I love it,' I said. 'Even now. I love it, as I love him.'

Her eyes were pitiless. 'And he, what would he think? If you bring into the world such a child. How would he thank you?'

I shrank away from her. 'Oh no,' I moaned. 'Please, no.'

'It will be difficult. Four and a half months. It will not be easy to arrange. But you say you have a little money. That will help.'

'Oh no,' I said. 'I can't. Please understand. I can't.'

'There is someone I know. It will take a little time. You will phone me, *ma petite,* in two days.'

'No. Please. No, no, no!'

She had regained the sofa. Stretching herself out, she dipped her hand delicately into the alabaster bowl and brought out another macaroon. 'You will think about it, *chérie*. And when you have thought, you will find the courage. You will telephone me. If not for yourself – ' she bit into the little cake, severing it neatly in two – 'for him.'

I tried to concentrate my whole mind upon Felix's face, the absorbed, loving face that I remembered, the little wry lines around the mouth, the gentleness in his eyes. But there seemed now to be two Felixes: the man I loved, whose cool control hid such a fierce and painful integrity; and the man the others saw, Meredith and Archie, Tarantin and Rostova, the man who was unable to love, who was selfish, unscrupulous, cynical, cruel. The Felix I knew was intensely private, could scarcely talk even to me about the things that caused him pain; but this other man, within hours of writing to me that he would never tell anyone what Aunt Jessica had said, had spoken of it freely to both Tarantin and Rostova. The Felix I knew, who had parted from me in such an agony of grief, could never, in the space of a day, have ceased to love me. But this other man had spent the next night with Rostova. And hadn't I, both before and after I had understood that I loved him, doubted him too? Hadn't he been prepared to manipulate me into obedience, hadn't he made promises and then been ready to break them?

Oh, but that was unjust, he had from the start been perfectly fair, he had done his best in the face of my hot-headed obstinacy to understand me, he had held back only to protect me from my own ignorance of the world and later, when he knew he loved me, because of my innocence which he so scrupulously feared to hurt. And had I not been wrong, despicably wrong, in my jealousy too?

But was I wrong now? If he had so easily gone back to his old mistress, might he not just as easily have found himself a new one, was he perhaps not even at this moment lying with his arms about her saying to her all the tender words he had said to me?

The Felix I loved could not be my brother: I did not care that I had no understanding of the relationship, I just knew with absolute certainty that what I felt for him I could not feel for a brother, even a brother I had not been brought up with, whose filial tie was unknown to me. But did the Felix I loved exist, had he ever existed except in my head? Already the cherished image of that face was dissolving, blurring into a terrifying confusion in which my certainty ebbed away. If everything else was in doubt maybe this too was doubtful. Perhaps Aunt Jessica had not lied after all.

I lay in the darkness of my room, tossing between damp sheets, racked with a monstrous, growing fear. Ghosts, he had said. 'So many things in my childhood that I understood by instinct but could not name.' And her voice: 'If only you could know all the suffering, my darling Felix, if one day I could tell you.' Child of that house, my love child. Oh God, no! How can you even consider such a risk? Oh no, please no! And he, how will he thank you for it? If you will not do it for yourself you will do it for him. . . .

'Madame Zena, Palmist and Clairvoyant', the sign on the shop front had said. She was a huge woman, obese, with a crop of hanging warts upon the folds of her neck that juddered when she moved. Her hands, I noticed, were by contrast very small and perfectly-formed with tiny shell-like nails, as if they belonged to someone else.

She led me through a door to the back of the shop, into a room that seemed half-sitting room, half-kitchen. I followed her, dazed. There was a smell of frying fat and of offal boiled for cats. The kitchen end of the room was partly screened off by a dingy curtain which had lost some of its rings.

'You've brought the money, dear?' she said.

My hands fumbled with the clasp of my handbag. 'Sixty pounds,' I said. My meagre savings and what a hard-eyed pawnbroker had been prepared to offer for two diamond pins.

The warts quivered. The little neat fingers took the notes, leafing through them meticulously. When she was satisfied she went over to the mantelpiece and stuffed the money into a china vase beside the clock. 'A souvenir from Margate', it said.

Then she turned and surveyed me critically.

'Have trouble with sums, do you, dear?'

'I – I'm sorry?' I said.

'They said you was three and a half months, the party I made the arrangement with.'

I looked down to where my hands clutched hold of my bag. My palms had made damp marks on the leather.

'Only it's more difficult the later it is, you see.'

Her eyes roved evaluatively to the pearls at my neck. I was glad I had taken off Felix's ring before I came.

'More of a difficulty all round. Particularly in the question of the fee.'

It was suffocating, airless, in that cramped room. I longed suddenly for the fresh air in the street. 'I haven't any more,' I said.

Perhaps she read my thoughts. 'Oh well,' she said quickly, 'what can't be mended can't be helped. I'm not one to turn away a young lady in need. Generous to a fault, dear, that's me.'

She went over to the curtain and pulled it back. I stared at the couch with its rubber sheet. My hands clutched my bag, my legs seemed to freeze.

'Well dear, no point in standing around chatting. Take off your underthings.'

Her back was to me, her neat little hands working away. I watched her, stupefied. Reaching up to a shelf and taking down a small bottle and a hypodermic syringe, she proceeded to fill the syringe with the contents of the bottle. Beside the sink were two lengths of rubber tubing. The first she attached to the jet of the gas ring. Into one end of the second she fitted the head of the syringe.

'Lie down then, love. Make yourself nice and comfy.'

I lay rigid, my arms clamped by my sides, not daring to look down at my body, no longer daring to look at her. I tried to shut my eyes, but they refused to stay closed.

'Now lift your dress up, dear. That's it.'

Her fingers were clammy on my skin. I could hear her making little reproving noises to herself, I shuddered under the gross invasion of her hand.

'You young ladies never learn, do you? Leaving things so late. It won't just go away, you know. Not by itself.'

Her face loomed over mine. The warts juddered. Her breath smelt of peppermint and decay.

I sat up. 'No,' I said. 'It doesn't matter. I've changed my mind.'

Firmly, she pushed me back. 'Don't you worry, dear. It'll soon be over. This'll be our secret, yours and mine.'

'No!' I said. 'I don't want you to!'

'But it won't be a proper secret, dear, if we don't both share it.'

Then she thrust the rubber tubing from the gas jet into my face.

CHAPTER TWENTY-NINE

Diary of Adele Ward.
Monks Last, Norfolk.

6th August, 1894.

M has been away these past two days, having found an excuse to return to London, but J, though she remains pale and drawn, appears unconcerned by his absence. I wonder what false promises he has made to ensure her compliance. Nevertheless, when there came for me by this morning's post a letter from him, I caught her, across the breakfast table, glancing longingly at the envelope. I, meanwhile, found myself in some agitation, knowing that the passing of every hour brought closer that inevitable event which would shatter her complacency; and we were still at the breakfast table when a servant appeared amidst great commotion to announce that Sir Arthur, unheralded and a full six weeks before he was expected, had returned from Ireland.

J's face wore for a moment such a pitiable expression of consternation that, in spite of everything, my heart went out to her; but, of course, in the presence of Papa and myself, she could say nothing, could only submit unresistingly to all Sir Arthur's kisses and exclamations of concern. I have since avoided being for an instant alone with her; yet, glancing up over luncheon, I found her eyes trained upon me with that bright, hard look which used to frighten me so in the nursery when I had taken possession of a toy she desired.

The afternoon being fine and sunny, we took tea on the west terrace, with the exception of Papa who has gone to King's Lynn to inspect a telescope offered for purchase. Despite Sir Arthur's gentle attempts to raise our spirits, an atmosphere of constraint pervaded our gathering which could not solely be explained by our mourning weeds; and when Sir Arthur, patting my head and turning with a smile to J, pronounced that I was the kindest and best sister in the world for, without my good sense in writing to him, he would never have known from the brave and stoical letters of his wife how much she now wanted the roses in her cheeks, I saw J's mouth tighten and I began involuntarily to tremble. When, an instant later, Baby Meredith appeared with his nurse desiring his Papa to show him the dragon flies on the lake, she could scarcely wait till Sir Arthur was out of earshot before she turned upon me.

'So it was you! I knew it. Well, you have failed, my dear, scheming little sister. I don't care about the scandal. There is nothing you or Arthur or anyone on this earth can do to stop the two of us being together.'

Though her bearing was to distant scrutiny controlled and though her voice scarcely rose above a whisper, her eyes blazed fire and she spat her words at me like venom. All at once, seeing in the intensity of her passion the pain and misery that must inevitably come to her, I felt my nursery fears subside and I was filled with pity.

'J, you do not know M – '

'Know him?' She gave a harsh laugh. 'He is everything to me and I to him. It is you who know nothing of him. What kind of wife could you ever be to him? I am his wife now and he my husband, if not in the world's eyes, in every way that Heaven counts important. We belong to each other body and soul – '

I stared at her, my pity growing, for I heard throbbing in her voice, her language, that deluded vision of love, by which I, permitting my febrile imagination too credulously to devour the sugary palliatives of novels, have allowed myself to be ensnared.

'Please, J, if you will not have a care for yourself, think at least of your duty to dear, kind Sir Arthur – '

She tossed her head contemptuously after his portly figure, where he and Baby sported together on the lawn. 'That spineless fool!'

'Then if you will not consider your husband please, please think of your child – '

'My child!' And I saw that she was not looking towards where Baby M gambolled about his father's legs but had all at once clutched her hands about her as if repressing a sudden spasm of pain. 'You may plead and whine all you wish, dear Adele – I shall only despise you for it. He is mine now, he will never return to

you. In two days we shall be in Switzerland together and nothing can stand in the way of it.'

'J,' I said, 'M will not come back to you. He wrote to me this morning saying he has been detained indefinitely in London and instructing me to return to him there as soon as possible, where he has some papers from our attorney which await my signature. He begs me to convey his gratitude for your hospitality and his regret that he is unable, in person, to –'

'No!' she burst out. 'That's not true!'

I took the letter from my work basket. 'Please. Read it for yourself. You will see that M indeed requests me to show it to you.'

As her eyes scanned the page what little blood there was drained from her face. She was dumbstruck for a moment; then she turned upon me in unrestrained fury. 'You evil little b—ch! I don't know how you have done this but I shall never forgive you for it. And I promise if ever I can find a way of revenging myself against you, I –'

But here Sir Arthur returned with Baby, and we were obliged upon an unconvincing pretence at small talk.

CHAPTER THIRTY

Felix was looking down at me. His face once again had that gentle, absorbed look and his eyes were filled with an infinite sadness. I wanted so much to tell him I loved him, to throw myself about his neck, but for some reason my arms were too heavy for me to lift them. I had the most curious sensation, as if from the tips of my toes lengths of fine silk were being drawn up inside me, drawn up and wound into a knot at my throat. And then I was not lying in the bed any more but somewhere above it, looking down. I saw that it was not Felix after all but my Cousin Meredith, with Sybil beside him. They were bending over the body in the bed, my body, as if with some concern. Surveying them impartially, I felt it was not a concern I could share.

'What did she say?' asked Sybil.

'Same thing she keeps saying. Just his name. By God, I'd like to get my hands on my bloody brother!'

'She brought it on herself,' said Sybil.

Meredith bent over the bed again. 'Poor little thing,' he said sympathetically.

Sybil snorted. 'I see! She's got you in her clutches now, has she?'

'Sybil, for pity's sake!'

'Well, she threw herself at him hard enough. Insinuating herself into his house, blackmailing him into taking her to France –'

'My dear, you know that's not true.'

'Then ask yourself, would any decent girl—'

'Sybil, not now. Not now, m'dear, after what the doctor said. Apparently there's never a lot of hope with septic poisoning. And anyway he says there's no fight in her.'

Sybil dabbed her lips with her handkerchief. 'It seems to me for the best,' she said. 'No man in his right senses would marry her now.'

He looked at her for a moment. Then, slumping heavily into a chair, he buried his head in his hands. 'Oh God!' he said. 'God help the lot of us.'

She tucked her handkerchief back into her sleeve. 'For heaven's sake pull yourself together. After all, it's not as if any of us need reproach ourselves. You can hardly blame her upbringing. It's as your mother always said. There's bad blood on that side of the family.'

Meredith looked up. His face was scarlet and he was struggling for breath. 'If you're searching for bad blood, Sybil, why don't you start with my wretched brother? It's been the same ever since I can remember. Taking, taking everything. Not caring. Not giving a damn for anyone else. Ever since we were boys. She gave him everything, there wasn't anything left, she gave everything to him.'

'Your mother,' said Sybil, 'was a good woman.'

'My mother,' said my Cousin Meredith, 'was a bitch!'

With the greatest reluctance I came down to rejoin the body in the bed. Then the pain began again and I could no longer hear what they were saying.

I breathed, I slept, I forced myself to eat. But that was all. It seemed to take an interminable time before I was strong enough to totter about my room. Where the ripeness had been there was now only skin stretched across bone. I could count every one of my ribs, my pelvis seemed to stick out at right angles. In bed my bones cut into me like knives. I could not cry, for Felix or for the death of my child. It was as if, like a flower that someone has snapped shut inside a heavy book for the dismal purpose of preserving it at any cost, in any state, there was only a semblance of life in me now, as if all the rich, pulsing juices of it had dried away.

After a while, deprived of the strength for active sorrow, I came gradually to a dull acceptance. If there was little present and no future there was at least the past. It ceased to matter whether I knew the real Felix de Lisle or whether he might or might not be my brother. There had been a man whom I had loved and who had loved me, as no brother and sister could surely be capable of loving. And that man, his being held forever in the softly focused images of memory, the warmth of his skin, the place at his shoulder which seemed so precisely designed for my head to nestle, the affectionate mockery of his smile, that man I loved still. There was a safety in the completeness of it, in its being incapable of development or change, that almost pleased me. If I was obliged to live I would rather live with what was past and gone; that, at least, no one could take away from me.

I began, very slowly, to get better. And as I improved, the pressure on my Cousin Meredith increased; Sybil was adamant, she would not for a moment longer than was strictly necessary tolerate me in her house.

He appeared one autumn afternoon in my room and drew up a chair to my bed. I could tell from the heaviness of his breathing and the way he kept screwing his monocle farther into his eye what he had come to say. My heart went out to him. There was so much of Uncle Arthur's kindness in him, even in his lectures and his obstinate insistence on doing his duty; but he had Uncle Arthur's weaknesses too, the same infirmity of will, the reluctance to do battle, the bewildered abdication in the face of demands made by a voice more powerful and persistent than his own. I felt sorry that I had become the cause of so much conflict in his life.

He made a final adjustment to his monocle and cleared his throat. 'Look here,' he said. 'Ought by rights to be giving you the lecture to end all lectures. But – well, the time's long gone for that. What's past is past. The point is what happens now, eh? That's the point.'

He paused, breathing heavily, as if, though it were indeed the point, it existed many miles beyond his reach.

'Fact is, Sybil and I have been discussing it. She – we both – think you should be sent – well, away somewhere, Switzerland, or something. For your health.'

He paused again, bracing himself for the onslaught of my reply.

I did not want to cause him any more trouble. And, besides, I no longer cared. 'All right,' I said.

He was visibly taken aback.

'Don't want you to think we're punishing you – '

'I don't,' I said.

'Of course I know it seems like a sort of banishment – '

'I don't mind,' I said.

He paused again, took out his monocle, inspected it, then jammed it back in place. It was as if, having come with ammunition for a long siege followed by difficult negotiations for peace, and finding the enemy instead prepared to surrender unconditionally at the first shot, he was somehow balked of his true purpose.

He coughed. 'Well, fact is Switzerland is Sybil's idea more than mine. Woman of strong moral principles, y'know. Takes a clear-cut line on these things. I – well, perhaps wrongly, I tend towards a broader view. More sinned against than sinning, that sort of thing – '

My apathy was stirred. I had never had the chance to defend Felix properly and now I wanted suddenly to explain that Meredith was wrong, that his hate was groundless, that Aunt Jessica's love was just as damaging as her contempt.

'I did nothing,' I said, 'that I did not do of my own free will and of my own choosing.'

'If my blasted brother had any sense of honour – '.

'Your brother,' I said, 'is intensely honourable. I think he's the most honourable person I've ever met.'

He stared at me for a moment. Then he reared up, wheezing. 'Now look here, Christabel. I've been damned generous up to now. Too generous. Most families of my father's generation would have thrown you out on the street. But because you've been ill, we've been soft with you – '

I stopped. It was always a mistake to put Meredith in a corner, he simply backed away from you and did not listen. Anyway, I could scarcely explain to him, of all people, Felix's true reason for leaving.

'I'm sorry,' I said.

'So I should think, my girl. After all the advantages this family's given you.' His monocle had fallen out. He replaced it. 'Anyway, we're getting off the point. Where was I?'

'Switzerland,' I said.

'Ah. Yes. Well, you could go to Switzerland, of course, that's one possibility.' He forced a heavy intake of breath. 'Or you could get married.'

So that was it. And being sent away was the sanction if I still could not be brought to heel.

'Sybil's right,' I said. 'I don't think any man would want to marry me now.'

'Cadwallander's a nice enough young chap, y'know. Had a lot of the rough corners rubbed off him since he's been running the family business. Shame old Cadwallander never got his peerage, but that's by the by. Still influential people in the constituency, good friends to have. And he's always asking about you. Been most distressed to hear about your illness.'

'That's kind of him,' I said.

'Yes, I thought so, m'dear. And since he's in London next week he's naturally anxious to visit you.'

'Oh. I see,' I said.

'You could do a lot worse, y'know.'

'Yes,' I said. 'And he could do a lot better.'

'Not sure he'd think so.'

'He will,' I said, 'when he finds out why I've really been ill.'

Meredith shifted in his chair. 'If he does find out, m'dear. But after all, what's past is past. No sense in upsetting the poor fellow. I'm pretty certain no one will tell him.'

Archie pushed his head round the door. He was carrying a bunch of chrysanthemums wrapped in tissue paper. He seemed older somehow, the furrow now permanent between his brows, his pink cheeks heavier, his bravado all but vanished. The sight of me in bed, propped up on pillows, made him timid. He carried the flowers like a defensive weapon.

I thanked him for them and asked him how he was.

'Mustn't grumble, what?' he said. 'Working man's lot a hard one, and all that sort of thing. All grist to the mill, don't y'know.'

I asked him how the family steel business was doing. He seemed relieved to be offered a ready-made topic of conversation.

'Mustn't grumble. . . . Guv'nor had a sticky year last year. . . . Bank requesting promissory notes, had to stop giving dividends on ordinary shares. . . . Had to lay off a few workers too, but then, old thing, they get more on relief than we can pay them, blighters don't know when they're well off. . . . Need a chap with new ideas, old Brice, the senior director, rather an old fogey, don't y'know. And then there's the question of money, what? Government policies taxing us out of bally existence, market flooded with cheap foreign imports. . . . Still, Baldwin's a steel man himself, should understand. . . . Need tariffs, need Protection, cut the Boche and the Frenchies out. . . . Need new ideas, a strong line. . . . Bit lonely with no one to talk to. . . . Still, an honest day's toil and all that rot. . . .'

It was an apparently endless flow, like a man returning from exile in a foreign country who, having been deprived for years of the opportunity to speak his native tongue, cannot restrain his outpourings, so great is his relief that he may be listened to and understood. But his growing pinkness suggested that he had not, for all that, lost sight of the ultimate purpose of his visit.

'Archie,' I said.

'Sorry, old girl. Good to get it off the old chest, don't y'know. Never asked you how you were bearing up.'

The flowers lay on the coverlet between us like a territorial barrier. I moved them and touched his hand.

'Archie, I think I know why you've come. And there's something I want you to understand.'

He gulped. The crimson shot up beyond his ears. 'Oh. Ah. Well, don't mean to rush you, old thing. Know you're a bit seedy, not up to much.'

I wished, how I wished that he would not always obfuscate things with an irrelevant flow of words.

'Archie, it's about Felix and me.'

The furrow between his eyebrows deepened. 'That bounder! Best not to say another word about him, what?'

I sighed. I knew I was going to do this badly, that he would not help me.

'Please, Archie. He's not a bounder. And I loved him very deeply – '

'Girlish infatuation. Good-looking blighter, I suppose, in a caddish sort of way – '

'Archie, I still love him.'

It threw him back for a moment. I could see him turning it over. But then with a small movement of his shoulders he shrugged it away.

'Grow out of it in time, old girl. Good steady chap to look after you, make you forget all that tosh. Blighter like that's no use to a decent girl, only after one thing.'

I drew in my breath. 'Felix and I were lovers, Archie. With my complete and unqualified consent.'

He looked aside, down at the coverlet, plucking it with his fingers, frowning at it in a bewildered manner. For a while he said nothing. I wished he had not once again forced me to hurt him, but there was relief in his silence nevertheless. I lay back upon the pillows waiting for the inevitable moment when he would get to his feet and go away.

Then he looked up. 'Bit of a strafer, what? Still, suppose it's the modern thing. Free love and all that. Suppose a chap's got to bite the bullet, move with the times – '

I raised my eyes to his like someone levelling a gun. 'Archie, I was carrying his child.'

There was a long silence. When he rose it was very suddenly, so that the flowers fell off the bed.

'Sorry, old girl. Very sorry. But couldn't take another man's leavings, don't y'know.'

That I was not banished to Switzerland I once again had politics to thank. For in October at the Conservative Party Conference at Plymouth Stanley Baldwin, arguing that import controls were now essential if the Government was ever to stop the rise in unemployment, came out in favour of Protection. It was such a complete reversal of all Bonar Law's pledges to maintain Free Trade that it compelled the Conservatives to go to the country. The election date was fixed for December. And the South Audley Street household, including, for failure of any more suitable arrangement, myself, moved North in Meredith's wake.

I had never been to the North of England before. The cobbled streets, the damp gritty air, the little, dingy back-to-back houses hunched against the driving sleet filled me with an uneasy depression. There seemed, in our travels to canvass Meredith's vote, to be two towns co-existing in unequal and reluctant partnership. In the one there were imposing civic buildings, shops bright with Christmas tinsel, trams filled with prosperous, well-fed people rattling out to the suburbs where, in a generous sprawl of neat houses with neat front gardens, maidservants kindled welcoming fires in cretonned drawing rooms. In the other, a maze of twisting streets and alleys, of tripe shops, pawnbrokers, loan offices and public houses crouched beneath the shadow of the iron gates and dark towers which, heavy with the roar of furnaces and labyrinthed with railway lines and clanging shunting yards, made up the satanic city of Brice and Cadwallander Ltd, steelworks. And, in the little children staggering home with steaming bowls from the chip shop, in the girls with their clogs and their headscarves jostling out of the cutlery factory at change of shift, in the muted queues outside the converted lock-up hospital that was now the Labour Exchange, there seemed to me something that was almost Dickensian, so that only the factory girls coming out again in a clatter of high heels and lipstick to the dance hall or the picture house seemed to make the bridge in time.

Meredith, ever-mindful of the longed-for Junior Ministry and that he stood in a steel town where cheap foreign imports were a perpetual bugbear, had eagerly embraced Protection. Sometimes he would order the car to pull up so that he could make an impromptu address to the loiterers on the street corners, the women with their bundles of washing or Sunday suits to pawn, the men in their caps and mercerized cotton scarves. A small crowd would usually gather, apparently glad of any diversion. Sometimes a stray voice would start chanting one of the electioneering songs made current by the popular press, but more often the crowd, hands in pockets, shoulders hunched, feet shuffling against the cold, would simply stare at the posters which read: 'Vote for Jobs, Vote de Lisle', in numbed and indifferent silence.

Occasionally we would see Meredith's Labour opponent a few streets away haranguing the same silent audience about food prices and Free Trade. He was a bluff man in a tweed suit, like Meredith a product of Eton and Cambridge, like Meredith a landowner, with an estate in the outlying countryside. It occurred to me that despite their rhetoric and the slogans on their posters, there must appear to the assembled onlookers very little difference between them. And in the pinched faces and dull eyes of the crowd there seemed to rise, through the steam of claim and counterclaim upon the frosty air, through the mist of promises and accusations, a deeper, harsher, as yet unspoken question which the Hobson's Choice of dearer food or higher unemployment could not even begin to answer.

Sybil had reluctantly given me a temporary amnesty provided that, so far as my limited energy allowed, I was prepared to do my share of the electioneering work. While the drawing-room manoeuvres of London were meat and drink to her, she clearly hated grass-roots politics, was interested in issues when they implied groupings to be joined or won over, but was bored by them as subjects of discussion for their own sake. She found the local County people provincial, despised the party workers and thought the town's burghers quite beyond the pale. She accepted, for Meredith's future, a martyrdom of duty and , in moments when she forgot how much she disliked and disapproved of me, clearly saw me as an ally in her suffering.

With his political interests and his commitment to Meredith, I was, to my embarrassment, now thrown often into Archie's company. But I did not find his new manner towards me, the restrained and distant approach suitable for dealings with a scarlet woman, altogether disagreeable. He had at least stopped calling me 'old girl'. After two weeks he had half-forgotten he was supposed to be cutting me, and seemed almost friendly again.

But, if elections were an irritating interruption to the real business of politics, there was nevertheless an unquestioned assumption of confidence in our camp. And looking round the hall at Meredith's political meetings I did not wonder at it. Here were rows of the warm and the well-fed from the suburbs, shopkeepers, small businessmen, civic officials, minor gentry, with the prospect of a roaring fire and hot punch and goose at Christmas, and not a cloth cap or mercerized scarf amongst them. Meredith, with his natural hesitancy and his shortness of breath, was not a compelling public speaker, but they applauded him rapturously as if, oblivious to the cut and thrust of political argument, they drew satisfaction merely from the sight of his huge, gentlemanly form, as if, like the statues in the square or the imposing Town Hall, he were a local institution, fixed, unshakeable, whom to challenge would be to unsettle the whole steady fabric of existence.

Only once was there any breach in this wall of complacency. Meredith, on the platform with Sybil and the Leader of the Council and other constituency notables, had just risen from the Union-Jack-draped table to speak when there was a disturbance at the back of the hall and a missile came flying towards him over the heads of the crowd. He ducked instinctively and the missile, a bag of flour, burst harmlessly in front of him. There was a pause while a man was ejected, then Meredith continued with his speech as if nothing had happened. A fine mist of flour hung in the air for a while veiling him from his audience and causing him every so often to cough. A white splash like a star blurred the red and blue configurations on the lower half of the Union Jack. But the audience applauded with their usual rapture. It was nothing.

When we came out there seemed suddenly a great many policemen in the street and a small disturbance surrounding a battered Austin Seven parked directly in front of the hall. A constable was staring at it doubtfully while a woman's voice, abrupt, forceful, burred with traces of the local accent, snapped: 'If you want it shifted, lad, then you'd best find some way of getting the bloody thing started.'

The chauffeur drove our car up alongside and as we walked towards it I saw that the constable, with a sigh, had bent to take the starting handle of the Austin and that the woman was Mrs Burton, our local doctor's wife.

I had not met Mrs Burton, although her husband, consulted on our arrival, had prescribed me a tonic and feeding up with plenty of bread and potatoes. She had something of a reputation in the district. It was rumoured that she had in younger days been a pillar of the suffragette movement and had spent a month in jail for breaking a civic window with a brick. She wore a bun and mannish tweed and an uncompromisingly gruff manner to match, and was known as the scourge of local dignitaries, political and religious alike. Meredith quailed before her, Archie was rumoured to flee at her approach. Sybil, of course, disliked her unreservedly.

'Oh,' the woman said, as we drew level with her, 'it's his Lordship. If some fool hadn't thrown flour at you I shouldn't be having all this fuss.'

Sybil drew her furs around her. 'I'm sure you'll be distressed to know,' she said, 'that it missed its mark.'

Mrs Burton snorted. 'I'm distressed they threw it at all,' she said. 'There's folk in this town starving. They've got better uses for a bag of flour than to waste it on your husband.'

But Mrs Burton and the bag of flour were only minute ripples in the calm pool of our certainty, like the graffiti announcing mass meetings for the unemployed on the wall of the Labour Exchange or the ill-attended rallies of the town's few ardent Communists. The constituency had always been safely Conservative and Sir Meredith de Lisle had been its choice for a by-election and two General Elections. Our certainty sustained us on polling day in the warm conviviality of Meredith's Committee Room visits as we watched his pledges coming in, and at the count, with Thermos flasks and sandwiches, in the draughty Town Hall. It was only at around one o'clock in the morning, seeing the two horizontal lines of ballot papers for each ward creep forward like tortoises in an infinitely protracted race, hearing suddenly an excited murmur grow, that we realized the unthinkable could happen. Meredith's agent began agitatedly to dash from table to table, ward to ward. Meredith himself looked bewildered, like a man stunned by a heavy object. Sybil, so ungracious in domestic battles, drew herself up to the public dignity in defeat for which she had from birth been trained.

That night Labour gained fifty seats and the Conservatives lost ninety, including Sir Meredith de Lisle's.

CHAPTER THIRTY-ONE

To avoid the post mortem I went to the library the next afternoon. On the steps I was surprised to hear my name called and, looking round, saw the severe felt hat and baggy tweed of Mrs Burton.

'It is Miss Ward, isn't it?'

I faltered, expecting her to make some sharp remark about Meredith's defeat. But instead I found she was looking me up and down with a diagnostic eye.

'Well, my husband was right when he said you were nowt but a bag of bones.'

I was so taken aback by her rudeness that for a moment I did not speak. Then, thinking suddenly that there was no malice in the abrupt voice, that her manner, like her dress, was perfunctory only as if she were short of time, as if some spartan instinct had compelled her to pare away all unnecessary frills, I burst out laughing.

To my amazement she responded with what, though it was gone in an instant, was definitely a smile.

'They say you play the piano, lass.'

'Y–yes,' I said.

'Got the energy to play it Wednesday week?'
'If I'm still here, yes.'
'Nothing fancy. Just a few Christmas carols. It's a do the Women's Health Society are giving for the little ones who won't have much of a time of it on Christmas day.'
'Yes. Of course.'
'Four o'clock Wednesday week, then. St Barnabus Church Hall.'

St Barnabus Church Hall was a hollow barn of a place with bare floorboards and a hammer-beam roof which no amount of stoking the temperamental wood-burning stove at the far end of it would ever render completely warm. Nevertheless, from benches on either side of twenty trestle tables spread for the occasion with pristine white cloths and laden with cakes, jellies and all manner of other festive fare, a sea of tiny faces greeted me as I walked in. There were children of all shapes and sizes, mostly under the age of ten, children with pinched, pale faces, children with coughs and runny noses, children giggling, children crying, larger children looking after troupes of small brothers and sisters, children with cold sores and rotting teeth, scrimpy children with spindle legs pathetically twisted and bowed. Although they were all evidently freshly scrubbed and dressed in their best it was also clear that for many best was woefully patched and turned or, in the case of shoes and trousers, borrowed for the occasion from other more fortunate members of the family regardless of discrepancy in size; and I was disagreeably surprised to discover it was not a picturesque myth that some children had no shoes at all.

An army of middle-aged ladies hovered in readiness beside the tables, led by Mrs Burton in a large white apron. But, though there hung in the air the atmosphere of anticipation and excitement to be expected at a children's party there was, too, a mutedness about it, a sense of awe, as if the sight of such quantities of food inspired not so much a careless pleasure but wariness. I thought again of my brief moment of true poverty in the hostel, felt once more the chill of that bleak, grimy room and of its utter hopelessness, a hopelessness from which I had so easily been able to escape.

But I did not have more time to reflect for, though I had come burdened with sheet music, Mrs Burton thrust a bowl of trifle and a ladle into my hands and set me to work.

I caught her in an interval when she had just managed to stop a small boy from asphyxiating his baby sister with chocolate cake.

'Suffer the little children,' she said, wiping her chocolate-smeared fingers on her apron. 'Sometimes I think I'm getting too old for this game. What d'you think of them? Grim lot, aren't they?'

'They're very sweet,' I said.

'If you can be sweet with rickets and consumption. Influenza does for a few of them this time of year too.'

'Where do they all come from?' I said.

'Some have parents too poorly to work. Others are the unemployed families from the cutlery factory. But most here have fathers laid off from Brice and Cadwallander.' And she went away to rescue a child who was being sick into his paper hat.

Later, when we had sung every carol in my repertoire and when the scrapping, sticky, replete horde had been packed off home with nuts and oranges distributed by the vicar got up as a rather myopic and adenoidal Father Christmas, we were left with a blissful silence and twenty trestle tables of debris. The army of ladies, with an efficiency born of long practice, set to work sweeping up, making tablecloths into bundles, bearing dirty crockery to the scullery.

'Well, Miss Ward,' said Mrs Burton, up to her elbows in soap suds, 'don't stand there gawping as if you'd never washed a dish in your life.'

I tried to conceal my embarrassment with a laugh.

She looked at me sideways, then thrust a tea towel into my hand. 'It's never too late to learn. I suppose you can't bake bread or boil an egg, neither?'

I thought with irony of my much-vaunted plans for work and independence. 'No,' I said. 'I'm afraid I'm quite useless.'

She gave me another of her unexpected, spartan grins. 'You've a grand way with the piano, any road. And happen you might be useful too, to me.'

'Oh?' I said.

'I'm an interferer, Miss Ward. There's folk around here say I spend so much time sticking my nose into other folk's business I'll get it cut off one day. And I was thinking of doing a spot of interfering tomorrow.'

'Yes?' I said.

'Well, it might be that I need your help.'

* * *

The woman who opened the door to us looked about thirty-five, she was heavily pregnant and carried a tiny child in her arms. Glancing past Mrs Burton at me, she pushed a lock of hair out of her eyes and screwed her careworn face into an expression of deep embarrassment.

'I were only expecting you, Mrs Burton. I'm not in a state for carriage folk – '

Mrs Burton laughed. It was an odd sound, like a gun going off. 'That's not carriage folk, lass. That's Miss Ward. She plays the piano and says she's useless. Don't you worry your head about her.'

We stepped directly from the street into a low cramped room. There seemed to be a great many small children under five, and in the corner, huddled over a meagre fire, an old man in a wooden rocking chair. But though there was an oppressive sense of too many people in too small a space, and though in the netted window a table covered with a blue cloth proudly sported a pot plant in a china bowl, the room itself was bare. Apart from the old man's seat at the fire there was one other chair pulled up to a deal table, nothing more. The floor was covered with tattered oilcloth which seemed to bear the marks where other furniture might once have stood. It was, despite the fire, bitterly cold. And though everything about the room gave the impression of scrupulous scrubbing and polishing there was, too, a smell, the ineradicable smell of poverty, musty like old clothes.

The deal table was littered with wire, thread, strips of felt and pieces of organza, all the equipment for the laborious handiwork of making artificial flowers. In a box lined with tissue paper several finished tea roses nestled, a bright frivolity set against their stark surroundings. Looking at them, I was suddenly reminded of Elsie and wondered whether she still sat hunched in the steamy workroom, spitting out pins as she coughed her little, rasping cough.

Mrs Burton introduced the woman to me as Mrs Mullins and the old man as her father-in-law. There were four little Mullinses in evidence, counting the baby, Sally. The other two children belonged to a neighbour and were being looked after in exchange for the coal. As the women talked the old man rocked slowly backwards and forwards, drinking tea from a stone jam jar and revolving phlegm with a rattle in his throat. The children charged round us in circles, clutching at our skirts.

In Mrs Mullins's arms the baby, who had seemed asleep, squirmed suddenly, spluttered and gave out a yellowish stream of vomit.

'Drat!' said the woman. 'That were t'last egg till Jack gets his dole. I saved it special.'

'Dole,' said the old man suddenly, to no one in particular. 'It's nowt but a crying shame our Jack begging for relief. Him fit as a fiddle and a skilled man.'

No one paid any attention. Mrs Burton went for water to the stand pipe in the kitchen and the baby was mopped up.

'Fourty-five shilling he were getting at Brice and Cadwallander,' said the old man into his jar of tea. 'Fourty-five bob's a ruddy sight better than nowt.'

'I came across someone throwing out these,' said Mrs Burton, proffering Mrs Mullins a brown paper parcel she had been carrying under her arm, 'and I happened to notice yesterday your Jem's selling calico again.'

The parcel contained a pair of child's breeches. Mrs Burton held the baby while the eldest Mullins was extricated from the mêlée and the new trousers measured up against his threadbare ones for size.

'Ruddy charity,' said the old man. 'That's where his fancy ideas gets us. Taking ruddy charity from folk.'

Mrs Mullins made a small movement with her head. 'Shhh, our Dad,' she said, with a patience apparently born of long repetition. 'No point in carrying on.'

Mr Mullins snorted. 'Well, he'd a good job till he got his head filled wi' all that highfalutin rubbish. "From each according to his ability, to each according to his need."' He spat a gob of phlegm into the grate. 'Gets hisself branded as a ruddy Bolshie. Then wonders why he's laid off.'

'There's plenty of other folk laid off from Brice and Cadwallander,' said Mrs Mullins.

'Ay,' said Mrs Burton. 'Or had their wages cut to the bone.'

'Capitalist system were good enough for my generation. If there weren't no money how'd folk live?'

'Strikes me,' said Mrs Burton, 'they couldn't live much worse than the way some do at the moment. And now,' she said briskly, looking round as if she had made a sudden discovery, although I was sure nothing had escaped her eye since she had entered the room, 'I don't see your Bobby anywhere.'

Mrs Mullins sighed. 'He were that poorly with his chest again this morning I let him lay in bed.'

Mrs Burton sucked in her lips disapprovingly. 'And you've not brought him round to surgery, like Doctor Burton said.'

'It were nowt but a touch of fever.'

'He said to bring him round.'

The woman's tired face creased as if with pain. 'If our Jack could get work . . . We're that behind wi' Doctor's bill – '

'It's never right,' said the old man. 'Bosses and workers, that's how it's always been – '

'Drat the bill!' said Mrs Burton. 'Let's us go and take a look at him.' And, without warning, she thrust baby Sally into my arms.

They disappeared up the stairs with most of the children following eagerly behind them.

'It were good enough in my day,' said the old man. 'Take us wages at end of week and be glad on't – '

I looked down at the baby. Having relieved herself of the unwanted egg, she slept now, a dead weight. Between her open lips I saw one new white front tooth. I thought suddenly that my own baby would have been just under a month old.

'Don't take me wrong, mind,' said Mr Mullins, addressing the fire, not me. 'She's a good lass, is that one. Works her fingers to t'bone making them ruddy flowers for Robinsons. Kept me out of workhouse when dust in fettling shop did for my chest. But I were at Brice and Cadwallander nigh on twenty-five year. Bosses know how to run works, lads like our Jack know nowt about it. Stop going to chapel, start reading books, and where does it get a man?' He gave a rattling cough and spat once more into the fire. 'Out on his ruddy ear, that's what.'

The women descended again. Mrs Mullins took the baby from me. 'He'll come tomorrow to see your Bobby,' said Mrs Burton, moving to go.

'About the bill,' said Mrs Mullins. 'We'll settle, I promise, when our Jack gets work. . . .'

'It's never right,' said the old man plaintively from his corner. 'If it were good enough for my generation, why then not for his? Bosses know how to run works, working men know their place – '

'And everything in the garden's lovely!' said Mrs Burton as the door closed behind us and we came over the carefully brown-stoned doorstep into the crisp, frosty air.

'That table,' she said, jerking her head backwards at the

window with its net and its proud potted plant. 'Orange boxes, under the cloth. Put there so's other folk won't know.' And she strode off to where the battered Austin was parked.

I followed her slowly. She looked at the horror in my face and gave one of her short, explosive laughs. 'Well, it's not Mayfair or Park Lane, lass. What d'you expect?'

I climbed into the passenger seat of the Austin and we set off jolting and rattling over the cobbles. 'What will happen to them?' I said.

'Oh, they'll go on living from hand to mouth. Jack Mullins'll not get work again. The second lad, Bobby, he's got TB and probably won't see his sixth birthday. The old man's lungs are rotten with silicosis, that'll take care of him. She'll go on having too many children. The Church will go on spouting platitudes. We've rid ourselves of your cousin and got a Labour man instead, but the politicians'll go on breathing out the same hot air. And the Mullinses will go on being poor. Folk say the poor have only themselves to blame, they say they're better off on the dole than working, even with the way they've cut it and cut it these last two years, they say Jack Mullins is either an agitator or a fool. But it's not true, lass. The poor are neither good nor bad. Just poor, that's all.'

I sat in silence for a while. 'And you brought me with you to be useful,' I said. 'But you didn't even need my help.'

'You looked after the baby, lass.'

'Yes,' I said quietly. 'I looked after the baby.'

She shot me a sideways glance. The car swerved to avoid a mangy dog lying in the middle of the road. 'Brice and Cadwallander,' she said, tangentially, as if her mind had been off reflecting elsewhere. 'There's nowt much else in this town, excepting the cutlery factory. It's ate up Josh Mullins, spat out Jack Mullins, and I've no doubt it'll take the Mullins lads into its maw one day. Take them in on indentures, keep them seven years as apprentices and one year as improvers, then lay them off the day they're due to earn a skilled man's wage.'

We were coming to the other part of town now, with its clean civic buildings and bright shops. A Salvation Army band was playing carols beneath the Christmas tree in the square. The car rattled noticeably less on the smoother roads.

'Season of goodwill,' she said. 'We're having a jumble sale, end of January, in case folk forget it doesn't have to be seasonal. For – ' and she rolled her tongue ironically round the words –

'the deserving poor. Happen if you're strong enough to go collecting votes for your cousin, you're strong enough to go round the houses out at Dingley Park, collecting a few of the gentry's cast-offs for me?'

'Yes,' I said. 'Of course.'

'If you can't drive a motor I've a bicycle to loan you. And you can start with your young Mr Cadwallander up in his baronial hall.'

'He's not my Mr Cadwallander,' I said.

She gave me another sharp glance. 'There's folk as say – ' She stopped, her eyes suddenly on the street ahead as the car juddered in and out of tramlines. 'Well, I reckon the least he owes us is a fat donation, any road. If someone could sweet-talk it out of him.'

My face spread in a slow smile of comprehension. She had extricated us from the tramlines now, was looking at me again.

'In this world, lass,' she said abruptly, as if concluding a business deal, 'there's nowt for nowt.'

Then, as if she regretted the abruptness, she flashed at me one of her instantaneous smiles.

'Besides, fresh air'll stop you looking like a wet weekend. There's enough consumption in this town without the rich folk adding to it.'

There had been much debate about what to do, meetings with Meredith's agent, private discussions with Sybil about whether to drop the constituency, stand for the next safe seat at a by-election, and shake the grime of the North from the family's heels forever. In the end nothing was fixed upon except a hasty departure for Christmas in London. When I announced that I should like to stay behind my decision was received with equanimity. After all, there was not much mischief I could get up to in such a godforsaken place, it saved despatching me expensively to Switzerland, and, to Sybil at least who, even though the political advantage had been so unfairly removed, saw other obvious elements of convenience, it meant that I might still be able to make a go of things with Archie.

I spent Christmas with the Burtons and afterwards started with a will upon the mission to convert Archie which Mrs Burton had outlined for me. Now that nothing was expected of me I seemed to get on with him a great deal better, feeling sorry for him rather than irritated. And he was so glad of a willing ear that we became almost friends again, until towards the beginning of spring we were spending two or three evenings a week together, either at the de Lisles' unwelcoming red-brick house or at his bleak mock-gothic mansion up on the hill above Dingley Park; he had even agreed to teach me to drive. I did seriously doubt that I could influence him for, though his accounts of his struggles with old Brice always made him out to be the hero, I could easily read between the lines his impotence and frustration; and besides, they seemed, Mrs Burton and he, to be speaking two completely different languages. But I did, from time to time, nevertheless determinedly try.

One evening I tackled him about the latest batch of lay-offs Brice and Cadwallander were rumoured to be considering.

'Look, old thing,' he blustered. 'You just haven't grasped it, don't y'know. Question of the readies. If we don't cut out our cloth and all that rot, we haven't the jolly old shekels to pay the preferential shareholders.'

'But the shareholders,' I said relentlessly, thinking of the well-fed, well-breeched people at Meredith's election meetings, 'aren't out of work and starving. And don't tell me again that your workers are better off on the dole, because I've seen them. Which is more than you ever have.'

'Ordinary shareholders don't get a bean, old thing. Haven't for two years.'

'There you are then!'

'No I'm not. Preferential shareholders expect a company to stump up. They're apt to get shirty at AGMs if the old doubloons aren't forthcoming.'

I took him through it all again, the degradation of not having work, almost worse for the men than the poverty, the way it made young men old before their time, loitering on the street corners, bereft, purposeless, the way the women slaved endlessly to make money stretch, taking in piecework or washing, queuing to join the eternal cycle at the pawnshop, redeemed on Saturday, pledged again on Monday, scrounging for their families the rejects from the slaughterhouse, slink or braxy, in the belief that diseased meat was better than no meat at all. I offered again to take him and show him. His face grew pinker, the furrow between his eyebrows deeper.

'It's the brass, old thing. Bank's breathing down our neck about the bally overdraft as it is. Hard world and all that. But there you are.'

I sighed. 'What you mean is that money's more important to you than men – that you're heartless, Archie.'

He reared up indignantly. 'I should jolly well say not. Even asked the works manager about your chap Mullins, the other day. Fellow thought I was cuckoo. Foreman says the blighter's a blasted Bolshie, wouldn't have him back at any price. Nothing doing there, I'm afraid.'

'Nothing doing anywhere,' I said.

He looked mournfully at his bitten fingernails. 'Be fair, old thing. Difficult times. Do my best.'

But two days later, after a board meeting, he appeared, bright pink and beaming.

'Not paying dividends on preferential shares.'

'Does that mean there won't be any lay-offs after all?'

'Argued like billy-o. Got the whole board round. No lay-offs. Not for the time being anyway.'

'Oh, Archie!' I was useful, at last I was useful. I was so pleased I kissed him on the cheek.

He bridled, began to stutter. 'Look here, old girl. Obviously things can't be – well, as they used to be. But – bygones be bygones, what? You're lonely, I'm lonely, both of us stuck in this wart on the face of the universe. What say we make the best of a bad job and – '

It had taken me a moment to understand his drift. 'No, Archie,' I said, as gently as I could. 'I'm very sorry, but I still love Felix.'

He was crestfallen for a couple of days, but then seemed to shrug it off. And I, it suddenly occurred to me, was better, no longer numbed, no longer actively unhappy. I had begun to put on a little weight, I could once more play the piano with unalloyed enjoyment. I had discovered a purpose, I was, in a modest way, useful. And it seemed to me now, with my renewed optimism, that I had not lost Felix forever, that I was simply waiting for him, and that if I could bear a while longer in limbo my patience must inevitably be rewarded.

One afternoon a week later I went up to Dingley Hill for my driving lesson and found Archie pacing the miniature baronial banqueting hall that was his drawing room with an agitated expression on his face.

When he saw me he looked first embarrassed and then almost afraid. Beginning to speak, stumbling, apparently thinking better of it, he thrust a copy of the *Daily Mail* silently into my hand.

It was only a small paragraph at the bottom of the page and it took me some time to find it:

> PARIS WEDDING OF U.S. HEIRESS
> Secret Romance with British Artist.
> *By Our Social Editress.*
> Miss Nancy Lanning Vandenbergh, daughter of the late Mr and Mrs Julius P Vandenbergh of Boston, Mass. and heiress to the $6,000,000 Grants Biscuits fortune, was married here quietly today. Her bridegroom was Mr Felix de Lisle, the British artist and stage designer.
>
> Mrs Vandenbergh de Lisle, who is 21, inherited her huge fortune when she was only sixteen, making her at that time one of the youngest millionairesses in the United States. Mr de Lisle is in Paris for the first performance of *Leda and the Swan*, the second work he has created with Vladimir Tarantin for the renowned Tarantin Russian Ballet, a work which was acclaimed with wild enthusiasm by the Gala Night audience . . .

It was April 1924, just one year and one month after he had left me.

Since my illness I had worn Felix's ring concealed beneath my dress on a chain about my neck. That night I took it off, the ring that was not his father's, and threw it on the fire. Three months later I married Archie.

CHAPTER THIRTY-TWO

Diary of Adele Ward.
Shakespeare Villas, Balham.

21st February, 1895.

M confined to bed with a recurrence of the indisposition which struck him down six weeks ago and which brought up such an ugly sore on his lip he was obliged to keep dabbing a handkerchief to his mouth to preserve his vanity. This time the doctor, on inspecting the rash, has diagnosed scarlatina. The patient does not require my ministrations, indeed seems positively to shun them, saying he is not on any account to be disturbed; so I have consigned him to the mercies of the maid-of-all-work and am left as usual, immured within the cheerless confines of these dank little rooms, to that desert of sketching and embroidery and trivial domesticity which M is pleased to call 'my own devices'.

Upon M, despite his frequent cursing of his lot, our reduced circumstances take the lesser toll: not all his acquaintance count themselves amongst the respectable, whose friendship is measured in pounds and guineas and declines in proportion to our possession of them. M may still cut a dash, with his moustachios and cane and lavender gloves at the Tivoli or the Empire. But for M's wife, a respectable married woman, our removal here renders life very different: except in the case of this indisposition of his, M is mostly absent; my two or three friends he has long since, to suit his own ends, estranged from me; and there are few of our former acquaintance who will leave cards in a neighbourhood inhabited by bank clerks and so ungenteelly plentiful of butchers' shops. Thus I, respectable Mrs Montague Ward, sit imprisoned within these walls like a stuffed parakeet beneath a glass dome. Even the refuge I once took in foolish dreaming of a Beau Sabreur or a Bertie Cecil is now denied me, for in the deceiving pages of those vapid romances I see only the most bitter and taunting irony.

Oh, and yet – when I consider this prison that is marriage, without whose chains a woman is of no account, yet within which is at best an empty void and at worst cruelty and oppression – oh, how I still long for the delusion of love which would make it tolerable. Is it truly only a delusion? Surely when I remember poor dear Mamma and the many years of happiness she and Papa gave each other, I must avow that love exists. Surely I have only to recollect dear Papa to reaffirm my faith that there is, after all, some good in this world –

But an end to this tirade of self-pity!! Though it is past eleven there is a knock at the door and, since M is ill abed and the maid would slumber on through Armageddon, I must go to answer it. . . .

22nd February, 1895.

I am numb. As I take up my pen to write this it is as if I had been deprived of all thought, all feeling.

When I answered the door last night I found on the step an ill-favoured woman approaching forty in a shawl and a drab stuff dress who asked with great perturbation of manner for Mr Montague Ward. I told her my husband was unwell and on no account wished to be disturbed, whereupon she began to wring her hands and hop from foot to foot as if she might no longer contain her agitation.

'I've been sent to fetch him, Mum, fetch him and no one else.'

'By whom, may I ask?'

'By my – by a certain party, Mum. On a matter of life and death.' She eyed me, hesitating: then her agitation seemed to conquer her apparent need for discretion. 'Oh please, Mum, wake him. It's his friend the General. He's been took, Mum, took –'

I felt myself grow cold as ice. 'The – General?'

'General Cavendish, Mum. Took terrible ill. And my – a certain party needs your husband's help.'

Suddenly I had no time for thought. 'Wait here,' I said. Seizing in a whirlwind my mantle and purse, I was instantly beside her on the doorstep. 'Please, take me to the General. Take me where he is immediately.' And, seeing that she was about to protest, considering this substitution for M no proper fulfilment of her order, I thrust a coin into her hand.

There was a hansom cab waiting at the kerb. It was very dark and I could by no means make out where we were going: we seemed to rattle on endlessly, over cobbles and tramlines, down squalid streets, as if we should never reach our destination. To my imploring questions as to my father's health my companion would vouchsafe no more than a repetition of: 'Took, Mum. Took terrible bad,' and, on my enquiring whether we were going to his Club, merely gave a strange little laugh.

'And, if I may be so bold, Mum – what may you be to the General?'

'I'm his daughter,' I said.

She seemed to subside into the seat as if the air had all at once been expelled from her. 'Oh Lor!' she said. 'That's been and done it!' But before I could ask her more we drew up at an indifferent-looking dwelling in a narrow street and began with great haste to mount the stairs to the first-floor apartments.

The vision that met us on the threshold made me step back, aghast. A creature in a heliotrope nightgown larded with lace, her eyebrows painted, her face powdered and crudely rouged, her hair hennaed and dressed, though with great disarray, in a style that mocked her evident half-century of years, stood with her hands pressed to her bosom, weeping copiously.

'Oh he's gone, Marie! Princie's gone! The doctor's left not five minutes ago. Not a spark of life in him, he said. My poor Princie, snuffed out like a candle, gone, gone!' And, clasping the hands of my ill-favoured companion, she began upon a renewed paroxysm of weeping, the tears charting great channels and tributaries in her painted cheeks.

I fancy I gasped for, all at once, as if aware of another presence, she peered toward where I stood in the darkness. 'But we must be strong, Marie. For my Princie's poor wifie and his little girls, we must be strong. Have you brought the gentleman, the one Princie said was a man of the world and would know how to avoid scandal?'

'Fine chance of that now,' said her maid, which I took the ill-favoured woman to be, although her manner towards her mistress was most disagreeably familiar. 'I been and done it, haven't I? I been and brought one of them little girls instead!'

The effect of this announcement upon the Creature was striking. Thrusting the maid aside, puckering her carmined mouth into a smile of fatuous adoration, she flung herself upon my neck. 'Oh, the poor wee thing, the poor little orphaned lamb! Oh, he talks ever so much about you, does my Princie – oh, what am I saying? – oh, you must be strong, we must all be strong! – talked about his little Jessica and – and you must be his sweet little Adele!'

I was drawn into a meanly-proportioned sitting room, a chamber crammed with gimcrack furniture, gaudy with mirrors, bedizened with bric-à-brac, cheap souvenirs and photographs in tinselled frames. Releasing myself from the Creature's embrace, which was repulsively odorous of cheap scent and gin, I stared about me, bewildered.

'What has happened to my father?'

'Oh, my love, my poor duck! He was just giving me my goodnight kiss when, "Twinkle," he says – he calls me Twinkle, you see, on account of my being the star in his firmament, so he says, and this little home of mine his Seventh Heaven – "Twinkle, there's a storm in my head." Then he's sick to his stomach and turns a horrible colour and falls back and – oh, you must be strong, my duck, will you take a little gin to fortify you? – no, I suppose you won't, seeing as you're a lady – oh, my Princie, my dear, dear love, gone, gone!'

Her words seemed to flow about me in a meaningless stream. Surely this tawdry room and the Creature within it could not be real, surely they were merely figments of my neurasthenic imagination?

'I wish to see my father,' I said.

She appeared taken aback. 'Oh, my love, I don't – well, the doctor's done his best to tidy him up but – a lady like you – he's not properly decent and – '

As if in a trance, paying no heed to her protestations, I walked past her and into the bedchamber.

An endeavour had been made to smooth the soiled and rumpled sheets and to lay out the man on the bed with some semblance of dignity, an endeavour rendered vain by the livid purple of the face, its blue lips twisted into a gruesome leer, and by the nakedness of the corpse, attired as it was only in combinations; someone, in mercy, had closed the dead eyes. I stared at this lifeless thing, this relic of a well-nourished, finely-built man of three score and ten; I recognized the broad span of the chest, the handsome white whiskers, thrown now into ghastly relief by the grim discoloration of the face, the high dome of the forehead beneath the crest of hair where I had been wont, as a child, in playful affection to run my fingers; but I saw in its nakedness, in the frightful countenance twisted by death into that last lascivious grin, nothing, not a whit of my proud, upright, honourable father, the father who had presided over our family prayers and mediated in our nursery quarrels and taught us to know our duty and been for twenty-three years the meaning, the purpose, the sole object of devotion of my dear Mamma's life. It was all at once as if he had never existed. Turning aside, I quitted the room.

The Creature hovered in the doorway, bolstering herself, between sobs, with gin and water.

'You must forgive him, my duck, you must forgive my poor Princie – we couldn't help ourselves, I had plenty of gentlemen make me offers but he was always the only one for me, my Princie, my Prince Charming – I call him that because I was playing in Cinderella at the Empire when I met him – well, I was appearing as the Prince to tell the truth, but I had the legs for it, principal boy, in those days, you see – and he came and took me out of the Halls, my Princie, and set me up in this little place and gave me all these lovely things – ' Here, gesturing at the tinselled room with a sniff, she wiped her eyes upon one heliotrope sleeve. 'Twenty years we had together, twenty blissful years – me waiting

here, keeping everything nice for him, him coming once a month, sometimes for a whole week at a time, when he could get away.' Again her mouth twisted into that girlish, adoring smile which, contrasting strangely with her brimming eyes and smeared, tear-cracked mask, gave her a ridiculous, clownish appearance. 'Twenty years – oh, I know it wasn't respectable, but we couldn't help ourselves – he didn't care about me not being his class, didn't care what the world said – he wanted to make an honest woman of me, my Princie, would have married me tomorrow if he was free – but what with his poor wife, your Mamma, being a helpless invalid all these years – well, he'd got his duty, it wouldn't have been right, I told him so –'

I had opened my mouth to inform her that she was deceived, that my Mamma, far from being an invalid for twenty years, had been in the best of health until her last illness and that my father, in consequence of that unhappy event, had moreover been a widower these past six months: but suddenly I restrained myself; and, glancing around that mean and vulgar room – that Seventh Heaven in which my father had so strenuously pursued his 'astronomical studies', leaving my Mamma to the fond belief that he was at his Club – observing the cheap trinkets that were the sole reward of this other unstinting devotion, seeing before me all at once, not a low, brazen creature, but a sad, ordinary little woman of advancing years whose youth, beauty, warmth and hope had all been squandered in vain, I was overwhelmed with the tears the lifeless thing on the bed had held no power to inspire: for I discerned in the brimming eyes of my father's mistress, in her foolish, girlish, esctatic smile, that delusion of true love – that vicious delusion which makes us women willing prey to the cruelty and treachery of men; and in the destruction of my own last dream, I could not shatter hers.

'I am so sorry,' I said, touching the heliotrope arm. 'So very sorry for it all.'

Sawstead Hall, Hampshire.

28th February, 1895.

After the distasteful arrangements of the past few days, my father has at last been laid to rest in the family mausoleum. Of his nearest kin, only Sir Arthur and I were present, M being still too unwell to attend and J being brought to bed four days ago of a second son, a confinement induced two months prematurely, so Sir Arthur says, by the shock of our father's sudden demise. Sir Arthur, despite his good nature, is distant with me and we avoid each other's eyes: yet this does not surprise me, given recent events and J's open hatred of me. Neither was I surprised, on my father's will being read, to discover that the portion of his wealth I might have considered my rightful inheritance is, on account of my 'weak and extravagant nature', left to me only in trust, with M as the sole trustee.

(For the woman in heliotrope there was no benefaction, nor even a mention.)

J's new son is to be christened Felix, which Sir Arthur informs me is in Latin 'happy' or 'O happy one!' I pray this will indeed be the child's inheritance; but I fear, like love, human happiness is a mere delusion.

CHAPTER THIRTY-THREE

'The Second Purser's table!' fumed Archie. 'Not the Captain's. Not even the Purser's. But the bally Second Purser's table!'

The narrow dimensions of our cabin caused him, in his jig of impotent fury, almost to collide with the steward who was endeavouring to unpack his dressing case. His now permanently pink face welled crimson, sending into stark relief the little fair moustache he had grown in order to increase his dignity. 'Bally insult!' he snarled after the steward, who had retreated into the bathroom to lay out his shaving kit. 'Call this a first-class cabin? Not enough room to swing a beastly pussycat. Not even on the bloody Captain's table. Don't pay good money to be bally well insulted!'

Five years of marriage had taught me better than to respond. I sat upon the bed, staring at the canary and black jazz pattern on the coverlet, feeling a familiar sense of fatigue. From somewhere within the heart of the great ship came a vibration, a deep, consistent, powerful purring. I concentrated upon it, willing my senses one with it till it could grow inside my head and drown out everything else.

'Giddy bloody limit, that's what it is. Look here, my man, you ankle along to your bally Purser and tell him I want to see him in this cabin smartish, or I'll jolly well know why.'

The steward, who had re-emerged from the bathroom, paused for a moment as if he were uncertain who was being addressed, then turned slowly towards Archie with that look of deaf-mute innocence which head waiters and club doormen reserve for persons of Archie's height and demeanour.

'Was there something the matter, sir?'

'I should bloody-well say there is. Want to see your Purser-chappie, pronto.'

'I think you'll find the Purser is busy in his office at the moment, sir.'

'Then he can damn-well unbusy himself, can't he! You ooze off and tell him so, and look slippy about it. Oh, and while you're at it you can fetch me a stiff whisky and soda.'

The steward stared blankly until Archie, comprehending, fumbled in his pocket and produced a note. Then, folding the money and putting it in his top pocket, he went away without a word.

'Bally cheek!' said Archie, to his retreating back.

I sighed. 'Don't you think it's a little early for whisky and soda?'

I should have known better. With the steward gone I was the only target left.

'I see. One measly whisky and we're going to come the old acid again, are we? Well I'll have a bally whisky if I bally-well want one. I'll have five bally whiskies, I'll get bloody-well whiffled, don't y'know. Without my lady wife shooting me pi looks like some bally schoolmarm.'

The ship's engines continued their steady purr. The rug beside the bed, I noticed, echoed the pattern on the coverlet.

'No blasted support to a chap. Wouldn't care if we travelled steerage. Well, I'm not going to be given the bum's rush by a bunch of Frenchie sea scouts. I'm going to have that Purser on toast. Captain's table or nothing. I'll give him the beans!'

I suppressed another sigh. I could not precisely date the point at which Archie's obsession with the symbols of his status had begun, but I thought it was when old Brice had sold out over his head to United Northern Steel. There was no point in arguing. It had been the same with the Rolls-Royce which had somehow become an essential replacement for his Bugatti, the same with his refusal to sell Dingley Hill and move to somewhere more comfortable, the same with the rows of over-formal, ageing clothes already unpacked and hanging in the cabin's maple-veneered wardrobe, my uniform as Archie Cadwallander's wife and a person of standing in the community.

I tore my eyes away from the geometric configurations on the rug and looked up at him. He stood, his bow tie awry, mopping his crimson forehead with his handkerchief, a square, ungainly figure in a crumpled grey suit, his attitude of belligerence already fading into pathos, as it always did after such outbursts.

'I need some fresh air, Archie,' I said, pulling on my coat. 'I think I'll go and explore the ship.'

It was like a great floating city, that liner, with its dining room wider than the church of the Madeleine, its four-storey tiers of little shops in the well of the Grand Foyer, its Parisian pavement café, its longest bar at sea, a city bright with chrome and mirror glass, cool with Pyrenean marble, sleek with mile upon curving mile of glossy blonde wood, a city designed and appointed exclusively for pleasure. From the Salon de Conversation came the sound of the ship's band already inveigled into the rhythms of 'Miss Annabelle Lee' by Bright Young Things, embarked before us at Cherbourg and determined to dance their way across the Atlantic. In his cage, for the delectation of onlookers, the pastry cook was sculpting the centrepiece for dinner. Near the bar, at the ship-board office of the Compagnie de St Phalle, a little huddle of American businessmen listened to the staccato chatter of the telegraph transmitting quotations from Wall Street and the Bourse, anxiously following the movement of the company clerks as they erased and chalked up share prices, hoping that the rally which had checked the previous Thursday's record, reckless selling would continue to hold up. I found my way onto the promenade deck. Here the swell of the ocean was more apparent and I swayed slightly to get the measure of its movement. Plymouth Sound had already disappeared beyond the horizon and now there was nothing but a flat grey expanse of sea, broken only by the creamy churning of our wake. I leant against the rail, looking back to where the land had been. A stiff breeze came off the water, tugging at my hair and pitching saltily against my cheek.

I felt sorry for Archie, but to be sorry was not enough. It was never enough, to marry without love. What had I felt then, confronted with the absolute proof of Felix's betrayal? Shock. And anger, oh yes, anger. But hadn't I been deluded too, deluded in my despair into thinking that if my real life, the joyous, vibrant, growing part of it had been so summarily cut off, I could at least find some purpose in doing good with what little that was left? Had I not set out with such bright ideals on my mission to Archie's satanic city, had I not been so determined that where others had failed I should succeed, that I should use my influence as his wife to bring compassion and enlightenment into his dealings with his workers? If I were not allowed to love Felix, could not love Archie, would I not expend all my pent-up reserves of love upon humanity instead?

It had not been so bad for the first year. Such was my naivety, so determinedly did I nurture my ideals despite the stony ground upon which I had sown them, that it was a long time before I could force myself to see that they had taken blight and must inevitably die. Even when I discovered that Archie had been deliberately disingenuous about the question of preferential shareholders, that the company's finances had made inevitable the decision not to pay them and that the matter of lay-offs had been a separate, unrelated issue, a false rumour only, concocted to force the union into accepting lower rates of pay, I still did not give up hope. I could, I would, change things.

I had reckoned without the fact that I had, by my marriage, whether I liked it or not, joined the enemy. It was one thing to be Christie Ward, uninvolved, independent, and go about with Mrs Burton. It was quite another to be Christie Cadwallander, the boss's wife. Not only did Archie now have a claim upon my loyalty and my discretion, he had also constructed a life for me with a position in society to be upheld, people to cultivate, duties to be performed and functions to be attended. I could not, he would reiterate indignantly, as Mrs Archie Cadwallander, dine with the Mayor one night and then be seen fraternizing with the hoi polloi the very next day. I could not cut the ribbon for the ceremonial opening of the new electrically-driven mill, and then consort with Communists and Bolshies and rabble-rousers. Mrs Burton was banned the house. But, though I continued to see her and to help with jumble sales and the other activities of the Women's Health Society – a discreet participation in local charitable work was acceptable, indeed correct, for Mrs Archie Cadwallander, provided it did not amount to any unsuitable emotional commitment – she, too, had begun to draw away from me, would take me into fewer of her schemes, would sometimes even abruptly stop speaking as I entered the room. For her, as much as for Archie, I had, by my marriage, become somebody else, no longer 'us' but 'them'. And if that were true for Mrs Burton who knew me, it was even truer for the legions of the poor and unemployed she tried to help.

Life contracted around me. While I grew to know more and more people I could nod to distantly, I saw increasingly fewer people I could talk or laugh with. The baronial wastes of Dingley Hill seemed to resound with their emptiness. It was an unlovely house, more unwelcoming and difficult to heat than Monks Last. I came to feel that its dank air had somehow seeped into my very bones, so that I was seldom without a cold or chilblains or rheumaticky pains, seldom really well.

The business had continued to founder, wages had continued to be cut, men to be laid off. I heard Archie's schemes grow more grandiose as the company's resources dwindled, watched his consumption of whisky rise as his sense of his own power and position diminished. The bitterest blow came in 1926 when Brice and Cadwallander could not raise the money to restart its furnaces after the General Strike. Old Brice, the majority shareholder, sold out to the consortium of United Northern Steel without consulting Archie or anyone else on the board until it was a *fait accompli*. More jobs were lost in the amalgamation, new investment was curtailed. Though Archie was now Chairman of the Board, old Brice having had a seizure and died soon after, he was head of Brice and Cadwallander in name only, the real power devolving to the holding company and to the accountant they had brought in as Company Secretary to try to put Brice and Cadwallander's financial house in order. And now there were rumours of worse to come. Meredith had regained his seat in the 1924 election and, while as ever balked of the Junior Ministry, had held onto it still in this year's massive Conservative defeat – though only by a whisker as a result of a Liberal splitting the vote. On his rare visits to his constituency, he would bring back whispers of the Chairman of the Bank of England's plan to reorganize the steel industry into regional groups, closing down all other plants. Brice and Cadwallander, inevitably, would be one of the companies to be closed down. Archie and Meredith would sit in the study over the whisky bottle pondering the inequities of fate for hour after hour, and Archie would be more than usually liverish and unreasonable the next morning.

But then an unlikely thing had happened. At the beginning of the year business had begun to pick up, there was even talk of a small boom, of paying preference dividends again. Archie had latched upon it as a vindication of everything he had ever said or done, a recognition of his rightful place in society. We had acquired the Rolls-Royce, we had awarded ourselves a holiday. And so there we were, he and I. It was 26th October, 1929. And we were setting out across the Atlantic, bound for New York.

New York. Why did the mention of it always remind me of Felix? 'Mr Felix de Lisle, the distinguished British Expressionist whose second one-man show has taken New York by storm . . .' 'At the New York Met another collaboration by that talented duo of avant-gardistes, Vladimir Tarantin and Felix de Lisle . . .' Oh, snippets from newspapers were all I heard of him now, he had apparently severed contact with everyone in London, had never once returned to England. Handsome, brilliant, much-acclaimed Felix, with his cosmopolitan existence and his famously rich socialite wife. I could not imagine his life, had no concrete setting in which to place it, could not envision Park Avenue or the East Side or the fabulous monoliths that pierced the Manhattan skyline. Would I be happier knowing, seeing it all, picturing him here or here? I was now so completely excluded from his existence that I could not imagine comfort from distant glimpses of its backdrop, only pain.

I looked out bleakly at the great grey waste of the sea. My cheeks stung with the direct force of the breeze, my lips tasted salty with it. Dimly, I became aware of two men posing for a photographer beside one of the ship's life belts a few yards away from me, a small man huddled in an astrakhan coat and a tall man with spiky hair and glasses. A woman with a pencil and pad was taking notes as the photographer composed his picture. The shutter clicked. And the tall man, giving a sudden shriek of 'Christie!', abandoned his position and leapt with outstretched arms towards me.

It was Stenko.

'Oh, Christie! How wonderful to see you!' We embraced joyfully. 'And you are beautiful as ever. You have not changed at all.'

I smiled. 'But you've changed, Stenko. You look – well, quite splendid.'

And indeed he did. Though his suit still flapped about his long, bony frame, it was elegantly cut, and even his intractable hair seemed smoother as if it received regular ministrations from a master barber. There was about him something relaxed, contented. If he still reminded me a little of an umbrella it was now a very smart and exclusive one from the faubourg St-Honoré. He had, I noticed, almost entirely ceased to stutter.

'Success suits you. I was so pleased about your piano concerto. I read the reviews of your concert with Horowitz, I wanted so much to go to it, but – well, we live a long way from London now and Archie had organized us into a Conservative Association dinner dance that evening – '

He was positively beaming. 'Oh, so much has happened. I hope for a first performance of my second symphony in Chicago this winter, I am working on a score for Teddy, there is suddenly so much to do – ' He looked over his shoulder at the hunched figure in the astrakhan coat. 'Poor Teddy. They are writing an article about him for *Vogue* and they follow us everywhere – '

There was something in the look, affectionate, almost protective, and in the use of that mysterious, intimate nickname which I had only heard from Felix's lips before that made me understand the change in him.

'Oh Stenko, I'm so glad you're happy.'

'But you, what about you, Christie? You are married now. But you still have time for the piano?'

I smiled. 'I'm afraid I don't play nearly as much as I should. Anyway, my husband says the piano's as dead as a Dodo now, when you can hear the Savoy Orpheans every night on the wireless.'

I had meant it as a joke, but perhaps the words came out more bitterly than I had intended. His long, pale face registered profound shock.

'But tell me,' I said hastily, 'what are you both doing on board? Is the Tarantin Ballet giving another New York season?'

'Oh, no. The company is in South America. Teddy and I are taking a holiday, we are travelling from Paris with – '

He did not have to say the name. His stopping short was enough, and the sudden confused, half-guilty look that came over him, followed by a shadow of his old lugubriousness.

'Felix is on board this ship?'

Stenko gave an embarrassed shuffle.

I wished all at once that Archie's outburst had not distracted me from reading the passenger list. I felt a strange impediment to my breathing, suddenly my legs seemed to be shaking.

'I haven't seen him for so long,' I said, forcing my voice to stay calm. 'How is he?'

'Much as always, Mrs Cadwallander,' said another voice at my elbow. Vladimir Tarantin had brushed off the journalists and stood with his broad astrakhan collar turned up against the breeze, huddled and yellow within its depths, so that he seemed to me somehow shrunken, not so much the Great God Tarantin now as a small, inimical gnome. 'He eats little, sleeps less. And he works sometimes – when his wife permits it. She likes the idea that she is married to an artist, you understand, so long as he does not do anything so unforgivable as to shut himself away and paint.'

His wife. I had, in the shock of realizing I was suddenly so close to him, forgotten about his wife for a moment. But now, in the glitter of Tarantin's black eyes, in the venom that spiked his reference to her, that venom which he had once reserved for me, she was all at once made real. I became instantly filled with a dread of meeting her, meeting them both up here on deck, bumping into them on my way to our cabin. My hands were shaking so much I was obliged to plunge them into the pockets of my coat.

There was a tiny embarrassed pause. I did not want Tarantin to observe my confusion, although the expression with which he surveyed me was one of indifference, as if I were a spent force, as if it would be an unwarrantable waste of energy to direct his malevolence needlessly at me now there was a more important target for it.

'I – I must go,' I said. 'My husband will be wondering where I am.'

'But we shall see more of you,' said Stenko, smiling once again, extending his hand. 'I have learnt to dance now. I am even brave enough for the Charleston. We shall Charleston together, you and I.'

'Oh, yes, Stenko,' I said, knowing all at once that I would not dance with him, that perhaps I should not even speak to him a second time, knowing that Felix's being on board had changed everything, that I should have to keep to my cabin now like a prisoner. 'Yes, of course. But – I really must go.'

When I regained our cabin Archie was evidently no longer on his first whisky.

'Where the blazes have you been?'

I turned my back on him to remove my coat. 'A most surprising thing happened. Who do you think I met on the promenade deck?'

'Know bloody well who you met! Not cuckoo, don't y'know.'

His face was crimson again, his eyes bulging. So he had eventually read the passenger list.

'I bumped into Stenko and Tarantin.'

'And who else, old girl? Who else did you just happen to bump into?'

'Archie, don't be silly.'

Suddenly he had cast the whisky aside, was grasping me by the wrists. 'Silly's what I'm not, old girl. Knew the bounder was on board all the time, didn't you? Went on deck to meet him. Think I'm potty, think I won't catch on!'

His fingers were bruising my flesh. 'Stop it, Archie!'

'Think you can canoodle with him while my back's turned. Think you can make a monkey's uncle out of me – '

I tore my hands free. 'Stop it, Archie, this instant! I didn't know Felix was here and I haven't seen him. What's more I don't want to see him, I don't ever – ' I was suddenly ridiculously close to tears. 'I don't want to see him, can't you understand!'

The violence of my outburst seemed to subdue him. Looking at him, I felt once again profoundly tired. I went over to the bed and lay down upon it.

Retrieving the whisky tumbler, he drained it to the dregs. 'Blighter's even on the bally Captain's table. Him and your two nancy-boy chums. Gave the steward a oncer but did he produce the bally Purser? Had to go and see the fellow myself and he choked me off with a lot of eyewash. But that louse de Lisle's on the Captain's table all right!'

I turned my head away. 'Felix is famous now. So are the other two – even Stenko. And Felix's wife is one of the richest women in America.'

Archie stared discontentedly into his empty glass. 'Carrying on like a bevy of bally film stars. Not a gentleman in the whole bunch. At least in England being a gentleman still counts for something, don't y'know.'

I sighed. A silence fell during which I concentrated my mind upon the purring of the engines in the hope that the sound would induce a merciful blankness.

'Oh, nearly forgot. Maisie Hartford's on board. Phoned and invited us to a jamboree in their suite. Cocktails before dinner.'

'I don't want cocktails,' I said. 'I'm not sure that I'll go in to dinner. I think I'm getting a headache.'

Suddenly he was animated again. 'You'll bloody-well go to Maisie's beano. You'll bloody-well stay where I can keep my eye on you.'

He was leaning over me now, breathing whisky into my face. 'Think I'm going to leave you alone so you can get cased up with him? Think I'm going to make it easy, what, so you can hawk your mutton?'

I turned aside sharply, out of his range. 'I've no idea what you think, Archie. And I don't care. You disgust me!'

There was another silence. My head was turned away from him so that I could not see his face. Then I felt his hand upon my shoulder, felt his breath wetly in my ear.

'Oh Christie, old thing, I'm sorry. Very sorry. Didn't mean it.'

He was pawing at me, trying to roll me back towards him.

'Touch of the green-eyed monster. Don't be too hard on a chap. Didn't mean it, don't y'know.'

His lips were nuzzling moistly at my cheek. I sat up to escape them.

'Don't let's have another barney, old girl. Can't bear the ice-age treatment, cuts a chap to the quick. Forgive and forget, eh? Kiss and make up.'

I moved my head so that his lips missed my mouth and found my cheek instead. They left behind them a damp smear.

'Love you, old thing. Want us to be chums again. Have a jolly time in America. Second honeymoon and that sort of rot.'

I looked at him in silence. I had heard it all before, so many times. His eyes were pleading, moist, almost tearful. I put out my hands and straightened his tie. 'All right, Archie. I'll try. We'll both try.'

'That's the ticket, old girl.' Then his arms were about me, he was squeezing me against his chest, his lips were again pressed damply to my ear. I remained in this embrace for some moments, inert, motionless, managing only by an effort of will to subdue my instinctive impulse to tear myself free.

'Say you don't love him any more, old girl.'

My will broke, I pushed him away. His hands still clung to my shoulders, his colour was rising and with it the violence in his eyes.

'Say you don't love him. Say it! Say it!'

'Archie, for God's sake – '

'Say it, Christie. Say you don't love him any more.'

His face was pressed close to mine, his hands were hurting me. I sighed. 'I don't love Felix any more, Archie.'

My voice was toneless, the words automatic, the empty rote of a familiar ritual. But my repeating them thus, for the hundredth, for the thousandth time, would make no difference. We would both continue to know they were a lie.

CHAPTER THIRTY-FOUR

'Gosh, what a crush!' exclaimed Maisie Hamilton Hartford, weighed down by a huge corsage of butterfly orchids. 'One simply wouldn't have imagined one knew so many people on one teeny-weeny ship!'

Certainly the martini drinkers wedged elbow to elbow in her stateroom and the large number of bon-voyage tributes, baskets of fruit, bouquets of flowers, even a monster lucky horseshoe of red and white carnations which served as a centrepiece and a trap to the unwary edging backwards in search of space to flex their shoulders, gave testimony to the breadth and diversity of Maisie's acquaintance. She had married a Philadelphia man whose father had made a small fortune in real estate and whose forefathers, she assured me, had come over on the *Mayflower*. They had a neat apartment on Riverside and a darling mansion in Newport, but it had been just divine to revisit Europe, for one couldn't help feeling a teeny bit homesick from time to time.

'Of course you've heard about Dolly,' she said, 'and her divine Austrian doctor! It all began with Charlie and that dreadful business of the divorce. Apparently she was quite desperate until she consulted Dr Rubenstein. Her superego was sublimated, her libido was regressing and her existential dichotomies had positively gone to pot.'

I looked anxiously for Archie and saw, to my despair, that with his usual determination after seven whiskies to be the life and soul of the party he had gathered a little audience around the horseshoe and was popping his head in and out of it and making faces, like someone posing in a seaside photographer's booth.

'Anyway, he said she'd got the most fascinating unconscious

mind he'd ever seen. So she experienced total transference and married him. Isn't that divine?'

I looked down at the olive becalmed in my martini. I no longer wanted to observe Archie and I dared not glance towards the door. Perhaps there would be a gale, perhaps we should all succumb to seasickness and Archie would let me stay in our cabin. Anything would be better than this paralysing anxiety, this waiting, dreading, living in fear of the moment he, they, would walk through that door. For Maisie must have invited them – she had certainly issued invitations to everyone else. Mr and Mrs Felix de Lisle. I did not want to see them, I could not bear to watch him with her. I wanted to shut myself away, lock myself in our cabin for the whole six days of the voyage, immure myself in safety with the past, not be forced to recognize the present, not be compelled so cruelly to stare it in the face, the bitter reality of what I had lost.

And yet, if I did not want to see him, why did my eyes nevertheless keep flickering furtively about the room? Why had I discarded the fussy printed georgette the stewardess had laid out for me and chosen instead the most understated frock I possessed, simple, waisted black velvet with a low back, ornamented only by one small diamond pin? He had betrayed me, had used Aunt Jessica's lie as an excuse to forget me, had cast me aside so easily, so completely. Why should I want to see him now, why did I tremble, long for it? He was as everyone had told me he was, heartless, cynical, incapable of loving. Why could I not be content with my secret store of memory? Why did I want to demonstrate to myself that it was only an illusion? What, now, could I possibly hope for from him?

Maisie was still extolling the virtues of Freudian psychology. The crowd was thinning, it was almost time for dinner, if he was going to appear it would be any moment, I must be ready, I must be calm. Archie had apparently tired of his game with the horseshoe and framed in its curve I could now see two middle-aged American women, one plump, one preternaturally thin, deep in conversation. Their sharp voices drifted across to me.

'I guess it's just like her,' the plump one was saying, 'to make herself so darned exclusive.'

'Hmmm,' said the thin one. 'Though it's not as if she really had any class. The Grants' millions are only second generation money.'

I realized with a shock that they were talking about Felix's wife.

'Perhaps it's that good-looking husband of hers. If you ask me, she's terrified someone will steal him away.'

'Oh, but he's quite boringly faithful. Mercedes Modlinger flirted with him for a whole hour at the Vanderbilts' *conversazione* and got nothing but a distant smile for her pains.'

'Still, with all that money, dear, one would be bound to worry a little. About his motives, I mean.'

'They say he's wealthy in his own right. And his paintings sell for hundreds of dollars. Peggy Guggenheim has one in her collection, Rosa Schumacher bought three. Carlton says they're quite an investment.'

'Al says art will never be as reliable as stocks and bonds.'

'All the same there was a little orangey-yellow painting in his show that would have looked just darling over the mantel in my salon.'

'American Telephone and Telegraph, Sears Roebuck. Safe as Fort Knox, Al says.'

'Safer than a handsome husband, anyway. Poor dear Nancy. I guess I'm glad Carlton is short and stout.'

'And I'm glad I married Al for his money, dear. So much more comforting than having it the other way around.'

I reeled away from them. It was only gossip, jealous gossip. The Felix I knew would never have married for money, it was completely out of character, he could only marry for love. And yet supposing it were true, supposing he didn't love her, supposing he still . . . No, it was a monstrous thought. But I had to see him now, he had to come to the party, it was almost over, so many people were leaving, but surely he would still come.

'I say,' said Archie blurrily, 'cheer up, old girl.'

'Oh, I think psychoanalysis is just too marvellous,' said Maisie. 'Fancy having someone whose sole function in life is to listen to one. Howard just opens *The New York Times* and goes humph.'

He was not coming, we were almost the last to leave, he would not come.

'I'm sure one has the most fascinating complexes, if only one knew.'

He would not come, I thought with sudden horror, because he realized I would be there. I had wanted to hide from him but it would be he who avoided me, he who stayed in his cabin for the duration of the voyage, he who still felt the shame and disgust Rostova and Tarantin had spoken of. And I wanted him, I wanted to see him now, I could not bear it any longer.

'Give us a smile, old thing,' said Archie. 'Remember, you promised. Chums again.'

'I mean,' said Maisie Hamilton Hartford, 'wouldn't it be too, too divine to discover one was really madly in love with one's father or one's brother?'

And then, just as we were going in to dinner, just as I had given up all hope, there he was, at the top of the Grand Staircase, waiting for someone.

He was looking away from us, a tall, straight figure, negligently elegant, his left hand in his trouser pocket, his right holding a cigarette. The suddenness of seeing him nearly pulled me up short, but Archie, again fulminating about the Second Purser's table, noticed nothing. I realized with a pounding heart that we should have to pass him to go into the dining room. We were almost upon him now, yet still he was not aware of us.

I had somehow expected him to have changed in those six years, or that my anger and misery, at least, would have changed the way I perceived him, would have made him smaller, meaner. But he was still as he had always been, a tall, proud, commandingly handsome man whose air of languid indifference suggested an easy superiority, an unconcerned mastery of the world around him. He was deeply tanned, the waistcoat beneath his dinner jacket was fashionably white, there was, too, about him now a cosmopolitan gloss. As we drew closer I could see that the six years had, after all, given their emphasis to the lines around his mouth and eyes, had rendered the clear-cut contours of his face harder, leaner. But it was still the face I knew, the face I had touched, the face I had seen in all the intimacy of love.

I stood for a moment, confused, shocked, in pain with longing for it, that face, unable to believe it was now, in all its secret lights and shades, closed to me, unable, above everything else, utterly unable to believe that I was looking at the face of my brother. Then he glanced round and saw me.

Perhaps I was mistaken, but there seemed, fleetingly, in his eyes, in a tiny involuntary movement of his lips, to appear a similar look of shock. But, whatever it was, it was gone in an instant. His eyes became guarded, his mouth curved into that smile, charming yet remote, which I had always observed him to bestow upon distant acquaintances.

'My dear Christie. And Cadwallander. This is an unexpected surprise.'

He did not move, nor even extend his hand. And, at that moment, there appeared beside him a small woman, blondish, tanned, very much got up with costume jewellery and clearly dressed in the latest creation of Schiaparelli.

In all my miserable imaginings, though I had never quite conjured up for Felix's wife a face, I had always pictured her as beautiful. But my imagination could never have encompassed the striking image of this woman. Beautiful she was not, but rather what is termed *belle-laide*. Her face had no particular distinction of feature, the mouth being somewhat too full, the eyes too widely spaced, the chin too negligible. But there was about the totality of it, about the way the sun-bronzed skin stretched paper-thin across its bones, a compelling quality nonetheless, a nervous intensity, so that, as with the flanks and fetlocks of a thoroughbred, you had the sense of veins and sinews barely concealed, exposed and made vulnerable by the slightest movement. Her lips were scarlet, her eyes dark with kohl and heavy-lidded with Vaseline. Over her gloves her arms were encased in slave bracelets to well above the elbow, deliberate, outrageous counterpoint to her Schiaparelli chic. She gave off a great sense of striving for effect, of expecting to impress with her originality, of being the sort of person who only feels secure when she is stared at. She was, I supposed, very much the modern woman, half-sophisticate, half-gamine, the kind men describe as fascinating. Looking at her, I became instantly aware of my height, my own gawky thinness, the severity of my plain black dress. She filled me at one and the same time with a wretched jealousy and a vague unease.

Felix's hand lightly touched her elbow. 'May I present Nancy, my wife –'

But at this point Archie, who had plunged his hands firmly into his trouser pockets, drew himself up to his full five foot six and said, not quite distinctly, but with all the force and emphasis of a man who has drunk half a bottle of Scotch: 'You keep your bally hands off *my* wife, de Lisle. Or I'll bally-well break your bally neck!'

And, in the instant before I was forced to trail miserably off in his wake, I saw to my amazement that there flickered in the strange woman's face a look of alarm, almost of fear.

* * *

The gale did not transpire, the sea remained millpond calm. We became acclimatized to our circumscribed life, a life of unstinting luxury in which everything was dedicated to our pleasure, in which there was nothing for us to do but drift from the beauty parlour to the café, to write letters in the library or exercise in the gym, to sip cocktails and, if the band was suitably tipped, to dance the Charleston and the Black Bottom till dawn. Our bodies became tuned to the hidden vibration of engines, on deck our legs assumed a confident sea dog's gait. The band played 'Ain't Misbehaving' and 'Blue Moon' and 'What Is This Thing Called Love?', the crew put on a boxing match for our amusement, the men laid bets on the Ship's Tote and listened to the chatter of the Brokerage Office telegraph. And I, dogged by Archie, ceaselessly watched, endlessly suspected, tried in vain to steel myself to my torment.

We had not met Felix and his wife again. But then Archie's jealous outburst had made sure of that; there would be no question of any social contact between us. Yet, if we did not speak to them, did not even exchange glances or nods, I seemed often to see them at a distance, in the café or dancing. In the great mausoleum of a dining room with its three shades of grey marble, lit eerily from below by electrified Lalique motifs and painfully from above by a thousand glaring bulbs set into the lofty ceiling, the Captain's table was clearly visible from the Second Purser's through the illuminated fountain, and I was forced to keep my eyes firmly upon my plate or the person next to me in order not to give way to the temptation always to be looking over at them. He appeared easy, unconcerned, laughing with Stenko and Tarantin, always attentive to her. She seemed to hang upon his smiles, his laughter, like a compass needle trained, unwavering, upon its lode star. I felt, in moments when Archie's eye was not upon me and my glance was irresistibly drawn, as if I were a small child standing out in the cold, my face pressed to a stranger's window within whose golden glow unimaginable delights existed, from which, though separated only by the infinitesimal thinness of the glass, I was hopelessly and irrevocably excluded. He never saw me, never caught my eye, never so much as looked in my direction. The pain of it, this slow, deliberate torture of being so near and yet so infinitely far away from him, seemed at times unbearable. I wanted so desperately to talk to him, to go up to him and confront him with the fact of my presence, to elicit something from him, a smile, a gesture, any token, however small, that would make some concession to my continuing existence. And yet bear it all I must, and laugh and make small talk and do my best to convince Archie that I did not care, that nothing mattered less to me.

The task of shadowing me proved irksome even to Archie himself. I did not share his enthusiasm for deck quoits or shuffleboard and my presence hindered him from playing hail-fellow-well-met at the bar. After the first day he accepted that Maisie might chaperone me, and so she and I fell into a routine of having our hair done and our nails manicured and making up a four for bridge.

On the morning of the third day, October 29th, however, I managed to shake off both of them. My nerves jangled from the necessity of being perpetually on guard. Maisie's chatter was beginning to drive me to screaming point. I wanted just to look at the sea and think.

Quite a crowd of men had already gathered outside the Compagnie de St Phalle office as I passed it, waiting for the doors to open so the wireless operator could telegraph their brokers with orders for the day's dealings. When I came up on deck stewards were moving along the rows of rug-cocooned passengers serving biscuits and soup. The October sun glinted fiercely on the unruffled sea. I put my face to the breeze, shielding my eyes with my hand, feeling a welcome dizziness as my lungs filled with sharp air. Then suddenly something struck me a harsh little blow on the ankle.

'Naughty!' cried a guttural female voice. 'Always when I turn my back you are naughty!'

'But I didn't mean it, Fräulein Wessel,' came back a child's voice, American, shrill. 'My hand slipped. I swear it.'

I turned. A stout woman in the uniform of a nanny was shaking a small boy by the shoulders. I bent down and picked up the missile. It was a toy car, an exact miniature replica of its original down to the flying stork on the bonnet, a grey Hispano Suiza perfect in every detail except for a missing front wheel.

The child broke free from the nanny and ran towards me. 'That's my motorcar,' he said. I stood there, holding it, staring at him.

'You will apologize to the lady,' said the nanny.

'I apologize. I didn't mean to throw it. Really I didn't.'

I continued to stare at him. Conscious that he had engaged my interest, half-pleased, half-embarrassed, the child wriggled, then said conversationally: 'We've been to the playroom. There's a real carousel, with white ponies and music to go round by.'

I handed him back the toy, my eyes still on his face. A child's face, smooth, uniform, with that clear gold skin some children have that shows dark shadows beneath the lower lashes. What could you tell from a child's face? It was merely the stupid coincidence of the model car playing tricks with my imagination, making me see in the high cheekbones, the set of the eyes, the slightly too-wide mouth, resemblances that could not be there. I did not need to know, it was better that I did not know it.

'A real carousel,' he said. 'It was awful fun!'

'Don't bother the lady. You know you should not bother grown-ups.'

'He's not bothering me,' I said. And then the impulse was too strong to conquer, I had bent down to him, had put my hands gently on his shoulders so that my eyes were level with his. 'What's your name?' I asked.

He looked sulky now, as if my excessive interest irritated him. 'My name is Nicholas Francis St John Vandenbergh de Lisle.'

I tried to laugh. 'That's an absurdly large name for someone so small.'

'I'm not small,' he said indignantly. 'I'm four and a half years old, I live on Long Island, New York State and in Paris, France, I'm learning to speak French and German, and I bet I can whip you at deck quoits any time.'

I struggled with things that, when Archie's resentment of our barren marriage let me forget them, I could now keep from my mind for months at a stretch, little shell-nailed hands leafing through a wad of notes, the smell of gas and Rostova's voice urging upon me that moment of craven doubt for which I would never forgive myself. 'Yes,' I said. 'I'm sure you can.'

He surveyed me impatiently with the air of someone who is quite familiar with the foibles of adults but has long since given up the bother of trying to understand them. 'Why,' he asked impartially, 'are you crying?'

'I'm not,' I said. 'I – stupidly looked directly into the sun.'

'Oh,' he said. 'You're right – that is dumb.' Then, losing interest, distracted suddenly by something I temporarily could not see, he shook himself free and ran back across the deck.

'We've been to the playroom! There's a real carousel with ponies and music!'

The woman was in mink, draped casually over flannel trousers. She stared at me as, feeling all at once ridiculous and curiously guilty, I struggled to my feet. The child ran past her to the man who followed, leapt at him, was caught up in his outstretched arms and raised to shoulder height. I saw for a moment on the man's face as the child's eyes came level with his, as one hand freed itself to ruffle the tousle of blond hair, that gentle, absorbed expression I so remembered.

'Wessel!' said Nancy de Lisle, giving me a look of absolute recognition. 'I thought I told you never to let the boy talk to strangers.' She had a brittle voice, high-strung like the rest of her, sharp as a razor blade scraping glass.

Felix looked up from the child and again I fancied I saw that fleeting tremor of shock, followed instantly by the resumption of his impenetrable coolness.

'Not strangers,' he said, lowering the child gently to the ground. 'Christabel is – well, I suppose your first cousin once-removed, Nicky. I'm sure she will allow you to call her aunt.'

The mother had seized the child, was holding him against her with both arms. We stood, the four of us, transfixed for an instant by the awkwardness of the meeting, by the strange scrupulousness of his introduction, by the impossibility of breaking apart in any elegant, casual way. I felt Nancy de Lisle's eyes levelled at mine, felt suddenly the child held between us as if in confrontation, felt her gaze burn with something that could almost be hate. Archie's drunken words had clearly done their work. Sensing my own vision begin to blur and waver, I mumbled something about Maisie waiting for me and turned away.

I had promised after luncheon to be Maisie's bridge partner against the two American women I had overheard talking at her party. But though we closeted ourselves in the Salon du Thé there was a strange atmosphere which made it difficult to concentrate. It was not precisely possible to locate its cause, but there was a restlessness, a sense of unease which seemed to flurry the smooth waters of our ship-board routine like a treacherous undertow. I had noticed it at first at luncheon, had been dimly aware of a dissonance but had been unable to put my finger on what disturbed me, until I was all at once conscious that there were very few men in the dining room. The fat woman had laughed and said that at any rate she knew where her husband, Al, was.

'Yes,' said the thin woman. 'Carlton went with him. It's like a drug to those men. Take them to Europe, show them the Parthenon, the Doges' Palace, make them go see the Louvre, they'd still rather be hunched over that darned ticker tape finding out what's happened on Wall Street.'

Then Howard Hamilton Hartford, who had seemed rather tight-lipped and had eaten and said very little, had been handed a message by a chasseur in the middle of the meal, and had gone away never to come back. He had not said to Maisie why.

'Looks like it's something big,' said the plump woman. 'I guess they're all counting on making a coup.'

We had continued with our Lobster Thermidor but all the same, coup or not, there was a strangeness about it which crept occasionally into the conversation, rendering our voices shriller, our laughter a little too loud. And when I made my way afterwards to the Salon du Thé I noticed that the oddly silent crowd trying to penetrate the narrow confines of the Brokerage Office was now so great that it had spilled into the corridor and even into the bar, while in all the other corridors there were female faces in plenty, but not a single man's.

Maisie and I were a rubber down when we became aware of the voices. Her concentration, never of the best, seemed to have deserted her entirely and she looked edgy and pale. She had just bid an abstracted three Clubs to my cautious one Spade, and I was wondering whether I could manage to prod her ankle with my toe without being apprehended, when the first man's voice came quite clearly from directly opposite the open door of the Salon du Thé.

'American Telephone and Telegraph dropped fourteen points!' There was something odd about the voice, a little bubble like incipient laughter, which the speaker was finding it difficult to restrain. 'American and Foreign Power down twenty-two and a half points. Sears Roebuck down sixteen and a quarter, General Electric down thirty!'

'Hang it, Mort,' said a second voice. 'It's like last Thursday. It'll rally, give it time.'

'Westinghouse Electric nineteen points down, orders no longer accepted on Trans-America!'

'The Bourse is holding up, Mort. It'll rally, you'll see.'

'Steel fallen to one sixty-seven, Dupont's dropped seventy before the market even opened!' The bubble in the voice was more insistent now, rising, rising, threatening to take over. 'Goddammit, Steel was two sixty-one in February, American Telephone and Telegraph was three ten and a quarter. And I just watched it drop from two twenty to two oh six!'

'Simmer down, Mort, have a drink.'

'Grants was quoted one thirteen only yesterday. Do you know what they're selling at now? Four, goddammit! A miserable, lousy four!'

'Have a drink, Mort, have a drink.'

'A miserable, lousy, stinking four!' The bubble rose, swelled. 'No I won't have a drink, I can't have a drink. I can't buy a lousy drink! Don't you understand? I'm washed up, finished, goddam ruined!'

The bubble burst with a rattle. There was a sudden high-pitched whine like a dog in pain. Then the four of us sat, silent, fixed with horror, listening to the sounds of a man crying, piteously and without restraint.

His friend must have taken him by the arm and led him away for we heard the sound gradually diminish. Then a second later we were confronted with Archie, his face larded with sweat and crimson, his eyes nearly popping from his head.

'You won't believe it,' he said breathlessly, with the excitement of someone witnessing a disaster which for once has happened to the other fellow. 'You won't bally-well believe it! Bottom's dropped out of Wall Street! Whole bloody market gone kaput, bunkered, dished, up the spout!'

CHAPTER THIRTY-FIVE

On a ship designed exclusively for pleasure there is no equipment to deal with an epidemic of despair.

Men used to commanding, isolated now from their brokers, accountants, advisors by a waste of ocean, watched impotently as the Brokerage Office clerks slaved on into the evening, chalking, erasing, chalking, erasing, writing on the blackboard the story of their ruin. By the time Wall Street closed at 3 p.m. a record seventeen million shares had been sold. On some stocks where brokers had been forbidden to accept any more orders the amount of shares outstanding had meant that millions of dollars had been nominally washed away overnight.

I spent a great deal of time with Maisie, offering her handkerchiefs and sal volatile and what words of consolation I could. Howard still retained some of his capital but what had gone would certainly be missed.

'He says we'll have to fire at least half the servants,' she moaned, her chin quivering. 'And our darling house in Newport – he simply can't see any way round it, it'll have to be sold.'

Walking the deserted deck, I found Stenko, his hair on end, his suit flapping, his long face made longer by a bewildered frown. Tarantin, worried about his South American backers and about a season in Chicago he had planned for the spring, had apparently retired to their cabin for the duration of the voyage.

'I do not understand m–m–m–oney, Christie,' he confided, temporarily succumbing to his stutter. 'I do not see how men can be ruined by promises and pieces of paper. Felix spends all day at the Brokerage Office now. Nancy has lost everything, you know. It is not just her shares in Grants but all her investments. It is terrible, Christie. The doctor is giving her sedatives. She is most d–d–d–istressed.'

Even Archie, after his initial enjoyment of the drama, was falling prey to the general despond. 'Of course, couldn't have such dickey-dealing in the City,' he kept saying, as if to reassure himself. 'Blighters on Wall Street only got themselves to blame, don't y'know. No savvy, think they're still winning the Wild West.'

Rumour had it that in London, although the 30th had brought a rash of selling, it was mostly in foreign shares and the market was still holding up. The Bourse, too, while it had closed on the Wednesday in a mood of apprehension, had not given way to hysteria.

'America's a far cry from England, what?' said Archie. 'City'll weather the storm, you'll see.'

Patout's great slabs of marble seemed to give off more than ever a tomb-like chill, the curving miles of veneered maple to mock with their bland glossiness. When you heard a sudden sound you drew up startled, never sure whether it was laughter or tears. On the Wednesday the ship turned about and dropped anchor for an hour in a vain search for a man overboard. On Thursday the Loiré and Olivier by-plane, which was launched, torpedo-like, from a catapult mechanism high on the afterdeck, burst with an ear-shattering detonation out over our wake, dipped back and circled a boat deck thronged but silent, on its way to deliver mail to Manhattan which, though it would arrive in three hours and seven minutes' time, a full twenty-four hours before the ship docked, would nevertheless arrive too late.

Wednesday's trading had shown a small rally with what gains there were sustained. But on Thursday the Exchange did not open till noon and on Friday it was to be closed completely to give the staff of the Exchange Houses a much-needed rest. When the Compagnie de St Phalle office closed on Thursday night, when the rustle of orders thrust upon the spike and the rattle of the telegraph ceased, there fell upon its environs, in the corridors and in the bar, a deep and funereal silence.

But, if trading had stopped, our routine of entertainment and indulgence, like some mechanical process which once set in train cannot be halted, continued around us, in spite of us, unabated. The orchestra played Hutch and Noel Coward, 'Spread a Little Happiness' and 'Singing in the Rain'. Barmen applied the secrets of their art to Prohibition-free Gimlets and Whisky Sours, albeit that when a man is searching for oblivion artistry is by the by. The pastry cook, in his cage, continued to create wonders out of *choux* and *millefeuilles* as if what had been torn down could be reconstructed by the right combination of beaten egg, water and flour. And for Thursday, our last night aboard, the Gala Night on the boat deck was still projected. There was to be champagne, and dancing beneath the stars, and coloured Japanese lanterns strung amidships from masts and rigging.

Beneath the shadows of the raked funnels, flanked by rows of huge lifeboats swinging from their davits, we sat at tables spread with white cloths, shivering slightly as the night wind came off the sea. The two American ladies seemed to have been deserted permanently by their husbands, Howard Hamilton Hartford was silent, present only in body, Maisie tearful, Archie becoming increasingly drunk. The band, inviting dancing, had just struck up 'A Nightingale Sang in Berkeley Square' when suddenly I was aware of someone standing over our table, swaying slightly but fixed there nevertheless with an intensity of purpose that would not be checked.

It was Nancy Vandenbergh de Lisle. And her eyes, oblivious of the rest of the company, were trained upon me.

She was wearing a Chanel sequined jacket with a green carnation, over a sweep of black satin. Wound around one of her wrists was a handkerchief of emerald chiffon, around the other a great many bracelets of ornate design. But if her dress suggested the utmost attention to effect her face formed a strange contrast with it. The skin beneath the tan was ashen, the mouth a crooked smear, the eyes, from a blur of kohl, were red-rimmed, underlined with livid shadows. There was in the whole high-strung structure of it a sense now not so much of veins and sinews scarcely protected but of every nerve-ending laid open, raw, tangible, painfully convulsed. Her lips worked, her fingers plucked at the emerald handkerchief as if she would tear it in two. Her eyes, seeing me, not seeing, were naked with hate.

'You think I don't know, don't you?' The razor-blade voice was slurred, barely on the edge of control. 'You think I don't notice you following him everywhere, eating him up with your eyes. Well, he's my husband, do you hear, mine, and he's going to stay that way! I have your measure, lady, and I'm cleverer than you are. I'll have him followed, I'll hire private detectives, I'll have you watched every step you take, every place you go. I saw you talking to my baby, I saw you try to turn him against me. Well he's my son, my baby, and nobody takes him away from me! Nobody, do you hear! I'll die first! And I'll make you wish you never lived, I'll get every decent house from Manhattan to Long Island closed against you, I'll make sure everyone you meet knows what you are. So just you take your eyes off my husband. And don't ever, ever come anywhere near my baby again! Because I know you, do you hear! I know, everyone on this ship knows! Even your own husband knows you for the scheming little tramp you are!'

She stood for a second, her nostrils dilated, every naked muscle aquiver. Then seizing a glass of champagne from the table she dashed the contents into my face and hurled it, splintering, to the floor.

Above the sound of its breaking her laughter came suddenly, just as sharp and high, rising within her, rising, overpowering her, holding her in its grip so that now not only her face twitched but every part of her was stretched and quivering. A tall figure appeared behind her, there was the crack of a hand coming down upon taut skin. She seemed for a moment completely still. Then her arms flew wide, her head drooped sideways, the green chiffon fell across her face and she crumpled like a broken doll. Felix caught her as she swayed, lifted her, put one arm around her waist to support her, with the other cradled her head against his chest. They remained for a second thus, she limp, helplessly sobbing, he with his arms about her, holding her to him. I saw the red stain on her right cheek, growing, the mark of his palm where he had slapped her, and above it his hand, infinitely gentle now, stroking her hair. Then, very slowly, he led her away.

The champagne ran from the curls on my forehead over my cheeks and down my neck and shoulders, spreading darkly across the front of my dress. Little beads of it clung to my eyelashes like sticky tears. I was conscious of an immense silence in which necks were craned, heads from tables all around us were turned towards me, staring. Maisie burst into tears, Archie mumbled something I could not hear. A whisper grew, women's voices were raised in question, fingers pointed, someone laughed. Slowly and carefully, not looking to either side of me, not touching the champagne stain on my dress, I rose to my feet. Then, drawing myself up, lifting my chin as high as it would go, I walked in a firm straight line to the nearest gangway and off the deck.

My composure lasted only until I was out of sight. In the deserted corridor, leaning my head against glossy wood, I stood for a moment, feeling the first flood of my tears mingle with the champagne, biting the back of my hand to choke the noise of my crying. But I could not stay there forever; someone, Maisie, Archie, would be down any minute. I did not want their fussing, their consolation, I wanted to be, as I had not been allowed to be for the five wretched days of our voyage, somewhere quiet and alone. Stumbling, I made my way down to the promenade deck.

In the darkness the ocean, illuminated eerily by light spilling from row upon row of portholes behind and above me, by the great, garish dazzle of that floating city, looked infinitely wide and deep. A velvet sky glimmered with stars. Leaning against the rail, not noticing the way the breeze swept my bare shoulders and tugged at my hair, I concentrated only upon where sky and sea merged together into that measureless darkness. I began to feel calmer. From the top deck strains of the band playing 'I'll See You Again' drifted oceanwards. I put my hands to my ears to shut the sound out. I closed my eyes.

But, though my eyes were shut, I could still see them, she leaning against him, giving up in total trust the full weight of her body, he with his arms around her, his hand in her hair, his face, his whole attitude gentle. And there came back to me with such force the memory of how he had once held me like that, touched me, softly stroked my face and hair, that I could almost feel his body against mine, feel his lips on my cheeks. I remembered the way he had looked at the child, that tender, concentrated, loving look which recently I had struggled still to picture until, in that instant of recognition, its imprint had been so painfully renewed. Whatever she was, he loved her. He loved her and he loved the child she had given him, her child, his son. He loved her, and when she had attacked me, humiliated me in front of everyone, it had been her he had instinctively turned to protect, her he had comforted, not me. The tears welled up in my eyes again at the misery of it and the unfairness. I shivered and sobbed in a paroxysm of jealousy. And Archie, it was all because of Archie and his drunken outbursts. If Archie had not brought it all about by his stupidity I could have kept my illusions, I need never have known, I need never have been faced with the completeness of my defeat.

I stood, racked with sobs, surrendering to the utter wretchedness of it all. Then something, perhaps the sheer violence of my jealousy, pulled me up. I looked out upon the waste of sea and sky and saw, with sudden painful clarity, the truth of my predicament. If I had been shamed and humiliated just now it was no more than I deserved.

I had never in all these six years brought myself to accept that Felix might really be my brother. Despite the abortion, despite the nagging doubts, the coincidences I could not explain, despite his own acceptance of it, I had continued in my heart to deny it. And I had come to use that denial as a contemptible excuse. Oh, how easy that excuse had made it for me to pretend that he had never really left me or stopped loving me, how readily I had used it as a justification for all my failures and inadequacies, how willingly I had let it blind me to reality. Why, even after all these years, when I had discovered he was on board the ship and that I was bound to meet him, I had somehow cherished the fantasy that the moment we saw each other nothing would have changed, that we would continue together where we had left off.

But everything had changed. He was married and had a child. I was married to Archie. It no longer mattered whether he might or might not be my brother. It was not my proper concern whether he loved his wife and son. It was not even admissible to speculate what his feelings might now be towards me. The past had been cancelled out irrevocably. His duty must above all be to his family, mine to my husband. He saw this duty, held to it unwaveringly, and that he did so from love it was not my place to lament or question. But I, how had I held to mine? Archie had married me with a knowledge that would have turned most men away from me, but how had I repaid him? Would not all his childish excesses, his exhibitionism, his drinking have been tempered if only I had tried a little harder to love him? Was not his jealousy, after all, justified? Had I not in every treacherous thought and look betrayed him, not just in these five days but for all the years of our marriage? And Felix's wife, had she not a right to her jealousy too? Oh, her reaction to Archie's outburst had been irrational, extreme, brought on by the shock of losing her fortune. But had she not unwittingly been correct in her suspicions? Could I have made Felix love me again, would I have held back for a moment?

I could not stop loving Felix, you did not turn off love like water from a tap. But I could try, day by day, to let my love diminish, to exist not within it but in spite of it, to bury it somewhere it could hurt me and not others. Archie had lived with the pain of being second-best for years. Nancy de Lisle had seen me, in her anguish, as the last intolerable goad that had driven her into hysteria. All I had suffered, other than what had been of my own making, was to have a glass of champagne thrown over me in public. I had sticky hair and a ruined dress, but it seemed I had otherwise got off rather lightly.

I wiped my eyes with the back of my hand. The orchestra was playing 'Glad Rag Doll'. A little upsurge in the breeze ruffled the water. I became all at once aware of someone standing at the rail near me. My heart lurched. I did not need to turn to know who it was.

'You're shivering, little one,' he said. 'May I put my jacket around you?'

Oh God but it was one thing to know your duty and another to hold to it, quite another, against the unexpected tenderness in his voice and his old affectionate way of addressing me, to resist the temptation to fling myself into his arms, to beg him, implore him to stop loving her and remember he had once said he loved me. I drew in my breath, tensed my shoulders in a vain attempt to control my trembling. I did not turn round. I did not want him to see my face, to know that I had been crying, to see how close I was to tears again. And besides I dared not look at him.

'Thank you, Felix. But I'm all right. I like the breeze. It's cold, but it concentrates the mind wonderfully.'

Despite my efforts at control, my voice sounded edgy, brittle. There was a pause. Then he said: 'Christie, I came to – '

I cut across him. 'Please don't be so disloyal as to apologize for her. I know she's upset and couldn't help it.'

'I agree,' he said quietly, 'that would be disloyal. But it's not why I came. I wanted to say how sorry *I* was. And to see if there was anything I could do.'

I struggled to keep back the catch in my throat. 'There's nothing,' I said. 'Really, I'm quite all right.'

There was another silence in which the band swung suddenly into 'Is Izzy Azzy Wozz?'

'Christie,' he said, very softly, 'please, at least look at me – '

'It would be wrong, too,' I said quickly, hearing again the edge in my voice, hearing my words tripping over one another in blind haste, 'for me to apologize for Archie. I don't think he imagined anyone would take him so seriously. He's got a long memory and he's never really forgiven you for his ending up in the Mountalbans' fountain.'

Beneath the strains of 'Is Izzy Azzy Wozz?' I could hear the water lapping against the ship's hull. I willed myself to concentrate on the calm, regular, watery whispering.

'She's ill,' he said, all at once. 'She had a wretched childhood and sometimes the world seems to turn upside down for her. Losing the money is more than she can bear.'

How gentle his voice was when he spoke of her. Despite my resolutions, I felt my jealousy surging back. I clenched my hands upon the rail.

'Why don't you tell her?' I said. 'If she knew – ' I battled with the words – 'if she knew the truth she'd realize there could be nothing between us.'

'I promised I would never tell anyone you were my sister, and I never have. My dear Christie, I owe you that.'

I thought of Tarantin and Rostova and knew he was lying. Suddenly, angrily, I wanted to lash out at him.

'Well, I absolve you from your promise,' I said. 'After all, it was years ago, it's finished, forgotten. You're married, so am I. We both have different lives now. I don't think about it any more. I'm afraid I've even lost your ring.'

As I spoke I felt the knot growing in my throat, knew that it was only myself I hurt with my stupidity, for, since he no longer cared for me, my anger could only glance off him. And yes, though he hesitated for a fraction, when his voice came again it was cool and even, turning my shaft back upon me as I deserved.

'I'm glad that's how you feel,' he said. 'I wanted very much to know that you were happy.'

My eyes burned, the obstacle in my throat threatened to overwhelm me. 'As you are happy?' I said.

'Yes,' he said, almost abruptly. 'As I am happy.'

Up on the top deck the saxophone, with a strident wail, began a solo. And far away, beyond it, I thought I heard someone calling my name.

He, too, said suddenly: 'Christie – '

The call came again, this time more distinctly. 'It's Archie,' I said. 'Please, Felix, leave me now. I'm quite all right, and there's no point in causing any more trouble. Please! Please go.'

I could feel him hesitate for a moment. But when, eventually, I turned round there was no one to be seen except the short, square figure of Archie, weaving rather unsteadily along the deck towards me.

'Why the blazes didn't you go to our cabin? And who was that with you? It was him, wasn't it, old girl? Gave me the slip so you could meet him. Turn my bally back for a minute and you're flinging yourself into the rotter's arms!'

'Archie, he only came to see how I was.'

He had me by the elbow, was holding me fast, frogmarching me along the deck. 'None of his bally business. I'm your husband, in case you've bloody-well forgotten. And I want you in our cabin, don't y'know, old girl. Now!'

He thrust me by the arm into the room so that I tripped on the rug and fell sideways against the wall. Then he slammed the door shut.

'Archie,' I said, 'there's no need for this fuss. I'm perfectly all right now.'

His face was purple, I saw from his eyes that he was very drunk. 'All right are you, old girl? Well, I'm tickled pink to hear it. Hoo-bloody-well-ray! Yo-blinking-ho!'

Then before I realized what he was doing he brought up the flat of his right hand and struck me with it across the face.

'That, old girl, is for meeting the blighter on the sly!'

He raised his hand a second time.

'And this one's for letting me down, for making me feel a bally sap in front of the whole bally boat!'

I reeled against the wall. My nose felt numb and there seemed to be a trickle of blood coming from it.

'Think old Archie's cuckoo, what? Think I won't tumble to your jolly pranks, think it takes some bug-house American filly to go off her rocker before poor old sap-headed Archie can add two and two? Well, the worm has turned, old thing, don't y'know. The worm has abso-bloody-lutely turned! You'll think another think the next time you try to pull the wool over old Archie's eyes. You're my other half and you'll bally-well behave like it. No more making Archie feel a prune in public. No more turning the cold shoulder every time a poor cove feels like canoodling. I'm going to get my greens, old thing, if it means you end up not walking for a week. You carried his bloody sprog, why can't you bally-well have mine? Not Archie's fault, nothing wrong with Archie! Want a son, old thing! Going to see you give me a son if I ruddy-well have to force you!'

He was tearing at me, nearly wrenching my arm from its socket, dragging me towards the bed. Stumbling over the rug again, I fell face-down across it. He fell on top of me, pulling and tugging until he had me half-rolled over. I tried to lash out with my arms and legs but he pinioned me with his body. His hands were fumbling with the bodice of my dress, his knee was thrust up hard between my thighs. His mouth came down upon mine, biting my lips, trying to force them apart with his tongue, covering my face with yeasty saliva. I struck out wildly at the back of his head, he grappled with my arm, bending it backwards. His other hand was yanking up the hem of my dress, ripping my stockings, his teeth were suddenly embedded in the base of my neck. My mouth was free, I let out a sharp cry. His hand went to my throat, pressing against it, forcing my head viciously backwards. I could not breathe, I felt myself going limp, I saw flashes of brightly coloured light.

The fact that I had all at once stopped struggling seemed to arrest him. I was aware of him staring down at me, puzzled, his face running with sweat, his pale hair falling into his eyes, his mouth smeared with the blood from my nose. We looked at each other in silence for a moment. Then, precisely, sharply bringing up my right knee, I thrust it with all my force into his groin.

He rolled sideways, moaning, clutching himself. I slid off the bed, ran to the bathroom, slammed and locked the door.

When I had bathed my face I sat upon the cold floor, hugging my knees, pressing my head against the tiled wall, rocking gently backwards and forwards.

After a while his groans turned to a high-pitched whining and then to sobs. There was a strange scraping noise as if he were crawling across the floor towards the bathroom, then a scrabbling of his hands upon the door.

'Sorry, old thing. Didn't mean it. Bit sozzled, don't y'know. One over the eight. Kiss and make up, please, old girl? Oh please, Christie. Don't be too hard on Archie. Poor old Archie. Please, Christie! Pl–ea–se!'

Yes, it was easy to make resolutions, easy to tell yourself to hold to your duty, but not always so very easy when you came to try.

CHAPTER THIRTY-SIX

Diary of Adele Ward.
Shakespeare Villas, Balham.

23rd April, 1895.

M returned home just before tea and rushed directly upstairs. Hearing from his room great commotion and turmoil, I followed him and was astonished to discover him packing a portmanteau. At first he would not heed my entreaties to explain what was the matter. Eventually, however, he rounded upon me with a snarl.

'That jackass Marjoribanks at the Club! He's accused me of cardsharping. In the good old days we'd have called each other out, settled the matter like gentlemen and that would have been the end of it. But a parvenu like Marjoribanks has no savoir-faire, no common decency. The booby's called in the police!'

'Oh, M,' I said, 'does that mean it's true? But we have my money now, you had no need. Oh M, you couldn't have –'

'No, dearest,' he replied, favouring me with a malevolent flash of his white teeth, while all the time bundling shoes and shirts into the portmanteau. 'I couldn't have.'

I surveyed him with alarm. 'But where are we going?'

Collar box in one hand, brushes in the other, he paused. '<u>We</u>, my dearest, are not going anywhere.'

I felt my blood grow chill and begin to drain away. 'But I –'

'My plans preclude the presence of my sweet, dear little wifie. And at last, thank G–d, I have no further need of her thousand a year.'

So that is why he has been so complacent these past two months, that is why we have not made use of my money to re-establish our household in the West End. Having been freed of further husbandly pretence by the death of my father, having suborned his crooked lawyers to make away with my inheritance, having ensured that I am now cut off from anyone who might offer me affection or come to my aid, he has laid his plans to run away with his latest Gaiety Girl, to cast me off like a pair of worn-out gloves. Heaven knows I hate him, heaven knows my life beneath his cruel yoke is a torture to me. Yet without him, abandoned in this place, alone, deprived by his disgrace of my own reputation, impoverished – for my thousand a year has dwindled to a mere hundred now – I am as <u>nothing</u>: I have no dignity, no function, no place in the world.

'But I am your wife!' I cried.

'My wife, my encumberance, my property. And, as such, dearest, I may dispose of you as I wish.'

I flung myself about his neck then, begging for mercy, but he hurled me away; I threw myself at his feet, twined my arms around his legs, sobbing, pleading, swearing I should do anything he wished if only he would not desert me; but with a cold sneer of: 'Anything, dearest?' he kicked me aside; I seized hold of his ankle as, fastening the portmanteau, he made for the door but, trampling my fingers with his unencumbered foot, he freed himself and, as I lay there upon the floor, choking, weeping, crying out to him to have pity on me, I heard his steps descend the stairs, the front door close and his waiting hansom cab roll away.

After a while I cried myself insensible, and now I have returned to consciousness the house is very still and I am alone.

Alone. M has gone, taking with him my youth, my hope, my dreams, my money, my very title to existence – that I am his wife. I have no family to turn to – his intrigue with J has seen to that. Even my precious mementoes of dear Mamma have not escaped him for, on regaining my room, I discover my jewel case has been forced and those few items it contained, mostly trifling keepsakes left to me in her will, have gone with the rest. He has spared me nothing.

What will become of me? Were I the heroine of one of those romances I used so avidly to read, an Ariadne deserted by her Hilarion, a Folle-Farine spurned by her beloved Arslàn, I should simply, mutely, lay myself down to die. And oh, I do indeed long most passionately for death!

24th April, 1895.

The sun is shining. An hour ago two constables called in search of M and, seeing I was a woman, alone and unprotected, dealt with me roughly until I was able to convince them I knew no more of his whereabouts than they. I should pray that justice overtakes him, yet I fear if he is apprehended they will bring him back. For I despise myself this morning, I am sickened by my craven cowardice in abasing and humiliating myself before him. ***I*** *plead with him, beg him to stay? Oh, merciful heaven, at last I am* ***free!***

I see it all now, what before I was too foolish, too ***womanly*** *to comprehend, the way the world works. Society depends upon a stable disposition of property and power. Men have the* ***power*** *and women are the* ***property****; accordingly we have settlements made upon us and are bought or sold as any commodity is bought and sold on the Exchange; our ownership thus established and sealed with high-flown words like 'duty' and 'morality', we must cheerfully submit to being disposed of at will; and if we reject this submission or are otherwise found wanting, we are cast out and become as nothing, for our failure, by imperilling that order of ownership, threatens* ***the very foundations of Society itself****.*

That is the logic of it. But we, mere chits of girls, still longing to put our hair up and attend our first ball, we maidens still with our giggles and our blushes, we are not renowned for our grasp of logic. So how may we be persuaded to accept this proposition by which Society stands or falls?

Why, by love. By the glory and the fire and the passion of love which is spelt out in novel after novel, romance after romance, adjective after mellifluous adjective, in pages which make our virgin hearts flutter and our blushes rise, in sentences rendered the more thrilling because our Mammas, being sadder and wiser, forbid us to read them; for our Mammas know, which we do not, that the glory, the fire and the passion are merely fictions, a tantalizing, honeyed dream to lead us into bondage.

From henceforth I shall abjure Society as I abjure its fiction, love. I shall be no one's property but my own. I have my health and strength, I have a hundred a year. I shall work; I shall trust only to myself; and I shall survive.

CHAPTER THIRTY-SEVEN

Archie's dogged assertion that we should escape the slump which had hit America was, of course, soon disproved.

By the beginning of 1930 the small boom in the steel industry was over, not a recovery from the decline but merely a brief interruption of it. Plans for reorganization still abounded. By the end of 1930, two of our furnaces were working at less than half capacity, two others closed down completely. It was commonplace now, I was told, to see a small crowd gather at six o'clock every morning outside the works gates, old men mostly who had been laid off some of them for four or five years, men in faded and patched overalls which would never see the grime of work again, convening thus with the regularity with which they had once, respected workers with skilled jobs, walked through those gates, in the vain hope of some day catching the foreman's eye.

The crowds on the street corners grew too, the gossipers filling in idle hours with a penn'orth of chips and an inquisition on their neighbours, the pinched, apathetic faces above threadbare jackets, the worn women and grubby, underfed children, not tens or scores of them now, but hundreds, waiting, loitering, whiling away the time until – until what?

With two and one half million out of work, a National Government, since it was above party dogma, was, we were assured, the country's best hope of getting things set to rights. In the 1931 election which resoundingly affirmed its tenure, Meredith, an eager advocate of the alliance between MacDonald and Baldwin, was returned with a much-increased majority. And the new government, with a 'doctor's mandate' and with the nation's interest impartially before it, set about implementing measures which, if they did not aim precisely to decrease the numbers unemployed, would certainly reduce their cost to the country.

One morning I passed the sewing room to find Alice, the girl who came in two days a week to do the mending, sobbing miserably as she sides-to-middled a sheet.

'It's our Dad,' she said, wiping her eyes on her apron. 'They've docked his money and it's all on account of me. They come round and asked a heap of questions, whether our Mam worked, even though she's been poorly three years with her chest, how much furniture cost, whether us had owt tucked away for a rainy day. Then when our Dad queued for his dole they said he'd been stopped ten shilling on account of me living at home and being in work. There were only nine shillings left over any road after rent and coal and clothing club and with me kid brothers there's five on us needs feeding out of that. Means Test they call it. Mean test I say it is! Only thing I can do is leave home but I've nowhere I can go.'

Judicious questioning of Mrs Burton revealed that the predicament of Alice's family was not now unusual. To Archie's intense irritation I offered her a vacant bed in one of the maids' rooms.

'Damn it, old girl, all got to make sacrifices, don't y'know. What about yours truly? – whole bally board of the company taken a twenty per cent pay cut just to show willing. Hard times, old thing. Means Test'll save the country twenty-four million pounds, so Meredith says. Unemployed got to do their bit like everyone else.'

Archie had indeed taken a cut in salary. Yet, despite that, our life up at Dingley Hill, in marked contrast with the bleakness of the town below, seemed to continue unchanged. If anything we lived more lavishly; for, with Brice and Cadwallander's growing instability, Archie's obsessional need to keep up appearances grew too, unreasoningly, frantically, like the struggles of a drowning man. We entertained splendidly and often, our presence could be relied upon at all the high-points of the local Season from County garden parties to the Hunt Ball. Sometimes we even made a rare escape to London where, eating poached salmon at Sybil's dinner table, listening to the popping of champagne corks and seeing everywhere about me silks and furs and limousines, I would again experience that bewildering feeling of having for a while simply stepped out of time, of having left our grey Northern streets behind as surely as if they had merely been an image conjured up by a forgotten history book.

One March morning of 1932, as we were driving from Dingley Hill to a luncheon party in the country, we noticed a large number of policemen in the centre of the town. Archie slid back the chauffeur's partition to enquire what was up.

'National Unemployment Workers Movement. Marching to present a petition to Town Hall.' The chauffeur, Calvert, was a local man, young, no more than nineteen. His brother, he said, was a special constable, on duty for the day. 'We'd best avoid Town Square on road back.'

There was some talk of the march over luncheon.

'Hunger March, indeed!' said our hostess. 'You can't tell me the unemployed are hungry, my dear, when they still have plenty of money to spend in the betting shops and public houses.'

'It's a put-up job,' said someone else. 'Everyone knows the NUWM is simply a front for the Communist Party.'

'Blasted Bolshies!' said Archie. 'Even the bally Socialists disown them.'

'All this fuss about the Means Test!' said our hostess. 'I met someone the other day who has a friend who's got something to do with the Public Assistance Committee, and he said when it comes down to it half the people on the dole don't want to do a hand's turn. They know when they're well off.'

'Can't expect a cove who *does* do an honest day's work to stump up 4/6 in the pound tax just to pay for the blighters who won't.'

'Still,' said our hostess, 'you'd better be careful on the way back, my dears. You read about those frightful riots in Salford? It said in the *Morning Post* they were throwing iron bedsteads, even the women, dropping them out of windows on top of the police.'

The chauffeur, with advice from his brother, had carefully planned our return route. We would approach the square from the north as usual, but instead of driving straight on we would turn off to the left just before we reached it, taking a detour that avoided all roads west through which the marchers, having presented their petition, would make their way for a rally and speeches on the Common. But when we arrived at our turning we found it blocked off by a police cordon.

'Change of plan,' I could hear a constable tell Calvert through the driver's window. 'Rumour is they'll try to storm Labour Exchange, break doors down and hold meeting there. You'd best turn right and go up Cobett Street.'

We could see the crowd in the square from where the car had stopped, a sea of serried grey caps, the faceless uniform of the working man, with here and there a banner or a hand-painted placard proclaiming: 'Down with the Means Test', 'We Must Have Bread', 'Struggle or Starve'. There must have been over five thousand, packed shoulder to shoulder, perched on the plinths of the statues, pressed with their backs against shuttered shop fronts, held off from the side roads by mounted police and fire engines with their hoses trained at the ready and from the Town Hall by its imposing flight of steps. At the top of the steps, from a huddled group of organizers and marshals dwarfed by the monumental grandeur of the portico, a man with a megaphone addressed them. Press photographers perched on the rooftops of neighbouring buildings. The delegation must at this moment be on the other side of the great carved and gilded doors, presenting the petition. Our new route would bring us to the road junction at the south-western tip of the square where, as we swung right again, we would for a moment travel directly past the demonstrators. Calvert reversed the car until we were level with the turning into Cobett Street, and we set off again.

When we came within sight of the square from the bottom of Cobett Street the speaker had lowered his megaphone and the Town Hall doors had just opened to let the delegation file out.

'Bally Bolshies!' muttered Archie, under his breath.

But the people I could see looked no more like organized political agitators than the row of fresh-faced young constables who linked arms to restrain them. They were the ordinary people of the town, the loiterers at street corners, the silent audience at Meredith's open-air speeches, the vain watchers outside Brice and Cadwallander's gates. As we drew level I saw not just men, but women and children as well, the little ones hoisted up to get a better view. Some of the older men wore their medals and ribbons from the Great War and the Ex-Service-men's band stood near the Town Hall steps, instruments silently cradled. Banners flapped in the bitter wind. And over everyone, watching, waiting for their representatives to appear beneath the massive stone portico, was a tense, expectant silence, a silence so purposeful, so complete that it was as if you could feel the concentrated power of five thousand wills pressing against the blank windows and granite walls, ready to make the whole pompous civic façade buckle and crash with the sheer force of their unity.

As if overawed himself by the spectacle, Calvert stopped the car for a second. And in that moment two things happened. The leader of the delegation appeared suddenly on the Town Hall steps, tore the megaphone from his colleague's hand and began to scream into it: 'The bastards! They won't even see us, comrades! They won't take our petition or even listen to us! They couldn't give a damn if we all of us starve!'

And someone spotted our Rolls-Royce.

The silence erupted into an angry roar. The crowd, which an instant before had been so still, began to seethe like a boiling sea, surging in one direction towards the Town Hall steps and in the other against the police cordon that protected us.

A stone hit the top of the car, another smashed against the bonnet, I saw a constable go down, the cordon of linked arms sag, the crowd burst through. A police horse, charging into them, was felled by a placard hurled at its fetlocks. And they were upon us, surrounding the car, screaming, howling, hammering upon the bodywork, beating at the windows, pelting us with stones. I saw a constable, baton raised to strike, his face no longer fresh with youth but ugly with fear. And then I could see nothing but the faces of the crowd, ugly too now, contorted with hate, pressed against the windows inches away from mine, spitting, jeering, men and women, tugging at the door handles, clinging to the bonnet, howling abuse. The car began to rock from side to side with an ominous, determined motion.

'Put your foot down!' Archie was screaming at Calvert. 'Drive on, you bloody idiot, or they'll turn us over!'

It was dark inside the car now, all light obliterated by the press of bodies around us, by those misshapen animal faces thrust against the glass, clawing at it, screaming obscenities. The rocking motion grew. It was suffocating, terrifying, we would be crushed, annihilated by the sheer weight of human bodies. Above us stones ricocheted deafeningly off the roof. I clung onto my leather strap to keep myself from falling. Archie, still shouting, sprawled across me as he tore at the curtains to shut out those terrible faces. I felt sick, I turned my head aside, I could not bear any longer to look at so much naked hate, to see how consumingly, violently we were hated. The chanting had disintegrated into the roar of battle. We were pitching, bucking, we would be over any minute. The noise, the movement, was overpowering. Then suddenly something hit us from the back with immense force, shooting the car forward as if it had been kicked by an elephant. There was a roaring sound like the bursting of a geyser. Every part of the car seemed to quiver with it, the shouting all around us turned to cries of panic. The faces fell away, through the half-drawn curtains the windows, the windscreen, seemed to blur as if they were melting. It took me some moments to realize it was water, they had turned the fire hoses on the crowd, were flushing, sluicing them off us with water.

When it cleared, I could see in front of us the mounted police begin a fresh charge, lashing out with their swordsticks. The rocking motion had ceased, and the thrust of the fire hoses. The car was suddenly quite still. And all at once I saw that the police cordon farther up, incredibly, had held, that the charge of horses had done its work and there was now a clear space in front of us.

'Drive on!' Archie screamed at Calvert. 'Drive on, you bloody fool, before we all get killed!'

Calvert seemed to hestitate for a moment as though paralysed with fear. Then he put his foot on the accelerator and the car jerked forwards. But at that moment, as if the pressure of the rioters being forced back at the rear had created an intolerable strain, like water dammed up in one place bursting out in a tidal wave from another, the cordon of linked arms ahead of us gave and a fresh section of the crowd, impelled not so much by violence as by the sheer press of bodies, spilled out into the road directly across our path.

'Drive on!' bellowed Archie. 'Drive into them, damn you! Put your foot down!'

'No, Archie!' I screamed. 'We'll hit someone!'

'It's us or them. Drive on, I tell you!'

'But there are women and children!'

'Drive on, Calvert. I order you to drive on! Drive on, or I'll make bloody sure you and your blasted brother and everyone else in your bally family never get a job in this town again!'

The car shot suddenly forward with great speed. I could still hear myself shouting: 'No, Archie! No, no!' What happened next seemed by contrast to happen very slowly. There was a scream as the crowd fell back, then a sickening thud. Something small and unnaturally light, something almost like a bundle of rags seemed to fly up over the bonnet, to hang in the air for a moment, then to come crashing down against the windscreen. I caught a glimpse of a hand with the fingers outspread, of a small shoe hurtling sideways quite separately in another direction. Then the bundle fell away into the road.

The car lurched, the back wheels shuddered. I flung myself at the partition that separated us from Calvert.

'Stop! Stop the car! Oh God, please stop the car!'

Archie grabbed me by the shoulders. I hung onto the side of the partition with my fingers, still screaming. He prised my hand free, hurling me backwards, sending me sprawling onto the floor.

'Don't listen to her! Drive on. It's us or them. Drive on, I tell you!'

The car swung wildly round a bend, then another, lurching across tramlines. I could still hear my own voice screaming: 'Stop! Oh God, it was a child! Please, oh my God, please stop!'

It was as if it were the voice of another person, automatic, dislocated from me. I realized I was still lying on the floor and that my knees and elbows hurt where I had fallen. I could see the back of Calvert's neck, the muscles rigid, set with horror, could see Archie, bolt upright in his seat, his hand clenched around the passenger strap, his face expressionless. I stopped screaming and slowly raised myself. The crowd was out of sight now, far behind, the roads empty as if the whole town had been depopulated by a sudden plague. We careered into Dingley Park, up the hill and through the open gateway of our drive. The gravel spat and hissed beneath our tyres. We reached the ornate porch with its gargoyles and spiked turrets and jolted to a halt. For a moment we sat where we were, not moving. Then Calvert, tearing open his door without stopping to attend to either of the passenger doors, flung himself away from the car and towards the laurel bushes. He began to vomit. I remembered thinking suddenly how young he was, how he still had no more than a faint blond down on his cheeks. We climbed out slowly after him. I went to put my hand on his shoulder but he jerked it away. He was vomiting and crying at the same time.

The Rolls-Royce stood in the driveway, its doors hanging

open, its lamps and windscreen shattered, its bodywork dented, one running board trailing, mudguards and bumpers buckled. Only the Silver Lady on the bonnet still flew poised and proud. But, tarnishing her outspread wings, there was a trickling, reddish-brown smear.

I had assayed the first few bars of the Chopin *ballade,* had thought the memories it held, softened by time, would comfort me. But my fingers, stiff and out of practice, stumbled over what they had once known so well and my mind refused to stay upon the music.

There was a police guard around the house for the night in case any of the demonstrators reassembled and tried to storm it. The inspector and his sergeant were still here too, talking to Archie in the study. The doctor – not Dr Burton but another doctor – had offered me a sedative. But did I need a sedative now, I who had only just awakened from a trance that seemed to have lasted these past eight years?

The child had been Sally Mullins. I remembered her one front tooth the morning I had held her – that had been eight years ago too. Not much of a life. Eight more years of that bare room, watching her mother destroy her eyesight making roses, watching the old man die by inches, wondering where the next meal was coming from. Not much of a life, but a life nonetheless. 'Bunch of ruddy animals,' Archie had said. 'It's us or them.' But if despair had pushed the crowd over the edge into that naked, animal hatred, could they, when we had remorselessly stripped them of all human dignity, be blamed? And why was it always them? There wasn't anything I could say to Mrs Mullins, no letter I could write, no gesture of recompense I could make. There were no excuses to be offered to Mrs Burton either. I had torn off all my clothes the moment I had reached our bedroom, shoes, stockings, underwear, everything, had bathed and left a note for my maid to burn them. But the clothes I wore now were just as tainted, my clothes, the carpet I stood on, the piano keys as I touched them. Everything we had, Archie and I, had been bought by the sacrifice of the Mullinses and thousands of others like them. They had been sacrificed to incompetent management, unwise investment, unimaginative planning, changes in government policy, even to keep down income tax, they had been sacrificed so that we, walled up in our gothic castle on the hill with three good meals a day and a place in Society, should feel no pain. And now there seemed no limit to the sacrifices we would ask them to make.

I had been clear in my duty to Archie, albeit tardily, and I had tried my best to fulfil it. But must I not ask now whether there was a premise behind that duty which a stronger obligation made it impossible to accept?

I tried again with the *ballade,* but still my fingers faltered painfully, like a child's.

Archie appeared in the drawing-room doorway. 'God rid of the blighters at last,' he said.

'Oh,' I said.

'Be an inquest, of course. Shouldn't have any trouble, though. Chief Constable's a chum of mine.'

I remembered suddenly the little cox who had gone down but had not come up.

'They'll want to chat to you in the morning. Must say, had a spot of bother convincing them you were too groggy to talk now. Did you have to make such an infernal din on the blasted thing the whole time? Heard you quite clearly in the study, don't y'know.'

'I wanted to talk to them,' I said.

'So you could spout a lot of hysterical rubbish? Think I'd chance that? No thank you.' He went over to the cocktail cabinet and poured himself a large whisky and soda. 'Anyway, give it a rest now, old thing. Had enough funeral dirges this evening, what? Tune in to Northern Regional, see if there's a dance band, something a bit jolly.'

His hand was already on the knob of the wireless. 'No, Archie,' I said. 'Please don't.'

His face as he bent was red and glistening. He must have taken a decanter of whisky into the study. Dutch courage.

'Look here,' he said, straightening. 'I wish you'd give up staring at me as if I was a bally murderer, don't y'know.'

I closed the lid of the piano slowly. 'Archie, we didn't even stop the car.'

'Should say not. Blighters would have killed us.'

'Us or them?'

'If you put it like that, yes. You heard what they were shouting.'

'Archie, she was a child. A nine-year-old child.'

'Brat shouldn't have run in front of the motor.'

'We drove at her. We drove deliberately straight into the crowd.'

Sighing, he took a large gulp of whisky. 'For pity's sake, old thing, don't start it all again. Not my fault, wasn't even bloody-well at the wheel.'

I felt a sudden familiar chill. 'Archie, you promised me, you promised you'd try to do something for poor Calvert.'

'And so I have, old girl. Done the only thing I could do under the circumstances. Given him his cards. Dangerous driving, don't y'know.'

'You ordered him to drive into that crowd. You even threatened him.'

He emptied his glass. He was swaying slightly. 'Look, old girl, you don't know a damned thing about it. You were doolally tap, having the vapours at the time. Fellow panicked, put his foot down, brat ran out under the wheels. That's what the rozzers believe, that's what'll be said at the inquest. My word against his. And you'll support me, old thing. Other half and all that.'

I stared at him for a while in silence. I knew now that there was no point in saying anything.

He had returned to the cocktail cabinet. 'Anyway,' he said, without looking up from the whisky decanter, 'only one half-starved brat, old thing. Parents probably not too bothered. One less mouth to feed.'

'Yes,' I said, very softly. 'What's one child, more or less?'

'By the by, old girl, why's Hodgson shifting stuff around in our bedroom?'

I drew in my breath. 'She's moving my things into the Blue Room.'

He looked up then, glass in one hand, decanter in the other. I steeled myself for the violence I knew would come, and then the tears. 'It's partly my fault, Archie, I should never have married you. And I'll stay until the inquest's over. But – but after that I'm leaving. I want a divorce.'

PART FOUR

THE NIGHTINGALE SINGS

CHAPTER THIRTY-EIGHT

Propped up between pink silk sheets against a great mound of monogrammed pillows, Mrs Silas P Schumacher had retired early to bed. With her wispy hair encased in a Lady Jayne Slumbernet, with her face liberally daubed with Vitagland Hormone Creme, and with the whole panoply topped off, as a rugger player wears a scrum cap, by her Patent Ganesh chin strap – 'restores lost contours, cures double chins, also keeps the mouth closed when asleep to prevent undesirable snoring' – she looked, despite the cock-feather trimming upon her negligée, every inch the frail sexagenarian her expensive army of masseurs and beauticians laboured daily to disguise. On her left-hand bedside table stood a phalanx of pill bottles from which it would be my duty as her lady companion to administer her nightly cocktail of vitamins, tonics and soporifics. On the right were library books, including the latest Edgar Wallace from which I would read to her until she fell asleep. Beside her, on his own pink pillow, resplendent in his rhinestone collar, lay Barrymore – after John – her Pomeranian, yielding sleepily to the caresses of her claw-like left hand.

The other hand, also twisted with arthritis, scrabbled ineffectually amongst the sheets. She lifted the mechanism of the Ganesh to admit speech, pushing it up beneath her lower lip like the strap of a Prussian officer's helmet.

'So where,' she exclaimed, 'did I put my spectacles?'

Then she gave a little laugh as we both chorused: 'They're on your nose, Mrs Schumacher.'

'So – spectacles I have – what you want me to read?'

I placed this week's copy of *The Lady* between her crabbed fingers.

'"How I Got Rid of Wrinkles at Sixty and Made Myself LOOK TWENTY YEARS YOUNGER"?'

'No, Mrs Schumacher, the next advertisement.'

'Which reminds me. Tomorrow early I have to be at the beauty parlour for my facial – '

'Mrs Schumacher, you're looking in the wrong place.'

'And then I have an appointment for twelve at the Hayman

Gallery. Rueben Hayman, may he live and prosper, says he's gotten a Ben Nicholson for me, swears he'll make me a special price, this I got to see – '

'Mrs Schumacher,' I said in desperation, pointing, 'not there. Farther down, next to the appeal for the unemployed. "House Sale in Norfolk" it begins.'

'Ach, honey! All this talk, my brain is tired. Read it me.'

I took up the magazine. '"Sotheby's announce the Sale of Contents of Monks Last, Norfolk, country residence of Sir Meredith de Lisle Bart, MP, to be held on 12th May 1935 at 2 p.m. – " '

'Yes dear, now I remember – the piece in *Country Life* on the real-estate auction you showed me a month back. So you think if they sell the tshatchkes maybe there's a painting or two I shouldn't miss?'

I laughed. I did not imagine that Monks Last, even though Sybil had apparently refurbished it, would be a fruitful source of Braques, Matisses and Picassos, and the family paintings in the hall were scarcely a likely addition to the by now renowned Schumacher Collection.

'No,' I said. 'I showed it to you because it interested me, because it's a house I know and – well, I wanted to ask you a favour.'

Mrs Schumacher removed her spectacles. 'So what kept you talking so long, dear? Anything you want, just ask.'

'I'd like to go to the sale. You see, I lived there once and . . .' I tailed off lamely. Even to myself I could not perfectly explain why I wanted to revisit a place which could only have wretched memories for me. Perhaps it was the very idea of the sale, of the dissolution of everything I remembered, that attracted me. Perhaps I felt that by taking one last look at the house, stripped bare, shorn of every painful evocation, I could exorcize the past once and for all and go cleanly into my new life, the life I would make in a month's time when Mrs Schumacher and I set sail for America.

'They sell your home, of course you be there.'

'It would only be for two days, Mrs Schumacher. I could take the early train on the 12th and be back in London by noon on the 13th. If you can manage without me – '

Mrs Schumacher chucked the sleeping Pomeranian under the chin, causing him to yelp plaintively. 'Christabel, everything's fixed, another word on this subject I don't want to hear.'

A single ramshackle taxi now ran from the station. Looking out of its window at green fields, at hedgerows golden with cowslips and purple with campion and wild orchids, at stone and red-brick cottages nestling comfortably amongst snowy banks of blackthorn in the bends of the road, I thought how cosy the morning sun made a landscape I had remembered only as bleak.

I had not visited Monks Last for five years. Sybil, though forced to tolerate me during my marriage to Archie, had seldom asked us there and had used my separation and eventual divorce as a welcome excuse for the family to sever all contact with me – I had only learnt of the sale of the estate from the article in *Country Life* I had shown Mrs Schumacher. I felt no animosity towards Sybil or Meredith; I was no more anxious than they to continue the connection. Indeed, with the exception of my regular correspondence with Dilly in India, I had ceased to keep up with anyone in my old life. Everything had changed for me now so completely that there seemed, quite apart from the limitations that poverty placed upon me, little point.

It had been hard at first. I had naturally refused any money from Archie and, finding myself one room in Chelsea, had set about earning my living by giving piano lessons. But, though the response to my handwritten card in the local newsagent's window had been adequate enough to bring me a precarious existence, my musical skills had not. Through lack of instruction and practice I had felt myself to be as much in need of a teacher as those I taught, and in the end, after eighteen months, no longer able to bear the sense that I was perpetrating upon my pupils an iniquitous confidence trick, I had given it up.

'CHAUFFEUSE-COMPANION wanted', the advertisement in *The Lady* had read. 'Must be gentlewoman, well-educated, humorous, adaptable, musical, enjoy reading aloud. Maid kept. No salary.' I had sent off my letter without much hope, in the knowledge that there were hundreds of applicants now for every job, and had been agreeably surprised even to be summoned to an interview. I had been even more surprised when, confronted by all four foot ten of Mrs Schumacher in peach silk lounging pyjamas and inch-long false eyelashes, I had been engaged on the spot, largely it seemed because she was certain she had seen me somewhere before, a conviction which both she and I found ourselves unable to explain but which had continued to trouble her throughout my employment.

Mr Silas P Schumacher, a one-time Brooklyn tailor who had transported himself to the West Coast and eventually to the very top of a large movie company, had died six years ago leaving his wife, who until then, unwelcome betrayer of his origins, had remained entombed and childless in a vast and echoing mansion in Beverly Hills, sole heir to so much money 'one crazy old woman knows from nothing how to spend it all'. Nevertheless, flighty, absent-minded, endlessly optimistic and generous to a fault, determinedly in pursuit of her lost youth, Rosa Schumacher was willing to try. Yet there was one point on which the native shrewdness that had eked out so long ago a scrimpy survival amongst the tenements of Brooklyn held firm. To keep her occupied during the Beverly Hills days, Silas Schumacher had permitted his wife to dabble in art. And dabble she had – to such effect that her fortune had not only survived the Crash but she was now possessed of one of the best and most comprehensive collections of modern painting in the world. I would still wonder, having narrowly prevented her from losing all her baggage in Paris or being bilked by a thoroughly suspect tour guide in Florence, to see her ears prick, her mascara-blurred eyes glitter, her tiny, over-painted mouth become a sharp line when confronted even in the unlikeliest of places with a likely acquisition, to observe her, relentlessly girlish to the last, paring a little more from the profit of the most hard-bitten gallery owner with every sweep of her outrageous eyelashes.

Mrs Schumacher and I, despite the odd circumstances of my employment, rubbed along together rather well. I did not mind walking Barrymore or buying toothpaste from Harrods or fetching endless Edgar Wallaces from the library, and the fact that I knew she needed me as her hands and eyes compensated me, selfishly, for the feeling of utter uselessness my failure as a music teacher had given me. So when she had suggested that once we had taken our fill of London and George V's Jubilee festivities I should go to live permanently with her in New York I had readily agreed.

There was, after all, nothing to keep me any longer in England. Two months ago even my divorce from Archie had at last become final. That it had taken so long had been due to a tragic and completely unconnected event. Late in 1932 the newspapers had reported the death of Felix's wife and son in an accidental drowning. The Hispano Suiza, parked on the shores of Lake Geneva, had slipped off its handbrake and had rolled, before anyone could prevent it, into the water, sinking with both its passengers trapped inside. There had been an inquest, demands from relatives for further enquiries, pictures of Felix at the funeral, a gaunt, bareheaded figure in a black overcoat, the contours of the face a pale, expressionless blur. I had no contact with Felix, I had not even known where to send a letter of sympathy. Yet Archie had become convinced, as if all of it, the accident, my desertion, were some intricate plot against him, that were he to divorce me I should instantly fly to Felix's side. Only his own meeting with someone who would make him a better wife than me had eventually persuaded him to give me my freedom.

But free I now was, free of Archie, of England, of all attachments – even perhaps at last free from Felix; for, brother or lover, there was, across the gulf of time which separated that life from this, little to be gained but needless pain in struggling to keep alive my distorted memories of him.

My attendance at the funeral rites of Monks Last would mark the final cutting of the bond. I did not know why, but I was all at once excited and nervous at the thought of it.

The house when I walked up the drive, looked, as the fields had looked, almost mellow in the sunshine. It seemed smaller than I remembered it, to cast a shorter shadow, as if the stark façade with its dirty, uncurtained windows had, with the stripping away of all the refinements of human occupation, also been divested of its menace. The lawns grew rank with coarse grass and weeds – since old Magnus had died it had clearly not been thought worthwhile to employ another gardener. On the croquet lawn where Sybil had planned, but never built, her swimming pool, a large marquee had been erected, and the auctioneers' clerk was already setting himself up a temporary office at a battered mahogany table placed between the verge of the lawn and the front steps. I found myself suddenly on guard for the appearance of Meredith or Sybil themselves amongst the little trickle of viewers who came, clutching catalogues, out of the front door into the brilliance of the May morning, but my first instincts had been right; the sale of the house and its furnishings had become merely a matter of business to which others could be left to attend.

I wondered why they had decided to sell. Looking around the drawing room, the first room I entered, and seeing tubular chairs and chrome occasional tables packed cheek by jowl with tired Edwardian armchairs, a Pembroke table, dumbwaiters and a pair of elephant's feet which must have been retrieved from one of the attics, I came to the conclusion that Sybil had perhaps simply tired of her attempts at modernity. The drawing room itself, despite the striking addition of copper dividing doors and concealed lighting, still seemed in its own strange way resolutely Georgian. The rest of the house appeared to have been equally unyielding for, beyond a similar transformation with mirrors and chrome in the smoking room and a Bauhaus-inspired electric fire in the hall, the march of design revolution seemed to peter out as though inexorably pushed back by damp and cobwebs and the dust of generations, the sheer weight of history effortlessly stilling the brash cries of 1930s chic.

It was like a pattern that had so far refused to be broken, the mournful obstinacy of that dark house, a pattern of all our family hopes and griefs echoed, repeated through generations, imbuing the very stone and plaster with its spirit. But break it would now, once every trace of our existence had been finally expunged. New patterns would form, windows would be unbricked to let in more light, children perhaps would one day laugh and play in the passages. You could see the change beginning already with the disorganization of the furniture, which had been collected together on the ground floor to facilitate the auction. I felt it now, answering my hopes, like a comforting, neutralizing force, defusing memory, reaffirming the safety of my distance from the past. Though I found the chaise longue, the Aubusson rug and the Bechstein crammed with everything else into the drawing room, the chaise was broken, the rug worn, and the Bechstein when I touched the keys gave out only the hollow discord of neglect. Though the great leather wing chair was there too, the chair in which Sir Arthur had died and which had stood like an insurmountable obstacle between Felix and me that terrible night in 1923, now, exiled from its traditional place in the smoking room, it looked only what it was, a dilapidated old chair badly in need of reupholstering, to be bought for a few shillings fo fill an unregarded corner in a guest room.

It was the same wherever I went, that laying of ghosts, that comforting distance. In my room the beech tree had overgrown the window, shutting out the light so that in my short-sleeved dress I shivered for an instant; but, stripped of their looming furniture, empty of everything save a couple of discarded mothballs and a dead beetle on the windowsill, the bare walls no longer conjured up the mysteriously palpable shadows which had nightly thrown terror across my pillow. Even Aunt Jessica's room seemed silent at last, ringing no more with those final dreadful whispers. From the murky glass of the schoolroom window, the view, with its white marquee and milling people upon the gravel, had taken on an almost festive air, like the last-minute preparations for a village fête. Some familiar pieces of furniture and porcelain were already missing, the family pictures too, presumably saved by Meredith for future de Lisles, had gone from the hall. The pattern was breaking, and with it, as I had hoped, the pattern of my whole past life.

Only in the kitchen, sitting in the chair once favoured by the kitchen cat, looking at the sun shining in through the open door across a jumble of pots and pans and chipped china grouped in numbered lots upon the table in a disorder Mrs Wix would never have permitted, did I all at once feel regret. I thought of Mrs Wix, who I would visit after the auction, blind now and bedridden with phlebitis in her cottage in the village, and suddenly I longed to bask in the frowsty warmth of a faraway winter's afternoon again and watch her big, capable hands punishing pastry and reaching out to stop me pilfering sultanas.

And, tasting the sweetness of the fruit on my tongue, feeling my fingers sticky with cake mixture, not sensing till too late the danger in their evocations, I found then, as though they mocked my complacency, my foolish presumption that I would ever gain mastery over them, the other memories flooding back, no longer blunted by time but as vivid as if they had been newly created: a tall, bareheaded figure limping determinedly in the wind, grey eyes assessing me impartially. 'I'm your Cousin Christabel.' 'Yes, I know.' 'Trust me now, and don't be frightened. I love you, little Christie, so very much . . . '

I was saved by the entrance of two middle-aged women who began clucking dismissively over Mrs Wix's chipped relics. I forced myself from the chair and out of the kitchen. I was free; the pattern was breaking, in a new life, from another country, I should not look back. If I walked into the dining room I should not see Meredith hunched defensively behind his *Times*, nor watch that pacing figure, nor hear again in endless repetition that inevitable conversation. I should not look back and I should not cry.

The dining room, packed like all the downstairs rooms with displaced furniture, was unrecognizable. I stood in its doorway, feeling again that comforting exorcism, relieved that my weakness in the kitchen had only been momentary. Then I gave a gasp of surprise. For there, amongst beds and tables brought down from the maids' rooms, was the schoolroom piano. Not just the piano, but the old armchair, the oilcloth-covered table, the black blackboard and easel, the map of the world and –

Suddenly I was pushing my way through the mass of furniture as if to see were not enough, as if only by touching would I believe. But it was true. Beneath the dust of years the walnut still yielded its remembered smoothness, my fingers still closed around the tarnished brass handles with the familiarity of long habit. Lot 104. My mother's old secretaire.

I stared at it in wonder. During the eighteen years I had believed it lost or destroyed it must have been up in one of the attics after all, stowed away there perhaps by an indolent Grover who had not bothered to fulfil Aunt Jessica's instructions to the letter, hidden with everything else from the schoolroom and forgotten. And if it had survived, had my secret then survived with it, the last relics of my mother's memory, the precious contents of the hidden drawer?

In an instant I was pushing aside the obstruction of a table, was down on my knees before the secretaire feeling for the concealed spring. It gave to my touch immediately. But the secret drawer beneath the desk flap did not open. I remembered how only with difficulty had I crammed my mother's diaries into its shallow space. It must be stuck. Rising to my feet, I tipped the secretaire carefully towards me and began to shake it. The drawer jerked open an inch, two inches, no more. Kneeling again, I tugged and pulled at it. Tantalizingly, I could see the scuffed green leather of the diaries now, could almost but not quite squeeze my fingers in to touch them. I began once more violently to shake the secretaire, to pull at the drawer, tearing my fingernails upon the unyielding wood.

Then, all of a sudden, I had an uncanny sense of someone watching me. I leapt to my feet, feeling obscurely guilty, turning to the door.

But there was no one. The doorway was empty, I was alone in the room, I must have imagined it. Yet, all the same, the guilt persisted. Though the secretaire was mine, I could not prove it nor even, supposing I could force the drawer open at last, could I establish that I had any claim on its contents. I no longer had anything to do with this house. I had no one to speak for me or even confirm my relationship to the de Lisles. If I removed what was inside the secretaire would I not technically be stealing, even though they were my possessions by right?

I carefully pushed the drawer shut again and let the catch spring back. Despite a pleasing elegance of design, the secretaire was old, the flap scarred, the veneer cracked, the wood brittle with lack of polish. It could appear remarkable only to me and would certainly fetch no more than a pound or two in the auction. Though it seemed an absurdity to acquire furniture when in a month's time I should be leaving the country, I was sure Mrs Schumacher would not mind once she learnt it was of sentimental value. I had seven pounds saved in my Post Office account which should be ample. I would put in a bid for the secretaire that afternoon.

The atmosphere in the marquee was stifling as the sun beat down upon the canvas and more and more people, drifting back late from luncheon, crammed into its confines. From my vantage point near one of the flaps I could see through the greenish gloom the auctioneer himself on his rostrum and, between the heads of the crowd, glimpses of the auctioneers' men carrying smaller pieces of furniture and other lots in and out of the tent for display as they came under the hammer. Bidding had been brisk but so far only the expected lots, a series of Meissen figures, some Sèvres porcelain and a magnificently inlaid tallboy which had graced Aunt Jessica's room, had fetched high prices. A little red-faced man in a tweed jacket a few yards away from me, clearly a dealer from King's Lynn or perhaps even from London, had bid successfully for all of them. Watching him notching up guineas with the minutest movement of his catalogue, pitting his will so determinedly against the competitive bidding, I was glad my mother's desk, albeit intriguingly described by the auctioneers as 'A Lady's Secretary after the style of Sheraton, possibly by Seddon, c. 1768', was a shabby old thing, unworthy of his interest.

Nevertheless, as we reached Lot 102, the schoolroom piano, I could feel a fluttering of nervousness, a dampness in my palms. Encouragingly, the piano fetched only five shillings, and the schoolroom armchair which came after it a mere half a crown. Then the auctioneers' men were carrying in my mother's secretaire, the crowd were peering on tiptoe at it, and the bidding for Lot 104 was beginning.

To my horror, the auctioneer started us at five guineas. I waved my hand frantically at him. Next to me, the red-faced dealer gave a flick of his catalogue. Bidding came as well from two other places in the marquee. I bid beyond my seven pound limit, up to ten guineas, then to thirteen, then to fifteen, eight pounds eight shillings more than I possessed in the world. But, beside me, the red-faced dealer continued his steady, relentless flick, flick of paper. And in what seemed only a matter of seconds I saw with disbelief, with despair, that I was beaten. My mother's secretaire and her diaries, which I had so unexpectedly regained, were now as lost to me as if Aunt Jessica had been true to her word and destroyed them all those years ago.

I watched, bewildered, as the bidding went up to thirty guineas, as the other bidders dropped out and now the fate of the secretaire seemed only to hang on the discreet flicker of the dealer's catalogue and the auctioneer's gavel which was falling, falling. Then another bidder from the far side of the tent jumped in, and suddenly the price was shooting up, not in ones now but fives. The dealer seemed to grow redder in the face, the movement of the paper less discreet. I craned my neck to catch a glimpse of his opponent but could see nothing but the mass of the crowd.

45–50–55–60 – I was almost dizzy with it. The audience, too, was completely silent, as if absorbed in the battle of wills. At seventy-five guineas the dealer began to raise his catalogue then, thinking better of it, shook his head with a sour smile, implying to one and all that anyone who would pay such a price for a small secretaire, even a Georgian one, was a fool with more money than sense. There was a rustle amongst the crowd as 104 was knocked down to the unseen bidder.

I stood for a while, fighting tears, no longer aware of what was going on around me, crushed with despair. Then all at once I realized I was simply being foolish. Whoever had bid seventy-five guineas had paid the money for the secretaire, not its hidden contents. The Stephenograph, the lavender sachet, my mother's diaries could be of no possible value to him – in all probability if he ever found them he would only throw them away. But they, above everything, were what was most precious to me. If I could only find the desk's new owner perhaps I could persuade him to give me the contents of the drawer or offer to buy them from him if he proved intractable.

I pushed my way out of the marquee and hurried round the side of it towards the house. The clerk behind his mahogany table, surely he would be able to tell me who had bought the secretaire, or at least the address to which it was to be delivered?

I waited impatiently in a small queue. When it came to my turn I was breathless and could scarcely speak.

The clerk, a dour, balding man, looked up from his paper disapprovingly. 'Madam,' he said, licking his tight lips, 'I am not empowered to disclose information regarding any buyer without prior authorization.'

'Oh, but please, I don't want to bother anyone. I don't even care about the secretaire. Just what's inside it, that's all – '

'Sorry, madam. We have our rules. It's more than my job's worth.'

I could feel the tears beginning to well up again. 'But you don't understand. It was my mother's desk – '

The clerk's lips pursed in irritation. 'Madam, you heard me the first time. Not without prior authorization.'

'Mrs Cadwallander needs no authorization,' said a quiet voice from behind him. 'The desk was bought for her.'

I should have known that voice anywhere. And yes, despite all my resolutions, it did still make my heart lurch to hear it.

CHAPTER THIRTY-NINE

Diary of Adele Ward. Volume the Third.
Silver Strands Boarding House, Weymouth.

22nd August, 1904.

This afternoon, as Bridie, who is truly not so much a maid-of-all-work as a veritable treasure, had promised to take upon herself the preparation of the suppers, I seized advantage of her generosity to stroll for a while along the Promenade.

Nine years, I recall it is, since M deserted me, six since I first came here. How much has occurred during that time, what grievous setbacks and small triumphs, what visions of the workhouse one moment and hopes of prosperity the next! Watching the young girls with their parasols and Gibson Bends parading arm in arm with their mashers, I found myself thinking of my own spent youth and of my drab brown dress which, like my other two well-worn gowns, I have long ago abandoned refurbishing with the lastest season's lace or passementerie. Who would recognize me now? Not M. Not J certainly, who, were she capable of relenting in her hatred, could never bring herself to acknowlege a sister who takes in paying boarders at a seaside lodging house!

And does this fall from Society's grace concern me? I am sorry to relate, not a whit! Oh, I may have freckles on my nose and roughened hands, and a day spent trifling with my embroidery or my paintbox may seem to me now an unimaginable luxury: yet I can scrub floors and black grates with a proficiency which would shame most housemaids; I have a better friend in Bridie than ever I had amongst my Mayfair acquaintance; in a good year I can extend my hundred per annum into two or three which, while it does not precisely allow for extravagance, gives us a comfortable living; and when I retire to bed at night, though my back aches from the day's toil, there is satisfaction in its twinges.

All in all, I found myself thinking as I walked on through the gardens, listening to the band on the Raft striking up 'Weymouth Chimes', I have, as I vowed I should, survived. Though the Season ends with the first week in September I have sufficient winter boarders to carry me through until Spring; the Misses Y will stay on, and that kind Mrs W from London is sending me a young man, an émigré from Roumania, who must take the sea air this winter for his health. Bridie and I shall go on gossiping, and quarrelling with the fishmonger, and despairing of the elder Miss Y's little dog; I shall continue to derive satisfaction from knowing by my boarders' smiles that they are content. Oh, there are no dizzy moments, no ecstasies, no heady storms of passion; there is nothing in this life of the romantic dream with which my girlish heart was once so foolishly deluded; but, in its very humdrum, bread-and-butter reality, there is peace.

How different from my cruel years of bondage with M! Preparing to retire for the night with my one indulgence, a volume of poetry – Mrs Barrett Browning is my special delight for the nonce –I find myself wondering where he is: swaggering at the stage door of some low theatre, incarcerated in a foreign gaol, perhaps? Wherever he may be, I am not grieved that it is far away.

25th August, 1904.

Mr R, our Roumanian, arriving today, proves to be no more than a boy of eighteen or nineteen and, apart from Mrs W's kind sponsorship, as poor as a church mouse. His history is indeed a sad one, his Papa having been imprisoned in Austro-Hungary for nationalist agitation and dying in a Magyar gaol, his Mamma expiring from consumption in London, whence she and her son had fled. The boy, it appears, has musical gifts and had taken up a piano scholarship at the Royal College until a doctor's examination warned he was likely to succumb to his mother's fate unless removed from the unhealthy town air.

All this we learn from Mrs W's letter of introduction, for the boy himself speaks little English apart from 'yes' and 'no', though he smiles a great deal and seems a pleasant and respectable sort of person. Bridie considers him very good-looking, like Rudolf Rassendyll from The Prisoner of Zenda, *she says, with his striking colouring and aquiline profile, and I grant he is tall and has nice eyes; but he is woefully thin with a sharp cough which brings a hectic flush to his cheeks. Nevertheless Bridie and I are resolved to feed him up and see what our bracing ozone may do, and I am deputed by Bridie to teach him English as soon as he is strong enough. I think Bridie has taken rather a <u>fancy</u> to him – she made a great business of brewing him cocoa and putting extra bottles in his bed.*

Oh how by our thoughts sometimes <u>we may summon up the devil!</u> How much do I regret my speculations of two days hence! I had just laid down my pen in preparation for bed when I heard the doorbell ring and Bridie appeared to say there was a gentleman asking for me: and when I descended to the front parlour I found it was <u>M</u>!

I scarcely recognized him at first, for he is greatly changed. His countenance is red and mottled, his handsome black hair greying and much depleted, and his walk has a rolling Jack Tar gait. Yet, when he spoke my name and called me 'dearest', I knew him at once and, pulling my peignoir tighter about me, drew back in horror.

'My dearest wifie,' he said with an ingratiating smile, 'are you not pleased to see your beloved husband come home at last?'

What could I do? I begged and pleaded with him to quit my house, yet he made no move to leave and I feared the disturbance of having him by some means ejected forcibly – though I knew not how – would awaken my boarders at so late an hour. He is unwell, he says, and down on his luck and, chancing to pass through Weymouth, wants no more than a roof over his head for the night.

I cannot forgive him for his cruelty and vile conduct. I feel uneasy merely at the thought of his being in the house. Yet he is my husband; and, though I believe I am absolved now from all duty to him, I cannot, on a wild night when he is ill and has no money in his pocket, consign him to the mercies of a bench on the Promenade. He will not wish to prolong his stay beyond a night; our existence here is as dull as ditchwater for one of M's proclivities. I have put him in the small top back bedroom and tomorrow morning I shall give him the five pounds I have put by for emergencies to speed him on his way.

PS. When I enquired how he had found me, for no one from my former life knows my whereabouts, not even Sir Arthur, he replied that he had traced me through my bankers – oh, how I curse the lingering spell of that wretched thousand a year!!!

CHAPTER FORTY

He was standing at the foot of the front steps, a cigarette between his long fingers, as if he had been there all the time within the shadows of the doorway, smoking, watching for me. It was, after those six years, after the twelve in which he had been lost to me, such a strange sensation to come upon him thus, a sensation at once of the infinitely familiar and of the unknown. His face was the face I remembered and yet there were lines around the mouth I did not recall, a new sharpness to the cheekbones, hints of premature silver at the temples. Though he was dressed with his customary elegance, silk shirt open at the neck upon a Charvet cravat, cream tussore jacket draped negligently over his shoulders, there was in the cut of his suit something indefinably foreign which, too, gave him a distanced, alien air. He leant upon a silver-topped cane and, with his eternal dislike of hats, had taken up against the sun the American habit of dark glasses so that there was a strangeness in that above all, like looking at a blind man, until you realized that the blindness was yours, being unable to see, in the eyes, all the motive power of the face.

I did not know how to greet him, this man who had once been my lover, was now a stranger, was perhaps, after all, my brother. In the end, though I took a pace towards him, I did nothing. He was smiling, but the masked eyes gave a distance to it, a reserve that emphasized his strangeness. I was all at once self-conscious in my simple, cotton-print dress and straw hat, wondering absurdly whether he would notice that my hair, drawn up beneath the straw into a flat chignon, was long again.

'I watched you in the dining room,' he said softly. 'I'd never seen the desk before, but I knew then it must once have been yours.'

So I had not imagined it, there had been someone there. 'Oh, Felix,' I stammered, 'it's very generous of you, but I couldn't – well, it's only the things in the drawer that are really important and if I'm going – I couldn't possibly accept – ' I paused, thinking how ungracious, even to my own ears, I sounded. 'Thank you, Felix. It was kind of you to realize how much it means to me.'

There was a silence, as if neither of us could think of anything further to say. It was I who broke it eventually: 'I was so sorry to hear about your wife and son.'

For the merest of moments there seemed in the lines around his mouth to be a tightening, like a spasm of pain, so that I instantly felt I had intruded. 'Everything passes in time,' he said. Then, throwing away his cigarette: 'I was sorry to hear from Meredith of your divorce.'

I smiled. 'My stain upon your family's honour? How is poor Meredith these days?'

'At last we have reason to be thankful for Ramsay MacDonald. Meredith has finally reached the dizzy heights of Junior Minister. Agriculture and Fisheries.'

We both laughed. It seemed to ease things, imperceptibly to bridge the gulf between us. I looked at him again, at the face I had once so lovingly explored with my kisses, the face that was like mine and not like it. My brother?

'You have not remarried,' he said. Although it was not a question there was, nevertheless, a questioning undertone to it.

'I'm happy on my own,' I said. 'It may be hard work sometimes, but I have my independence. And that's, above all, what I've always wanted.'

'Yes,' he said. 'I remember.' And there was in his smile now a faint trace of his old mockery. 'Come, let's find your newly-acquired Georgian secretary and see if, between us, we can't force open your mysterious drawer.'

I followed him up the steps and through into the hall. The cane was not an affectation; he was, I observed, limping slightly. The secretaire had been returned with other sold lots to the dining room, where it stood against a wall. I sprang the concealed catch and while he, casting aside the cane, tilted and shook the desk, I tried in vain to pull out the drawer. But it was no good. Whatever we did, it would not open more than a couple of inches.

'It's the diaries,' I said, out of breath with my exertions. 'They must have jammed it at the back.'

He looked thoughtful for a moment, then, wandering off amongst the other furniture, came back eventually with a wooden ruler he had found in the drawer of the schoolroom table. I watched him as, with obvious pain, he knelt down and slowly and carefully began to ease the ruler through the narrow opening, between the wood and the leather of the diaries. His face, concentrating, was so close as I knelt beside him that I could have put out my hand and touched it. Finally he gave a small exclamation of triumph as the end of the ruler reached the back of the drawer.

'Now, if you use that to press down as hard as you can upon the diaries, I'll try to shift the drawer.'

It gave suddenly, in a rush, with all the pent-up force of the released spring, almost throwing us both off balance. For a moment we were face to face, breathless, slightly dishevelled by our endeavours, smiling delightedly at our success. And there was in the proximity of our bodies, in the unconscious intimacy of the task we had just shared, such a sense of recognition, of slipping back effortlessly into an old pattern, that I felt for that instant the barriers between us fall away as if they had never existed. Was this what it was like when love died, I wondered, the familiarity remaining behind like a habit? Or was it perhaps what it was like to have a brother, someone you knew and did not know, the two of you coming always from different directions but to the same centre, held by a bond you knew instinctively but not in reason? I wished all at once very much that I could see his eyes behind the glasses.

He straightened himself painfully while I took one by one from the open drawer the Stephenograph, the lavender sachet, the strings of pearls and the two volumes of my mother's diary that had escaped Aunt Jessica, turning each object over in my hands, fondling it lovingly, before I passed it to him. Closing the drawer and getting to my feet, I let my hands play over the secretaire's scarred walnut again, glad now, so glad that it too had been restored to me.

'I don't suppose Mrs Schumacher will really mind,' I said, more to myself than to him. 'It's not a very big desk, there must be room for it in a packing crate somewhere – '

He looked up from the little pile of my mother's belongings. 'You're going abroad?'

'Yes, next month. To America. To start a new life.'

'I see.'

'You must tell me what it's like. To live there permanently, I mean.'

'Yes. Yes, of course.' He was glancing round for his stick and there was now something in his manner that dispelled the last echoes of our moment's intimacy, raised all the barriers again. I was embarrassed at my tactlessness, feeling that my mention of America must have come to him as another unwarrantable intrusion on his grief.

'Well,' he said, moving to the door, 'you must tell me where to send the desk in the meantime. And we'll try to find someone to make a parcel of these things so you can take them with you today.'

I followed him back into the hall. Despite the sunshine pouring in through the open front door there was still a chill of damp in the air that made me recoil. Watching him give my little pile of possessions to one of the auctioneers' men to be packed up in brown paper and string, I felt again the strangeness of my being there with him, the whole paradoxical mixture of our intimacy and our constraint. I was certain that after so many years I had persuaded myself out of loving him, and yet the bond had been there all the same in the moment of our opening the drawer, firm, enduring, stronger than time.

He had believed from the first that he was my brother, had said he had understood instinctively that what Aunt Jessica had told him was true. Propped against the hall panelling beside us was the great gilded mirror that had hung over the mantelpiece in the drawing room and, looking at our images reflected in it, two tall figures, the faces different in the detail of their composition and yet, like variations upon a single theme, sufficiently similar nevertheless, I did not doubt that an outsider would detect, as Dilly had, the family resemblance, nor unquestioningly believe we were brother and sister. Had I used my love for him simply to blind myself to what, for anyone else, would have been obvious? Was this strangeness now merely the instinctive sense of it he had experienced, freed within me at last from sentimental delusion, coming to consciousness? I stared at the two looking-glass images in perplexity, scarcely recognizing them, suddenly feeling even my own identity confused.

His reflection, turning, seeming to follow my eyeline, appeared in the instant of meeting my reflected gaze to feel it too, to pause transfixed for a moment, then, as if he read what was in my mind, to draw back with a scarcely perceptible shiver of distaste.

'I've always hated this house,' he said. 'Let's go outside into the sun.'

From the front steps we could hear the auctioneer's steady litany, singing the dissolution of Monks Last, smashing the pattern of the past with every decisive blow of his gavel. After the mustiness of the hall the air smelt sweet with honeysuckle and flowering grasses, the afternoon sun burned warm upon the bare skin of my arms.

Felix lit a cigarette. 'Would you like to go back to the marquee? The Bechstein should come up within the next half hour. I'd be happy to make you a present of it.'

I laughed at his profligacy. 'Oh Felix, you've already been far too generous. And besides, while I'm sure Mrs Schumacher won't mind the desk, she might raise an eyebrow at crossing the Atlantic with a grand piano.'

He threw away his spent match. 'Yes, of course, I had forgotten.'

'But what about you? There must be some things here you're sorry to see go.'

He drew upon his cigarette, looking straight ahead of him at the marquee and beyond it, and when he spoke there was a bitterness in his voice that chilled me. 'My dear Christabel, I have already lost everything I value. There is nothing in this house I should miss.'

Then, as if he regretted the bitterness, or at least the self-revelation in it, he turned away abruptly. 'Come, let's leave them to it. We'll walk for a little.'

My eyes went doubtfully to his stick, paused there a fraction too long. He flicked at the gravel with the tip of it irritably.

'It's nothing. Merely a last-ditch attempt by the doctors to prove they were right all along. There are good days and bad days. And the bad days I ignore.'

Suitably reproved, I fell in beside him and we set off, along the front of the house, skirting the west terrace where all those years ago I had bumped into him sketching, in the direction of the lake. The noise of the auction was behind us and now the air was full of subtler sounds, the whirr of dragon fly wings, the soft chatter of grasshoppers.

I looked back at the impassive west face of the house. 'Why did Meredith decide to sell?' I asked.

'Money,' he said. 'The income from the capital our – his father left won't stretch as far as it did and a Junior Minister's salary doesn't amount to much – not if you're married to Sybil, anyway. I've been more fortunate, I suppose. I live on what I can earn and people still seem foolish enough to buy my paintings. Besides – ' and here once more was the undertone of pain – 'I have no dependants. But Meredith in the main exists on his investments. So, after generations, the de Lisles have decided to give up being landed gentry.'

We had doubled back across the west lawn and now, walking on in silence, came to the door leading into the walled kitchen garden. Here, with the overgrown paths, the beds full of dock and dead-nettles, the espaliered plum trees thrusting out crippled arms in a forlorn attempt to straighten themselves, the signs of Magnus's passing were still more obvious.

'Meredith offered the estate to me,' Felix said suddenly, 'before he put it up for auction. Of course he was oblivious to the irony of it. Quite apart from my dislike of the house, I should feel, even if I had paid for the privilege, an arrant impostor as master of it. It seems dishonourable enough to bear a name I am not entitled to.'

I stared at him, surprised again by the bitterness in his voice and, as I had been when I had first known him, by the unexpectedly personal, the unlooked-for break in his control. His mouth was sardonic. I wished once more that I could see his eyes.

'But that's ridiculous,' I said. 'Even if – if what Aunt Jessica told you were true, you would still have every right to the estate from the Cavendish side of the family.'

He gave a little sharp laugh. 'Ah yes, the Cavendishes. The de Lisles, the Cavendishes and the Wards. Let us not, my dear Christie – ' and here he flicked viciously with his cane at a clump of dead-nettles – 'let us not, above all, forget the Wards.'

We had crossed what had been the strawberry bed and had begun to walk down the central path towards the apple tree and the water butt where once I had sat and watched him walk with Aunt Jessica on a sunny afternoon eighteen years before; and in that instant I saw it, the pattern again – mother, son, sister, brother – saw it with an almost superstitious shiver, and saw too that perhaps it was not breaking but only changing, subtly, stealthily reforming itself.

'Damn them!' I said. 'Damn the de Lisles, the Cavendishes and the Wards!'

'Yes, my little sister,' he said softly. 'Damn, damn them.'

At the intersection of paths Magnus's old bench, too weather-beaten to be worthy of auction, stood beside the water butt where it had always been. It seemed inevitable that we should sit on it. We remained in silence for a while, he smoking, I looking out across the tangle of weeds to where the bees busied themselves with the plum blossom.

'Who did buy the estate in the end?' I asked.

To my amazement he began to laugh, this time with genuine amusement. 'You mean you haven't heard? Oh my dear Christie, at least there is a little rough justice in the world. Do you remember Corporal Routledge?'

'The man who died beside you in the shell hole? The blacksmith's son?'

'Well, it seems the eldest Routledge brother went to Canada after the war and made his fortune. And when he came back to find Monks Last up for auction the opportunity was irresistible. He intends to let out the land, apparently, and turn the house and grounds into a country club.'

'Oh.' My vague imaginings of people making a home of the place, a family with children who, being happy there, would lift the bleakness like a curse, conflicted oddly with the idea of tennis courts and ping-pong rooms and cocktail bars. 'Isn't that rather awful?'

'Yes, I suppose it is, if you're disposed to be sentimental about the house. But it'll bring money and jobs into the village, which badly needs both. And that's more useful than sentiment.'

I smiled. 'So the croquet lawn will after all become a swimming pool.'

'And Monks Last, having taken so much over the years, will finally give a little back.'

He threw away his cigarette and looked at his watch. 'Anatole is arriving with the car at four. Are you catching the train back to London tonight?'

I explained that I was staying at the Rose in the village and intended to visit Mrs Wix.

'Then we shall pick up your parcel and Anatole shall drive you there.' He rose stiffly. 'I'm at the Blue Boar in King's Lynn. Perhaps, if I send the car for you this evening, you will allow me to give you dinner.'

Later I wondered why he had issued the invitation. I realized, as I sat talking to Mrs Wix, toying with a glass of the cream sherry I had taken her, as I fussed over the only other of my few frocks I had brought with me, a white rayon cinema dress printed with black and pink lozenges which suddenly looked out-of-date and shabby, that it had made me unaccountably nervous, as nervous as I had been as a girl. And nervous I was still as I walked into the panelled saloon bar of the Blue Boar, seeing him before he saw me, a handsome, dark-suited figure, strangely incongruous amongst the tweedy farmers and corn chandlers. It had again that disturbing sense of familiarity, watching him look up, rise to greet me, just as meeting Anatole as he held open the door of the racing-green Bentley, his perennial smile appearing to broaden with genuine pleasure at seeing me, had felt so familiar, so comfortable, like coming home. But there the familiarity ended. Felix had once again resumed his impenetrable reserve. Though he no longer wore the dark glasses, and though I did not quite dare to meet his eyes, I knew they would be as carefully empty now as when I had first met him. It was as if the moment when we had managed to open the drawer of the secretaire had never existed, as if we were chance acquaintances, nothing more.

Yet there was about his detachment something different too. In the bar, in the gloom of the nearly-empty dining room over sinewy duckling and soggy cabbage, I had more space to observe him than I had found at the auction. Though he was not obviously in pain as he had been during the afternoon, I noticed how thin and ill he looked without the disguise of the glasses. He drank little, though the claret had admirably survived the Blue Boar's ministrations, and ate hardly at all. After a while it struck me with the force of shock what the change in him was. Before, beneath his indifference there had always been a sense of fierce energy, of passion held in check by that careful, disciplined coolness, so that in his very restraint there was something highly-charged. But now the tension was gone, in its place was only lassitude, a profound exhaustion in which the smallest movement seemed too great an effort. It was as if, drained by an excess of emotion, he had become at last too tired for feeling. The indifference was no longer a mask.

He talked little and I, anxious more than ever not to intrude upon what was closed to me, sensing the loss of his wife and child in wait like an ambush for the most casual question about his life since we had parted, found myself chattering on about Mrs Wix and my failure at the music lessons and Mrs Schumacher and even Dilly's letters from India, so much was it left to my part to make at least a pretence at conversation. It occurred to me that there were now so many areas of my life too – Archie, the divorce, the loss of my own child – which I could not and would not talk about that conversation was, besides, in any proper sense impossible between us. He appeared to be trying to listen to my chatter but again I had the feeling it was an effort for him, that he was involuntarily drifting off somewhere else; and once, when I accidentally met his eyes, they too seemed focused elsewhere, and there was something about them as well, not emotion, for they were perfectly inexpressive, but a curious disturbance of their symmetry which I could not precisely define.

'I'm sorry,' I said. 'You mustn't let me rattle on at you like this.'

He smiled then, as if he were making a conscious attempt to concentrate. 'My dear Christie, you don't rattle on. I'm delighted you're so well and so happy.'

But nevertheless, though he insisted on accompanying me on the drive back to the Rose and on my returning to London in the Bentley the next morning instead of by train, I felt that he was not delighted, that everything, even his generosity in buying the secretaire, had been merely a kind of politeness. I could not think why I felt so disappointed about a meeting which after all could hold out nothing for me, or why, since I was so certain I had ceased to love him, when the car drew up outside Mrs Schumacher's house in Clarges Street I was suddenly so sad. We had said scarcely anything to each other on the drive back and, looking at that closed face, the long, thin fingers languidly lifting the cigarette, I had kept repeating to myself: 'This is my brother, my brother.' The idea confused me, there was still something within me that refused to accept it. Yet, if he were not my brother, he must now be nothing at all to me.

Still, I told myself, it did not matter. I was going away, in a month's time I would be in America. Brother or not, I was convinced I should not see him again before I left, that though he knew where I was he would not seek me out. I was convinced of it not just because of his manner towards me, but for another reason which I was aware of only when I was up in my room unpacking my bag; for in all the hours we had been together, when he had taken my coat, opened the car door to let me get out, pulled back my chair in the hotel dining room, even when he had helped me open the drawer of the secretaire, he had not once, not even fleetingly or by accident, ever touched me, as if he had deliberately, scrupulously avoided doing so.

CHAPTER FORTY-ONE

I was convinced I should not see him again, and yet one afternoon a week later when I returned from walking Barrymore the parlour maid informed me that a gentleman had called and I heard voices and laughter from the drawing room.

My heart inexplicably began to thump. Still clutching my parcels, I hovered for a second outside the drawing room door. But Barrymore, off the lead, would not allow me to make a furtive entrance. He burst through, yelping and squeaking with his usual homecoming delight. And there they were, Mrs Schumacher reclining on the sofa in a befrilled fuschia tea gown and Felix by the cocktail cabinet, shaker in his hands, mixing her a martini and laughing at something she had said, precisely as if they were old friends.

They looked round as I entered and Barrymore, like a small white missile, hurtled onto Mrs Schumacher's lap.

'Christabel! Martians could visit, you wouldn't mention it. Felix de Lisle is your cousin, and do you say one word on the subject?'

Felix smiled wryly as he fitted the martini glass into her little claw of a hand. 'She wasn't any more informative about you, I'm afraid. She mentioned a Mrs Schumacher but said absolutely nothing to connect you with the Schumacher Collection.'

I stared at Felix. He held my gaze imperturbably.

'But Felix de Lisle, the painter!' The eyelashes fluttered like butterflies. 'Felix de Lisle whose work I am crazy for, whose pictures I bought in New York, the war painting and the two cubist still lifes! You know him – he's even a relative – and we're in London three months, you don't say a word. Only by chance I get to meet him, because he comes to deliver your desk.'

'Oh.' For some reason, perhaps because of my very reluctance to answer the questions I knew it would invite, I had omitted to mention the secretaire. 'Oh Mrs Schumacher, I'm so sorry.'

'For the desk you shouldn't apologize. It's a fine piece, so – ' and here she groped unsuccessfully for a suitable adjective – 'so historical. And so kind of Mr de Lisle – though it should scorch your tongue to mention him yet – to take all this trouble delivering it in person.'

The note of innuendo in her voice, the deductions she would immediately and erroneously draw, embarrassed me. 'I think I'll go to my room and look at it, if you don't mind.'

'Do that, dear. But hurry back, have a martini with us. This Mr de Lisle you forgot you knew has invited us both to Boulestin's for dinner.'

Up in my room I willed my hands to stop their ridiculous trembling. Why had he, on such a flimsy pretext, come back? But later, sipping my martini and watching the two of them on the sofa, Mrs Schumacher patting his arm with her gnarled claw, fussing with the blonde curls of her transformation, flirting with all the outrageous bravado of her sixty years, and Felix being charming in return, I was obscurely happy, glad that I had seen him once more before I left England for good.

He was different again tonight, I thought, closer to the Felix I had loved. Oh, he still wore his habitual air of detachment, but the bitterness and the exhaustion appeared to have gone, his laughter seemed genuine and his easiness unforced. He no longer carried the stick, I noticed, and, though his face in repose still bore traces of that haggard look, there was about it too a renewed vitality, as if behind the cool façade the spring of his energy were once more coiled.

Watching him covertly above my martini glass, I was alarmed to discover that, while Mrs Schumacher held him in full, discursive flow, his eyes were fixed upon me. To my irritation, I felt myself blush. And, as if an eddy had appeared in the flood, Mrs Schumacher's conversation reached a hiatus and stopped. There was a second of silence, then she announced most unconvincingly that she had forgotten to make a very important telephone call.

'But you'll look after Mr de Lisle for me won't you, dear?' she said, dumping a protesting Barrymore in my lap. 'Maybe it'll help you remember you're acquainted.' And, to my chagrin, hidden from Felix by the door, she screwed up the eyelashes into a conspiratorial wink.

Felix had risen and was standing before the mantelpiece lighting a cigarette. The silence continued and now there was a curious tension about it. To break it, I said: 'It was good of you to take such care over the desk.'

He drew upon the cigarette and his expression was all at once serious. 'My dear Christie, you know I came in the hope of seeing you.'

My hand quivered suddenly so that I spilled some of my drink on Barrymore, who licked it off indignantly.

'Oh?' I said.

'Yes. I've been thinking about you a great deal since we met. I – '

He paused. I put my other hand to the rim of my glass to stop it shaking.

'You should know that I no longer touch the money I was left in Sir Arthur's will. I haven't since – ' He paused again, made a brief, almost helpless gesture with his cigarette, then continued rapidly. 'The income from it is considerably smaller than it was. Nevertheless, over the years it has mounted up to quite a reasonable sum. I should like to make it over to you, together with the capital and any further income it may earn.'

I stared at him. It was ridiculously, impossibly generous of him. And yet at the same time it frightened me too. The secretaire, the Bechstein and now this, such profligate giving of things where once, more generously, he had given of himself.

'Oh Felix, I don't know what to say. It's so very kind of you, but there's no need – '

'Yes, Christie, there is a need. It seems to me the family has treated you most unfairly. As – as your closest blood relative I find it impossible to stand by and watch you struggling for your living with nothing and no one to protect you. I should like you to have the money. And, in addition, as I realize that when you give up your job you will be homeless, I should like to offer you a place in my house until you have decided what to do with your life. There is a great deal of room at Cheyne Walk, as you know, and since I now use very little of it I'm sure we can exist together without getting in each other's way – '

I had continued to stare at him, speechless. Now, within me, there was a feeling of something sinking. 'Felix, thank you but – '

'There is no reason to thank me. I am merely attempting, rather late, to fulfil my duty, the duty any brother has to his sister – '

'Duty?' I was suddenly overwhelmed with an unreasoning anger that brought me to the verge of tears. I stood up, catapulting Barrymore ignominiously from my lap. 'Felix, you have no duty that I know of to me. I don't need your money, or your patronage, or your ideas of how I should rearrange my life. I'm perfectly happy, thank you, just as I am!'

'Here?' he said, glancing at Barrymore, who was attempting to restore his ruffled dignity upon the sofa. 'Here, where you are?'

'Nothing but a glorified servant? Well, isn't that what you were going to say?'

'Here, where you are not free.' His voice had tightened perceptibly. 'You used to place such value upon your freedom. The money would restore it to you, you could begin your piano studies again.'

'That was only a childish fantasy,' I said. 'I accept I haven't the talent, I accept myself as I am. And yes, here I am free, despite what you say. Because I can be myself, because I don't have to conform to someone else's idea of me, Archie's or the family's or your idea of what your – sister – should or shouldn't do. I'm not seventeen any longer, Felix. I don't have to answer any more to the de Lisles!'

'Oh my dear Christabel, forgive me!' And now I felt his anger sparking off mine. 'I had assumed that since you were no longer seventeen you would cease to cling to your seventeen-year-old notions of romantic poverty. Or your obstinate seventeen-year-old pride!'

'How dare you!' I was trembling with anger now. I had a

sudden recollection of him a few moments before being charming to Mrs Schumacher and felt all at once the disloyalty of it. 'And how dare you go behind poor Mrs Schumacher's back like this! I suppose you think it's perfectly all right to be sugar and spice while she's in the room and then sneer at my life here when she's gone. What does she matter to you? Oh, she buys your paintings so you can tell me proudly you earn your own living. But for the rest she's just a foolish old woman to you, isn't she? Well, she may be silly sometimes. But she's also sweet and generous and very, very kind. And I'm happy here because she needs me. Yes, she needs me, Felix, unlike – '

I broke off, suddenly alarmed by the force of the anger he had ignited in me, by the way I could feel it flaring between us, my eyes burning with it, his face no longer guarded but white hot.

'Thank you, my dear Christabel,' he said acidly, turning away. 'I see you have also retained your seventeen-year-old estimation of my character.'

'Oh Felix, I'm sorry.' At once I realized how rude and ungracious I had been. Subsiding onto the sofa beside Barrymore, I allowed two tears that also shamed me to fall invisibly on the white fur of the dog's head, causing the animal to look up with a pained expression.

'I really am sorry. I didn't mean it. I can't thank you enough for your generosity. But there is truly no need, not out of duty – I really couldn't, couldn't accept . . .' I tailed off miserably, looking down at my hands.

'I understand,' he said quietly. 'But don't answer me yet. Give yourself time to think about it.'

When I glanced up he was standing before the mantelpiece, cool and detached again. And when, a few moments later, Mrs Schumacher fluttered back into the room with an explanation for the length of her telephone call which made the inventive powers of Edgar Wallace pale by comparison, it was as if the conversation had never happened. Yet it stayed with me nevertheless, filling me with a misery which seemed so disproportionate to its cause that I was irritable and scratchy with it.

Mrs Schumacher, of course, was highly excited at the prospect of dinner and, in the interval of Felix going off to change before coming in the car to collect us, had got herself up like a veritable wedding cake, persuading her maid to squeeze her into her most uplifting Beautiform Garment and donning every available diamond and pearl that had not been deposited for safekeeping at the bank. Me she had compelled into my one respectable evening dress, the low-backed rose quartz satin she had browbeaten me into accepting as a present on my last birthday.

'Well,' she said, surveying the tallness and the shortness of us in her looking glass and giving a disapproving upward slap to her double chins, 'for old Rosa Schumacher I can't say so much, but you, dear, all dressed up for your gentleman caller, you look as pretty as a picture.'

I gave way to my edginess. 'Mrs Schumacher, once and for all, Felix de Lisle is not my "gentleman caller".'

Though I felt instantly ashamed at taking my bad temper out on her, she shrugged it off good-humouredly.

'If I were young and gemütlich he'd be mine, believe me. You know,' and here she looked up at me thoughtfully, 'I'm still getting this feeling I've seen you before.'

'It's probably Felix,' I said, concealing my scratchiness in a pretence of fastening the clasp of her necklace. 'People say we look very alike.'

'They do, dear?' said Mrs Schumacher vaguely. 'Well, I guess all you British aristocrats do – maybe it's something in the shape of your noses. But no, I never met your cousin before, that it can't be. Nevertheless, I'm wondering . . .' she tweaked pensively at the fringe of her transformation, then appeared to go off on another track. 'I told you he's promised we can go visit his studio, see his paintings. Oh Christabel honey, for that I can't wait!'

But wait she would have to, poor, dear Mrs Schumacher. For though, as we were getting out of the Bentley after what for me had been an uncomfortable dinner, Felix had once again asked me to think over his proposal, I had already made my decision. I wrote to him the next day, an awkward, stilted letter that went through numerous drafts before I could finish it.

Dear Felix,

Once again I should like to apologize for seeming to throw your great generosity back in your face. I do appreciate your considerable kindness in offering me your inheritance and a home beneath your roof. But I cannot accept either. Please do not think this is obstinate pride. Even if we are brother and sister, I cannot believe this gives you any obligation towards me, and I should be distressed to think you continued to be concerned by it when you have your own life to concern you. I am content with my lot, more content now than I have been for many years.

Thank you, all the same, for thinking of me. It was nice to see you, if fleetingly. Perhaps, should you ever be in New York, we shall meet again one day.

I could not think how to close it, for I could not write 'with love', and 'yours sincerely' seemed ridiculously inappropriate. In the end, I just signed my name. Then I rushed out and thrust the envelope into the mouth of the nearest post box as if to hold onto it a moment longer would burn my fingers.

Three days later I was alone in the house when the parlour maid annnounced that there was a Monsieur de Tarantin asking to see me. I was relieved that Mrs Schumacher's beauty salon appointment prevented her from discovering the extent of my exalted acquaintance; but I was also alarmed. For, whatever Vladimir Tarantin wanted of me after all these years, it could surely be nothing good.

He was shown into the drawing room. He seemed even smaller than I remembered him and no longer ageless but old. The corrugated hair, though still unctuous with brilliantine, was grizzled, the dark face not so much creased now as wrinkled, shrivelled like a desiccated walnut; and there was a strain, a shiftiness about him too, so that he would not quite meet my gaze almost as if he were embarrassed. He did not offer me his hand, but dipped his head in a little sharp bow, clicking together his heels.

'Mrs Cadwallander – '

'I don't use that name now,' I said.

'Miss Ward, then. You will be surprised to see me.'

Keeping my voice as neutral as possible, I said that I was.

His hands played with the hat in his lap, then abruptly cast it aside. 'Miss Ward, I come to make you an apology.'

I stared at him, wanting to draw away, wondering if this were some kind of trick. But no, all the lines and creases of his face were working in great agitation, his tongue nervously moistened his thin lips as if he were indeed searching for unfamiliar words and was having great difficulty in finding them.

'I see you distrust me. This gives me no surprise. For very many years I have done you a great wrong.'

'Monsieur de Tarantin, I – '

His hand went up, flashing the gold of his rings. 'No. I must finish. Miss Ward, I am flesh and blood like any other man. But the needs of that flesh, you must understand, are . . .'

Here, despite his having expressly forbidden interruption, he paused, seeming again to search for words.

Embarrassed, feeling, in spite of myself, a sudden compassion for him, I said softly: 'I think I do understand.'

Momentarily his eyes blazed. 'Do you? How could you possibly? And yet, perhaps . . .' Pulling his handkerchief from his sleeve, he dabbed his lips. 'It is my misfortune, Miss Ward, many years ago, to fall in love with someone who cannot love me. His nature does not allow it and I know this. But I am a beggar, so I make do with the crumbs. He is my friend and he loves no one else. Then a girl comes, a child almost. And before this child is spread, like a great feast, everything I long for, suffer for, and may not have. But what does this child do, this girl who can offer him nothing beside me – for his art, for his intellect, for all the true things of the soul, nothing! – what does she do? She looks at the feast and she tramples on it –'

'Monsieur de Tarantin, that is not—'

Again the hand went up. 'Miss Ward, this is what I see, you understand. Oh, he will not hear a word against you. Stenko, too, is forever telling me how good you are, how kind, how you cannot hurt a fly. But I know that such a man, once he loves, will not stop loving. So if it is all ended between you it must be because you have ended it. Imagine my anger, my rage for him! When you come asking me where he is I think only how I must protect him from this bitch, this callous little whore who cares nothing for him. How am I to know the truth, Miss Ward? How am I to know you and Felix are brother and sister?'

I stared at him. 'But you did know. He told you all those years ago.'

He glanced at me in amazement for a moment, then he threw back his head in laughter. 'If you believe that you do not know my friend very well. He told me nothing. Oh, he came to me, said he must go away suddenly, and the pain in his face, that I could see. But he told me nothing. Only now can I know you are not to blame, that you, like me, love where you must not love, that you have suffered a little what I Vladimir Tarantin, have suffered. So, from my heart I, give you my apology.'

I watched him uneasily. Though his contrition appeared genuine, though we seemed to have come to the end of the conversation, he made no move to rise and had the air of preparing a further speech as if, far from finishing, we had only just begun. Unworthily, I wondered whether perhaps, after all this time, he had decided to blackmail me.

'Monsieur de Tarantin, it was good of you to come. But really there is no need for apologies. Everything is past, over and done with.' I paused. 'One thing puzzles me, though. If you did not know our secret twelve years ago how do you know it now?' Then I remembered that, on the boat, I had absolved Felix from his promise. 'Has he at last confided in you?'

'My dear Miss Ward, of course not. He said nothing then, he will say nothing now.' Suddenly the lines and creases quivered and flowed together into an expression that, for Vladimir Tarantin, was as close to shame as I would ever see. Going to his breast pocket he produced a crumpled and singed sheet of paper. 'I am afraid I have read this.'

I took it from him. It was my letter.

'Base to the last, Miss Ward, as you see.' His lips twisted self-deprecatingly. 'But my motives are perhaps not so evil as you imagine. I was with him when he opened it and it had on him such an effect that I believed – I cannot explain to you why – it was from someone else. He threw it on the fire but, as you observe, it did not burn. So – I stole it. I am not glad to confess this to you, but I am glad I now know what I know.'

Looking from him to the letter in my hands, I felt anger at his impertinence, at his unwarranted intrusion into my life. 'Monsieur de Tarantin, why have you come here?'

'My dear Miss Ward, as I have said, to apologize. But also to – to ask your help.' Again he pulled out his handkerchief and dabbed his lips. 'I have said that Felix cannot love me. But perhaps that is not true. Oh, he cannot be to me what Stenko is, but – ' he fluttered the handkerchief as if again lost for words – 'well, I must admit to you that I, Vladimir Tarantin, am not without my faults. I am jealous, I am a hard taskmaster, they tell me sometimes – ' another half-incredulous gesture with the handkerchief – 'that I am altogether unreasonable. But for seventeen years Felix has worked with me, he has suffered my jealousy, he has, as you say, "put up" with me. I do not have friends, Miss Ward, only lovers. He is the only true friend I possess. And in that, do you not think, there is a great love?'

I saw with horror that his hard black eyes were now glittering with tears. He made no attempt to disguise or staunch them, but continued as if they were not there.

'So, Miss Ward, I wish to repay that love. And to do that I must ask your help. Please – what your letter says he has offered you, please change your mind and accept it.'

Distrusting his tears and the note of melodrama that had entered his voice, I felt all my suspicion flood back. 'He has sent you here, hasn't he? He asked you to come.'

'My dear Miss Ward, no. He knows nothing of this, you must never tell him – he is a proud man, he will never forgive me. I come because he needs your help. Please, write another letter, tell him you have changed your mind, you will agree to his offer, you will go to live with him.' To my dismay, he was on his knees before me, pressing my hand in his. 'Please, Miss Ward, if you love him, do this for him.'

The pressure of his hand was crushing my fingers. I forced myself not to draw away from it and from the bitter, pungent scent of his brilliantine. The tears were still in his eyes and his face now had that softness hard men's faces take on with age, a dissolution of once-tight muscles that blurs the features to reveal a curious, almost pathetic femininity. Meeting his gaze, I could no longer doubt that his emotion was genuine.

'But why? Why is it so important I go and live with him?'

'Because he needs help. Oh, he will not pay attention to me. But to you he will listen. Because you love him.'

'Monsieur de Tarantin, love is a living thing. Cease to feed it and it dies.'

'I do not believe your love is dead.'

'He killed it. It was his duty. As my brother.'

'Help him then, as his sister.'

'Must I have my duty too, Monsieur de Tarantin?'

The bitterness in my voice surprised both of us. He released my hand and got to his feet.

'Besides, you haven't explained,' I said, more gently. 'Why does he need my help?'

'My dear Miss Ward, he has suffered, suffered so much.'

The bitterness came back and with it a corrosive, selfish anger as I remembered the barren years with Archie, the loss of my baby. 'We have all suffered, Monsieur de Tarantin.'

'Oh, but you do not understand.' The tears had gone, were suddenly replaced by a fiery agitation of voice and gesture. 'What happened in Geneva – it was terrible.'

'The death of his wife and son? Yes, of course I understand it must have been.'

He dismissed my interruption with an impatient flash of his rings. 'But afterwards. Police, examining magistrates, the funeral. As always, he is perfectly calm. Too calm. And then he becomes ill. Pleurisy, pneumonia. Of course, he will not see a doctor. Anatole wires me he is in a delirium. For three days and three nights I sit in that hospital certain he will die. He does not die, but he recovers very slowly, and there is again the old trouble with his back. He becomes strange, withdrawn. One day, he disappears altogether. No one knows where – North Africa, I heard a rumour, but who can tell for certain? Then, just as suddenly, he reappears in London. And he is – well, Miss Ward, you have seen how he is.'

I remembered how he had been in Norfolk. But in London he had seemed better. 'It is grief,' I said. 'It will pass.'

'No, it is more than that. He is still ill. And there are – ' he appeared to begin to say something, then to think better of it – 'there are other things.' He was bending over me now, the almond scent of his brilliantine sharp in my nostrils. And again, in his eyes, in every ridge and crevice of his mobile, simian face was a fierce pleading. 'Miss Ward, I think he has lost the wish to live.'

'Oh, but that's melodramatic, ridiculous!'

'Please, write to him once more. Tell him you accept his offer.'

I thought of Felix's talk of duty and how it had hurt me. I must push from my mind all memory of his haggard face, his need for the stick, his exhaustion. I feared to be hurt now, I had carefully built myself a life where such pain could not touch me.

'No,' I said gently, overcoming my repugnance and taking Vladimir Tarantin's hand lightly in mine. 'I know you have come to me out of great friendship for him. But you must understand, what you ask is impossible. I am going to America in three weeks. And I cannot change my mind.'

Yet once he had left me my certainty seemed to desert me too. I did not doubt that Tarantin was right, that, despite his dismissive remarks about doctors, the pain in his back was real, that he was still far from well. But what good could my being at Cheyne Walk possibly do? I could not talk to him, I could not reach him, so how could I possibly be of any help? Better to follow my own plans, shut my ears to Tarantin's pleas. Yet why had Tarantin gone to such lengths to see me when it must have cost him all his pride? And why was he spying on Felix, reading his letters, he who was Felix's closest friend?

Haunted by visions I could no longer banish of Felix alone, giving way to the suffering he would not show to others, I began to see my own craven desire for self-preservation as contemptible. Did I not, after all, have a duty to him too? If Felix was ill and needed me, if his life were somehow threatened, how could I think only of my life, my safety? The doubts, the sense of my own selfishness worked upon me like the pricking of needles until I snapped at Mrs Schumacher, ignored Barrymore, became abstracted and forgot things.

One evening a week later, while I was reading Mrs Schumacher to sleep with Ruby M Ayres, I faltered and lost my place so many times that she eventually raised the strap of the Patent Ganesh and pondered me thoughfully.

'You know, boobela,' she said, lifting the dog's muzzle to her face, 'I got the feeling Christabel's heart ain't with us today, I think maybe it's off dancing with that gentleman admirer of hers.'

I snapped the book shut with violence. 'Mrs Schumacher!' I exploded. 'How many times do I have to tell you that he is not, not, not my admirer!' Then I startled us both by bursting into tears.

Her arm was round me in a moment, Barrymore, who only half an hour before I had roughly pushed away, was licking my hand.

'Christabel, honey, forgive this foolish old woman – may she be marinated in cabbage – forgive her teasing. To hurt you we never meant, did we, *hundchen*?'

I fumbled for my handkerchief. 'I'm so sorry, Mrs Schumacher. How stupid of me!'

The faded eyes, naked of lashes, surveyed me sadly from their folds of flesh. Barrymore, whining, pushed his wet black nose into my lap.

'So I know better my tongue should be cut out than I should pry into your business. But *liebchen*, this grief and misery, this I can't bear to see. Ach, is it so impossible you should tell this crazy old bubba your troubles?'

So, wiping my eyes, I told her what I could, editing out Tarantin and his apology and the real reason for Felix's sense of obligation to me. 'Really it's not what you imagine, Mrs Schumacher. Felix is my – ' I still could not bring myself to say the word – 'just a relative of mine. It's simply that I can't bear to think of him alone and ill and if there is something I can do I feel I ought to do it. But I want to go to America, too, with you. Oh, I'm utterly confused by it all. I just don't know what's right any longer.'

Mrs Schumacher tickled Barrymore's ears thoughfully. 'You know, pooch,' she said, 'maybe it's time we call up that Mr de Lisle, fix to go see his paintings.'

CHAPTER FORTY-TWO

'Ach, Mr de Lisle, one tiresome old woman, how happy you make her already – that she should be so privileged to breathe the air which gives you inspiration, that she should stand upon the same spot you put the finishing brush strokes to your design for *Icarus* your portraits of Anna Rostova! This moment we'll treasure, Barrymore and me, till the end of our days, won't we, *hundchen*?'

I cringed. Mrs Schumacher, jangling with bracelets, got up, in a Princess Marina picture hat overgrown with tea roses, as if for the Royal Enclosure at Ascot, seemed, from the moment we had stepped across the threshold of Cheyne Walk, to have become a caricature of herself. She had scarcely drawn breath as we climbed the stairs, pronouncing the house 'refined', its decor 'classy' and, as Anatole drew aside to admit us into Felix's presence, the studio 'cultured'. Nevertheless I was glad her monopoly of the conversation prevented any exchange between Felix and myself. And I thought I detected something else in her too, beneath the gushing, an undercurrent of suppressed excitement, like Barrymore anticipating the moment you would call upon the maid to dish up his chicken, ears pricked, muzzle pointing, eyes watchfully aglitter. The house seemed chilly and inhospitable, surprising not because it had changed after so many years but because it felt as if nothing had changed at all, as if time had stopped for it. Oh, of course everything had been shut up all the years Felix had been abroad. But even in the studio I was perplexed by the same feeling, as though somewhere long ago a clock had stopped never to be wound up. Yes, some things within the room had been altered or rearranged – there were packing cases in one corner and a huge pile of canvases stacked, backs outward, against the far wall where the screen had once been. But the clutter remained and amongst it, though here and there overlaid with the new and unfamiliar, all the old heterogeneous objects I had once regarded with so much affection. And over everything, dancing in a golden haze across the sunlight shafting in through the great windows, softly powdering the paint tubes on the mantelpiece and the curling photographs and the heaps of discarded sketches, was dust, fine and uniform, so even in its distribution that you only noticed it where some movement had disturbed it. Glancing down at a pile of books I was suddenly afraid to look more closely at the topmost volume lest I should still encounter the page at which it had been open twelve years before. But perhaps, once again, that was only the effect of Tarantin's words upon my imagination.

Certainly, as Felix came forward from the window seat to greet us, I tried, so far as my embarrassment over the letter would allow, to scrutinize his face for signs of pain. And yes, I saw again the silver at his temples, the taut skin across his cheekbones, the sharply etched lines about his mouth. And when, on Mrs Schumacher's renewed exclamations of delight and her pronouncement that she wanted to see everything, every last painting, nothing could be a surfeit to her, he and Anatole began to shift the canvases from the stack against the wall, I fancied that there was still an awkwardness about his movements and that in Anatole's manner towards him as well there was something curious, wary, almost protective. But I could only observe him covertly; and besides, he wore, for Mrs Schumacher, all the armour of his charm, polished, impenetrable, the carefully veiled eyes giving away nothing.

I sat in a chair with Barrymore in my lap, an uninvolved observer, while the three of them busied themselves with the paintings. There were canvases of all sizes, some so large it took both Felix and Anatole to move them. Watching them turned one after the other, face up, for Mrs Schumacher's inspection, I saw how his style had changed, how he had developed away from Expressionism and from the Cubism that had followed it into abstraction, into an anarchy of shape and colour that left me bewildered. They were mysterious, inaccessible, these paintings, holding out no point of reference from which I could approach them. I supposed it must be my inadequacy, my failure of understanding, but it seemed to me the tension which had given his work such power was missing. Oh, the savagery was still there and the pain – the scream Tarantin had once mentioned; but the discipline, the sense of warring elements held in fine balance together, was gone: and what was left, inchoate, brutish, spoke the incomprehensible private language of nightmares. There were a surprising number of unfinished canvases; and I noticed then that one thing about the studio had changed: there was no work in progress on the easel.

Mrs Schumacher did not seem to share my disappointment in the paintings. With each new revelation she would flutter her eyelashes and clasp her claws together and utter fresh ecstatic cries. But nevertheless, there was too, still beneath her girlish excess, that dogginess, that quivering watchfulness of Barrymore anticipating a scent: she was not satisfied, she had not found what she wanted, yet she was still hunting, still counting on whatever it was all the same.

Felix and Anatole had reached the last canvas in the stack, one of the larger paintings, about six foot by four, face to the wall like the rest. Anatole's hands were moving to turn it when Felix stopped him with a slight shake of the head. It was the smallest of gestures, barely perceptible, but it had a quite remarkable effect on Mrs Schumacher. She paused stock-still. It was as if you could see her ruff bristle, her hackles rise, her nose prickle with it.

'That last picture, Mr de Lisle, you don't want I should see it?'

'My dear Mrs Schumacher, it wouldn't interest you.'

'To me, Mr de Lisle, art is like a box of candies. Anything and everything is interesting.'

Felix made no move to touch the picture. In fact, he walked away from it. 'It's a painting I did a long time ago, Mrs Schumacher. I'm afraid it bears no relation to my present work.' And he motioned to Anatole to begin restacking the paintings.

But Mrs Schumacher had taken the scent and now she was in full cry. 'Ach, Mr de Lisle, a foolish old woman, such an admirer of yours – surely you won't disappoint her?'

Felix had taken the jade box from the mantelpiece and was in the act of extracting a Muratti from it. There was a hint of irritation in the way he flipped open the lid. 'My dear Mrs Schumacher, I have already explained the painting is of no interest.'

'Who can say where our interests lie, Mr de Lisle? Or how maybe we share them?'

Felix stood, the box in his hand, looking at her for a moment. There seemed to pass between her pricked, doggy eagerness and his stillness, like electricity, a silent communication. He snapped the box shut.

'Very well. Anatole, turn the painting round.'

I watched; gave an involuntary gasp: then stared in astonishment.

'Ah, Mr de Lisle!' said Mrs Schumacher with some triumph but not a trace of surprise. 'It's a portrait of our dear Christabel.'

It was a full-length portrait, composed from the sketches he had made of me the day before we had gone to France, the day of Archie's proposal and Rostova's séance. I sat propped up on cushions in the window seat sleeping, my head supported by my hand, my feet curled up under me, the book still open in my lap. From behind me, through the great window, the last rays of a wintry sun flooded in, transforming my hair into a halo of burnished copper, catching half my face in its pale luminescence, throwing the other half into shadow. It was so strange to see myself thus, larger than life, held for ever, sleeping peacefully, in my seventeen-year-old happiness, that I could at first perceive only the strangeness, not the painting itself. But when I looked again I saw that it was unlike anything else he had done, that while it had some of the distorted perspective, the angularity of the rest of his early work, it had captured too the reflectiveness of the sketches, captured and held it not with anger or pain, but with a pervasive, wistful tenderness, calm, still, and infinitely sad.

Suddenly I did not know where to look, wanted to say something to him but did not know how to. But when I did look up he was lighting his cigarette, his face turned away.

'Dear Mr de Lisle,' said Mrs Schumacher, ears back now, ready for the kill, 'I adore your British modesty! Not an interesting painting? It's a fine painting, a very fine painting indeed. I thought so already when I saw it hanging in the Silberstein Hayman Gallery in New York.'

Felix drew upon his cigarette but his face did not move a muscle.

'Oh, it wasn't in the gallery – it was in the back office. And no signature, so how should I know it's yours? Maybe I should have figured this out only, as you mentioned, there are some differences in style. I offered Solly Silberstein a cheque you wouldn't believe, but he's like somebody zipped his lips together, won't let on who is the artist, just says this painting ain't for sale, even to Rockefeller.'

'It is still not for sale.'

'Mr de Lisle, I guess you don't understand. Finding it again, knowing dear Christabel – no question, I must have it. Only name your price.'

'I could not put a price on it, Mrs Schumacher. As you point out, I did not even sign it.'

'But you did, Mr de Lisle. The signature has been painted over.'

'Nevertheless, unsigned, it can have no possible value.'

'To me, to crazy old Rosa Schumacher, it has great sentimental value.'

'Come, Mrs Schumacher. You are blessed with the original.'

'Let's not play games, Mr de Lisle. I know what I'm blessed with – an eye for a fine painting and too many dollars. Now name your figure.'

I stirred uncomfortably, looking at the painting but feeling as if it were me who was being bargained over.

'Mrs Schumacher, I could not take your money. I have explained the painting is not for sale.' Felix drew upon his cigarette and his eyes were as impenetrable as ever. 'I should like to give it to you.'

Mrs Schumacher's eyelashes fluttered, her claws went up to her mouth. 'You're a prince, Mr de Lisle! But I couldn't accept such a present. Maybe I might make you promises but I couldn't, you understand, guarantee you anything in return.'

Felix looked at her thoughtfully and again, between her fluttering and his stillness, there seemed to pass some unspoken exchange. 'Then I shall lend it to you,' he said.

'I couldn't offer security on such a loan.'

'I require none. I know if I ever need the painting back you will return it to me.'

'This, believe me, Mr de Lisle, I pray you won't need.'

'Yes, Mrs Schumacher,' said Felix softly. 'I pray so too.'

There was a moment of silence. Then suddenly they were both smiling.

'Your hand on it, Mr de Lisle.'

Felix took the little painted claw. 'My hand upon it, Mrs Schumacher.' And he raised the crooked fingers lightly to his lips.

'So now,' said Mrs Schumacher, eyelashes batting, bangles jangling, tea roses bobbing with delight. 'You admit to the painting, maybe you'll do me the honour to sign it.'

We sat and watched in silence while, like some concluding ceremony to their bargain, Felix took a brush, dipped it in paint, and wrote his signature in the bottom right-hand corner. Then Mrs Schumacher, leaving instructions that when the paint was dry the canvas should be crated and sent directly to Southampton docks, declared that we had taken up far too much of his precious time and must be away.

In the car on the journey back to Clarges Street, sitting in the front passenger seat with Barrymore in her lap, she was still fluttering and exclaiming, but I sensed a tiredness in her too, a drooping of every fold of flesh beneath the panstick, as if the afternoon's endeavours had left her drained.

'Oh, Mrs Schumacher,' I said, as I pulled the car up at some Belisha beacons, 'I'm afraid I'm still no wiser about what I should do.'

'Ach, Barrymore,' she exclaimed, chucking the dog beneath his chin, 'she's a good girl but crazy yet! It's a fine painting, honey, and the man who painted it – whatever he may be to you – he should need your help, you should go to him. But I guess you'd made up your mind to do that anyway. Before you even spoke to me you'd decided.'

'But, Mrs Schumacher – '

'We'll manage, dear. And we'll have the painting, won't we, boobela,' here she lifted up the dog and for a few moments buried her face in his ruff, 'to remember dear Christabel by?'

'Oh, Mrs Schumacher!' At that moment we drew up in a queue of traffic and, seizing the opportunity, I leant over and kissed her.

'Sush, dear! You find things don't – well, you should change your mind any time, there's always a home for you in New York. Just write me, I'll cable the money for your passage.'

I sent Felix another letter apologizing for my over-hasty decision and saying that, while I still could not accept the money, I should be grateful for his offer of a home. He replied, without comment, that he would be pleased to welcome me whenever it suited me. And so, at the end of May, I moved into Cheyne Walk.

I do not know what I had expected. I suppose I had imagined that, with Tarantin's protestations of his need of me, he would, even though he had only asked me out of duty, be in some way glad of my company. But, from the very first evening, I scarcely saw him. He remained shut in the studio, seemed seldom to leave it or go out, appeared even to sleep there, and when I tried to discover what he did by himself for all those hours, Anatole, giving his inevitable inscrutable smile, replied only with a firmness which betokened 'no admittance' that Monsieur de Lisle was working. On the occasions when I did meet Felix, in the corridor outside the studio or wandering about the house, often in his dressing gown and sometimes, surprisingly for one who was usually so effortlessly elegant, unshaven, he seemed to come upon me almost with irritation, to draw back as if carefully preserving his distance. I no longer saw the slightest glimpse of the Felix who had visited Clarges Street and charmed Mrs Schumacher; instead the exhaustion I had observed in Norfolk hung upon him like a pall, so that I began to understand that the Clarges Street Felix had been achieved only by considerable effort. I understood too that when he had said the Cheyne Walk house was big enough for us to exist together without getting under each other's feet he had meant it quite literally. He appeared to find nothing to say to me, positively to discourage conversation and, in the space that he held always scrupulously between us, I once again had the sense of his avoiding even accidental contact, as if my very physical presence were distasteful to him.

If I seldom encountered Felix, however, Tarantin, often with Stenko too, called virtually every day. He seemed to come regardless of whether Felix would see him – indeed the studio door was frequently as firmly closed to him as it was to me – seemed to make me now the prime object of his visits, as if, like a doctor attending a difficult case, he felt responsible for my well-being, for charting the minutest details of my condition and progress. Finding his protectiveness as all-embracing as, before, his malevolence had been, and being grateful for company in my solitude, I began to be genuinely glad to see him and to miss him on the days he did not appear. Stenko, of course, I was always pleased to see, the new, confident, successful Stenko who did not stutter and who was no longer prey to lowering thunderstorms of Slavonic gloom; although occasionally I would catch him pondering me with something of the old umbrella Stenko about him, darkly spread as if the sun had suddenly gone in.

One day he appeared with a sheaf of paper which he thrust shyly into my hand.

'It is a piano sonata. I compose for you, Christie. So you will never again compare yourself badly with a wireless set.'

I felt at once both profoundly touched and bereft. 'Oh, Stenko, I – it's so lovely of you but I couldn't play it now. It's much too difficult.'

'My music is not difficult to play. Only, for some critics, difficult to understand.'

'But my fingers won't work for me any more, Stenko. I must learn to accept that I haven't enough talent.'

All of a sudden the umbrella began opening and closing, seized with a jerky, comical anger. He tore at his spiky hair, he waved his arms, he jumped in outrage from foot to foot. 'Accept, nothing! What is this accept? You cannot play because you do not play! I find you a teacher, I work with you myself. We work and work until you play my sonata. I make you try again, I force you. And damn your bloody wireless set!'

I stared at him, compelling myself to see the comedy, the rubbed-off shades of Vladimir Tarantin, willing myself to laugh in order not to cry. 'Oh, Stenko, you're sweet to me. But there's no point.'

'Of course there is point. Perhaps you will not now be a great concert pianist. No matter. You will still give pleasure to someone, you will do something for the person who needs this most. You, Christie! Yourself!'

'Oh, Stenko, I—'

'Please. No more "Oh Stenko". No more excuses. We will start tomorrow. You have a talent and you will not kill it. You will not give up.' Suddenly he cast his eyes ceilingwards, in the direction of the studio. 'There is already in this house too much giving up.'

I was grateful for his friendship, I acceded to his plan for my rehabilitation; but I did so as much to fill the emptiness of my days as anything, I could not believe there was truly any point in it. Indeed, I was beginning to find my whole life at Cheyne Walk more and more pointless.

I had been wrong in believing the house had not changed. But the change was a subtle one and consisted not so much in things being rearranged as in their gradually, piece by piece, being taken away. It was not just the absence of its former disorganized life, the visitors dropping in on the off-chance and settling themselves with a newspaper or a cup of Anatole's splendid coffee. Once the dust sheets, as a concession to my presence, had been removed, I saw that objects and pieces of furniture were missing too, a sofa table here, a lamp or a pair of candlesticks there, a Bokhara rug, the snuff bottles on the drawing room mantelpiece. And, as I drifted aimlessly from room to empty room, it seemed to me that this process of depletion continued, invisibly, stealthily, so that I would come week by week upon new gaps. It was as if the house were slowly drawing in upon itself, like some threatened creature, pulling in its tentacles, concentrating all the substance of its being upon its imperilled nucleus, the dark, solitary presence behind the closed studio door immersed in grief.

One afternoon I came home to discover that the icon paintings in the drawing room had gone. No effort had been made to conceal their disappearance; the two panels on which they had hung on either side of the great velvet drapes still stood in their accustomed place, puzzling, desolately empty. Later, bumping into Felix during one of his rare appearances downstairs, I asked him about the paintings. He merely shrugged his shoulders irritably.

'I'd grown tired of them.'

'But they were beautiful. And so much a part of the room.'

He turned then on his way back upstairs and there seemed again to be about his eyes that strangeness I could not identify. 'My dear Christie, when one has lost the only two people in the world one has truly loved there seems little point in waxing sentimental over a couple of paintings.'

The words cut me like a knife. Watching his retreating back, I felt crushed with a sudden sense of my own loneliness. I understood that the loss of his wife and child was insupportable, I wished profoundly that I could comfort him. But I was excluded by his grief from his life, his thoughts, from all possibility of helping him; and worse still, there was for me in that exclusion a contemptible jealousy that cried out against this giving of everything to the dead, that longed selfishly for the tenderness and affection which were no longer my right, for the place in which they had justly supplanted me. I tried to master it; but the pain his words had inflicted remained, leaving me abject and wretched.

When Tarantin came the next day I told him about the icons. His little eyes glittered, the eyes of the doctor once again, discovering a new symptom, weighing it against his diagnosis.

'So! Maybe he is short of money.'

I said I thought this was unlikely.

He snorted. 'To have money he must sell paintings. You have seen his recent work?'

I nodded.

'And what is your opinion of it?'

'I – don't think I understand it very well.'

'Understand? Nonsense! It is rubbish. I think he knows this too. So now he does nothing. I have a plan for a film of *Firebird,* an utterly new project, but he will not listen. They ask him to paint a mural for the new League of Nations Building in Geneva, a mural celebrating Peace – he says since they let Japan invade Manchuria, collective security is dead, he is not skilled enough to paint hot air. Always excuses not to work. Oh, he tells you he is working all day, work, work, work. But since he has been in London he has produced nothing. I snarl at him, Reuben Hayman is beside himself. But – nothing!'

'Then what does he do up there all alone?'

Tarantin's rings flashed in a gesture of despair. 'My dear Christie, who knows? You are our hope of finding out.'

I sighed, thinking of the icons again and of Felix's words to me that evening. Perhaps the icons had been sold, but the need for money appeared too simple an explanation for what was happening to the house and to both of us in it. There was such a sense of finality about it, in his withdrawing so completely, in his deliberate, gradual giving up of everything, that it reminded me of Tarantin's original appeal to me which all at once no longer seemed melodramatic. Was there not in this letting go a kind of edging out of life, a chill submission to the dead that whispered like an insidious draught in every empty room, every silent corridor? Feeling once again the pain of it, my own selfish pain at my exclusion, I shook my head miserably.

'Teddy, don't place your hope in me. I can't help him, can't even come near him. And I don't think I can stay here much longer. I don't think I can bear to.'

Tarantin's wrinkles gathered into a little knot of concern. 'My dear girl, it is difficult. But we must have patience. Just a few more weeks. Something will happen, you will see.'

But, as June drew into July and the weeks dragged past, I could not share his optimism. My days at Cheyne Walk seemed to have become an unremitting battle against misery and loneliness. I worked at the piano with Stenko, through Mrs Schumacher I had acquired a part-time job chauffeuring another visiting American widow around London, but the job would finish at the end of the Season and there were anyway the long lonely evenings to be filled, evenings made emptier by the glimpses of light beneath the studio door, by the constant awareness of Felix's presence, so close and yet separated from me by an unbridgeable void. Comfort came from nowhere; it was as if everthing I touched conspired to increase my misery. Even the sight of my mother's diaries, set out amongst my few possessions, on my bedside table, stung me with a sense of unexpected betrayal, semed only to bring me face to face with what I had so obstinately tried to avoid. Reaching the point of Felix's birth in 1895, I had long since abandoned reading them. How could I, confronted in page after page with my mother's dawning knowledge of my father's infidelity, with such irrefutable evidence of his betrayal of her, continue to assert that Aunt Jessica had lied? My mother had not doubted whose child Aunt Jessica carried. It did not matter that I could not understand the relationship – Felix was my brother and I must accept it. He was my brother, his only feeling for me now was a sense of duty, his only love was for the dead. I began to give way to despair.

One Saturday, feeling the need to escape from the oppressive gloom of the house, I had gone for a walk and was returning back along the Embankment when I encountered an extraordinary procession coming in the opposite direction, heading from Chelsea towards Vauxhall. Four limousines and two vans, all black, travelled in cavalcade at some speed, the first limousine flanked on each side by six motorcycle outriders in black uniforms, goggles and high black boots, and the whole procession escorted at the gallop by mounted police. Silver belt buckles flashed in the sun, I caught a glimpse of more uniforms inside the cars, of armbands, as the outriders roared past, emblazoned with the Roman axe, the insignia of the British Union of Fascists. The cavalcade must be making its way from Black House, the Fascist headquarters in Chelsea, to a rally in the East End. There was something so unexpected in coming upon it thus, in an empty street at the height of a July day when everything around it was bathed in the drowsy peace of the sun, something at once so incongruous and so sinister that I stopped involuntarily to watch it pass. As I did so, the last car pulled suddenly out of the cavalcade and drew up at the kerb about fifty yards from me. The nearside door was opened and a woman climbed out. Then the limousine slid away to join the rest of the procession.

Crossing the road, the woman went up to the stone parapet and looked out across the river. She seemed to be taking in great gulps of fresh air, but there was something about the set of her shoulders and her hands upon the parapet that suggested it was not illness she was trying to subdue, but anger. She looked about my age, was of the build euphemistically called 'comfortable', and there seemed to be something disconcertingly familiar about her.

Suddenly I began to run towards her. The sound of my feet and of my voice yelling made her look round.

'Dillo!' I screamed.

'Christie!' she shrieked with surprise.

And we fell into each other's arms.

'But I thought you were in India!'

'And I thought you were in America!'

'I – I changed my plans. I wrote to you.'

'And I to you. We must have crossed in the post, damn and blast the Post Office!'

'But what are you doing here, Dillo? And with those people? Don't say you've joined them?'

'Good Lord, no. I was kidnapped.' Then, seeing my look of alarm, she laughed. 'Oh, only by poor old Dolly. You know she's just married this frightful Fitzallen person who's a sort of lieutenant of Mosley's? Well, she's got awfully keen about the whole Black Shirt thing, keeps insisting I go to a rally. I didn't know too much about it, and besides Dolly's gone a trifle potty, what with all the divorces and everything, so I thought it best to humour the poor thing. But when it came down to it, Christie, I couldn't – not even for poor potty Dolly. But I suppose it's just her way of getting back at her second ex, poor old Dr Rubenstein. I couldn't stomach the conversation they were having in the car so I made them let me out post-haste!'

Despite herself, she was beginning to flush, to quiver with anger again. 'Anyway,' she said, 'I've explained to you why I'm not a Fascist, now you explain why you're not in America with your Mrs Schumacher.'

I hesitated. Finally I told her only that because of unforeseen family circumstances I was temporarily living at Cheyne Walk.

'With your Cousin Felix? You know, Christie, I never could understand why you didn't marry him, you were both so—'

Something in my face must have stopped her. 'Oh goodness!' she said. 'We can't stand here forever. Let's find a cab and go somewhere we can talk properly.'

It was logical, since it was only just up the road, to invite her to Cheyne Walk, yet I did not want to return to the house or take her into it. So when she announced that, since her parents were at Critchley, she had been lent the house in Berkeley Square, and suggested that I go back with her to meet her three daughters, I readily agreed. I spent the afternoon there and most of the evening. She had returned to England without Robbie to put her two eldest girls into St Monica's and we chatted on about how she was missing him and about their life in India. I was at first reticent about my existence at Cheyne Walk, but finally, on being pressed, I confessed that I did not think the arrangement with Felix was working (though I did not explain why) and mentioned that I had been seriously considering joining Mrs Schumacher in America after all.

Dilly clasped her hands together in delight. 'Well, it's perfectly simple, old dear. If your Cousin Felix is being beastly, why don't you move in here? There's plenty of room and we'd adore to have you. Then you can book your passage to New York to coincide with when I have to go back to Poona. That gives you all the time in the world to make your arrangements, and meanwhile you and I can have fun.'

I hesitated, but not for very long. Already, after one evening in her company and away from Cheyne Walk, I felt better, if not precisely happy then no longer in active pain. And to rejoin Mrs Schumacher was the only eventual solution to my problem. By the end of the evening it was all decided. I had only to tell Felix of my intended departure, and this I resolved to do the next day, before I had time to dither about my decision.

CHAPTER FORTY-THREE

Diary of Adele Ward.
Silver Strands Boarding House, Weymouth.

2nd December, 1904.

D R's English now much improved. I endeavour to set aside an hour each day to tutor him and he spends most afternoons with Bridie and me in the kitchen watching us prepare the suppers, while Bridie makes him recite the names of everything by rote, including the pots and pans!! I shame to say we sometimes cannot restrain ourselves from laughing uproariously at his mistakes, but he takes it all in good part, smiling and laughing with us. He is intelligent and quick to learn and in the space of these few short months has become quite one of the household. In the evenings he has found work playing the piano in the Palm Court of the Burden Hotel: although Bridie and I were concerned lest he should overtax his strength, he is too proud to exist, without thought of repayment, solely on the generosity of Mrs W.

M is confined to bed again today with another of his headaches. I confess I at first believed his indisposition merely a further excuse to postpone quitting this house, but, taking breakfast to him this morning, I observed him to be genuinely in pain. I suppose he is not much trouble to us, all things considered; the Misses Y have accepted the fiction that our separation has been due to his absence in the Colonial Service all these years; he takes his meals in his room, for which I am grateful, since he has developed an uncouth habit of spilling and slurping his food which is most disagreeable to watch; and, provided I can spare him a few shillings from the housekeeping, he will happily spend all day away from the house. Yet his temper has become exceedingly unpredictable of late and Bridie and I always feel uncomfortable when he is in the room. We have concocted so many plots to achieve his departure yet, since he is, alas, my lawful husband, there seems little we can do.

If M's health declines, D R's mercifully seems to have taken a turn for the better. He coughs less, has more colour in his cheeks and seems to be gaining weight. I suppose Bridie and I do make rather a fuss over him; and after all, though he is still a boy, there is no trace of the mollycoddle about him; indeed his character shows a strength and independence far beyond his years, with something inexpressibly fine in his proud, intelligent features which comes no doubt from the suffering he has already endured. Nevertheless – perhaps it is his mischievous smile or that we have the advantage over him in English – I cannot help feeling motherly towards him, as if he were the son my unfortunate marriage has not granted me, although when I confessed this to Bridie she at once burst into fits of laughter.

'Oh Lor, Mum! The way you talk anyone would think you was an old crone. Motherly, indeed! There can't be more than ten years between you and him.'

'Ten years, Bridie,' I said, rather severely, 'is a very great deal of time.'

'All my eye, Mum! There's young gentlemen I've seen swaggering out of the swell hotels with ladies on their arms their grandmas was in pinnies with.'

I chose not to respond but to busy myself with my pastry; for Bridie, though she is the sweetest, most generous soul in the world, is given to imposing a rather earthy note on matters involving purity of feeling.

3rd December, 1904.

This morning when I entered my private parlour I discovered, nestling amongst my housekeeping books, a little spray of lilies of the valley tied with crimson ribbon – a posy which, very much surprised and touched, I realized could only have come from D R. Inhaling delicate fragrance from the waxen bells I thought how interminable the winter seems, what an age it is since last I breathed the scent of flowers; and all of a sudden, the little posy appeared infinitely precious to me. Alas, when I enquired of D R where he had found such blossoms out of season he only gave a mysterious wink, so that I am rather afraid he must have purloined them from one of the epergnes at the Burden Hotel. However, it is such a charming gesture and his smile is altogether so winning that I could not find it in my heart to reprove him. What a dear, sweet boy he is! If Bridie will not allow that I am of an age to be a mother to him, then at least he inspires in me the protectiveness of an elder sister for a mischievous yet vulnerable young brother. And indeed his kindness could not have been more welcome, for the remainder of the day has been most disagreeable.

The elder Miss Y came to me in considerable distress, complaining that M has on several occasions brutally kicked her beloved spaniel. I broached the matter with M immediately, informing him that he is only under my roof on sufferance *and that if such an episode occurs again I shall use whatever means necessary to evict him. I do not care that he takes his flashes of temper out on me, but I will not have him behave in any way which endangers the little livelihood Bridie and I have worked so industriously these past six years to establish.*

M, surprisingly, was most apologetic: the pain in his head makes him sometimes lash out unthinkingly but he sincerely regrets his actions and will never again have such a lapse. His expression was curiously pathetic, almost childlike. Yet, though I could not detect liquor on his breath, his speech was slurred as if he had been drinking.

4th December, 1904.

This evening, the sisters Y having retired early, Bridie having gone on a visit to her mother and D R for once not being required at the Burden, the two of us spent the time most agreeably at the piano in the front parlour. Though it is somewhat out of tune, D has a fine touch and, with me turning the pages and singing, we gave a duet of all the old melodies – 'Lost Chord', 'In The Gloaming', 'The Better Land', 'Pale Hands I loved Beside the Shalimar'. There was such a delicious poignancy in the music, which brought tears to my eyes and yet made us laugh a great deal at our own sentimentality; the room with its blazing fire and drawn curtains seemed so cosy and far-removed from the chill December night outside; and there was such a companionable sense in the two of us playing and singing and laughing – indeed just as brother and sister might – that all at once I felt suffused with an indefinable warmth, as if, for the first time since those days of innocence at home in my own dear Hampshire, when my heart – blind, foolish heart – fluttered for Ouida's dashing guardsman in giddy ignorance of the world, I were, not in a negative way of absence of care or misery, but positively, unashamedly, happy.

It was at this juncture, when our heads were bent together over the music and my heart was full, that M burst in, red in the face and foul-mouthed, accusing me of deliberately causing *all the clocks in the house to tick louder in order to torment him.*

I began to laugh, but then perceived that he was serious.

'D'you imagine I'm a fool, dearest?' he screamed. 'I know what you're scheming, I know d——n well you're all scheming against me!' Then he stormed from the room.

CHAPTER FORTY-FOUR

Knocking on the door of the studio, waiting for an answer and hearing none, I felt with a shock a sense of the pattern again, the pattern at Monks Last as we had walked where he and Aunt Jessica had walked, not breaking but re-forming. But now, where it had begun for Felix and me on that night so long ago after Lady Ambleside's ball, I would break it for good. I could not help him, it was useless to continue suffering needlessly, I had taken my decision and I must hold to it. Nevertheless, the sense of repeated history made my hand tremble as I knocked again and, still hearing no reply, pushed the door open.

Though the afternoon sun blazed outside, the blinds were drawn, casting the room into a gloomy underwater shadow in which objects loomed darkly, in which splotches of light, the whiteness of paper, the glint of silver or glass, rose up mysteriously like the glimmer of retreating fish. Felix sat in the window, his back to it, his eyes focused upon the far end of the room. He was utterly, completely still, as if he had been sitting thus for many hours. It seemed to take some moments for him to notice me standing in the doorway and then he acknowledged my presence only by a small listless movement of the head. His face was expressionless, his eyes empty. Since he said nothing, I stepped over the threshold and closed the door.

'Well,' he said eventually in a voice that betokened not so much irritation as infinite weariness, 'you have chosen to disturb me. So I suppose you are going to explain why.'

I began, but found my voice was shaking. I took a deep breath. Then I told him about meeting Dilly, and wanting to stay with her and how I had decided that it would be sensible, after all, if I made arrangements to go to New York. He listened to me impassively, almost as if he only half-heard me.

When he saw that I had finished he surveyed me in silence for a moment. Then he said, in the same tones of weariness: 'I have been expecting it. It was a mistake for you to come. I should not have allowed Mrs Schumacher to persuade you.'

'Mrs Schumacher didn't persuade me. I came – ' and here that odd, unreasoning anger rose in me again – 'I came because I felt I too had a duty.'

His lips twisted ironically for an instant. 'Which, of course, you do not. When are you intending to go?'

'At the end of the week, if that is convenient for you.'

'Certainly. Why not go this afternoon, if that's what you want?'

His indifference stung me. 'All right. This afternoon, then.'

'Very well.'

The anger grew in me. I wanted suddenly to shout, to throw something, to do anything that would break that wall of weary indifference. But I was struck also by the hopelessness of it. I said nothing.

'I suppose,' he said softly, 'I must not insult you by asking you whether you are in need of money.'

'No,' I said. 'Thank you, but I am in need of nothing.' Again I hesitated, still wanting to give way to my anger, to compel him in some way to recognize it. But he had turned his head aside as if he had now completely lost interest in my existence.

'I shall ask Anatole to tell you when I am leaving,' I said stiffly. Then I forced myself to open the door and, without looking back, walk out of it.

Once in my room, I sat upon the bed staring bleakly at the wardrobe. I had not wanted the pattern to break, I had wanted him to stop me, had expected it. And now, when I had forced the situation, had compelled him to demonstrate how little he felt for me, I was too late faced with what I had striven so hard to deny. I loved him. I loved him as much now as I had twelve years ago. All these miserable weeks at Cheyne Walk had served to prove was that nothing had changed except that my love was no longer returned. I wished profoundly that I had gone to New York while I had still lived in the safety of my own self-deception.

I had not the heart to begin packing, and besides I should have to telephone Dilly to tell her to expect me earlier than we had arranged. Eventually, with an effort, I raised myself from the bed and drifted downstairs. The studio door was, as ever, fast shut. I wandered into the drawing room, that room I had loved and which now, with its wilted hangings, its bare mantelpiece, its denuded panels, gave out no longer a passionate clamour of colour and texture but a muted, sad, expiring note. It was probably the last time I should ever enter it. There was some music on the piano, from yesterday's lesson with Stenko, the Chopin Ballade I had once played at Monks Last, had then to my own surprise, played tolerably well. Now my fingers faltered every few notes, became, with my effort of concentration, leaden, mechanical, no longer lifting the music from the page but seeming to crush it, rendering it banal. I began to be angry with myself, forcing my fingers back over and over again to retrieve missed notes, to master limping runs and trills. But it was as if my hands would not obey my brain. I found myself, as my frustration communicated itself throughout my body, playing louder and louder, growing stiff with tension, making more and more mistakes. My muscles ached, my fingertips burned, the whole room seemed filled with the ugliness and the hopelessness of it. And suddenly I heard a voice, shouting above my discord, jagged too with scarcely controlled rage.

I stopped playing and looked round. Felix was standing in the doorway. His face and his knuckles where they clenched upon the door knob were white.

'If you must play the piece so badly, please don't play it at all.'

I stared at him. 'Felix, that may be just but it is scarcely kind – '

He was not listening to me. His exhaustion had vanished, his mouth was hard with anger, his body with it; it seemed to impel him suddenly across the room until he was level with the piano, towering over me.

'Well or badly, I don't wish you to play it, do you understand? I don't wish to be disturbed by it!'

Once more I felt my own anger, striking off his, rising to the limits of its control. 'I'm sorry, Felix, if I have disturbed you. But I assure you it won't happen ever again. I'm going to my room, this instant, to pack!'

I rose from the piano stool, slamming the keyboard shut. As I did so, clumsy in my rage, I caught the fingers of my left hand in the lid. Clasping them to me, I let out a small cry of pain. His hands moved involuntarily towards mine, were within an inch of touching me when suddenly, as if he feared that my flesh would burn him, they drew back. An extraordinary expression, a look almost of horror, crossed his face. I stared at him for a moment.

So I was right. He dreaded even to touch me. Ugliness and shame he had talked of in his farewell letter. And now that was all that remained to him of our love. Incest, an ugly word, and guilt, perhaps an uglier one. Well, I would not stay to suffer the pain of his revulsion. Tightening my other hand over my bruised fingers, determined not to show how I was hurt, I drew myself up to sweep past him. But he was blocking my way.

'Why?' he demanded suddenly. 'Why are you leaving like this? Is it so impossible for there to be any friendship between us?'

'Friendship?' I faced him, rigid with pain and anger. 'My God, Felix, how? How, when we cannot even be comfortable in the same room together?'

'If that is how you feel, why did you change your mind? Why did you bother to come here in the first place?'

'Because I was worried for you. Teddy told me how ill you'd been, I could see that you were in pain and – and that you'd never got over it, the accident, losing both of them, everyone you loved. I wanted to help you, I thought by being here – I ought to have known you'd never let me.'

'So you came out of pity?' His mouth was hard, his face deathly pale. 'Well, you are right, my dear Christie, I don't want Teddy's meddling and I don't, above all I don't need your pity – '

'And I don't need your cruel sense of duty!' I was shaking with anger. 'Oh, your fastidiousness about your obligations is admirable, Felix. Particularly when it seems to cost you so dear. But to be reminded, day by day, of just how great that cost is – ! Perhaps you are my brother, perhaps what we did was wrong. But it was twelve years ago, it's over, finished with. I can't stand being punished for it any longer. I can't bear daily to be reminded of how my very presence is repugnant to you – '

He stared at me for a moment. Then suddenly he gave a great savage laugh. 'My dear little sister, that's rich! When every day you put me in so much pain I am obliged to – Dear God, I thought I was safe from you, I thought I was protected by the fact that you had ceased to love me, had told me so, had made it plain that even your divorce didn't alter it. I thought no matter what I felt I could be a brother to you at last. I hadn't reckoned with the nightmare of having you in this house, of knowing that even after twelve years I cannot change what I am. Over and done with, Christie? Well, it may be for you. God help me, I am still cursed with it, cursed so I am afraid to be near you, afraid to touch you or look at you because I want you so much – ' He advanced upon me, his eyes blazing. 'Damn you, I accept that you cannot love me! But I won't have you mock me with it!'

I had opened my mouth to speak. But, seizing me by the wrists and pulling me towards him, he brought his lips down hard upon mine. His mouth was violent and mine answered it with violence. There seemed to rise between us, not passion, but the combustion of our mutual anger, two live currents lethally united, exploding into voracious, consuming flame. We bit, bruised, tore at each other. He forced me backwards into the curving side of the piano, imprisoning me there, body arched and twisted in excruciating pain. I raked the nape of his neck with my fingernails, wanting to draw blood, wanting to make him cry out with it, snarling, biting, wanting suddenly to destroy him, feeling it in him too, white-hot, blinding, annihilating, the denial, each of the other, of anything beyond that growing, resentful, destructive rage. All at once I was frightened of the strength of it, of how it was conducted like lightning between the two of us. My body went rigid, I wrenched my head aside. He let go of me immediately and I saw for an instant in his face a look of horror that recognized, answered mine. He turned abruptly away.

'Oh God, forgive me! My dear little sister, forgive me if you can!'

I felt the weight of self-disgust in his voice, felt it in my own misery and confusion like an attack. If I still doubted that he was my brother his conviction of it was absolute, unshakeable. Everything, even the evidence of the diaries, seemed to support him. And now there was this between us, as strong in me as in him, not love, not tenderness, but the utter abnegation of both, as if all we had once felt for each other had been perverted and made ugly. If he wanted me, it was not with joy or pleasure but with a loathsome compulsion he thought of as a curse. And it was in me too, that bitter destructive force. I was suddenly overwhelmed with despair.

'Oh Felix,' I said helplessly, 'I can forgive you anything. Only please – please don't obliterate me.'

'Obliterate you?' He spun round and instantly the anger was there between us again, live and dangerous. 'My dear Christie, much as I might wish to, I cannot do that. Oh, I suppose there have been days when I have not thought of you, some days here and there in the last twelve years when mercifully I haven't seen you or heard your voice, when your sweet face hasn't been there to torture me or the touch of your sweet beautiful body or the vision of it yielding joyfully in Archie Cadwallander's bed!'

'I had no choice but to marry Archie!'

'You wanted it. You would not have married unless you had wanted to.'

'I wanted nothing, Felix. There wasn't anything after you'd gone. It was easy for you, you had another life. But I had nothing.'

'Easy? Dear God, I think I'd always been alone till I met you, but it was only afterwards I knew what true loneliness was. I thought I understood pain but there is no physical pain to compare with what I felt during those first months in Paris. And then when you went North and I knew it could only be for one reason, to be with Cadwallander – '

'How could you know? You weren't there.'

'Do you suppose I was capable of simply turning my back on you? Do you suppose I didn't make certain every day as far as I could where you were and what you were doing? And when I knew you would marry him, that it was only a matter of time – I thought if I couldn't take some action it would kill me. I wanted to come back and tear you away from him – '

'But you didn't come back.'

'How could I? What could I offer you? I'd already wronged you enough out of ignorance. Was I, knowing how wrong it was, to force you to continue with it? If it was still there like a sickness in me at least I could make sure you weren't at risk from it. If I loved you the only loving thing I could do was to leave you alone, to let you be happy.'

'Happy? Oh Felix, how could you believe – after I'd lost – when there was nothing left? When I knew you were in love with someone else?'

He stared at me as if he did not understand. His face was very pale.

'It was wrong of me to marry Archie – wrong for him. But I just gave in. There seemed nothing else to do once I knew about your marriage.'

'In love? With Nancy?' His lips were bloodless. 'Oh, little sister, haven't I made it clear to you, haven't I explained that all these years, these twelve wretched, abominable years, I've never been able to love any woman but you? Against everything decent and honourable, against everything in you that is precious to me, against nature itself I have it in me like a contagion that refuses to be cured. I love the one woman in the world it is a sickness to love. And for that, as I deserve, I have been punished. I have been punished so that as long as I live I shall always remember – always see – '

His face worked as if the last vestiges of his control were slipping away. I watched him, bewildered.

'I don't understand,' I said. 'Do you mean the accident?'

'Accident?' He stared at me but did not see. 'There was no accident. God, Nancy had two old aunts in Boston who wanted an inquiry to dig up what I'd paid a fortune in bribes to conceal. I thought at least, since it was intended for me, only I should know what she really – '

He turned suddenly towards the mantelpiece, seemed to struggle with his emotion as though with a physical force, his whole body taut, his head back, his fists clenched, and as I watched I felt the anger die between us as if he were drawing it into him, turning it upon himself.

'Please, Felix,' I said. 'Help me to understand – '

Very slowly his shoulders came down, the taut sinews in his neck relaxed, he seemed to gain mastery over what he had been fighting. But, though he half-turned towards me, he did not look at me, and I felt him grow distant as if now the anger was gone all point of contact between us had vanished too, so that I was not even certain whether he knew I had spoken.

'It took three days to winch the car up from the lake,' he said. 'The drowned look very dead after three days. He had been so beautiful, my son, I had been so utterly unprepared for how fiercely I should love him. There was the rage, of course, that howling pointless fury. But the guilt too – she knew that would be there – as if it had been I who'd killed him. She knew. That's why she did it.'

I stared at him, horrified. I wanted to say something, to go to him, to put my arms around him, but every aspect of his tall, proud, embattled figure shut me out. And all at once, as I thought how little I had understood, how meanly jealous of his wife I had been, it seemed to me that my exclusion was just; and there came to me, like a knife thrust, such a sharp consciousness of my own guilt, of the child I had killed, weakly, from doubt, from cowardice, his son perhaps also, that I was glad his head was turned away so he could not read in my face how I too had injured him.

He did not speak for some moments. Instead, taking out his

silver case, he lit a cigarette and stood propped against the mantelpiece, his head in his hand, drawing in deep draughts of smoke. His weariness had returned as if his internal battle had overwhelmed him. I watched him helplessly, crushed by my inability to reach him, feeling how I stood on false pretences with him, miserably tainted by my own guilt.

When at last he spoke he still did not look towards me but remained with his eyes focused far away, beyond the two empty panels that had once held the icons, beyond the dark velvet, as if he were no longer aware of the room or anything in it. He spoke quickly, painfully, as though rehearsing a dialogue he had often had with himself, for which he could imagine no other audience. Beneath the weariness I could hear the anger working in his voice, bleak now, self-directed.

'I could not love her and I should not have married her. But I wanted a commitment. I knew I had no right to be jealous of Cadwallander. I knew the only way I could honour my love for you was to keep you safe from me, to put as much distance between us both as possible. And besides, she seemed so lost, so bereft of everything. I didn't know about the money then, I only discovered that when I read the newspapers the day after the wedding – she hadn't seen fit to tell me about it because she thought, quite rightly, that I would find it an obstacle to our marriage. But then I had only known her a month, I really understood nothing about her.

'It wasn't a promising beginning, that omission of hers. But at the time I still thought it would work. After all, plenty of people marry without love. I thought at least I could protect her and care for her and if there were a lack in me I could make certain she should never know it. And then, of course, later – ' he smiled suddenly to himself – 'there was Nicky. Dear, impossibly naughty, preposterously alive Nicky.'

He drew upon his cigarette and I noticed that his hand was shaking.

'Anyway, it did not work. She would not let it. Oh, I suppose it was not her fault, simply the effects of her wretched childhood, of being treated as if she were merely a sum of dollars on a balance sheet. From the start, she was morbidly jealous. She resented my work, my friends, even my love for our child. The universe, according to her, was peopled with my mistresses. And since she was determined to catch me out in my unfaithfulness it was, of course, only a matter of time before she stumbled on at least part of the truth.'

'Oh God,' I said. 'Archie's stupid outburst on the boat!'

He paused as if surprised by the interruption, but still did not look round or make any acknowledgement of my presence.

'It was long before that. She found the painting. She found it and I suppose she saw in it – what Mrs Schumacher saw. She tried to destroy it and I had to persuade Reuben Hayman's partner to hide it for me. But after that there was no peace. It did not help that I would not, could not talk about it. She had her evidence, she had a focus now for the violence and the scenes. It had been difficult enough to come to terms with the wrong I had done you and all I had forfeited by it. But now the extent of my loss was thrown in my face every day. I tried to understand, to be gentle with her, I tried as much for Nicky's sake as hers. But in the end – ' and here he drew long and deep on his cigarette – 'in the end it was all I could do not to hate her.

'And then there came that nightmare voyage. My dear, beautiful little sister, all in black, with her flaming hair and that clear, pure sweetness of hers. Oh, it didn't take Cadwallander to make a idiot of himself, Nancy recognized the original of the painting instantly. And, of course, now she was certain I would betray her. I couldn't tell her the truth – the only way I could protect the beautiful Mrs Cadwallander was to pretend she had become a stranger to me, that nothing mattered less than her presence on board that ship. And even that was not, as it turned out, protection enough. 'Besides – ' he gave a sudden bitter laugh – 'perhaps Nancy was right. When I saw you there, my dear little sister, and was faced with everything I had lost, I was seized with a wild notion that after all those years the perversity of my desire no longer mattered, that I could step off the ship with you and disappear and to hell with morality and ugly names. But then you disabused me of such foolishness by telling me what, after all, I should have most wanted to hear – that you were happy and had forgotten me. And anyway I could not have taken my son from Nancy and I could not have left him.

'So we went on, Nancy and I. After the Crash things became much worse, once the money had gone she seemed to lose all grip on reality. Doctors, nursing homes – nothing helped. For three years we went on, three hideous, violent years. Yet I would willingly have continued for a lifetime if I thought I could have prevented – could have saved – '

Here he stopped as if the anger had suddenly mastered him. His face worked, his fingers, fumbling for another cigarette, trembled so much he could hardly strike the match to light it. He buried his head in his hand for a moment. When he continued his voice was level again, though so quiet it was only just audible.

'It was logical, of course, when you thought about it. She could kill herself, she'd tried twice before, but it wouldn't be enough, she couldn't be sure I'd feel properly guilty. She could kill me, but I'd become indifferent to life – that might even be a kindness. No, there was only one way to make sure I remembered how I'd failed her, one way to be certain I'd go on for the rest of my days blaming myself, only one perfect way I could be punished for loving where I should not love. I knew that car, I'd had it for years, it could not have slipped off the handbrake. She drove quite deliberately into the water. She would kill herself but that wasn't important. What counted was punishing me. By murdering my son.'

He stood, leaning against the mantelpiece, his face averted, his head in his hand. Again I wanted to go to him, to tell him I loved him, but again I could not. Nothing in his voice or attitude admitted me. It was as if he were at home with the hate and the guilt, had accepted them, had embraced their corrosiveness almost with pleasure. The distance between us now seemed infinite, and once more I felt my inability to comfort him or even to reach him like a reproach, a reproach for my own guilt which, answering his, filled me now with a wretchedness as utter as when, so long ago, waking ashamed and empty in a darkened room, I had come to a consciousness of the destruction to which I had so weakly consented.

'Felix. Oh God, forgive me. Both your children are dead.'

He looked up then, stared at me, seeing me with surprise, not comprehending. My lips were very dry. I compelled myself to rid my voice of all traces of emotion.

'I allowed myself to be persuaded that our baby would be born deformed. I had an abortion.'

It seemed to sink in slowly. He continued to stare at me for a while. Suddenly his lips twisted, he turned his head away. I watched numbly as he seemed to take my confession to himself, separate me from it and add it to his own burden of grief. I thought I had never felt more isolated, more wretchedly ashamed in my life.

Then all at once he had turned towards me, the closed look had fallen away, his eyes were upon me as if for the first time since I had come into his house he saw me clearly, saw me not with the anger or reproach I had dreaded, but with a mixture of shock and agonized tenderness.

'Oh my dear little one, they said you had been ill – before you went North – but I never for a second imagined – '

'Felix, I'm sorry, so sorry.'

'Sorry? You? Oh my darling Christie, what in heaven's name have I done to you?'

Then his arms were around me and mine about his neck and I felt myself enfolded in the familiar, comforting strength of him.

We stood like that for a long time, holding each other close, silently grieving for the death of his son, for our unborn child, for the twelve, bitter, sterile years we had been parted from each other, all anger gone, the distance bridged, words unnecessary. After a while he lowered his arms and gently moved apart from me.

'Oh Christie, forgive me for not knowing, for not understanding. I thought at least if my life was wretched my going had saved you from suffering. Now I understand why you ceased to love me.'

'But I didn't,' I said softly. 'I lied to you on the boat. I lied because we were both married to other people and – and I thought it was you who had forgotten me. I was hurt and jealous and angry and for that I'm sorry too. But I've never stopped loving you. Oh, perhaps I've tried sometimes but it hasn't been any use. I love you just as much now as I did twelve years ago.'

'Oh my darling Christie, my dear, dear little one!' His lips parted, his breath seemed to catch, his arms went out to me again. Then, in an instant, he withdrew them. 'Dear God, it is wrong even for me to kiss you properly.'

I put my hand up and touched his cheek. 'Felix, if it is wrong, we are both wrong, if you are guilty, I am guilty. But I don't believe – there must be something, some hope . . .'

He took my hand and pressed it to his lips. Then with his eyes still on my face, with a suppressed shudder that told me the effort it cost him, he drew away from me. But his hand still held mine fast, interlacing my fingers with his.

'At least we can talk,' he said. 'If you will stay, that is?'

'Stay?' I had completely forgotten I was supposed to be going to Dilly's. Suddenly I was laughing, my hand tightening on his. 'Oh, Felix, if you want me to, yes, oh yes I'll stay.'

So we sat on the day bed, still holding hands, and talked, and I told him about Brice and Cadwallander and Mrs Burton and my marriage to Archie, and, after a while, when I could bear to, about the abortion. He listened in silence, but when I came to the part Rostova had played in it, even when I mentioned her name, his face seemed to darken, and I knew then, before he told me, that it was as Tarantin had said and that he had confided in no one. It was I who had stupidly let Rostova trick the information out of me, I who had told her Felix was my brother.

'Oh Felix, I wanted your baby so badly.'

His eyes filled with a sharp sadness. 'I wanted that too, little one. I wanted us to be married, you to have my children, everything we have lost. I have tried so hard to find some way of forgiving my mother. But I cannot forgive her love – if such a shabby thing deserves the name – for destroying ours.'

His face now, gentle, sad, was the face I had struggled so long to remember, the closed look, the white, impenetrable stiffness of it, gone utterly. As we talked we had moved imperceptibly closer together so that not only our hands touched but our arms, our shoulders, mine resting lightly against his, and in the proximity of our bodies was again the familiar consoling warmth, that sense, not of space between us, but of constraints falling away, of lines and divisions merging into a fine clear communication that transcended our separateness. Suddenly everything in me cried out that he was not, could not be my brother.

'It is not destroyed,' I said.

He smiled. His arm came up around my shoulders, turning me towards him so my face looked directly into his. 'My dear little sister. You were such a very beautiful child and now you are an even more beautiful woman. Oh God, how I have missed you!'

He bent then and kissed me gently on the forehead. When his lips withdrew his hand still rested lightly on my shoulder, his eyes, finding mine, held them, and there seemed to come into him a tension which, in the careful lightness of his touch and the intensity of his gaze, passed to me too, making me fear I would begin to tremble.

'Unpin your hair,' he said softly.

Putting up my arms to do as I was bidden, turning my head aside, I could feel his eyes upon me still, watching as one by one I drew out the long pins that held my hair in its decorous pleat, watching as, lock by rebellious lock, it fell in a heavy copper mass about my shoulders. I heard him give what I thought was a sigh. Then his hand was at the nape of my neck, gently forcing me to turn my head, to look at him again.

His eyes were cloudy now, the set of his jaw almost hard. His other hand shook as it came up to brush aside a stray tendril of red that fell across my cheek. I held his gaze but within me a tighness grew as if I no longer dared to breathe. His lips were parted, his left hand explored the contours of my chin and throat while all the time his right worked at my neck, drawing the mass of my hair, slowly, carefully around his fingers into a tight knot.

Slowly, slowly, with the movement of his hand, my head went back. I caught my breath. I arched my neck against him. We were for an instant both held there perfectly still. Then a shiver passed between us like the sound of something breaking, and his lips found mine.

His kiss was gentle at first, then, as I responded to it, harder, fraught with urgency. I felt his lips, the dance of his tongue upon mine, as something I had waited in starvation for, something so infinitely familiar and yet through the length of my deprivation so unexpected that it came to me at once both with recognition and a perturbing, tantalizing strangeness. His hands were in my hair, mine about his neck, he was little by little easing me down against the cushions so that I lay beneath him.

Then suddenly he seemed to freeze. Sensing it, I too became still and, opening my eyes, looked up into his face. For an instant, forgetting, I did not understand. Then I saw in his eyes, flooding back, all the guilt and the horror, saw that he stared down at me with disbelief, felt in him, growing like a monstrous shadow, the realization of what he had come close to.

He tore away from me, springing off the day bed, whirling towards the mantelpiece. For a second, catching sight of himself in the looking glass above it, seeming to see there too in his own image the horror reflected back, he was immobilized.

Then: 'Oh God in heaven, no!' he screamed. 'No, no, no!'

And seizing from the mantelshelf the only object now upon it, the ivory figurine, he hurled it with all his force into the glass.

CHAPTER FORTY-FIVE

Later, standing before the mantelpiece, looking up and seeing my own reflection savagely bisected in the cracked glass, I felt it as an image of our uncertainty. In the moment of his shattering the mirror it had seemed as if everything that had so suddenly been laid open between us, the old intimacy, the recognition of our love, had been shattered with it. But then he had sent a message by Anatole asking me to dine with him and when he had reappeared all trace of that violent self-abhorrence had gone, his manner was gentle, affectionate, as if he wished to reassure me. Yet, in the hours of his absence, the full weight of his exhaustion had returned too; though he had shaved and dressed with apparent care, there was in the very fastidiousness of it a sense of effort, of pain suppressed; and in the smile with which he greeted me there was a sadness which seemed to set me at a distance again. We stood, two people in evening dress, watching Anatole mix cocktails, preparing to take dinner together with every appearance of normal domestic routine, yet, in our silence, our constraint, our scrupulous observance of the space between us, there resounded like the splintering of the glass the harsh impossibility of our situation.

When Anatole had left the room Felix looked at me without speaking for some moments. Then, putting aside his cocktail untouched, he came and pressed my hand gently to his lips.

'Little one, forgive me for this afternoon. I love you so very dearly. I love your sweetness, your goodness, your generosity, every part of you. But I cannot love you without wanting you.'

'There is nothing to forgive,' I said softly. 'You know it is the same for me.'

'Yes, little Christie, I know that now.' He made a movement as if he would touch me again, then with a wry smile turned away. 'I know that and it gives me joy – and at the same time it makes my keeping you here the more unpardonable. If I believe I can offer you any happiness, I am simply deceiving myself.'

'But I love you,' I said. 'I want to stay. Loving you is my happiness.'

His lips twisted sardonically. 'Are you happy now?'

'That's unfair.' I turned from him, towards the mirror. 'I don't – I can't believe there is no hope.'

'Hope? Oh, my dear little sister, you were hope itself once to me, I think the only hope I ever had. But my mother killed that twelve years ago with her wretched confession. And perhaps, in any case, you could have expected little in return.' I watched him in the glass come towards me again, watched our two reflections move together, those two faces that were different and yet so alike, the Cavendish face, separated now only by the great shafting crack in the glass. 'My dear little one, you've always had such a luminous innocence about you. You are so precious to me and I am so afraid of hurting you. I feared it then and I am terrified of it now.'

There was in his face not desire but an expression of infinite sadness. He bent and, almost as if he were testing himself, kissed my bare shoulder, so lightly that his lips scarcely touched my skin. And, as he raised his head and our eyes, in the mirror, met, it came to me again how tired and ill he looked, and I saw suddenly, with shock, something else too in the reflected eyes, that strangeness, the curious disturbance of their symmetry I did not understand. I had opened my mouth to speak but I stopped short. For a second I held his gaze. And no, it was not a trick, a distortion of the broken glass, but there, disquieting, unaccountable, chilling me all at once with the thought that there was something else that stood between us, something beyond that treacherous similarity of our images in the mirror. But he seemed to read my face, for in an instant his eyes had left mine, he had turned away.

'Come, my darling, let's go in to dinner. Whatever we decide we must do in the end, I should like to spend one selfish evening just enjoying having you back.'

His voice was light, he was smiling now, holding out his hand to me. And in the dining room I began to wonder if, after all, what I had seen in the looking glass had been only my imagination. There was such a homecoming sweetness in sitting across the table from him, surrounded by familiar objects, the silver, the bowls of flowers, the crystal, seeing him, through the candlelight that flickered between us, surveying me with his old, affectionate, half-mocking smile. Suddenly the memory of everything we had lost, the full force of that loss and of how, though so much had been changed by it, somehow nothing important had changed at all, spurred me to a despairing rebellion.

'Oh, Felix, I don't believe it. I can't believe I shouldn't love you, that it's unnatural, something to be ashamed of. I can't, can't believe we are brother and sister.'

Felix smiled wearily. 'Don't, little one. That way madness lies.'

'But is it madness? Oh, if it were one of us, perhaps. But both of us? And would we have gone on loving each other for so long in spite of everything? Wouldn't we change somehow if it were true? I suppose I can't understand properly, I don't know what it's like to have a brother or sister. But I'm sure I'd feel differently towards you, it would happen automatically, I shouldn't have to struggle with it. And you, you at least have a brother, you must know something of what that bond is like.'

He laughed. 'My darling, it's hardly a useful comparison.'

I sighed. 'Oh, don't mock me, Felix. I know I'm not explaining myself very well. But there must all the same be a difference – brother, sister, no matter which – a difference in the bond, a difference in kind.'

Seeing my seriousness, he too became serious again. He looked for a while at the crimson glow of the wine in his glass, then he said: 'I don't know what I feel for Meredith, Christie. Shame, I suppose, that the name he bears with honour I have no right to. And apart from that? Well, something more than for a stranger, perhaps, but exactly what, I can't define. My mother brought us up on the principle of divide and rule. In all our childish rivalries he got the rougher justice. For that he not unnaturally dislikes me, and for it and for not knowing him because of it I feel a deep regret. Perhaps if I had been brought up with a sister it would have been the same. But we were not brought up together, little one. We didn't have time to nurture a nice healthy contempt for each other. You didn't come to understand my mother's version of family love till much later.'

The bitterness in his voice arrested me for a moment. The candle flame had thrown his face half into shadow, emphasizing where there was light the sharp angle of his cheekbone, the proud, hard lines of his mouth and jaw, and I thought again how gaunt he looked, as if the bitterness and the guilt were burning him away.

'But I did understand it,' I said quietly. 'She would have done anything to stop us marrying. She would have lied to you. At the time I was convinced that she had. And even now I'm still not certain – '

'She didn't have to lie, Christie. What she told me was the truth.'

Desperately I pushed from my mind the evidence of the diaries. 'But she died before we could ever make her prove it. It might have been true but it might just as easily have been something she made up simply because she'd loved my father. We didn't put it to the test, we didn't even question it – '

To my surprise he burst suddenly into sardonic laughter. 'Didn't question it? Oh, my dear little sister, do you believe I just went away, gave you up, accepted it all without a single objection? I went through boxes of papers, travelled miles, worked through long nights in a kind of frantic desperation trying to prove it couldn't be true. But I arrived only at what my instinct had told me was correct all along. Sir Arthur de Lisle could not have been my father.'

He had not touched his wine and had almost from the start abandoned any attempt to eat. Now he pushed his plate aside and drew out his cigarette case.

'Although I told everyone I was going abroad, I didn't leave immediately. I waited until my mother's funeral was over, you had all returned to London and Monks Last was shut up, then I went back. I spent several days going through my mother's papers and anything that was left of Sir Arthur's, but I found nothing to help me. Instead, I unearthed one piece of information which depressed me deeply. My mother had always claimed, without my ever attaching any importance to it, that I had been born two months prematurely. If that were so, there was still room for doubt. But if her pregnancy had gone the full nine months the likelihood of her story being true increased dramatically. At the time I was conceived, Sir Arthur would have been in Ireland selling his estate, and could not possibly have been my father.

'It seemed to me that if my mother had gone into labour two months before her time there would have been difficulties at my birth, but I didn't remember any stories to that effect, or any reports that I had been a sickly baby. So I decided to consult the drunken Dr Blair, who had been in attendance at my mother's confinement. After half a bottle of whisky he was quite forthcoming – yes, I had been a fine, healthy child, he remembered it well, no, there were no problems. Two months premature, a nine pound baby? But at that point, even despite the whisky, he became suspicious and decided to clam up, and besides I wasn't sure that, through the mists of Glenfiddich, I was prepared to rely on his memory. I remembered that my old nurse had retired to Dorset and so, with some difficulty, I traced her. Her reaction when, after two hours, I steeled myself to ask her the same questions, was much more straightforward and even more damning. She simply burst into tears.'

He paused, drawing upon his cigarette, and again the dancing flame etched deep shadows in his face.

'So you see, little Christie, my mother did not have to lie. Sir Arthur was in Wexford at the time I was conceived. But Montgomery Ward was at Monks Last – she even kept dated photographs of the two of them beside the lake. Put that together with everything else we know and I'm afraid there is no room for doubt. And you and I are damned by it.'

No room for doubt. Yes, everything in my mother's diaries confirmed what he said, hopelessly, completely, so that I almost wished I had never recovered them. And yet my instinct cried out against this overwhelming welter of evidence, demanding, contrary to all reason, that there must be something else, something we had missed.

'It's not conclusive,' I said, despairingly. 'If we went back, searched again?'

He shook his head. 'For what, little one? A miracle? Besides, both Blair and my nurse are dead now. And, after twelve years, there can't be any hope of unearthing anything new. Unless – ' he looked up at me suddenly – 'unless your mother – '

My face must have told him everything that was in the diaries for he did not even bother to finish his sentence. We sat in silence for a while, not looking at each other, he smoking, I staring into the candle flame. Our despair seemed to descend upon us like darkness, muting the brightness of the flame and the sparkle of the crystal, drawing the walls of the room in closer upon us as if we would be engulfed in their shadow.

At length I said softly: 'What shall we do?'

The sulphur flared as he lit another Muratti and for a moment there was something in his face that seemed once more to distance me so that I wondered what he had been thinking about and was inexplicably afraid of finding out. But when he looked up at me I saw only that sharp, tender sadness again.

'I know what we should do, little one. I should persuade you to accept the financial settlement I offered you – '

'I won't accept it. Not ever.'

'I should find some way of making you listen to reason. And then we should go our separate ways again.'

'Oh, Felix, is that what you want?'

He gestured wearily with his cigarette. 'No, my darling, of course it isn't. But I don't see what else is left to us.'

I felt the hopelessness overwhelm me once more. 'But, if we love each other, there must be some other way – '

His lips twisted bitterly. 'Oh yes, of course there are other ways. We could lie to ourselves, lie to each other, pretend my mother died before I was ever able to speak to her. We could become lovers again, we could even marry – after all, Sir Arthur appears as my father on my birth certificate, there is no reason in law why we should not. Of course, we should live in mortal fear of making you pregnant again. Anna – ' and here, as he had before at the mention of her, his face darkened, his mouth became grim – 'Anna at least is right about that, we are too close in blood on both sides. But apart from that we could make some pretence at a marriage, live together in a way as mean and unnatural and furtive as the lie itself. And I could watch myself destroying you, your goodness, your innocence, everything about you that is precious to me, destroying it a little more day by day.'

He paused, and I saw the weariness come over him once more. 'Oh, my dear, dear little one, before I knew you I understood "love" only as a word people used when they wanted to wound or trap someone. You, my darling, taught me that it could mean something else, something strong and generous, with a kind of glorious freedom, even, in its commitment. But my mother, with one sentence, destroyed all that and left in its place a tainted thing she could better understand.'

'No, Felix,' I said softly. 'Perhaps your mother destroyed the possibility of our ever marrying, of ever even being lovers again. But she didn't, she couldn't destroy our love. We still have that.'

'Oh, but little one, could we ever live with it? When we remember it whole could we live with it crippled?'

'We could learn to. If that is all we can have.'

Beyond the candle flame he surveyed me thoughtfully for a while in silence. Then, with a sigh, he said: 'Even if I thought I was capable of it, I don't think I could ask that of you. You are very lovely and still young. You could marry again, make another life. If you stay with me it will be half a life, nothing more.'

'I am only half-alive without you,' I said.

'That's absurd. When you've survived these twelve dreadful years untouched, become, if anything, only more beautiful.'

'Oh, I've survived. I survived Archie. But it wasn't a life.'

'My dear child, you need not marry another Archie.'

'But it would simply be another survival. I know that now. You are my life, you always have been.'

His eyes were on my face, searching it for a moment. Then he reached across the table and took my hand. 'And you mine, little one. It's impossible, a torture to live with you as you suggest. And yet, now that I've found you, it's impossible to give you up.'

His fingers wove themselves gently into the spaces between mine. Looking into his face, I returned their pressure.

He smiled at me. 'Can we do it, little Christie?'

'Perhaps it will become easier in time.'

'I cannot change what I am. I cannot love you like a brother.'

'And I can't even imagine what it's like to be a sister. Oh Felix, I can only try to love you as best I can.'

His lips curved wryly. 'I think you already love me, little one, far more than I deserve.'

Our fingers closed tightly together like the sealing of a pact. Between us the candle guttered, throwing strange shadows across his face. Then all at once I felt a change in the pressure of his hand, saw, when the light welled up again, that his expression had altered, that where before had been only tenderness he now wore a stricken look, was deathly pale, seemed to struggle in agony with something for a moment so that every muscle of his face was stretched taut.

He withdrew his hand abruptly. 'It's no good, little Christie. I cannot ask it of you. And besides – ' his face seemed to close against me as he spoke, to become a grim, cold mask – 'besides, it is probably too late.'

I stared at him, thinking suddenly of Tarantin's warnings, feeling again an inexplicable dread. 'Too late? Oh Felix, why? Please, if there is something the matter, something more, please, oh please tell me.'

His eyes were impenetrable, his mouth hard. 'There is nothing, Christie. Nothing that need concern you.'

'Then why too late? Oh Felix, if you are in pain, if you are ill – Tarantin told me how desperately ill you were in Geneva – '

'Tarantin?' His voice was suddenly icy with anger. 'Damn Teddy and his meddling! He has no business talking to you – '

'But he's your friend. His anxiety for you is natural – '

'I don't need or want Teddy's interference in my life.' He was white with anger, his lips bloodless, a cold, cruel line. 'And I don't wish you to become so friendly with him. You distrusted him before. I advise you to distrust what he says to you now.'

I stared at him, incredulous. 'But he has nothing but concern and love for you, Felix. And I understand now that he means me no harm. He only wants to help both of us. Oh Felix, he knows – '

I stopped short, remembering my promise to Tarantin that I would not tell Felix of his visit to me or that he had stolen my letter. But Felix's eyes were upon me, intent, inexorable.

'Knows what?' he asked, in a voice that was suddenly dangerously soft. 'What does Teddy know?'

Confused, all at once afraid of those relentless eyes, I turned my head away. Why was Felix at daggers drawn with Tarantin, Tarantin whom he had always defended to me before? And what did Tarantin want of me? Whom had he supposed my letter to be from? What was there between the two of them? And whom was I to trust, Tarantin, in whose friendship I now believed, or Felix whom I loved?

'Knows or guesses – it can't matter,' I said miserably. 'He only means to help us.'

Again that quiet, chilling voice: 'Guesses what, Christie?'

'Guesses the true relationship between us. And knows we still love each other. But he'll keep our secret. I understand that now. Because he cares about you so much he won't do anything to hurt either of us.'

He seemed to hear me with relief. Gradually his expression softened. 'No, Teddy won't hurt you, little Christie.' Then, as if the weariness had descended upon him again, he sighed. 'That power, it seems, is uniquely reserved for me.'

An uncomfortable silence fell between us. He seemed to become preoccupied with his own thoughts so that once more, watching the candlelight throw his features into relief, unable to read his expression but sensing him draw yet farther away from me, I was suddenly afraid of knowing what was in his mind.

Eventually he looked up, seemed to hesitate for a moment, then said: 'You have read your mother's diaries, little one. What – what sort of man was my father?'

I smiled, relieved, thinking I understood him. 'You are not a bit like him, Felix, if that's what you mean. Oh, in appearance perhaps, yes – according to my mother he was very handsome when he was young. But in no other respect.'

'You sound very certain.'

'Of course I'm certain. I know you. I know your integrity and your sense of honour prevent you from in any way resembling him.'

He surveyed me for an instant and there seemed to play upon his lips a little, bitter, self-mocking smile. 'Your faith in me, my dear Christie, is touching.' Then, all at once, as if he had come to some unexplained decision, he pushed back his chair and stood up.

I rose too, alarmed by his expression and the tone of his voice. 'Oh Felix, please tell me –'

'My dear little sister, don't look so dramatic.' He waved me aside with a weary gesture. 'You must forgive me for leaving you, but I have some work I must finish tonight.'

'But it's nearly midnight.'

'You know I prefer to work at night. It spares me the useless quest for sleep.' Then, seeing that I still looked alarmed, relenting, he smiled. 'Oh, my dear child, there's no need for that horrified expression. It's simply that I am still occasionally plagued with bad dreams.'

I stared at him helplessly, dreading his going yet unable to prevent him, not knowing any longer how things stood between us, what we had decided or whether indeed we had decided anything at all.

'But we will talk more in the morning?' I said.

'Yes. Yes, of course.' As he looked at me, all his tenderness seemed to return. And, coming up to me, placing his hands upon my shoulders, he stood, holding me a little away from him, gazing at me silently for some moments. His eyes seemed to explore my face as if they were imprinting afresh its features upon his memory and their tenderness was all at once tinged with that deep sadness I had seen before in the glass.

'My darling Christie,' he said very softly, 'whatever happens, never forget how very much I have always loved you.' Then he kissed me lightly on the forehead and was gone.

I stared after him, stopped, wanting to follow him, to beg him to come back, knowing I could not. Standing in the empty doorway, I shivered, suddenly ice cold. For it was not just that, in the way he looked at me, in his parting words, he had reminded me of another night long ago at Monks Last. But, as he had searched my face and my eyes had held his, I had glimpsed in them not only the sadness but also again that strange diffusion of their focus as if they surveyed me from a long way off; and I had understood suddenly the disturbance of their symmetry, had seen that both pupils were curiously contracted and of unequal size, so that like a threatening chord there rang in my memory something which, though I could not comprehend it, inexplicably increased my fear.

Bad dreams, he had said. I needed to see him, talk to him, draw out of him somehow what this other thing was that stood between us, this secret thing that gave him bad dreams. Impatient of the sleep that would not come, driven by my need to know, to know now, I rose early, before even the servants were awake. But the studio door was firmly closed, the empty passages, the denuded rooms were sunk in a tomb-like silence. I sat in the study, in the drawing room, in the dining room, waiting. Anatole came and offered me breakfast, which I could not eat. The shadows grew longer, the sun settled in bright squares upon the carpet. Anatole came to enquire about lunch. And still the studio door stayed closed.

I could not settle to anything. Stenko was not expected, there was for once no sign of Tarantin. I contemplated going out, but abandoned the idea as if superstitiously fearing to miss him, he who no longer went anywhere, did not leave the house, did not leave the studio, had closed the door against me now as if I did not exist. I tried to tell myself that it was not important, not in any way unusual in the pattern of his reclusiveness, that I was certain of his love and it did not matter if nothing were decided, if the strain of our situation caused him to withdraw from me; he simply wanted time to think and we had time, all the time in the world, if only I could find the patience to wait.

By the evening I could stand it no longer. But Anatole's smile was as inscrutable as ever.

'Monsieur de Lisle is working, madame. He sends his apologies.'

'Will you tell him, Anatole, tell him I – I must see him.'

'I am sorry, madame. He has given orders he is not to be disturbed.' I searched his face for some sign, some telltale crack in the eternal smile, and found nothing. And yet perhaps there was in its very fixity something, a rigid determined loyalty that added to my fear.

For afraid I was now in earnest. Whatever Felix did up there hour after hour he did not work. Tarantin had asserted it, the paintings with their nightmarish evidence of his disintegrating talent, the empty easel, the silence proved it. Looking into the drawing room mirror at the great crack where he had tried to shatter his own reflection I was afraid of his pain, afraid of his haggard look and his exhaustion; and of what I had seen in his eyes and of his words to me which had been so much like a parting. I was afraid most of all.

I do not know how I got through that night. The next morning I realized that, whatever Felix's instructions were, however much I knew I must respect his freedom, I could remain alone with my fears no longer. With deliberation I climbed the stairs in the direction of the studio. I was almost at the door when Anatole, materializing from the shadows, glided across the landing and stood blocking my way.

'I am sorry, madame. Monsieur de Lisle is not to be disturbed.'

'So you say, Anatole. But I must disturb him.'

A curious transformation occurred in the smile, the minutest succession of movements around the corners of the mouth, so that without it ever precisely vanishing it contrived to look first torn, then apologetic, before fixing itself into a look of unbending determination.

'No, madame. He would not wish it.'

There was a note in his voice I had never heard before. And suddenly I saw in the bared teeth, the rigid lips, a flash of menace like an unsheathed knife. I stared at him. Still smiling, he began to move forward slowly, interposing his body between me and the landing, so that to pass him or even hold my ground I would have to engage in a physical struggle. Mesmerized with shock, I retreated before him, down the stairs. I was on the third stair when there was the sound of the front door knocker. I heard a maid go to answer it and then Tarantin's voice. Turning from Anatole, I ran down the stairs and across the hall, almost falling into Tarantin's arms.

'My dear girl, whatever—'

'Oh Teddy, I'm so glad you've come!' And, despite myself, I burst into tears.

He put his arm around my shoulders, proffered me the handkerchief from his sleeve and shepherded me into the study where he firmly closed the door. But although he was kindness itself there was something strange in his manner, a suppressed excitement which, no matter how they schooled themselves into a concerned expression, danced in all the creases of his face, glittered in his black, monkey's eyes.

'So! Something has happened between you and Felix. Something has happened at last!'

'Oh Teddy – '

'Yes, yes. Quickly! You must tell me everything.'

I began haltingly to explain the events of the last two days, but it seemed I could not tell my story fast enough for Tarantin, for he urged me on with frequent 'yes, yeses' and impatient flashes of his rings. When I began upon Felix's strange behaviour and his subsequent retreat he was grave for a moment, his lips pursed, his head on one side, but his gravity was that of the doctor listening triumphantly to the confirmation of his diagnosis, it served only to increase his excitement till every muscle in his small, lithe body seemed aquiver with it.

'Oh Teddy, what can we do?'

'Do?' He suddenly pulled out his watch and inspected it anxiously. 'Yes, it is only a quarter past ten, Stenko is outside in the car, we have plenty of time.' Glancing warily at the closed door he all at once lowered his voice to a stage whisper. 'We will go on a visit, dear girl. To an old acquaintance.'

CHAPTER FORTY-SIX

Anna Rostova. Even the name filled me with apprehension. For now I remembered what I had seen in Felix's eyes, where I had seen it before. I had supposed her far away, in another country, somewhere her shimmering snaky presence could be no threat to us. But now, with Stenko at the wheel of Tarantin's Lagonda coupé, we were driving through London to meet her. Felix's mistress. He had given her up, yet she had returned the night of the seance, returned with hints of some subtle threat to menace me. And later, before he had left England, though he had not told her the truth, he had gone to see her, gone from my arms to hers. I wondered suddenly whether it had always been so, whether he had ever really left her, whether all this time, even now, there continued that secret midnight dance between them.

We had set off, with Tarantin supervising Stenko's somewhat haphazard driving, in the direction of the West End, but now we doubled back to rejoin the Embankment at Vauxhall Bridge.

'They will suspect. Perhaps we do not deceive them. But the need is there and it is desperate. They have no choice, they will take the chance.'

'Oh Teddy, what need? Where are we going?'

Tarantin was crouched in the back seat with his arms resting on the leather behind my head so that, in the proximity of his face to mine, in the closeness of his breathing, I could still sense that pent-up purposeful excitement.

'We have followed them, Stenko and I. Week after week, once I was certain. I cannot stop it, Felix will not listen to me. But you, you have the power to end it.'

'End what? Oh Teddy, please explain. Why are we going to see Rostova?'

His jet-bead eyes still glittered as I turned to look at him, but I glimpsed something beside the excitement in them now, something implacable.

'You will see,' he said. 'You will see.' And, holding the intensity of his gaze for a moment, I no longer found his melodrama ridiculous.

We were driving through the City in the direction of the docks. Presently the tarmac road gave place to cobbles and the buildings on our left to drab shops and little, low, soot-blackened dwellings, hatched higgledy-piggledy in a maze of grim streets and squalid alleys. Two old crones outside the Public Wash House struggled with a mound of laundry in a crippled pram. In the doorway of the Seaman's Mission, a drunk babbled incomprehensibly to himself. A tailor's shop, its shattered frontage boarded and padlocked, bore the painted legend: 'Hail Mosley! Kill The Dirty Jews!'

Turning off West India Dock Road, past the huddled emporia of the Chinese Quarter down a narrow street where a gaggle of filthy children played with an old tyre and women seated on their doorsteps looked after us suspiciously, we drew to a halt outside a tenement building.

I stared up at the broken windows, the balconies festooned with dingy washing.

'Anna Rostova? Here?'

Tarantin acknowledged my amazement only with a terse little nod. 'Come,' he said, helping me out of the car. 'Stenko will drive about until we are ready. We do not, anyway, wish to advertise our presence here.'

He took my arm and we entered a dark hallway and began to climb the stone stairs. The climb seemed interminable. Here too the walls were scrawled with graffiti, and the air was rancid with stale cabbage and frying fat and the overpowering stench of urine. Our footsteps rang out hollowly, echoing down the stairwell and, from all around us, through thin walls and half-closed doors, came the cacophany of a seething, mutinous, multifarious life, babies crying, voices raised in altercation, Al Bowly blaring from a distant wireless set, a dog yapping, someone nearby coughing as if to bring up their lungs. On the fourth landing we stopped and Tarantin paused to take off his hat and mop his forehead.

'So!' he said. 'Finally we are here. Shall we go in?'

The door was not locked. The room we entered was in profound darkness, so that it was only through a vague sense of some presence stirring within it, a droning sound like the distant hum of an engine, that we were aware of its occupancy; through that, and through the smell. For, if the stench on the stairway had been oppressive, here the air made the muscles of my throat contract. It was a curious, fetid, cloying smell, compounded of human secretions but with an overriding sickly sweetness to it, the smell of the charnel house.

I stood with my hand clamped over my mouth while Tarantin, striking a match, lit the gas mantle. The scene that rose up out of the darkness made me edge backwards towards the door. The room was bare apart from a rickety construction of orange boxes in one corner and a soiled mattress covered with what looked like a heap of rags in another. All light from the window had been blocked out with thick layers of newspaper. The cracked linoleum appeared to have been used indiscriminately as a sewer and I saw now that the strange buzzing came from flies, crawling, swarming everywhere, but humming most thickly around a gilded birdcage which stood near my feet and was, apart from some clutter on top of the orange boxes and a few photographs, curling with damp, pinned to the far wall, the only evidence of the room's tenant. I stared down at the birdcage and, understanding the reason for the flies' attention, quickly averted my eyes, willing myself to choke back my nausea. And at that moment the bundle of rags took life and moved.

'*Merde!* But you are early, *mon cher.*'

I gasped in horror. For the voice, throaty, purring, was unmistakable. And I saw then that the photographs, now faded and stained, barely recognizable, had once looked out at me from jewelled frames in a very different room.

Tarantin, as if for protection against the fetid air, took out a cigar. 'My dear Anna Nikolayevna, we must disappoint you. He is not early. But I hope for his sake we are not too late.'

There was an expletive and the rags heaved. A leg came into view, a purplish, ulcerated leg like an old woman's with the toenails yellow and curving into claws underneath the foot, then an emaciated arm and then a face, a face that mocked the faded images gazing down at it from the walls, such a face that I looked away for a moment aghast. But the eyes were the same; greenish-yellow unblinking eyes, crazed as if they had drunk the light. They focused with difficulty upon us, seeming first alarmed and then baleful.

'*Merde!* Le Bon Dieu Tarantin! Why have you come? I do not need such little gods now when I have all creation in my power. I spit on them, I who touch the sea and sky, I who command the air they breathe, I crush under my feet like beetles such *bétises*!'

'You, Anna Nikolayevna?' said Tarantin, calmly lighting his cigar. 'I did not know the Snow Queen has such powers.'

'*Sot!* I am not Snow Queen now. I am Firebird!'

'So the snow was not enough, Anna Nikolayevna? You could not kill yourself with cocaine, so now you trust morphia to do it.'

'I am Firebird. It is I who command the earth and air – '

Tarantin gave a scornful laugh. 'You, Anna Nikolayevna? You are nothing but a filthy bag of rotting bones.' And suddenly he swooped down and seized the emaciated arm by the wrist.

She wrestled with him. 'I am Firebird! When I dance the earth is blinded with it. And when I sing – '

'Yes, my dear Anna?' He was stronger by far than she, he held her arm twisted back so she was forced to look into his face. 'When you sing?'

'When I sing my Prince hears me. My Prince hears and I open *tout à fait* my golden wings and his blood fills with my fire and I give him all my power, *le monde entier.*'

'This is what you give your Prince!' He wrenched her arm round suddenly so that the inner skin of it was exposed to me. 'Look Christie. Look very well. This is Anna Nikolayevna's gift.'

I stared, horrified. I remembered how those white arms had

moved fluent as the air itself, music's embodiment. I remembered how diamonds and emeralds had glittered on those wrists. I wanted to turn away but Tarantin's eyes were on my face, compelling me to look.

'So! Soon our Firebird will have no veins to stick her needle in. Oh, she cannot smell the stench or feel her rotting flesh. The morphia takes care of that, does it not, my dear Anna Nikolayevna? But always there must be more, more. For if there is not, our Firebird falls to earth with a so-unpleasant crash.'

She struggled, drew back her crusted lips in a snarl. But all the time he held her fast and his bright, implacable eyes were fixed on mine, forcing me to understand what I fought not to, fought to push from my mind as too terrible even for thought.

'Oh Teddy, no. I can't believe – '

'You cannot imagine, my dear Christie, how such a pathetic creature feeds this great appetite? Well, she has friends in the Chinese Quarter. But she must have money. So our all-powerful Goddess puts aside fire and air for a while and tries a little vulgar commerce. She sells. And – '

Suddenly he stiffened and I saw that his ears were straining after some sound only he had caught.

'And here, Anna Nikolayevna, is someone come to buy.'

I heard it now too, the sound of footsteps echoing in the stairwell, footsteps climbing towards our door. All at once Rostova's body went rigid, her eyes took on a wild expression. And in that moment Tarantin, still holding her with his left hand, threw aside the cigar and dived in amongst the soiled rags with his right. She thrashed, flailed, tried to bite the hand that gripped her, but he was too strong, he held her easily. Suddenly giving an exclamation of triumph, he withdrew from the filthy heap a small white package and, almost before I was aware of what he was doing, flung it towards me. My hands caught it automatically. I looked down at it, bewildered. Through the paper, my fingers felt something malleable and powdery.

'Your handbag!' Tarantin snapped, clamping his free hand over Rostova's mouth as she began to let loose a volley of expletives. 'Quickly! And stay quiet.'

The footsteps came on steadily up the stairs. We stood in silence listening to them. I held my breath, praying they would not stop on our landing, praying they would go on upwards, that I would not have to face him, that it was all an invention of Tarantin's, that he would not at any moment come through that door. But no, I sighed with relief, they were not his footsteps, they were too rapid, too closely-spaced for a tall man, Tarantin was wrong after all, they would go on up, they were not coming here, they could not –

The footsteps stopped. The door handle turned. And in the doorway stood Anatole.

'Ah, my dear Anna Nikolayevna,' observed Tarantin, 'your Prince finds you so repulsive he will not even come himself. He sends a messenger.'

I stared at Anatole. He had gone as white as a sheet and there was in his expression no trace of a smile.

'Oh, Anatole,' I said, 'how could you? How could you do his dirty work for him?'

The man looked back at me for a moment. It was a strange look, not guilty, not frightened, the look of someone holding their ground. 'Madame,' he said, 'you cannot know – you do not understand.' And, before we could stop him, he whirled round and was gone.

Tarantin flung Rostova back upon the mattress, where she lay, gnashing her teeth and pouring out an incoherent stream of abuse. Then he turned to me, and all at once his excitement had left him, every crease of his face was puckered and sad. He spread his hands helplessly.

'So you see, dear girl. Now you see.'

'Oh God, Teddy! For how long?'

A chuckle that made my flesh creep came from the mattress. '*Toujours!* Always he has been mine. It is in his blood, the fire of the gods is in him. Oh, sometimes he has denied the power of Firebird, *le pauvre fou.* But not for long. His blood betrays him, *mon cher Félix,* always he will return to me.'

I remembered suddenly the words the glass had spelt in the seance, the glass I had believed Tarantin had pushed. 'Blood will betray – ' Oh God in heaven, it was not possible that all the time I had loved Felix it had been true, that I had never known him, had always been deceived. I gazed in horror at the thing on the mattress, the death's-head thing with which he had such secret kinship, which presaged what he would become.

Tarantin snorted, all his purposeful intensity upon him again. 'Nonsence, Anna Nikolayevna! Must we listen to more of your evil rubbish? I have the talisman against it now.'

Once more that derisive, throaty laugh came from the mattress. '*Merde!* The Great God Tarantin! What talisman?'

Tarantin took my arm, drawing me towards her. The yellow-green eyes gazed up at me with scorn. 'Ah, *la petite.* The little innocent who gives to *cher Félix* her so-sweet, so-touching love. Oh, of course the pederast Tarantin must admire such love, *contre nature comme lui-même.* But I give to Félix another love, a love *sans corps,* a love which speaks in the pure fire of the spirit, which folds us in its divine flame and purges us *de toute au monde.* We love as Gods, Félix and I. And as Gods we crush your creeping animal love!' The festering lips pursed and spat. 'We crush it, *ma petite,* as once I crush the filthy spawn you want to hatch for him!'

Tarantin stared at her for a moment, then at me. 'What is she saying?'

I forced myself to look at the thing in the bed, the remains of the woman who had persuaded me that I must kill my child. 'Nothing, Teddy. It doesn't matter.'

Tarantin's lips drew back savagely. Lunging at the mattress, he took the thing by the throat and began to shake it. 'Tell me, Anna Nikolayevna! Tell me, before I finish you, what new evil is this?'

'No, Teddy!' I screamed. 'No! Please, no!'

Reluctantly he let go of her. She fell back choking amongst the rags.

'Very well,' he said, between gritted teeth. 'We will leave her to the mercy of her dirty needle. Come, Christie. We will take her obscene merchandise with us, so a little of her evil may be destroyed.' Bringing out his wallet, he tossed a handful of notes contemptuously towards the mattress. 'There, Anna Nikolayevna. There is your blood money.'

Outside in the street he took his handkerchief from his sleeve and carefully wiped his hands where he had touched her. Then he threw the handkerchief away.

'So!' he said, looking back at the tenement as we climbed into the car. 'She has come home, Anna Nikolayevna Rostova, the divine goddess of the Tarantin Ballet, Hannah Rozsas, the little waif I rescue from a Budapest slum. She danced like an angel. And now she will die like a dog.'

I sat in the passenger seat next to Stenko, taking in great gulps of fresh air, clutching my handbag with its deadly contents. 'Oh Teddy, I still can't believe it. Always, she said. And when she said it, so much slipped into place, things I didn't understand all those years ago. But I still can't – I don't want to believe it. Please, Teddy, tell me it isn't true.'

'My dear, you have seen and heard it for yourself.'

'How long have you known?'

'For certain, only since he came back to London. But it is possible with discipline to conceal the habit for years. She is at the finish, she no longer cares.'

His arms were once again propped on the back of my seat, his face close to mine. I turned to look at him. 'And he – is he now beyond caring, too?'

Tarantin paused. The jet-bead eyes became for a moment opaque. 'You understand why I beg you to come back. It must be stopped. You must stop him.'

I stared at him, at Stenko spread for thunder at the wheel, at the handbag resting so innocently in my lap. 'Oh, but how? If you can't, how can I?'

'Only you know that. You will find a way.'

I thought of how controlled and strong Felix had always appeared, so very much in command of himself, and remembered the closed areas of him, the Felix de Lisle he had never let me know. It was into this closed territory I must now venture; yet his defences were impregnable, he would never let me in. And I was frightened as well, terrified suddenly of what, if I succeeded, would be revealed to me.

'Teddy, I'm not sure that I can. I'm not even sure any longer how I stand with him.'

Tarantin snorted. 'When already he has told you how much he loves you?'

'I believed – I thought he did – but now I don't know, after this I feel I don't know him any more.'

'But you love him. At least you will not still deny this to me.'

'Yes. Yes, I love him. But everything is so hopeless between us.'

Tarantin's eyes flashed. 'Sister, mistress? – I do not know, I do not care! I know only this. Apart from his son, you are the person he has always loved most in this world. How do I know it? Well, I tell you something I have not said before. When he comes to see me that night twelve years ago, how am I so certain that something terrible has happened between you? Not because he tells me. On the contrary, he talks only of his plans to go away, talks to me without the slightest emotion. But as he talks, the tears begin in his eyes. I do not know if he feels them, even understands that they are there. He is a cold proud man who does not show his emotions, and all the time he is talking about his work and when he will return to Paris, and all the time the tears are running down his face. I say nothing – I know him too well and, besides, I, Vladimir Tarantin, am burning with jealousy for the person who can make him feel so much. I have never seen him like it, before or since. I have never spoken of it to him. I tell you now, so you will know whatever Rostova is you are stronger.'

The car pulled up outside Cheyne Walk. For a moment the three of us sat in silence, not moving. I looked at the handbag with its parcel of death. Then I looked round at Tarantin. 'And if I can find a way, if I can persuade him?'

'I know a doctor who is expert in these things. He will come if I telephone him.'

I moved to get out of the car. 'Then I shall be in touch with you, Teddy.'

'No.' It was Stenko, speaking for the first time, putting his arm across me to prevent my opening the door. 'We will come with you, Christie.'

I smiled. 'Thank you, Stenko. But I think I should go alone.'

'Dear girl, no. Stenko is right.' Tarantin put his hand on my shoulder. 'His man will have returned by now, he will now know what has happened. You must not confront him without us. He needs the morphia badly, you understand, and – '

'You mean,' I said slowly, 'that I won't be safe?'

Tarantin gave a helpless flash of the gold rings. 'It is the drug, Christie. Or the lack of it. You have seen Rostova. He may do things he would not – well, he may perhaps threaten you or even – perhaps he may be a little violent.'

I looked down at the handbag and shivered. 'But if he loves me?'

'Please, Christie,' Stenko said. 'Better we should come with you.'

I opened the bag and took out my front door key. 'No. If I'm to persuade him of anything, I must do it myself.'

'Then you will give the morphia to us before you go,' said Tarantin. 'Stenko and I will destroy it. To take it into the house, to have it when you see him is foolish. Please, dear girl, you will not put yourself in unnecessary danger.'

I looked down at the white envelope nestling between my purse and my powder compact. I loved Felix de Lisle, I had loved him all my life, and yet who did I love? The time we had spent together those twelve long years ago had been so brief, how could I possibly have known him? But know I must, now, whether it was Rostova's Felix de Lisle or the man I loved who met me when I crossed the threshold of Cheyne Walk. For knowing that was more important than anything, even than knowing whether he was my brother.

I snapped the bag shut. 'Thank you, both of you. But I must go alone and as I am.'

CHAPTER FORTY-SEVEN

Diary of Adele Ward.
Silver Strands Boarding House, Weymouth.

5th February, 1905.

This morning, hearing screams from the kitchen, I found Bridie cowering in a corner while M, who in his insane rage had smashed all the china on the dresser, berated her with threats and foul language. It appears he believes she and I are poisoning his food. Eventually he left, swearing he would eat no more meals in this house, and I managed to calm Bridie somewhat. But I cannot find it in me to reproach her when she says, as she has so often lately, that if M continues beneath this roof she must give me warning.

What should I do without dear Bridie? The departure of the Misses Y was hard enough to bear, yet after the disappearance of the dog, I could scarcely in all conscience plead with them to relent, despite M's denials. Oh, poor Bridie! It is bad enough that I owe her a fortnight's wages, due to M's constant draining of my resources. But if I give him money I am able to keep him from the house for hours at a time, thereby at least affording us a respite in which we may all breathe more easily. Oh, if only there were some way we could be rid of him altogether. Entreat him as I may as to the pain in his head, he will not consult a doctor; and, were I to call out the local constable, what could he do? M is my husband, my roof is his roof, and beneath it he may be as violent and unreasonable as he pleases.

D alone is a rock to me – dear D, my devoted brother by adoption. While we do not speak of M, I catch him on occasion watching me with a brother's protective glance; and this afternoon, though I have tried to conceal my financial difficulties from him, he came and without a word pressed an envelope into my hand which I found to contain a portion of his hard-earned wages. Touched nearly to tears, I explained that I could not accept such a gift. Shaking his head and with a curious expression on his face, he appeared to begin upon an objection; but then, perhaps missing the English words, he fell silent.

6th February, 1905.

I had just laid down my pen last night when my bedroom door was flung open, and there was M, his face contorted in a grimace of malevolent cunning. With a gasp I rose from the secretary; but before I could prevent him he had stepped across the threshold and had locked the door behind him. I opened my mouth to scream; he clamped his foul hand over my lips, holding me fast. I began to struggle but my feeble efforts were no match for his insane strength. With horror I realized he was dragging me to the bed.

'So, my dearest little wifie,' he hissed in a voice of terrifying softness, 'your beloved husband has come home and he will have what is his right! I've seen you spooning with your little pet, your foreign puppy. But remember your duty to me, dearest. I won't have you cuckold me with a pup of a boy. Struggle, would you, dearest? Try to bite my hand, would you? I'll take my rights as your husband, if I have to beat your prim little face to pulp!'

Flinging me down upon the mattress, he thrust the vile weight of his body on top of me. I began to fight with all my strength then, as wild and insane as he was, trying to claw at his face with my fingers, to free my mouth somehow from that repulsive suffocating grip. I saw his eyes, staring and red with blood, saw his lips drawn back in a wolfish leer. My stomach heaved, my struggles redoubled in a frenzy, I managed at last to wrench my head free and scream. I screamed, screamed until my lungs felt they would burst.

All of a sudden he seemed to be arrested. 'Oh no!' he gasped. 'Oh G–d, be merciful! Don't make that noise. It's like a knife in my brain!' Then, his words becoming jumbled and nonsensical, he fell forward, clutching his head, jerking and pitching in the throes of a violent convulsion.

I became aware of hammering on the door and the voices of Bridie and D. Dragging myself, weak and trembling, from the bed, I ran to turn the key in the lock. D was into the room first, his face white, his mouth hard, seizing me by the shoulders and gazing at me as if he feared to find me mortally injured: Bridie came after, weeping hysterically. We dreaded, all three of us, for a moment to approach the prone body of M. But, as we stared in terror at him, he appeared to come to himself, and letting out a high-pitched whine, began all at once to sob unrestrainedly like a child. So, eventually, I was able to lead him, harmless and still sobbing, back to his own room.

Though we considered it best to lock him in, this morning he appeared dazed and only partly conscious, his words again coming in an incomprehensible jumble. D went to fetch the doctor who, after a brief examination of his patient, asked leave to consult a colleague for a second opinion. The two physicians are upstairs in the sickroom now, where they have been for some time.

7th February, 1905.

I could not bring myself to write this yesterday.

After the two medical men had left M's bedside they came and sought me out in my private parlour. With grave faces they began all at once to ask me the most indelicate questions concerning intimate details of my married life. I forbore to answer at first, profoundly shocked by this impertinence. Whereupon they explained that M is sick of a disease which, having worked its evil in his blood for many years, has eventually attacked his brain; that this disease, which I cannot even now bring my pen to name, is a result of M's degraded and immoral way of life; and that because I am his wife I too might be in grave danger of its unspeakable contamination. I could scarcely comprehend the full force of their words, but I endeavoured, despite many blushes, to answer their questions, which they said must go back to the very first days of my marriage, and at length I seemed to satisfy them for, despite their appearing a little surprised at my answers and one of them raising his eyebrows and staring at me narrowly a good deal, with manifest relief they pronounced me beyond doubt free from all risk of infection.

As to M, they say the disease can be checked only in its initial stages; now he is past all hope and will decline gradually into madness. Describing his violence and the fear with which he blights our household, I begged them, since no care of mine can help him, to admit him to some hospital where he may be properly looked after. But, shaking their heads, they said that it is early days yet; though it will come to it, his condition is not at present grave enough to incarcerate him in an asylum; having reached this crisis, he will probably thereafter become docile for a time and perfectly tractable.

Docile he undoubtedly is, for when, this morning, realizing he must still be fed and otherwise attended to, I brought myself to look in upon him, he seemed, though he has regained the faculty of speech, weak and almost babyish. Oh, must I now as his wife bear, on top of everything else, the intolerable burden of nursing him? My manly and upright M, my noble hero? It revolts me to be in the same room with him, let alone to touch him.

*After the doctors had gone, I sat alone for a while, crushed by despair and humiliation, feeling as though, despite their reassurances, I too were tainted. Finally D came to me and, seeing my stricken look, taking my hands in his, begged me to tell him what was the matter. I could not, even to him, bring myself to utter the **truth**; I told him only that M was mad and that there was no cure for it. I wanted very much to cry but, perhaps from shock, the tears would not come. Stroking my hair and gathering me into his arms he held me for a while with my cheek against his, comforting me; and thinking suddenly that it was many years, more than I could remember, since anyone showed me such tenderness or put their arms around me, finding such consolation in the warmth of his body and the touch of his skin against mine, I felt the tears welling up at last and was instantly ashamed of myself. Smiling, however, and taking my handkerchief, he softly wiped the moisture from my cheeks, looking at me all the while with eyes that were at once grave and gentle. Suddenly I recalled M's foul accusations. Oh how greatly they profane the purity of feeling between us! But could such a monster as M ever comprehend an emotion as far removed from his own bestial appetites as heaven is from hell? If I am fond of D and he perhaps returns that fondness, it is with the **chaste** and **sacred** affection brother holds for sister. My dearest boy, so brave and loyal. How he protects and cares for his sister in her wretchedness; and how I feel his strength imparting strength to me in order that I may take up this new burden my duty as M's wife compels me to shoulder.*

*Yet supposing M does not remain docile? Supposing, rotten as he is with vile disease, he tries once again to **force himself upon me?***

CHAPTER FORTY-EIGHT

My bag had a longish handle to it and fastened with a clasp at the top. Winding the strap of the handle round my wrist as tightly as I could, I worked my fingers through the gap above the fastening, sliding them down over the side of the bag and round its base, so that it was clutched tightly to my side with my arm covering the clasp, a precaution which, though it might not withstand a prolonged struggle, meant that my ugly burden could not easily be wrenched from my grip. Then I opened the door and went in.

He was standing waiting for me at the top of the stairs, standing there so quiet and still it was an instant before I was aware of him. He was clean-shaven and fully-dressed and he looked as he had always looked, very tall and straight and lean, perfectly in command of himself. I stared up at him with shock, remembering vividly the decaying thing in that vile room, not knowing how I had expected him to be, wondering suddenly whether everything I had seen and heard had simply been part of some dreadful nightmare which would vanish now I was back on familiar ground.

Then he began to come slowly down the staircase towards me. At the foot of the stairs he paused. His eyes rested for a moment on the handbag I clutched so firmly before travelling upwards to my face and there was something now in his expression, in his very stillness that filled me with apprehension, made me know I had hoped in vain.

'My dear Christie,' he said evenly, 'I think you have something that belongs to me.'

My hand grasped the bag more tightly. He was about three yards away, his eyes still trained upon me. I held his gaze defiantly, in silence.

'Christie, don't be stupid. This serves no purpose.'

He was only a couple of feet from me now and I could see in his eyes with their ominously contracted pupils that veiled, strange look. His movements were deliberate, unhurried, the hunter slowly and carefully stalking his quarry. I held my ground until he was almost upon me, then turned abruptly and, keeping tight hold upon the bag, made for the drawing room. I could hear his footsteps on the marble behind me, following but not quickening their pace. Every room was a cul-de-sac in which he could trap me, there was nowhere except the front door by which I could make my escape, he had no need to hurry to be certain of me. He came softly after me across the drawing-room carpet, waiting for the moment I would reach the mantelpiece and would be obliged to turn and face him. I felt my hand upon the bag sticky with sweat. I stopped and turned.

'My dear little Christie, Teddy has no business involving you in this. But now that you know, you must be sensible. If you have the package he stopped Anatole from collecting, you must give it to me.'

His voice was measured, calm, but there was in its very reasonableness an undercurrent of threat.

'No, Felix,' I said.

'Little one, I know in your own brave, sweet way you mean to help. But you must understand there is only one way you can help me. And that is to give me what you have.'

'No,' I said.

A flicker of irritation crossed his lips. 'If you have some romantic notion that you will change things, you must abandon it.' He moved a step closer to me. 'I do not wish you to be hurt.'

I looked steadily at him. His face, apart from what I saw in his eyes, was the face I loved, the face I had known, gentle, affectionate, filled with tenderness. I saw now how the mouth was set hard, how the little muscle above his jaw worked. I took a deep breath and clenched my hand upon the bag. He moved closer to me.

'Christie, I need that parcel. You must give it to me.'

'No, Felix.'

Still closer. He held out his hand. 'Please. Don't be foolish.'

'No.'

He was a foot away from me, his face pale, his mouth a thin line. 'Give it to me, Christie.'

'If you want it, you must take it.'

'You must believe that I shall.'

'I do believe it. You're a great deal stronger than me. I can't give you much of a fight. But fight I will, Felix. With everything I have. If you want Rostova's filthy wares, you'll have at least to break my arm.'

He seemed to struggle with himself, looked for an instant torn with anguish. Then I saw his face harden, his eyes go dark. He crossed what remained of the space between us and stood over me, menacingly tall. I felt myself go rigid, dug my fingers into the leather of the bag. His hand closed around my arm. I drew in my breath. His fingers tightened on my flesh. I thought that it did not matter, nothing mattered any more; if this was what I must know, if this was how I must lose him then it was not important, I must not grieve for it, for I had lost nothing, all I had ever possessed had been an illusion. I clenched the muscles of my arm, pressed the bag against my ribs so that it hurt me. Holding my breath, I closed my eyes.

His fingers tightened, tightened – then relaxed and fell away.

I felt my muscles gradually slacken, felt my arm throb where his fingers had bruised me, felt in the very consciousness of my pain an overwhelming relief. I opened my eyes. His back was to me, he had moved over to the window where he stood framed by the two empty panels that had held the icons. Something wet trickled down the side of my nose and I realized with surprise that I was crying. 'Oh Felix, oh my darling, I knew—'

He swung round upon me angrily. 'My dear Christie, you know nothing. And you're foolish to place such confidence in my love. In another hour, when the pain starts, I shan't be so squeamish. I shan't care if I break your arm or even kill you. I love you, but I need the morphia more.'

I glanced down at the bag, still pressed against my ribs. The tears tasted salty on my lips. 'Felix, why? In God's name, why? I've seen Rostova, I know what it can do. How could you destroy yourself like this?'

'Christie, it must not concern you. I realize now it was criminally wrong of me ever to ask you to come to this house.'

'But I love you, Felix. I want to help you. Tarantin has a doctor who can—'

'Damn Teddy! Damn his eternal desire to play God! Damn him for ever letting you get caught up in this!'

I stared at him and was suddenly angry. 'Oh Felix, how could you? How could you of all people let Rostova destroy you? How could you let this turn you against Tarantin? How could you even get Anatole mixed up in it, sending him on your vile errands?'

'Anatole went to Limehouse today because I did not trust myself to go. I thought after you had told me what Anna had done to you I should be in grave danger of breaking her neck.'

'Then how could he consent to it? He's always been so loyal, so – '

'And he is loyal still.' His voice was sharp with impatience. 'You do him a deep injustice. He is as opposed to this as you are. But he is more sensible. He accepts what must be accepted. When I am too ill to know or care what I am doing, he takes it upon himself to look after me. He has a curious dedication to keeping me alive.'

I gazed, horror-stricken, at the pale, set face. 'And is that now a matter of such indifference to you?'

He took out his cigarette case. 'My dear Christie, I am obliged to care only about what is in your handbag. Try, like Anatole, to be sensible and accept it. Don't force me to hurt you.'

I continued to gaze at him in dismay, at the man I had, minutes before, suddenly felt so confident of knowing, who was now once again a stranger to me. I had won no battles, crossed no barriers. I began to sob uncontrollably.

He looked up from lighting his cigarette. His expression became for an instant more gentle. 'Please, little one, don't cry. It isn't worth it.'

'At least help me to understand, Felix. At least tell me why.'

He gave a little dry smile. 'Isn't it enough that you know the full extent of my degradation? Do you wish me to make excuses for myself as well?'

With my free hand, the hand that did not clutch the bag, I wiped my face, struggling to control my tears. 'But Rostova said – Oh, Felix, she made it sound as if she had always had this as a hold over you.'

He drew deeply upon his cigarette. The self-mocking smile still played upon his lips. 'Anna and I come from the same place, that is all.'

I stared at him, puzzled. 'Does that mean – did you – do you love her?'

I thought of the filthy, rotting thing on the mattress. 'And you and I – do we come from the same place?'

'No, little one. From very different places.'

His face was all at once suffused with regret, as if with a longing for something irrevocably lost to him. Watching him, I felt my tears well up again.

'But if we love each other – Oh why, Felix? Because of this? Because of Anna?'

Again he smiled that dry, self-mocking smile. 'No. Not because of Anna. But she has always understood it. She used to taunt me with it. That night in London, the night after I left you, she knew then.'

I felt my heart sink. 'And that was why you went to see her?'

He stared at me, surprised. 'Dear God, no. The last person in the world I wanted to see that night was Anna. I had been forced for practical reasons to visit Teddy, but I could barely talk to him, I was in a kind of mad despair with knowing what I had done to you, driven wild with the pain of it, wanting to do something violent and not knowing what. In the end, since there seemed no possibility of sleep and I couldn't face going home, I decided to go to the "43" and get myself blind drunk. I failed, even in that. But while I was there I saw Anna. She was with Brilliant Chang, the dope pedlar. She was bored by her experiments with cocaine and wanted to try something more exciting.'

'And she offered you morphia?'

'She understood that I would not accept, that I should be angry. It was a game she played. I remember she smiled and said: "You think you are so very strong. But it is a powerful God, you will not cheat it in the end." She knew how much I hated her fascination with drugs and by some evil instinct she had worked out why.'

My tears had ceased. I stood very still with my eyes upon his face, not daring to interrupt him now, scarcely daring to breathe. But he seemed all at once to recollect himself, for he broke off abruptly with a small gesture of impatience.

'Little Christie, there is no point in this. I need the morphia and I must have it.' And he moved suddenly from the window, towards me.

My hold on the bag had relaxed. Tightening it, I backed away from him. He came on after me, his expression cold and intent. Then something, perhaps the fear I could not disguise, seemed to check him. He stopped before the mantelpiece, surveyed me for an instant, turned aside.

'Please, Felix,' I said very softly, 'I want so much to understand.'

He drew upon his cigarette, moved away from me with sigh of exasperation, began restlessly to pace to and fro between the mantelpiece and the window. Eventually he said:

'It was my souvenir from the war, Christie. I should have died in that shell hole with Routledge, but since I did not they had an obligation to keep me alive. Oh, the medicos weren't to blame –

what could they do? If you were in pain they gave you pain-killing injections. If the pain persisted, they simply increased the dose. By the time I returned to Monks Last after my spells in various hospitals I had been pumped so full of morphia I was completely dependent on it. Oh, of course that drunken idiot Blair never realized. He was all set to continue the process. But I knew it was the begining of a gruesome life-long servitude. So after three weeks of enduring agony, being offered day after day what I craved in torment for and knew I must resist, being scolded by the nurse and reproached by my mother, I somehow managed to get the better of it. Nobody knew, the symptoms of my struggle were simply put down to shell shock. And the struggle didn't stop, of course – there was the nonsense with my back to fight now I no longer had the drug to stop me squaring up to it, and the craving remained for some while afterwards.'

He paused to extinguish his cigarette.

'But you conquered it,' I said.

'Yes. It left me eventually. Teddy's man in Paris taught me other ways of controlling my pain, by meditation, by exercising the will. I believed I was free.'

I looked down at the strap of the handbag knotted round my wrist. 'Then why – '

He had gone to his pocket for his cigarette case again. He smiled bitterly. 'Anna was right after all. It is a powerful God and difficult to cheat. After the accident, after Nicky died – ' he paused for a moment to light another Muratti – 'when I was ill in Geneva, the pain in my back returned with a vengeance and I seemed to lose all resistance to it. They gave me morphia. I was too weak and ill to understand what was happening, and by the time I knew it was too late. Besides, I had ceased to care. I needed morphia, I needed it, I discovered, in larger and larger doses. When I left the hospital I found myself a crooked doctor who would supply my needs with no questions asked. I no longer examined my motives. I had lost you, I had lost my son, I could not escape my guilt for what I had brought upon both of you. I cannot tell you where the need to control the pain left off and where my longing for the oblivion morphia brought took over. I began to build my life around it. I stopped going out, stopped seeing people. Eventually I decided to rent a villa in Tangiers where I could live in seclusion and give myself over utterly to it.'

He paused. The savage little smile flickered on his lips once more. 'There are weeks, months in Tangiers I simply don't remember. Anatole took over all the practical aspects of my life, drove the car, paid the bills, fed me when for days I forgot to eat, dressed me when I was too weak to manage it. I had developed an increasing tolerance to the drug, I needed massive amounts, forty, fifty grains a day, to reproduce the effect two or three grains had once achieved so easily. I had persuaded myself that the strange waking dreams I experienced improved my painting. But now the dreams became appalling nightmares where I saw grotesque creatures devouring one another, human heads sliced apart like onions. There was no escape in sleep, I could not sleep, it was as if I should never sleep again. I could no longer paint and my vision became so seriously disturbed I began to be afraid I was losing my sight. So – ' he paused, drawing upon the cigarette, then resumed his restless pacing – 'I decided to stop.'

His restlessness had increased as he talked, I could feel a disquieting tension growing in him. 'I decided to stop, little Christie, but I could not. This time the pain of not having morphia was much worse, unimaginably worse, than any physical pain I had endured. Oh, I managed in slow and grinding agony to reduce the dose until, apart from the occasional setback, I can usually survive now on a mere three grains a day. I returned to England, I picked up some semblance of normal life, I found you again and amongst the many ways I deluded myself about my relationship with you I persuaded myself I could conceal my wretched dependence. But you know it now, Christie. And you must understand it for what it is – a squalid slavery from which I shall not escape.'

He had grown very pale and the little muscle continued to work above his jaw. I looked at him, at the tall, commanding figure framed dark against the light of the window, at the controlled, set face, the lips still curving with that mordant self-contempt, and felt once more overwhelmed with relief. He had not chosen this destruction willingly. Rostova had not won yet.

'But you can escape. Perhaps not by yourself. But you're no longer alone?' I wanted all at once to go to him, forget the handbag, the need for space between us, wanted to hold him, to touch that pale, proud, embattled face. 'Please, Felix, let me help you. Tarantin's doctor will come if I telephone, please let me do it – '

His eyes flickered to the bag for a moment, his lips twisted, he drew away from me as if from a contagion. 'No, Christie.'

'But why? If he could help you – '

'No.'

'But if you want to be free, if you want to stop it?'

He turned, and his face was expressionless. 'I don't want to.'

I stared at him, not understanding. 'But you said – Oh, Felix, you can't, it's like passing a death sentence on yourself. Please let me help you. Please at least see this doctor. Please, my darling, if you love me – '

'Don't!' he said sharply. 'Don't ask me to choose between your love and morphia. If you do, I must choose morphia.'

'Oh Felix, no – '

'I must choose morphia, my dear little sister. Because, as you well know, I may not choose you.'

I gazed at him in silence, aghast.

'Oh, little one, I had already wronged you enough before I compounded it by asking you back into the house. This at least makes everything simple and clear between us.' He laughed bitterly, moved away towards the mantelpiece. 'There is some irony in it too. It has one small blessing, my wretched weakness. It achieves what reason and decency and any sense of honour I may still have left seem quite unable to do. In sufficient quantities, morphia deadens my need of you. When you are gone I may become a brother to you at last. And for the rest – ' he sounded suddenly profoundly tired – 'I no longer care. There is, after all, a kind of justice in it.'

'Justice?' I burst out. 'Oh God, no, Felix! Rostova consented to it, she wanted what she has become. That, if you like, is a kind of justice. But you—'

'Anna's way is my way. I always knew that, my guilt is in not holding to it. As I have said, Anna and I come from the same place, we belong there where we can only harm ourselves.'

I moved towards him, and now both our faces were reflected in the glass above the mantelpiece, divided, held separate by the savage line of the crack. 'What place, Felix? What do you mean? I don't understand.'

'Oh, little Christie, even before, when you first came to Cheyne Walk and I could not get you out of my mind, I knew it. The pattern was fixed then, of Monks Last, of the war, of this. You were like some bright dream of innocence I might long for but must not have. But I persuaded myself into a sort of crazy hope, I took what I longed for, I thought I might change what I was. Change? Oh God, I who had been so concerned about hurting you – if I had sat down deliberately and concocted a scheme for it I could not have been more successful and more damaging. So I accept now what I am. And if this is part of it, I accept it too.'

I stared at the two reflections bisected by the crack in the glass. 'Accept it? But it's a kind of suicide.'

'Perhaps. There is a rightness about it. Beyond that I neither know nor care.'

I felt suddenly the anger grow in me again. 'I never suspected you, Felix, of being a coward.'

He looked up then and his lips twisted bitterly. 'Didn't you, little Christie? After all, I seduced my sister and made her pregnant, I bear at least part of the guilt for my son's death, I couldn't even die decently in the trenches when plenty of better men did. Why not add cowardice to the mixture? It's simply another part – my inheritance, if you like. My noble inheritance as the bastard son of Montague Ward.'

He had moved so the crack again ran like a gash across his reflected image, splintering, refracting it as when he had first hurled the ivory figure into the glass. And, meeting his eyes, the eyes of the reflection so like and unlike mine, seeing in them that bitter self-contempt, I thought all at once that I knew, knew that other hidden territory in him as if I looked with his eyes into the mirror. I turned away. The anger within me took heat and boiled over.

'Damn you, Felix! Damn your cruel sense of honour! By what right do you take all the guilt upon your own shoulders, by what right do you judge yourself so harshly? What use is honour if it is set so high it can't allow anything to meet it, won't admit of any good? So this is fair, this is just, you've passed sentence upon yourself, have you, with all the mercy of a hanging judge? Well, I reject your judgement, I reject it utterly! There is no pattern, no inheritance. What our father was—'

He had whirled away from me. The muscle near his mouth quivered, in his eyes now too there was anger. 'A spoiler, little Christie. A spoiler, and a crook.'

'Whatever he was, you are not like him. The only inheritance you – both of us – have from him is what he and your mother did. And you can't take that upon yourself. You didn't make the past, you aren't bound by it. There isn't a pattern, not one that can't be broken. And as for the rest – even if so much in life is set crooked you can't take the guilt for it all. I can't begin to imagine what the war was like – '

'It was a despicable war!'

'But you were a good soldier in it. Routledge's death agony didn't keep you alive. You lived because you cared more about his dying than your own. You can't pass sentence on yourself for that. You can't blame yourself because, through your courage, you survived where others died.'

'Others with more courage? And better lives to live?'

'You can't measure, you can't judge. You have no right!' I was trembling with rage. 'And you and I, Felix, you have no right to all the guilt for that. If there is guilt for what we did out of ignorance, then we share it. There was nothing between us that did not happen with my willing consent. And when you left – oh, at the time I was bewildered and angry, I thought you had stopped loving me – but now I understand it as an act of great love. You can't – it is arrogance to absolve me from blame by taking everything upon yourself. It's worse than arrogance, for in denying me blame you deny my love, you deny my existence, you obliterate me.'

'It seems I have a happy knack, my dear Christie, of destroying what I love.'

'Your son, you mean? Whom your wife killed, as she killed herself, in a fit of insane jealousy? Oh, Felix, you cannot hold yourself accountable for what was beyond all help, all reason – '

'I failed to save him.'

'You failed? You failed only where it was human, unavoidable to fail. But your inhuman sense of honour won't allow that, will it? It can make concessions for others, but to yourself it will concede nothing. So you'll take the guilt, yours and everyone else's. And you'll rot, like Anna Rostova, because that's what your honour tells you you deserve. Well it's not honourable, Felix, this death sentence of yours. It's a wanton, useless waste. And I won't consent to it!'

I paused, feeling my eyes scalded with tears again. His restlessness had grown so that, in his pacing, in every line of his body, it communicated itself like a live charge.

'Felix, I love you so much. Please let me send for Tarantin's doctor. I can't bear this hopelessness, this giving up. I can't bear the waste of all that is strong and good – everything I love about you. I can't bear the destruction of all your great gifts. You were a fine painter once – '

He laughed sardonically. 'Cruel use of the past tense, little Christie.'

'You can be, you will be again. And you and I, even if we must live as brother and sister, surely there is some future for us, some hope. Oh please, my darling, listen to me, let me telephone Tarantin, let me help you. Please.'

He paused in his pacing for a moment, looked at me, looked away. Then he said quietly: 'My dear little Christie, if you want to help me I'm afraid there is only one thing you can do.'

I stared at him with shock, understanding slowly that all my anger, all my pleading had changed nothing. He had begun to move closer to me and now the tension jangled in his every movement, I saw that the hand which held the cigarette was trembling and that he had started to shiver. In my anger I had forgotten the handbag and its evil contents. Following his eyes and realizing the danger in that growing tension, I tightened my grip, clutching the bag to me again with both hands. He came on, gradually, inexorably. Clinging to the bag, my eyes upon his face, I backed away.

'Oh please, Felix. You are my hope, my life. If you died I should not wish to live. You hurt me, Felix. You hurt me by this as you could never hurt me before.'

He was close enough to touch me now.

'Little Christie,' he said, in a voice that was harsh with the struggle for control, 'please, my dear, dear little one, give me the morphia. If I end up taking it by force I shan't simply be indifferent to life, I shall wish very positively to be rid of it.'

I glanced down at the handbag, at the knotted strap about my wrist, at the leather shiny with sweat where my fingers gripped it. Then I looked up at him, met his eyes, saw the pain of the struggle in them, saw that his lips were bloodless, his fists clenched with the effort of keeping the space between us, saw how they fought each other, his love for me and his need for the morphia, saw it all with a terrible, numbing despair.

There was only one defence left to me. I drew a deep breath. 'All right,' I said softly. 'I accept your judgement, Felix, harsh as it is. And I'll give you Rostova's little parcel of poison. On one condition. If there is guilt, you must accept that we are both guilty. If by continuing to love me you stand condemned, then so must I for loving you. And my life, too, Felix, hasn't been so blameless. I agreed to the abortion – do you think I shall ever completely forgive myself for that? I wasn't a good wife to

Archie – I tried, but I couldn't love him. I couldn't change the poverty around me either; though I wanted to, I wasn't strong enough or good enough, in the end I became as much a part of the world I abominated as Brice and Cadwallander itself. I know what it is to feel jealousy and hate and to be mean and low and unloving. There isn't any guilt you feel I don't know and share, Felix. So if it is just for you to poison yourself with morphia then it's just that I should too. I shall give you Rostova's package. And you can initiate me.'

I saw in his eyes a look of astonishment, followed by one of disbelief. 'Christie, don't be ridiculous.'

'There's nothing ridiculous about it, Felix. I love you, I couldn't bear life without you. This way we need never be parted. The only trouble is I don't know how to begin. You'll have to show me.'

I began to withdraw my arm from the strap of the bag, edging my hand painfully over the clasp. He stared at me.

'Little Christie, don't play silly games.'

'It's not a game, Felix. I realize I have no other choice. But I need you to tell me what I must do.'

I had my hand free and began to unwind the strap from my wrist. There was a scarlet weal where it had cut into my flesh. I felt his eyes upon me, knew I had made it now all too easy for him to take what he wanted, waited for him to move. But, though I could feel the tension in him as strong as ever, he did not. I glanced up, glimpsed in his eyes still the disbelief; but it was tempered with the beginnings of uncertainty.

'Christie, don't be stupid. Give that to me.'

I met his eyes, held his glance calmly, defiantly, willed myself to show my intention was unshakeable. 'Yes, I'll give it to you. If you'll promise to help me.'

He essayed a laugh. 'This is absurd. Of course I won't.'

'Then if you won't I'll have to find out for myself.'

'My dear child, you couldn't possibly—'

'Couldn't I, Felix? I can, I will. I suppose you heat the stuff in some way, make a solution of it. And then, like Rostova, you use a hypodermic—'

'Christie, stop it!'

'I've never injected myself, but I think I could give an injection.'

Praying that I sounded convincing, I began to move towards the door. 'Mrs Schumacher used to have vitamin injections once a week.'

'Christie, this is stupid and dangerous—'

'You make a tourniquet to restrict the blood flow. And then you pump with your hand till the veins stand out. All I have to do is find your hypodermic, Felix.' I was nearly at the door now, I had him with me, he was moving after me.

'Don't be an idiot! You can't play at this—'

'All I have to do is find it, Felix.'

'You can't play with hypodermics, you'll kill yourself.'

'In your bedroom? No, in the studio, of course – '

'Christie—'

'In the studio desk, in the drawer – that's it!'

'Christie! No!'

'I love you, Felix, I want to do this, you won't stop me!'

'You bloody little idiot! God in Heaven, no!'

He was upon me then but I had reached the doorway and I was prepared for him. Still clutching the handbag, I tore across the hall and up the stairs. Halfway up he caught me by the elbow, tried to wrench my arm back, pinion me against the bannisters. We struggled, I lashed out with the handbag, tore myself free. Gasping for breath now, I hurled myself up the remaining stairs and towards the studio. I could feel him behind me, gaining on me, knew in another moment he would catch me once more. I flung myself at the studio door, tore at the handle. The door flew open just as his fingers seized my wrist. In the sharpness of the movement with which my arm shot out as he slammed me backwards into the doorframe the strap that held the bag snapped, sending it flying out at a tangent, scudding across the landing floor. He had me caught fast, one arm wedged painfully behind my back, crushed against the doorjamb by the weight of his body, the other held in a grip of steel by his left hand while his right had me by the jaw, forcing my head aside, pressing my right cheekbone into the wood.

'You senseless, crazy little fool! Not ever, do you hear? Not ever, Christie, not as long as I live!'

I wrenched my head free, looked up at him, saw in the eyes staring down at me utter horror. I had expended my slender reserves of acting ability, could no longer sustain my pretence; I felt a sudden profound exhaustion. 'Now you know,' I said wearily, 'how what you do to yourself hurts me.'

He relaxed his hold on me. There was an expression on his face I was not sure I understood. Then I remembered the bag, looked beyond him, saw it a few yards away from us, noticed with dismay that it had burst open and that Rostova's envelope had shot out of it, splitting and shedding a trail of white powder across the floor. We both stared at it in silence for a moment. My pretence had been a desperate last resort, I had no further weapons against him. I felt my exhaustion change to a sense of total defeat.

Then, abruptly, he turned away. 'You said Teddy's doctor would come if you telephoned? Perhaps you would get him here as soon as you can.'

CHAPTER FORTY-NINE

When I had made my peace with Anatole, I waited in the study with Stenko while Tarantin and the doctor talked to Felix. Finally Stenko, too, was summoned upstairs to the studio, and for what seemed an interminable time I was alone, wondering apprehensively what their conference signified, nervous lest Felix should have gone back on his decision. When Anatole at last announced that I was needed in the studio I was alarmed to walk in upon the doctor giving Felix an injection, but Tarantin, observing my horror, patted my arm.

'Codeine, dear girl. It will help him until tomorrow. After that – ' the gold rings flashed deprecatingly – 'well, you know our friend. Always he chooses the hard way. No comfortable sanatorium for him. He has decided from tomorrow morning he will be locked in his room like a prisoner until he is over the worst. Anatole and the other servants will be sent away for three weeks. The only help he will accept is for Stenko and me to be his jailers.'

I smiled, relieved. 'And I shall be his nurse.'

Felix had rolled down his sleeve and was lighting a cigarette. 'No, little one,' he said gently. 'I want you to stay with Lady Dilly as you planned.'

I stared at him, not understanding. 'But if you're going to be ill and in pain I must be with you.'

He shook his head. 'My darling, I shall miss you very much, but I want you to go to Berkeley Square tomorrow morning. It will only be for three weeks.'

'Three weeks! Oh Felix, why? Don't you trust me?'

'Of course I do.' Coming over to me, he put his hands upon my shoulders. The self-mocking smile flickered upon his lips but his eyes were grave. 'Little Christie, perhaps, as you said, I am a coward.' I opened my mouth to object but he silenced me with a shake of his head. 'I don't deserve your love and I am very afraid of losing it. The next couple of weeks, particularly the next few days, will be – well – ' again there was the sardonic twist to his lips – 'I don't think I want you to see me like that. And I don't want to inflict the unpleasantness and brutishness of it on you.'

'Felix, I love you. I don't care—'

He touched my cheek. 'But I do, little one,' he said softly. 'Please leave me to Teddy and Stenko.'

'After all, dear girl,' interjected Tarantin wryly, 'we have put up with each other's vile moods, he and I, for so long, a little more will be *une bagatelle*.'

I looked up at Felix. His eyes were gentle but there was also a firmness in them that did not waver.

'You make me feel useless,' I said. 'I want to do something to help you.'

He smiled. 'My little one, you have already done more, far more than enough.' He bent to kiss my cheek. 'It won't be for long. And in the meantime Teddy has agreed to be my messenger. He will come and see you at Lady Dilly's every day until we can be together again.'

And so it was all decided. The decision, the sudden making of arrangements and packing of suitcases seemed to throw us into an unexpected euphoria that belied the grim period of pain and separation which would face us the next morning. Perhaps it was the unburdening of all our secrets that seemed to come with the acknowledgement of Felix's need for morphia which caused us to be so inexplicably light-hearted. With my ready consent, he had made open to Tarantin and Stenko the true situation between us so that there need be no more pretence on any side. He said it strangely, with his arm around my waist and with a kind of solemn joy, almost as if he were announcing our betrothal. Over dinner Tarantin and Stenko toasted us with champagne and wished us well and all four of us seemed to laugh and smile a great deal. Only Felix's inability to eat or drink and the marks of pain and tension when his face was in repose, inescapable reminders of his coming ordeal, cast shadows over the festive atmosphere. At eleven o'clock the doctor called to give him another injection and shortly afterwards, a sudden weariness falling upon us as if we had exhausted ourselves with our own bonhomie, we all retired to bed.

I lay, despite my exhaustion, a long time awake and must have just sunk into the depths of first sleep when I was woken again by the sense of someone moving in the darkness of my room. I jerked myself bolt upright, fumbling for the switch of the bedside lamp.

He stood near the foot of the bed, a dark figure in the black silk dressing gown. Some instinctive reaction had made my hand go to the wayward straps of my nightdress so that my arm was held protectively across my breasts. He smiled dryly.

'My dear little sister, don't be frightened. I could not make love to you now, with all the will in the world. I wasn't able to sleep and I had a crazy longing to take one last look at you. I didn't mean to wake you up.'

Closing the door, he came over and sat beside me on the bed. I saw that he was very pale and held himself stiffly as if he were struggling not to shiver.

'Is it bad?' I said.

He shook his head. 'The codeine helps. It holds off the worst of it.' He put out a hand and gently drew back a stray tendril of my hair. 'Oh, my dear little one, can you forgive this wretched weakness?'

I looked at the pale, proud face with its hard jaw and sardonic lips, at the muscles of it taut, controlling, concealing the pain that betrayed itself only in his eyes, battling with their tenderness for me. 'There is nothing,' I said softly, 'to forgive.'

Then, putting my arms around him, I drew him down slowly till his head was cradled on my breast. He lay like that for a while, he with his hands in my hair and his lips touching the bare skin at the division of my breasts, I with my fingers gently caressing the nape of his neck, feeling the tight muscles of his shoulders, the hard nakedness of him beneath the silk of the dressing gown. After some time, however, sensing his growing tension, realizing he no longer wanted to be touched, I withdrew my arms and he moved so that he lay above the bedclothes beside me with his head turned towards me and his hand resting on my shoulder. His fingers for a moment lightly traced the line upwards to the hollow at the base of my throat, then down to the naked curve of my left breast where the fallen strap of my nightdress had exposed it. In his touch, in the intensity of his gaze, was an infinite tenderness and also something calm, contemplative, as if, in this lying together chastely, brother and sister at last, he had found a measure of acceptance.

His hand moved upwards again, coming to rest in my hair. His voice was almost a whisper: 'My darling little Christie, my sister, my love, my wife, my dearest friend – if this is all we can have, let us take it. Let us take it and live with all the joy we can.'

I turned my head and pressed my lips against his wrist where it had lain across my cheek. His eyes were still on me and, despite the pain that was now evident in his face, he was smiling.

'Yes,' I said, smiling too. 'With all the joy.'

We lay together in silence after that, not touching, meeting each other only with our eyes. I felt myself slipping into sleep once more, struggling against it, wanting my eyes open as long as possible to take in and hold for memory every line and contour of that loved, loving face, for I knew when I awoke in the morning he would no longer be there. And, as I fought the heaviness of my eyelids, seeing him blurrily now, feeling myself drifting away, I made inwardly a solemn resolve. I should not let the weeks of my absence slip idly by, I would use them to begin again upon the quest he had abandoned as hopeless, I should take nothing for granted, leave nothing out of count, until I had proved what my instinct, in defiance of all the facts, now cried out passionately must be true: he could not be my brother.

'I say,' said Miles Millington, removing the head of his Dick Whittington's Cat costume and mopping away the sweat it had brought in great beads to his brow, 'have you heard the latest?'

'Oh God!' sighed Venetia Millington (Venetia Mainwaring that was), looking rather fetching as Dick himself in a leather jerkin and high green boots. 'Not more about the awful Mr Hitler. No one in this country wants another war.'

'Oh gosh, no,' said Miles, who was having some difficulty controlling his tail. 'I mean the latest joke, actually.'

'Apparently it's no joke at all,' said Maisie Hamilton Hartford, a crinolined Sleeping Beauty. 'Doing the Season now, I mean. Not like our day. Three dances a night and not a wink of sleep. Everyone ends up positively shredded.'

'Knock, knock. Who's there? Max.'

'These fancy-dress bunfights really are too ghastly for words,' said Dilly. 'Dandini! With my legs! But Christie was the only one slim enough for the Cinderella costume and they were absolutely the last two get-ups Bermans had.'

'Max who? Max-no-difference!'

'Dressing up seems positively to bring out the worst in people. Miles looks as if he's got the mange. And have you seen Crikey?'

'Max-no-difference? Knock, knock, who's there, Max? . . .'

'I think it's perfectly frightful.'

'Oh,' said Miles Millington, crestfallen, 'I thought it was pretty jolly funny, actually.'

'It's not funny at all,' said Dilly, waxing eloquent. 'I wouldn't mind so much if the wretched man wasn't my partner. But who's ever seen Sinbad the Sailor in a dinner jacket? I don't care if his nanny did send him to a children's party as a playing card so he couldn't sit down or play sardines. And as for his one concession to the proceedings, his so-called sea-monster!'

'It looked rather like a lobster to me,' said Maisie, reflectively.

'It *is* a lobster, an antediluvian lobster with one gammy claw that's clearly survived years of rejection in the fish tank of some third-class restaurant only to finish up here being trailed around like a Pomeranian on the end of a piece of string.'

'Rather a fish out of water, what?' said Miles Millington with a strangled guffaw.

'Anyway, I've told him he can't possibly bring it in to supper. He can leave it to play in the fountain. Apart from anything else, the sight of mayonnaise is likely to make it feel most uncomfortable.'

'Eleven million people voted for collective security in the Peace Ballot,' said Venetia Millington to no one in particular. 'We can't possibly have another war.'

It was the last party of the Season, before everyone left London for the Cap d'Antibes or the Scottish grouse moors. Mercedes Modlinger, 'American millionairess and socialite', was giving an English Pantomine Ball. Lord and Lady Mountalban had lent Critchley Castle for the occasion and fifteen hundred people, Widow Twankeys embarrassed by their petticoats, Man Fridays with sweat-runnelled bootblack and wilting grass skirts, Priscilla the Cows who wished heartily they had come as something else, were consuming venison and plovers' eggs, dancing to the music of Geraldo and wondering why the capricious English climate should have unkindly dealt so much fur, feather and false hair one of the hottest nights of the year. The great hall had been transformed into the House of Cards, the newly-built swimming pool was Father Neptune's Kingdom, the large marquee, with trellis and papier-mâché and several miles of crêpe paper, had been decked out as Jack's beanstalk and, in the Italian Garden, festooned with fairy lights as the Sleeping Beauty's Bower, the peacocks fled in panic from mechanical swans ploughing, miniature-railway-like, across the grass, spouting fountains of pink champagne. Dilly, despite protesting the utter ghastly impossibility of it all, had insisted on my presence and had found us both partners, Crikey for herself and an old friend of Robbie's, a Grenadier Guardsman, for me. Though conversation did not seem to be Captain Fellowes's strongest suit, I found his politeness agreeable and his silences a considerable blessing. For I was drifting through the evening in a state of suppressed excitement, fizzing inwardly with it, abstracted, preoccupied, seeing and hearing everything around me as if it had taken on an unreal element and the only reality, making my stomach light and my heart lurch with the consciousness of it, was the idea, the revelation that bubbled and grew inside my head.

I had been at Berkeley Square for two weeks now. Tarantin, true to Felix's promise, had visited me every day and had been kindness itself, so that even Dilly was moved to confess that 'when one got to know him he didn't seem quite the unsavoury little tick one supposed'. I had not, of course, told Dilly the whole truth, only that Felix was ill and needed peace and quiet, and she was too much my friend, even if she questioned it, to probe further. From Tarantin I learnt that the first eight days had been the worst but that Felix, though still very weak, was beginning to be able to eat again and was sleeping a great deal. Although I had written every day he had not replied to my letters, but Tarantin had explained this was only to be expected, he had been too ill to write, too ill for anything. On the tenth day Tarantin had come with the news that Rostova was dead, had been found blue and cold with the needle still hanging in an etiolated vein, victim of an accidental overdose. When I had expressed regret at such a squandering of life, he had merely smiled grimly.

'So our Firebird has plunged to earth. *Tant pis!* Our friend's supply is now cut off. If he wishes to go back it will be more difficult for him.'

I looked at him, aghast. 'Does he want to go back?'

The gold rings quelled my apprehension with a dismissive flash. 'No. He has been very hard and determined. Now he has come so far he will not give up.'

I smiled. He would not give up, and it was only a week until we could be together again. Together. And with what new hope, what promise for the future, as if all the clouds had suddenly been swept away, as if everything that had happened to us had been no more than a bad dream. I had only to work a little more, think a little harder, find the one piece of the jigsaw puzzle I lacked. And then – oh, then . . .

I had told nobody, not mentioned it to Tarantin nor even hinted at it in my letters to Felix, had been evasive with Dilly when she had expressed an amused astonishment at my preoccupation, my mysterious trips to libraries, my sudden obsession with birth certificates, my frantic flurry of correspondence. Yet I had understood it that first night in Berkeley Square when, obedient to my resolve and taking the easiest and most obvious starting point, I had sat down to re-read my mother's diaries. I had begun with a heavy heart, for what could I expect to find there that I had not found already, what except the depressing proof, beyond reasonable doubt, that Aunt Jessica had spoken the truth? And then it had come to me in a flash. I had been decoyed, decoyed by my own desire for disbelief into seeing, questioning only that truth, those facts. My mother's marriage to Montgomery Ward had been a failure. His affair with Aunt Jessica had been proof of that failure but not the reason for it. The reason, oh the reason, that was different, the answer to another question I had never asked myself, the key to a whole sequence of events I had missed. I went on reading far into the night, past the point of Aunt Jessica's confinement where before I had lost heart and stopped, cursing myself for my feebleness, scarcely believing the idea that was now taking shape in my head, yet seeing it, with every word I read, confirmed to me. I woke the next morning and gazed about me puzzled, as if the perspective of everything had shifted subtly. I stared at my face in the looking glass, touched my features tentatively, distrustfully, as if I expected them to dissolve before my eyes into something alien. I was right. I could not fully comprehend it and yet I knew I was right. But to be certain, to satisfy myself, to convince Felix, I must have proof. And illness, death, the war, the inaccessible boundaries of a foreign country, thirty years' vagary of human destiny, all could cheat me of it. The Royal

College of Music, that was the starting point, they must have a register of students. Yet, to start, I needed a name. I railed against my poor mother for her habit of using initials. Who, oh who, was DR?

'They say,' said Howard Hamilton Hartford, a ruggedly New World Mother Goose, 'now Baldwin's taken over the premiership from MacDonald he'll have to hit the campaign trail. And I guess collective security's the ticket that wins the votes.'

I blinked. I had drifted off again. We were at supper in the House of Cards.

'Soldier's job to fight,' said my Guards Officer, helping me to salmon trout *en gelée* with asparagus. 'No point in asking questions. King and Country. If there's a war, there's a war.'

'Even Baldwin wouldn't dare go to the hustings with rearmament,' said Dora Chantry. 'Think of the Oxford Union debate. Think of the East Fulham by-election – a Labour majority of seven thousand on a pacifist platform.'

'Balderdash!' said Miles Millington, who was finding his paws something of an impediment to wielding a knife and fork. 'Collective security's a dead duck. Japan and Germany both out of the League of Nations, Mussolini cutting up rough, Howard's chaps never even in it in the first place – Baldwin may talk about Collective Security, but when he wins the election he'll start carolling another tune – '

'Oh, must we talk politics!' sighed Maisie.

'The Labour Party will never stand for rearmament,' said Dora Chantry's partner earnestly.

'We're rearming already,' said Miles Millington. 'I have it from the jolly old gee-gee's mouth. Meredith de Lisle hinted as much over luncheon at White's the other day, and he's a Minister, practically in the Cabinet, actually. And Archie Cadwallander agreed with him, said the slump in steel's over, business is booming – ' He looked up suddenly with his mouth full of venison. 'Oh, I say. Sorry, Christie.'

'Not at all,' I said. 'How was Archie?'

'Top hole, actually. Wetting the head of his brand-new son and heir. Now, as I was saying – '

'Oh really!' said Dilly. 'Let's talk about something else. My sister and Mosley's awful Fitzallen have just come in, and I can't face another row.'

Lady Dolly, a Mainbocher Aladdin, had indeed sat down with her husband not far away from us. I saw Dilly flush slightly and

Dora Chantry and her partner draw back in frozen disgust. I was suddenly tired, my brain numbed with the effort of trying to fix itself upon something in its distant recesses that escaped me, everything was unreal again, the people, the conversation blurring, sliding away, I wanted to go somewhere quiet by myself and think.

'If we don't talk politics,' said Dora Chantry militantly, 'how are we to protect democracy? How are we to prevent it from being ground under the heel of the Fascist boot?'

'I agree,' said Dilly. 'Just let's not talk about it now.'

'I'd rather have Crikey droning on about the Test Match,' said Maisie.

'We all agree about the Fascists, Dora,' said Howard. 'But you can't kid us your Red friends are so big on democracy either.'

'Which reminds me,' said Dilly. 'Wherever is Crikey?'

'Watering W G, no doubt.'

'Communism, Fascism – it's the ordinary people who suffer in a war,' said Venetia Millington.

'W G?'

'The lobster. That's what Crikey calls it. After W G Grace.'

'Rearmament doesn't actually mean war,' said Miles Millington.

'Communism *is* for the ordinary people,' said Dora. 'Government for the people by the people – '

'Why do you think the Germans so adore the Führer?' said Lady Dolly to a sympathizer farther down the table. 'He is the embodiment of the people's all-powerful will.'

'It strikes me,' said Dilly, 'politicians always talk most about the interests of the people when they mean something quite opposite.'

'It's a question of jolly old economics, actually,' said Miles Millington. 'Rearmament would mean jobs for the unemployed.'

'It's a question of territory,' said Howard Hartford.

'Germany doesn't want to fight England,' said Lady Dolly. 'It's Bolshevik Russia that's the threat.'

'I can't sit here and listen to this,' said Dora Chantry. 'It's a question of morality. If you'd worked with the Jewish refugees as I have – '

'But is it moral, under any circumstances, to kill people?' said Venetia Millington helplessly.

'A few more tanks and battleships don't mean we're going to kill people, old dear,' said Miles. 'Jobs for the chap in the street. Raise morale.'

'In Germany there's a sense of purpose. Hitler Youth isn't demoralized like British youth,' said Lady Dolly.

'War's the rotten side of human nature,' said Dilly, 'when people stop loving individuals and starting to love causes.'

'Then all that's left is to fight honourably,' said my Guards Officer. 'No other answer.'

'Old Bunty Rosslair's got the answer,' said Crikey, reappearing suddenly, lobsterless. 'Says we should invite Mr Hitler over for a spot of grouse shooting. That'll show him what's what.'

'Oh, for heaven's sake!' said Dilly. 'Let's move to the terrace and have a breath of fresh air.'

It was cooler on the terrace and I felt the beginnings of a night breeze ruffle my hair and my Cinderella rags. Dora and her partner, looking gloomy, drifted off, murmuring about the drive back to London. Miles Millington took Maisie away to dance and Howard persuaded a protesting Dilly to follow their example. My Guards Officer fell into a conversation about the pros and cons of body-line bowling with Crikey, while I listened to a despondent Venetia telling me about her children and wondering whether indeed it was right to bring any child into such a world as ours. Before us lay spread the whole glittering, expensive panoply of Mrs Modlinger's hospitality. The conflicting strains of the two bands echoed across the sleeping countryside, filling the empty fields with 'Night and Day', 'I'll Follow My Secret Heart', 'I Get a Kick Out of You'. Car doors slammed, a peacock squawked, voices and laughter drifted from the Italian Garden, and sudden screams from the swimming pool – the usual sport had begun, I assumed, of giving a watery shock to the unsuspecting. Above it all, a clear moon hung in a velvet sky, mocking Mrs Modlinger's fairy lights. The last party of the Season. And still there niggled something in the back of my brain, something I knew I must at all costs remember but which, eluding me, caused, by the sheer effort of my concentration upon it, a foggy, suffocating feeling as if my skull were slowly filling with cotton wool.

'Of course,' Venetia was saying, 'it's germ warfare that worries me most.'

One band was playing 'The Continental', the other 'We're in the Money'.

'Do you know, Professor Joad says a single bomb from an aeroplane could poison every living thing in an area of three-quarters of a square mile.'

The second band began upon 'A Nightingale Sang in Berkeley Square'.

'Lobsters!' said Dilly's voice suddenly, in tones of apoplexy. 'I'll give you lobsters, you miserable wretch! Young Binnie Featherstonehaugh and her partner decide to go for a dip in the pool, and what do they find? Not one miserable crustacean but hosts of them. In our pool!'

'A Nightingale Sang in Berkeley Square'. I felt the cotton wool lifting, suddenly my hands were shaking, I tried to shut the voices out.

'Binnie Featherstonehaugh starkers in a pool full of W G's!' sniggered Crikey. 'Bet she was tickled pink, eh?'

The band was still playing it, the tune mingling with 'Deep Purple' now. I wanted to jump up, to shout out.

'She was not,' said Dilly. 'And neither were W G and his little friends. Lobsters don't care for chlorine. They're all dead.'

'Everything in an area of three-quarters of a square mile,' said Venetia Millington dismally.

'You're a pill, Crikey!' said Dilly. 'An utter, unspeakable pill! And it's high time we made you take your own medicine. Howard! Captain Fellowes! To the pool with him!'

'Oh, I say! Oh, that's a bit strong! Put me down, you chaps! Oh gosh! Dash it, it was only a jape, raise a few chuckles, Binnie Featherstonehaugh in her birthday suit with – Oh, Crikey!' squealed Crikey.

'Sometimes,' said Dilly, ignoring his diminishing cries and dusting her hands together as if she were expunging every trace of his existence, 'sometimes I think the whole world has gone mad!'

'Oh, Dillo!' I said, hugging her. 'It's not mad, not all of it. Something marvellous has just happened!'

'Really, Christie! I wouldn't call a pool full of chlorinated crustaceans anything to write home about.'

'Listen to the music!'

'Music? It sounds like a ghastly mixture of "Deep Purple" and "A Nightingale Sang in Berkeley Square".'

'Precisely, Dillo. Nightingales. "Thou wast not born for death, immortal Bird".'

'Just as I said, the world's gone potty. Still, the girl comes from a most peculiar family, you know. One cousin a Government Minister and the other – '

'Keats, Dillo. "Ode to a Nightingale", Keats!'

A tired volume of Keats whose pages fell out when you opened it, which had once belonged to my mother and which had been lost for ever when Aunt Jessica had made her swoop upon the schoolroom. A volume of Keats with a faded inscription on the flyleaf.

'Oh Dillo, I'm sorry about the lobsters and I'm sorry, Venetia, sorry about everything, and I'm sorry I'm so incoherent because I can't explain properly now, but oh, I'm so happy – Oh God, I'm so happy I could sing!'

I had found a name for D R.

CHAPTER FIFTY

Diary of Adele Ward.
Silver Strands Boarding House, Weymouth.

15th February, 1905.

M has been gone from the house two days now. I suppose I should feel anxiety lest he is lying in a gutter or an alley somewhere, but I confess only to fear that he will return. With Bridie gone and the spectre of poverty looming once again before me, D is my sole consolation. Dear D, my ever-vigilant brother. While he is here I feel safe and protected. But during these nights as I wait for him to return home from the Burden, as I wonder whether M is out there somewhere lurking in the darkness, every noise, every creak on the stair terrifies me. In vain do I try to distract myself with the little volume of Keats, D's dear present. My nerves jangle. There it is again, a sound like a stealthy footstep softly crossing the landing – the wind perhaps, or D returning, or merely my overwrought imagination. . . . Listen, Adele . . . There is nothing, nothing. It is only the old house settling on its foundtions, only the windows rattling, only.

* * *

16th February, 1905.

When I opened my door the landing was in darkness, yet I was certain I had remembered to leave the gas burning in the hall below for D's return. Only the moonlight from the little window at the end of the passage faintly illuminated the staircase and the sweep of its balustrade. I paused, listening, wondering why the gas was extinguished, quivering with fear. I held my breath. But everywhere there was silence. Nothing moved: Only shadows in the hall and on the staircase which my imagination made palpable, nothing more. Feeling chilled, wishing I had not quitted the warmth of my bedroom, I turned towards the door – when suddenly from behind they came at me, hands clutched about my throat, choking me, something ice-cold pressed against my cheek. I smelt the rank breath, felt it moist upon my neck, saw that the coldness on my cheek was the blade of the big kitchen knife, the one I kept honed razor-sharp for meat, its point not an inch from my eyes. I opened my mouth to scream but the knife moved to my throat, the blade tilted so that I could feel, like a tickle, the deadly caress of its cutting edge. The thing began to speak in my ear, keening, gloating, not words but mutterings and animal grunts ending in low guttural laughter. Its left arm fastened across my bosom, forcing me backwards against its tainted body; I felt a vile pressure through the thin cambric of my nightgown, felt with unspeakable horror excitement growing in the monstrous loins. My head was thrust back and suddenly above the blade of the knife I saw the thing's mouth, open, drooling, struggling to press the loathsome contamination of its lips upon mine. The knife no longer touched my throat, I screamed – and all at once, with the force of an enormous impact, the hand with the blade jerked sideways, the thing, staggering in the grip of an unseen assailant, released its hold.

I fell against the wall. When I recovered my balance I saw two figures, one hunched and simian, the other tall and lean, locked in combat at the head of the stairs. I heard the creature growling, snarling, saw moonlight flash upon the knife blade as two opposing arms arched upwards, grappling for its possession. Then the blade spun free and with a terrible shriek the thing, losing its balance, fell backwards. There was the soft thud of a body bouncing step by step down the staircase, a crash as it hit the marble floor of the hallway; then silence.

D bent to pick up the knife. Running to him, I flung my arms about his neck. Slowly, fearfully, we moved together to the balustrade and peered down at the shadowy, inert heap at the foot of the stairs.

I heard myself say: 'Is he dead? Oh, is he dead?' And it was dawning upon me how devoutly I wished it, when the dark mass stirred; rose on its haunches; with a howl of pain and rage lifted its head towards us, teeth bared; and, slouching low upon the ground, its arms swinging apelike before it, turned tail and slunk from the house through the open front door.

I must have fainted away. When I came to myself I was lying upon the sofa in my bedroom with D bending over me, holding smelling salts to my nostrils. Blinking at the brightness of the light, I gazed up at him for some moments, seeing before me not a boy's face now, but a man's, the features hard and determined though the eyes were tender with anxiety for me. My saviour, my darling, selfless, valiant brother! Overwhelmed with relief at being back in my own snug room with him beside me, I fell into his arms, burying my head in his chest, where I stayed for some while, listening to the beating of his heart and feeling the warmth of his body steal over my senses like a comforting spell. Then, all of a sudden, I recollected the danger of our situation.

'Oh, D, he may come back. He may come back tonight!'

He stroked my cheek to calm me. 'Everything is bolted up – I lock everything.'

'But even so I'm afraid. He's cunning, he will find his way in somehow.'

'Then tonight I sleep outside your door. And – ' here with a grim smile he produced the knife he had taken from M on the landing – 'if he comes, I kill him.'

For the first time I noticed that the hand which held the knife was bound with a blood-soaked handkerchief. 'Oh, D, how selfish I am, thinking only of my own safety. Here, let me look – oh, my dear, are you badly hurt?'

In the heat of the struggle he must have grasped the knife blade which had slashed a deep slanting wound across his palm. Taking out my little medicine chest and using water from the carafe by my bed, I bathed and bandaged the injury, feeling as I worked his eyes, sharp with the pain my ministrations must of necessity cause him, fixed all the while upon my face.

'You shan't sleep in the passage, I won't permit it. We shall lock the door and keep the gas burning and you shall stay here on the

sofa tonight.' My work completed, his injured hand still in mine, I bent to kiss him on the cheek. 'Oh, D, you're so very good to me. M has driven everyone else out of the house. Why do you stay?'

To my surprise, his eyes, which continued to be trained upon my face, appeared to darken strangely. 'You know, I think.'

I was aware all at once that my nightgown was still unbuttoned at the throat where, in my faint, he had loosened it. I drew my hands sharply away. 'That's foolish talk. You're young, only a boy. You mustn't be carried away by such ridiculous fancies – '

'Fancies?' He smiled at me dryly. 'I think I am not so stupid I do not know what is fancies and what is love.'

I sprang up from the sofa, turning away from him. 'You know nothing of love! Oh, I used to dream like you. I used to bury my head in romances and long for some great and glorious emotion to sweep me off my feet. So I married M. Love? If there is such a thing as love then it only exists in the baser side of nature, it is only a vile appetite, gone as soon as it is sated. The bestial, degraded thing that is my husband – he is the embodiment of love in all its perversions and diseases. That's your love, D, that monstrous thing!'

Perhaps, though he cannot have mistaken my vehemence, I spoke too fast for him properly to understand my meaning, for he gave me only a strange smile, half-sorrowful, half-disbelieving. 'You will make of that man the whole world?'

Relenting, smitten suddenly by the thought that I had hurt him, he who was so kind and gentle to me, I turned back to him and, smiling, softly touched his wounded hand. 'Please, my dear – I am deeply grateful for your fondness for me, a fondness which you know I return. But you must not call it love. You must understand – I am older, ten years older than you. And whatever M may be, I am still his wife, a married woman. Please, you must promise never to speak to me in such a way again.'

Not answering me, appearing to examine my face for a moment, he once more smiled that strange, almost compassionate smile I did not understand. Then, to my relief, he shrugged his shoulders, laughing. 'So. Perhaps, after all, I sleep in the passage.'

Restraining him, horrified to think that by my words I should now inflict discomfort and hardship on one whose sole dedication these pasts weeks has been to protect me from suffering, whose very penance outside on the cold, bare boards would be further in my cause, I shook my head. 'No. Please! Things between us shall be as they were.'

And later I was grateful, as always, for his presence for, every minute movement of the wind or creak upon the stairs setting my nerves ajar, I could not sleep; and falling to thinking of what would happen when the sun rose, of how many sunrises, how many years I might be called upon to live with this burden of terror, I became prey to such despair that after a while I could not prevent myself from weeping uncontrollably: so that eventually D, forsaking the sofa, lay down beside me on the bed and took me in his arms. Perhaps, given my stern words and the fact that I was attired only in my nightgown, I should have resisted him; but he, after all, was fully dressed; and besides, he was so tender and gentle, my dear, dear brother again, with no thought but to stroke my hair and lull me gradually to sleep.

This morning, however, I woke with some surprise to feel the unfamiliar weight of an arm across me and to hear the soft rise and fall of another's breathing. Opening my eyes I saw D's head beside mine on the pillow; and, in an instant, never having watched him asleep before, observing the unguarded face, the lips pale and slightly parted, the strong, finely-etched profile contrasting unexpectedly with the almost feminine length of the lashes which swept his cheeks, I was so overwhelmed with sisterly tenderness for him that, without thinking, I reached out and touched him gently, just below the sleeping curve of his mouth. Whereupon, waking immediately and giving me first a lazy smile, he leaned over and kissed me lingeringly upon the lips.

It was, I pray, but a matter of seconds before, feeling his hand above the cambric of my nightgown move softly upwards to caress my bosom and sensing, as his body shifted closer against me, my own body stir strangely to meet it, I realized with shock I had returned his kiss. Drawing away abruptly, I heard him give a long, shuddering sigh. 'Oh, Adele –'

'You must not call me that,' I said, starting up and clutching my nightgown about me. 'I am Mrs Ward, Montague Ward's wife. You must never call me that, or – or do what you have just done again. Last night you made me a promise – I did not think you of all people would be so dishonourable as to break your word.'

He lay for a moment with his head turned away and when he spoke his voice was, as I had never heard it before, constricted with anger. 'I make no promise – Mrs Ward.' And suddenly I remembered that he had not, but had only laughed and given me that strange, compassionate smile.

Hearing the anger in his voice I was all at once consumed with guilt, guilt that I had hurt him, guilt that I had not instantly spurned his kiss, guilt for the curious and improper sensations it had aroused in me. However, in a moment, he had swung his long legs off the bed and was stretching himself and smiling at me as if nothing untoward had occurred between us.

Though this morning we sought out the doctor and, describing M's condition, extracted a firm undertaking that once he could be captured he would be taken directly to the St Saviour Asylum and detained under lock and key, the police so far achieved no success in their search for him. Thus we are obliged to spend another night behind bolts and bars.

D once more volunteered to keep cold and painful vigil outside my room; but, as before, I cannot bear to think of his enduring such wretchedness on my behalf, so it is agreed he will again sleep on my sofa. Yet, as he lies stretched out there, while I sit at the secretary writing this, I know it is improper for him to be in the room with me. I know it is improper for him to be alone with me in this house in the absence of my husband.

Oh, but yet can it be? Can there be anything immodest in this fine <u>pure</u> feeling between us, anything except that he, being still a boy, must mistake our tender friendship for that other base, carnal thing which burns, like the disease which is its retribution, in M? Why, there is no trace of M in D, only that selfless and tender affection for which I hold him so dear. And I, if I so much forgot myself as to allow him to kiss me, was I not simply prey for an instant to my own foolish nature which, while it now repudiates those dreams of my youth, those unrealities culled from the fevered pages of forbidden novels, still in unguarded moments somehow longs for them as one might long for childhood innocence again? No, there is nothing between D and myself but the pure and enduring affection that is natural between <u>brother and sister.</u> And if, even now, as I steal a sidelong glance at him and observe all at once how tired he looks, how pale and drawn his face is – for such has been his strength these past few days that I forget his youth and that he is still far from well, still sometimes troubled with that debilitating cough – if even now I yearn to put my arms about him and run my fingers through his hair, to kiss his poor wounded hand and press his dear head to my breast, it is *only with a sister's tender feeling, nothing more. How consoling it is to know he is near me, how peaceful in this snug room with its warm light and glowing fire. Only the knife, its cruel shaft resting between his fingers, reminds me of the danger that threatens us.*

CHAPTER FIFTY-ONE

The porter looked up from his crossword puzzle and a cup of curdled tea. 'Professor Radescu? Old Court, Miss F. Staircase. Through the arch and on your left.'

Thanking him, I heard my voice unnaturally tremulous and shrill. I still could not believe how ridiculously easy it had been. Not dead, not in another country, but traceable within ten days by the simple expedient of some telephone calls and a letter. And even then I could have been frustrated by his going away; what were the chances of his actually being in residence during a long vacation rather than climbing in the Alps or researching manuscripts in some foreign library? It had all been so simple it frightened me. My hand clutched the brown paper parcel beneath my right arm more tightly. The queasiness I had felt in the train grew.

My euphoria, sustained by my quest, had lasted until I received his reply to my letter. Up till then he had still been partly a figment of my imagination built out of snatches of tear-stained calligraphy, not a real person with handwriting of his own who used blue ink from an unreliable fountain pen. And besides I had had no time, no room to ask myself questions. I would be moving back to Cheyne Walk, I would see Felix again, I wouldn't wait for proof, I was bursting to tell him. How, oh how from him of all people could I ever hold such a thing back?

It was Tarantin's visit the day before I was due to leave Dilly's that put the first damper on my crazy, ungovernable excitement. He was looking in every line and crease crestfallen, the jet-bead eyes avoided mine almost with embarrassment, but I was at first too up in the air even to notice.

'Dear girl,' he said at length, taking out his handkerchief and dabbing his lips with it, 'our friend sends me with a request which I know you will find most disagreeable. But I beg you to have patience. He asks you to give him another week.'

I stared at him uncomprehendingly.

The handkerchief described an apologetic gesture. 'He is not himself yet. Now there is no more morphia he suffers somewhat with the old trouble of his back.'

'But Teddy, I'm dying to see him, I have some wonderful news for him. Why should that stop me coming home to Cheyne Walk?'

'Dear girl, you must try to understand.'

'I don't understand, Teddy, I don't understand at all. Three weeks he said, and the three weeks are up. There's something wrong, isn't there? Something you haven't told me.'

'Please, Christie, I know it is difficult but you must try to trust me.' And the creases formed themselves into such a convoluted pattern of distress that I was instantly ashamed of myself. 'He is – well, you must remember he took morphia first of all for the pain. Oh, he will not go back, but now he must find another way. It depresses him, you understand, and he is not himself – '

'But—'

The handkerchief flapped deprecatingly. 'He means it as a kindness, he wishes to save you hurt. He is, as I said, depressed. And we both know – ' here the creases twitched wryly – 'that in such moods our friend has sometimes a savage tongue.'

'Oh, Teddy – '

'Only another week, dear girl. One more week.'

Another week stretching before me. And then the next day the letter had arrived, as impersonal, uncommunicative as my own. 'Dear Miss Ward . . . remember your mother, of course . . . doubt if the rest of my memory holds up, but happy to give you any recollections of pre-war Weymouth that may help.' And suddenly I was consumed with nervousness, of myself, of him, of being mistaken, of somehow stirring up a hornet's nest that would, simply to gratify my own selfish ends, hurt and embarrass people. I had climbed into the train at Liverpool Street in a kind of daze, willing myself not to think of everything that could go wrong, had told myself even at Cambridge Station, in the taxi going into town, that there was still time to turn back, forget the whole business. And yet there was too much at stake, I must go through with it. So there I was, walking across a peaceful college court in the sunlight of an August morning. The clock on the tower struck twelve. I clutched my brown paper parcel and willed my legs not to shake.

I met no one on F Staircase; only a profound silence in which my footsteps jarred like an intrusion. On the third landing to my right was a painted name board: 'Prof. D J Radescu.' The IN/OUT sign was slotted to IN. The oak door was open, there was still no sound anywhere. I took a deep breath and knocked on the inner door.

It was a large room with gothic windows curtained in faded chintz through which the sun streamed in upon a dusty but comfortable disorder. Two cello cases and a carved music stand filled one corner, in another were more music stands of the collapsible variety; and everywhere there were books, piled haphazardly upon the dilapidated Brussels carpet, taxing with their unlooked-for weight the springs of a sagging horsehair sofa, books and scores and music paper in teetering columns upon the chenille-draped grand piano. It was the room of someone whose preoccupations left no space for the refinements of decoration. It gave off, in the sunlight, from its panelled walls and heavy furniture, a mellow, well-worn sepia look like the patina of old leather, and smelt pleasantly of pipe tobacco.

The man who had risen from an armchair at the far end of it on answering my knock was tall and very thin and stooped slightly. Though the onset of middle age had whittled any spare flesh from his face, hollowing his cheeks, emphasizing his high forehead and rendering almost beaky the pronounced aquiline of his nose, he had clearly in his youth been a good-looking man, and even now in his gaunt angularity there was something striking. Striking, too, was his hair, a thick, curling mop on top of that thin face, a tangled, ungovernable mane which would in a year or two be completely white but in whose pepper and salt it was still just possible to see traces of paprika, the vibrant flame of its original red.

Professor Dinu Radescu, D Mus., LRAM, ARMC, LTCL. Feeling that I was staring at him oddly and that he could not help but notice it, I blushed. But he was smiling, unconcerned, his eyes behind tortoiseshell-rimmed spectacles surveying me with abstracted good nature.

'Miss Ward? Yes, of course, I am expecting you, I remember your letter. Do come in and sit down, won't you.'

He had a pleasant voice, light, with no trace of an accent, yet there was something in its timbre and in its very precision that suggested nevertheless the constraints of an alien language meticulously learnt. He moved some books to make space for me on the sofa.

'It – it's good of you to see me like this,' I said.

'Not at all. I remember your mother with great affection and I'm very sorry to hear she is dead. She was a good friend to me in difficult times.' He smiled. 'In fact, without her I should never have learnt English. She taught me mainly from Mrs Beaton, I recall – while I'd fumble asking my way in the street I had the most encylopaedic knowledge of the names of kitchen utensils and could have held my own in any conversation provided it was restricted to the merits of tureens and fish kettles.'

I echoed his laughter nervously. 'And Keats,' I said. 'You read Keats together.'

He looked at me, surprised for a moment. 'Ah yes. Adele was very fond of the Romantics. But then she had had little enough truth and beauty in her own life, poor thing. You know – ' and here I felt him scrutinize me more carefully, felt myself blush again as I wondered if I would pass muster, suddenly desperately craving his approval for my little tip-tilted hat and the cream linen costume I had, with the indecision of someone dressing for a long-lost lover, finally selected from my wardrobe – 'you know, you really are very like her to look at, Miss Ward. Except, of course – ' and his eyes hesitated all at once upon the curls of my fringe beneath the cream straw – 'for your colouring.'

Was it my imagination, or had there been suddenly a note of puzzlement in his voice? He turned away, went over to a corner cupboard. 'You will take a little sherry? It is, after all, past noon.'

He was a few minutes finding glasses and the right decanter and I used the time in a nervous perusal of my surroundings for evidence of how he would receive what I had come to say. There seemed little enough token of any personal life amongst the clutter of work, no photographs of wife or children, no domestic touches that suggested a female hand; rather his frayed shirt cuffs, the missing button on his jacket, the glimpses I caught, as he went out to the gyp to run glasses under the tap, of a small bedroom off the main room, coldly spartan, through the half-open door, spoke of a solitary bachelor existence in which any ripples made by my imminent disclosure would spread with no further danger than to the object of it himself. Nevertheless my hands were shaking uncontrollably now. Pushing my brown paper parcel out of sight beneath the arm of the sofa, I took one of the bound scores from the pile next to me and began to flick through it in an attempt at unconcern. It was a Brahms Piano Concerto, the Second. Returning with my sherry and finding me thus employed, he again gave me a vague, good natured smile, in which was there now, nonetheless, a glimmer of additional interest?

'You're a musician, Miss Ward?'

'I used to – well, I once studied the piano. But, through circumstances I regret, I've rather given up.'

The low table beside the sofa wobbled. He jammed a stray score under one leg to steady it before putting down my glass. 'That seems a pity.'

'Yes,' I said, sounding suddenly surprisingly resolute to myself, 'but I mean to change all that now. It was wrong to give up, and it's still not too late to try again. I have a very good friend who – ' I paused. He was bound to have heard of Stenko Sokolov, had perhaps even met him, I had a perfect escape route if I wanted it, I could talk about Stenko and music, chat and drink my sherry and go, without ever mentioning the real reason for my visit, without ever forcing upon him facts he would not wish to confront, that were perhaps, after all, not so much facts as pure conjecture, that would sound merely hollow when I spoke them out loud.

He had retired to his armchair with his sherry and was taking out a tobacco pouch and a pipe. Looking at him, at the tall thin shape making angles within the frame of the chair, at the greying hair that still showed traces of red, I was certain my theory did hold water. I felt the queasiness rise within me again, knew I could not drink the sherry. But I could never have lifted the glass an inch from the table, let alone to my mouth, without spilling it anyway.

'What I mean is,' I said lamely, 'I love the piano. So I intend seriously to try again.'

'And I hope you'll have every success.' He raised his glass a fraction, smiling. 'But now, Miss Ward, you must tell me how I can help you with your researches.'

I gulped. The palms of my hands were wet. 'Professor Radescu, what I said in my letter was not strictly true. I'm not doing research, at least not for a book anyway.'

His eyebrows went up, he lowered his glass, surveyed me for a second, his glance suddenly no longer vague. But all he said was a noncommittal 'Ah'.

I could not think how best to continue. 'You see, my mother died when I was ten. You knew her and – well, I – '

He had put down his glass and was filling his pipe. He seemed unconcerned enough but, though perhaps it was still only my imagination, I sensed in his very apperance of ease a guardedness, as if a little of my tension had communicated itself. However, when he glanced up he looked merely curious. 'Go on, Miss Ward.'

'Professor Radescu, what I need to ask you is going to seem at best impertinent. At worst it will probably result in your throwing me out of this room and telling me never to pester you again. And it involves my talking about things that are – well, not commonly mentioned freely in society and certainly not by a person of my sex. But you must believe that I haven't come out of any prurient motive. In fact, I really wouldn't have come at all if, for a particular reason, it didn't have the most profound bearing on my whole life. I – I beg you, please, not to think too badly of me – '

He paused in the act of lighting his pipe. 'My dear Miss Ward, you seem, though I don't know you, to be a charming young woman, and I can't imagine there is anything you could say which would force me to eject you from the premises.'

He was smiling, yet the abstractedness had gone; I had definitely put him on his guard now. I could not get the measure of him, felt myself floundering. Did he realize the extent of his danger?

'My mother's marriage to Montague Ward was, as you are aware, not a happy one.'

'Yes,' he said, drawing on his pipe. 'Poor Adele. The man – forgive me – was a brute.'

'And died in a lunatic asylum two years after I was born,' I said. 'The man I was brought up to think of as my father, although, of course, I never knew him.' I looked down at my hands. I could hear that my voice was shaking. 'Montague Ward died of tertiary syphilis, Professor Radescu.'

'So that was it,' he said quietly. 'If she knew, your mother, of course, would not have told me.'

'She knew,' I said. 'She was deeply ashamed of it, but she certainly knew. The doctors were forced to be frank with her in order to make sure she was free from contagion. The dormant period after the first infection until the onset of the tertiary stages of the disease can be anything from ten to twenty years. It seems probable that Montague Ward contracted it in 1894 soon after he had – after he had returned to London from a summer spent in Norfolk. But the doctors could not know that. They were obliged to ask her about the full twelve years of her married life and from her answers they deduced that she had never been in any danger.'

He had taken the pipe from his mouth. 'Miss Ward, I don't see – '

'She was not in danger because up until the sixth of February 1905, the day she spoke to the doctors, her marriage had never been consummated. Thirteen days later, according to the records of the St Saviour Asylum for the Insane, Montague Ward was admitted within its walls never to be released.' I took a deep breath. 'Professor Radescu, Montague Ward could not have been my father.'

He was frowning. 'My dear Miss Ward – '

'He could not have been my father unless, in his insanity, he had at some time during those thirteen days taken my mother by force. But, though he attempted it, he didn't succeed. You know he didn't, because you were there. You were her only friend, you stayed with her all the time, protecting her, you were even prepared to kill him if he harmed her – '

He had lowered his pipe now and, though the spectacles prevented me from perfectly reading his eyes, it seemed to me that some of the good nature had drained out of them.

'Miss Ward, did your mother tell you all this?'

'No, but she kept a diary. I've pieced it together from that.'

'I see.' He said it very quietly, but all at once there was about him an alertness, as if he saw the danger clearly at last, was watching and waiting for it, rallying his forces to defend himself. His face had hardened. I felt my heart sink.

'Professor Radescu, I need to find my real father, not just for myself, but for someone else too, someone who won't be properly convinced of all I'm saying unless I have some kind of proof. Forgive me, but it's very important to me – '

'Presumably your mother's diary tells you everything you need to know.'

'It doesn't, it can't. Because after the sixteenth of February, 1905 it just stops. Apart from one short entry three days before my birth, she never wrote in it again.'

He had returned to his pipe, his mouth worked upon it. Though he appeared to survey me still with a dry, almost impartial interest, I felt the hardness grow in every muscle of his face as if he were setting himself against me like granite.

'Oh, Professor Radescu,' I said desperately, 'you knew my mother. She had a horror of the physical side of love, a horror which was reinforced by her marriage and – by certain events after it. February sixteenth is nine months, almost thirty-eight weeks exactly, before the day I was born. I don't believe my real father knew of my birth or even that she was expecting a child. I believe that because of what happened between them their relationship cooled and he went away. But one thing he would know, one thing he is the only other person in the world who can know, one thing which should surely convince him that the child conceived on February sixteenth 1905 must, beyond reasonable doubt, be his. My mother was a virgin until I was conceived, Professor Radescu. Only my real father would know that.'

There was a moment of utter silence. Then, casting aside his pipe, he rose from his chair. There was in his manner now nothing absent or rumpled, but only the quiet force of controlled anger. 'My dear Miss Ward, I promised not to throw you out and I shall keep my promise. But for a seemingly intelligent woman you appear to be subject to the most grotesque flights of fancy. Almost nothing you have said is based on indisputable fact, everything is mere speculation and conjecture. You have allowed your imagination to run away with you, you have leapt over all the mass of other logical possibilities simply to seize the one that suits your purpose best, you have put two and two together, Miss Ward, and made four hundred. Even if you could prove Montague Ward was not your father, and your case there is by no means watertight, the conclusions you go on to draw afterwards are tendentious in the extreme. You are speculating about events that happened thirty years ago, making deductions from things that cannot possibly be remembered with any degree of accuracy – '

'There are the diaries,' I said.

'Ah yes, the diaries. Does it not occur to you, Miss Ward, that if your mother chose to omit the crucial event on which you place such emphasis she might have left out other things as well? I had the greatest respect and fondness for her, and I don't wish to seem ungentlemanly, but—'

'Is it possible she had other lovers? You knew her, Professor. You know she didn't.'

He stared at me sharply and suddenly there seemed to enter into his face that puzzlement he had shown first on taking in my tallness and thinness and my red hair. He appeared to struggle with it for a moment, then successfully repress it. But when he spoke his voice was more gentle: 'My dear Miss Ward, even if part of what you said were accurate, even if your mother were still a virgin on the date you mention and even if nine months later she did give birth to you, it would still not necessarily follow that the man who took her virginity was your father.'

I returned his gaze as levelly as I could. 'No,' I said softly, 'it would not necessarily follow. Though you must agree it is more than likely. However I can't prove it. I can't prove anything. My only hope lies in the man himself. For I think his own instincts will tell him it is true.'

He took my words, held them for an instant, then seemed to recoil from them as if from the force of shock. I picked up my brown paper parcel from the sofa and proffered it to him.

'Please,' I said, 'you have been very good to listen to me and I have no right to ask you anything more. But would you, before you dismiss me as mad or mischievous or both, read my mother's diaries? Please?'

He looked at me but made no move to take the parcel. I put it down upon the table beside his armchair and turned away, feeling suddenly heavy with despair.

'Miss Ward – ' Taking off his glasses, he pinched the bridge of his nose between his finger and thumb as if trying to collect his thoughts. His eyes, I noticed, were green, like mine.

'Miss Ward, you must forgive me – ' he was fumbling for his watch, had all at once resumed his rumpled, abstracted air – 'I had quite forgotten I have arranged to meet a colleague for luncheon. Perhaps if you could give me – if you could return in two hours' time? . . . '

Two hours. I found a tea shop on King's Parade and sat over cheese scones and a pot of Earl Grey, not touching either, staring out of the window but scarcely aware of the world going by outside. I believed it utterly, any doubt I might have secretly harboured had disppeared, that same inner voice which had cried out so insistently against Felix being my brother now asserted with equal force that this was, must be, my father. I sensed that he believed it too, at least in part. But would he ever admit to it? I understood his anger and his shock; though it was of so much importance to me, it could only be an unpleasant discovery for him. Speculating on his possible, perhaps inevitable rejection of me, I was suddenly racked with pain. I had worried that he would not like or approve of me, but I had not thought of my liking him, of liking him, despite the unpropitious circumstances of our meeting, so that now the thought of never knowing him, never even seeing him again, filled me with an overwhelming anguish. I was all at once irrationally afraid; the two hours seemed to loom menacingly before me like a vast mountain I should never scale. Supposing he never intended to be there when I returned? had used the two hours merely as a tactful and dignified way of making his escape? Supposing . . . When the time at last came, my feet pounded up F Staircase, I was panting, scarcely able to get my breath. On hearing his answer to my knock I almost fell in through the door.

He was sitting exactly as I had left him, in his armchair, the pipe in his mouth, his brow furrowed, his eyes abstracted. It was as if everything in the room had stopped dead for the two hours I had been away from it. His pipe was out and only a pile of spent tobacco in the ashtray testified to his ever having lit it. The brown paper parcel containing the diaries was, I noticed with consternation, also untouched, still securely bound with my knots on the table where I had placed it.

'Ah, Miss Ward.' Again his fingers compressed the bridge of his nose beneath his glasses. 'It's a beautiful day and I usually think better in the open air. Shall we go for a walk?'

My heart sank as I followed him down into the sunlit court. So that was it – he had decided I was mad or dangerous and was going to make impossible demands upon him, so he would take care he answered me somewhere open and public, somewhere I could not cause a scene. He could not even find it in him to trust me.

We walked without speaking through Old Court, beneath an arch and out onto the Backs. Just before we reached the river the professor took a large key from his jacket pocket and we passed through a door marked 'PRIVATE, FELLOWS ONLY' into a small, untidy walled garden. There was the scent of roses and mignonette, a dim buzzing of bees; butterflies fluttered intoxicatedly above the heady purple tassels of a buddleia bush. We found a rustic seat amongst a profusion of lavender and sat down upon it. I did not dare look at him.

'Well, Miss Ward,' he said, putting a match to his pipe, 'it is as I said before. You have a hypothesis only and a rather tenuous one at that. Oh, there are some probabilities, I agree, but very few hard facts. Your theory, as you pointed out, doesn't constitute proof of anything unless you can persuade the man concerned to believe it. And perhaps there are good reasons why he might not want to believe.'

His voice was dry, neutral, as if he were dissecting a mathematical problem. I still could not bear to look at him.

'We all like the world to seem straightforward, Miss Ward, and we will go to great lengths to deceive ourselves that it is so. A coincidence there, a resemblance there – we'll make of them what suits us best, we'll construct our own pattern out of life's disorder and be damned to the things that disturb it. You've constructed one pattern, Miss Ward, I another. And at my age one clings to one's construction like a life raft. To have it dismantled beneath one – '

'Please, I do understand,' I said.

'Do you? When the dismantling might involve facing guilt and self-recrimination? Then perhaps you'll forgive me for not wanting to disturb my pattern but to pick holes in yours instead.'

I felt numb with despair. 'You didn't read the diaries,' I said.

'I didn't need to.' He was busy for a moment applying another match to his pipe. 'I didn't need to, Miss Ward. Because it all happened exactly as you described it.'

I caught my breath, whirled round. The sunlight, catching his spectacles, seemed to impart to his eyes for an instant a glitter of sharply-recollected sorrow.

'Your mother was not alone in her virginity, Miss Ward. She was the first woman I ever loved, and I loved her very dearly, wanted to marry her and damn the difference in our ages, would have waited for her till she was free. But, as you say, her life with that brute Ward had damaged her, she was afraid of love, had no understanding of it except in the context of his brutishness.' He sighed. 'I was an insensitive fool! I believed she cared for me and that in time her natural impulses would conquer her repugnance. But after that night things were irrevocably changed between us. She seemed consumed with guilt, she could scarcely even bring herself to look me in the face. By April of that year my health had improved enough for me to return to London and take up my scholarship again. She urged me to go and in the end I thought it was better that I should. I wrote to her, of course, but she never replied – only now do I understand precisely why. I thought of her, I never forgot her, but I was a young man and – ' he gestured vaguely with his pipe – 'like all young men I found other distractions. I never saw her again. So I never knew there was a child.'

I had opened my mouth to speak but he went on, reflectively now, staring out towards where a bumblebee weighed down the full-blown petals of a crimson rose. 'As I said, we become adept at deceiving ourselves, don't we? I fancy a part of me wasn't particularly surprised to receive your letter, or even to be faced with that abominable hair of mine recreated into a thing of staggering beauty in you. I don't think that part of me was even surprised at what you had to say. But the other part, the part that likes things tidy and can't bear to think that the illusory terra firma it has constructed for itself is actually quicksand, that part, you understand, quite cravenly couldn't bring itself to – ' his lips twisted ruefully – 'Oh, my dear, I'm sorry I was sharp with you.'

I put out my hand experimentally and placed it on his. He did not withdraw. 'There's no need to be sorry,' I said.

We looked at our two hands in bemused wonder for a moment, two thin hands with long fingers, mine pale, his darker, bonier, flecked with the liver spots of impending age. His fingers closed around mine.

'My dear, I've turned fifty. My wife, bless her, died three years ago and my children are all grown up and living their own lives. There's no one my youthful indiscretions can really hurt now. Except you, of course. And, I suppose, myself. So, while you were away, I began to think that to refuse such a gift – such a very beautiful gift – given to me at an age when I could scarcely hope for anything so unexpected and joyful was – well, simply churlish. And wrong. For, my dear, your challenge to me strikes home. Looking at you, remembering your mother, I cannot deny what, ridiculous, extraordinary and alarming as it is, my every instinct tells me is the truth.'

We stared at each other for an instant almost in disbelief. I looked at the gaunt, bony face, at the eyes behind the glasses, the hair like mine, the jaw too which had a hint of familiarity about it, and thought that though I did not know that face at all I had yet somehow known it always, like a part of me I had missed.

'Christabel?' he said shyly, making it sound like a question.

'Christie,' I said. 'What shall I call you?'

'Dinu,' he said. 'It is a little late for anything else.'

We bent towards each other and kissed, the confused kiss of two people who have not yet worked out the implications of their relationship, not quite missing mouths nor satisfactorily finding cheeks. Then, suddenly, as if a formality had been got out of the way, as if formalities no longer counted and I could dance and shout and sing, could abandon myself to a positive lunacy of joy, I flung my arms around his neck.

'Oh, thank you, Dinu. Thank you! Thank you!'

He drew me gently away from him and looked at me and I saw now that his whole face was spread in a smile of irradiating glee.

'My dear child, to think I have a daughter! And such a very, very beautiful daughter too.'

An idea occurred to me. 'You mean I am your only daughter?'

He nodded.

A jubilant, crazy laughter began to bubble in my throat. 'Then I have a brother?'

'Three. One in America, one in Leipzig and the youngest is an undergraduate here, although at the moment he is probably up to no good with a party of friends on the Italian Lakes.' He was all at once serious again. 'I don't know how yet, I shall have to consider what way to manage it – but perhaps you will meet them one day. And now – ' he glanced down at my unadorned ring finger – 'you have told me nothing of yourself, Christie. You mentioned mysteriously that you had some particular reason for finding me, but you did not explain it.'

I looked at him. 'I should like – may I bring someone to see you?'

'Yes, of course.' Behind the spectacles I thought I perceived a sudden mischievous glint. 'Shall I approve of him?'

'I think you will, very much. Despite his being Montague Ward's son.'

CHAPTER FIFTY-TWO

He is not my brother. He is not my brother the train with all its wheels and pistons seemed to shout, rollicking towards London, lurching across points, screaming under bridges and yet grinding through the miles that separated us with unbearable slowness all the same, not my brother running down the long platform, not my brother – Oh God why were there never any taxicabs when you wanted one? – not my brother in traffic jams at Holborn and Park Lane, not, as we drew up to Cheyne Walk, oh he couldn't keep me away now, he wouldn't want to, not when he knew, not when he heard, not, not, not my brother!

It was Stenko who met me at the door, looking worried, recovering his stutter for a moment. 'But C–C–C–ristie, Teddy told me Felix is not to be d–d–d–isturbed – '

I flung my arms around him, sending him staggering backwards, his glasses awry. 'Oh, Stenko, he's not my brother, he's not my brother!'

The umbrella opened, closed, turned inside out with the force of it, he looked at me for a second then uttered a sort of Cossack war whoop which I could still hear as I galloped up the stairs. The studio door was closed but I did not stop or knock upon it. An excited, irrepressible laughter was bubbling in my throat, my feet seemed scarcely to touch the ground, I burst through the door as if there were no doors, no barriers any more, nothing in the world that would ever now be closed to me.

He was in his dressing gown, lying propped upon the cushions of the couch, a cigarette between his fingers, a discarded book at his side. He surveyed me coldly, as if I were an irritating stranger. 'I asked you, Christie, not to come here.'

For a split second I was taken aback. I do not know how I had expected him to be, my brilliant, beautiful Cousin Felix; I suppose I had assumed now the worst was over he would have lost his haggard appearance, would be completely recovered, in every respect as I had known him before. Nothing had prepared me for how thin and ill he looked.

'You will forgive me,' he said dryly, 'if I don't get up.'

I hesitated, but only for a moment. If he were still in pain I had the means to mend it, I had the means to change everything now, I had – Oh God, the laughter, joyous, unstoppable, came to my throat again. I flew to the couch and, throwing my arms about his shoulders, buried my face in his neck.

'Oh my darling, I know you asked me for more time, but when you hear you'll understand, when I tell you – '

He accepted my embrace but did not respond to it. I felt his hand lightly on my back but sensed too, in his whole body, a defensive tension of muscles, which, as if drawn up in resistance to some other force, tolerated but did not welcome my touch. He smiled faintly but his eyes were cold and far away. I thought of how his expression would change when I told him, though of it and wanted my arms around him again, wanted to hug him and kiss him and never stop.

'Oh Felix, I've got such wonderful, wonderful news – ' My words tumbled over one another, the laughter kept bursting out and getting in the way, I searched for the beginning of my story and could not find it, began in another place, became tangled up and had to go back again; but eventually, brokenly, incoherently, I managed to tell him everything, the facts of my mother's unconsummated marriage, of Montague Ward's syphilitic madness, of finding my father, of meeting him, talking to him, of how ridiculously easy and yet how difficult it had been, till my voice was cracked and I was out of breath, trembling with the joy and excitement of it.

He had not questioned or interrupted me and now I had finished there was a silence. Gazing down at him I saw in his face, not the joy I was certain must answer mine, but a strange look I did not understand, a contraction of the mouth and jaw as if he were bracing himself against intolerable pain. I thought, suddenly aghast, that in my excitement I had not explained properly, that my incoherence had obscured my vital point.

'Oh my darling, don't you see?' I said. 'Aunt Jessica didn't lie, but she only told you half the truth. We're not brother and sister, we never have been. We are what we first believed we were, cousins, nothing more.'

He seemed to ride whatever it was, begin to master it. His lips twisted mordantly. 'The picture of my father grows prettier by the minute.'

I gazed at him in astonishment. 'Oh Felix, that doesn't matter. You're not a bit like Montague Ward, you never will be. What matters is that we're free to love each other, free to get married and be together and nothing now, nothing can stop us – '

'Christie, it isn't possible, I can't believe – ' The expression I did not understand was still there, as if somehow he were deliberately trying to close his mind to everything I had said, to blank it out as if the words had not been spoken.

'Oh, I know it seems incredible. I'm still dizzy with it myself. But it's true, Felix, oh my darling, it's true. And I want you to meet my father, I know you'll get on well together, in fact – ' I thought suddenly of the two of them, my father and my future husband, two tall, handsome, distinguished men, and my heart lurched for joy – 'in fact, if you're like anyone you're more like him, I know you'll both take to each other famously – '

'Oh God, not now.' He spoke almost in a whisper, as if to himself. 'Not now, after all these years, when I can't – when it can't make any difference.'

'No difference?' I felt suddenly, in my inability to make him understand, something akin to panic. 'Oh my darling, don't you see? – All those twelve dreadful years, they've gone, every bit of them, we can be lovers, we can marry, we can be ridiculously, gloriously happy at last!'

There was another silence. I watched incredulously as he seemed to brace himself for a second time against that inexplicable onslaught. Then, as if he had successfully gained the upper hand of whatever it was, his face grew set again, as cold and impenetrable as when I had first entered the room.

'No, Christie,' he said very quietly, in a voice almost devoid of inflection.

I stared at him disbelievingly. 'But Felix, we—'

'My dear child, I didn't wish you to see me like this, and yet I suppose I was bound to be faced with the task of explaining to you sooner or later. In 1917, when I recovered from my encounter with the Kaiser's bullet against all the doctors' predictions, they told me I was lucky but that the damage was still there and I could expect to have increasing trouble with it as I grew older. Well, it seems they now have their revenge. My luck has run out, rather sooner than I expected.'

I continued to stare at him, not understanding.

'Christie – ' and as before his voice was very level, matter of fact, as if from what he was telling me he had abstracted his own involvement – 'at the moment I suppose I might just manage a walk to the other side of this room. Teddy's doctor says there may be some small improvement, but he tells me I should not hope for anything much. It seems I should be wise to learn to accept it.'

I gazed at him for a moment with shock. 'So that's why – why you wouldn't let me come back – why you – Oh Felix, no!' I flung my arms around his neck. 'Oh no, my darling. We won't accept it. The doctors were wrong the last time, you fought it and won – '

'My dear shild, I was twenty-two then.' He unwound me from him, held me gently but firmly at a distance. 'Now I'm afraid Teddy's man is probably right to be pessimistic.'

'Then we'll find other doctors, get other opinions. Oh Felix, you have so much courage – and I'll do anything I can to help. We'll fight it together, we'll—'

'Christie, you haven't understood.' And now in the careful evenness of his tone there was all at once an undercurrent. 'There can be no "we". Do you imagine I would ever marry you under these circumstances? Do you imagine for one moment I would let you spend the rest of your life tied to a cripple?'

I stared at him, horrified. 'But Felix, I love you, it can't change that – '

'It can and will change everything.' The undercurrent was taking strength, boiling, angry. 'As long as I'm forced to lie here I can't work and, even with your romantic disregard for money, I scarcely think you'd relish living in poverty.'

'I don't care, it doesn't make any difference. Provided we're together, it doesn't matter.'

'Dear God, Christie, be sensible for once. It's time to stop dreaming.' With a supreme effort, he forced himself into a sitting position and I saw his face twisting in pain and anger. 'Do you imagine I haven't thought, this past month, when I knew what I was asking you to tie yourself to, do you imagine I haven't understood? And do you think your incredible, wonderful, dreadful news makes any difference? A dream, child, that was all we had. A beautiful idyll for a few brief weeks twelve long years ago. And now I understand that we're exceptionally lucky, you and I. We've never had to look beyond the dream as most people do. Perhaps we should be grateful to my mother for keeping us apart all these years, for allowing us our romantic delusions and never forcing us to put them to the test – '

'No, Felix. No. Our love has been tested, there isn't any test now it couldn't withstand.'

'There it comes again – that word "love". Yes I've loved you, little Christie, in every way I'm capable of, for twelve years. But I'm no longer sure what I mean by it. That I'll make you happy? That I'll guarantee not to destroy everything that is joyful and precious between us? Oh, it's an easy word to say, "love", a fine and flexible word, capable of taking on a multitude of meanings. My mother was inordinately fond of it – she used it to emasculate her husband and make her children despise each other, to wreck her sister's life, to torment you and tear us both apart. My wife, God help her, if she were ever called upon to justify the killing of my son, would probably have said she did that out of love. In France there are fields of crosses testifying to the virtues of love, boys, some of them mere children, lives wasted, talents squandered, blown to sticky, unrecognizable bits for love of King and Country. But the meaning we give the word, little Christie, with its splendid promise of all things creative and good – does that love exist, can you look about you and tell me, hand on heart, you see our love in operation anywhere? Oh, there's an appetite I'll grant you, the appetite that killed my father. But "love" as we mean it? Not as an excuse or a justification or a weapon, but as a force of itself for freedom and good? The world, as perhaps you may have noticed, isn't precisely a respecter of the free and the good. The natural impulse of humanity is to limit and crush, the driving force of human passion isn't to create but to destroy. And you and I, my dear Christie, for all we profess to care for each other, for all the splendour of our romantic dream, should we acquit ourselves any better? Should we, by some miracle, be the exception that proves the rule? Oh God, wake up, child! The dream is over. This is the reality, this humiliation, this squalid futility of my having nothing to offer you except the chance to live in some filthy lodging house with bedpans and wheelchairs and you nursing me night and day and hating me, and my hating myself for the sheer degrading uselessness of it. How long would our dream last us then, Christie?'

I gazed at him, bewildered. 'But it wouldn't be like that, Felix. I know myself, I know you – '

'You know me?' All of a sudden he seized me by the shoulders, forcing my eyes to hold contact with his. 'Dear God, Christie, look at me, see me properly for once and not through the rose-coloured glasses of the dream. I'm tired, worn out by life, a contemptible shell of a man who until last month needed morphia even to exist. I'm my mother's son, Christie – and the son of my noble father – '

I looked at him, dazed, seeing only the anger blazing savagely in his eyes and in the cruel curve of his lips.

'I know what I am, Christie. I haven't your blind faith. I'm obliged to see reality as it is. Oh, it was a glorious dream we had, all those years ago. Do you think I could bear to watch you wondering what became of it, how you could have been so deceived? Do you think I could stand seeing you shackled to me and loathing me for it, while I crucified you with my jealousy in revenge? Do you think I would willingly commit you to that squalid little pantomime of despair? No, if I've ever cared anything for you, Christie, I should let you keep your beautiful dream of love. Cherish it, little one, save it for some other man, don't waste it on me. I can only see the danger in it.'

A silence fell, a long, numb silence. He lay back upon the cushions again, his face once more a cold, impenetrable mask. I stared at him, seemed to do so for a great while. Something, perhaps it was a sob or perhaps a scream, rose in my throat. I stifled it with difficulty, swallowing hard until it was gone. I got up from the couch with my eyes still on him, feeling myself grow stiff and icy and pale.

'If you are in danger from anything, Felix,' I said, 'it is not from love.'

Then I turned on my heel and left.

I do not remember how I got back to Berkeley Square. I don't remember anything very much until I was all at once looking at Dilly, and she was asking me what the matter was and I was opening my mouth, attempting to answer her, but no sound was coming out. And then I was in Dilly's bedroom, lying on her bed, trying to drink the brandy she had given me and choking and sobbing, sobbing as if I would never stop.

When I could speak, she sat with her arm around me and I told her everything, from the very begining, from Felix's returning from the war and Aunt Jessica's taking the diaries, leaving out only all mention of the morphia and the real reason why I had moved into Berkeley Square. While I talked, Dilly's eyes grew wider and wider. Finally, as I reached my conclusion, a small furrow etched itself between her brows.

'Oh Christie, and I never knew! How perfectly dreadful.'

I wiped my eyes and tried to laugh. 'Not so dreadful if the story had the traditional happy ending. And today I thought it would.'

'But is he really so ill?'

I sighed. 'I don't know. Tarantin says he's depressed. And he's never paid any attention to doctors before. But perhaps now – oh Dillo, perhaps that's not what he's really saying.'

The furrow between Dilly's brows deepened. 'You mean the stuff about his illness is an excuse and he really believes all that bosh about love?'

'Perhaps it's not bosh. As he says, we only had those few weeks of happiness all those years ago. Perhaps I have been dreaming.'

'You don't believe that for an instant and neither do I. Neither can he, or I'd go round to Cheyne Walk this minute and shake him – he simply wouldn't deserve you.'

Despite myself, I was laughing properly now. 'Oh Dillo! But you're partisan.'

She squeezed my hand. 'Of course I am, you silly old thing. I love you too, in case you'd forgotten.' Her thoughtful frown returned.

'You know, it strikes me, of the two of you it's he who's the dreamer. He seems to judge the world by impossible standards – beginning with himself. Oh, I know, what with your unspeakable Aunt Jessica and his nasty wife, it's been fairly thoroughly proved to him so far that for him to love anyone is pretty much of a disaster. But he does seem to have taken his beastly father very much to heart, too, as if it were a confirmation of something he recognized in himself all along. From all you've said, he's so convinced you couldn't love him if you knew him properly he's hell bent on making himself impossible to love anyway.'

I felt the tears starting again. 'But I do know him, I know him as well as I know myself. I know he's not incapable of loving or being loved. There's so much good in him. And the bits he sees, the bits he thinks unworthy of love – they're in all of us, part of our humanity. It isn't given to us to be perfect – '

Dilly gave a wry smile. 'Oh, I agree. Inside the average worm there's good and evil in equal mixture. You accept that, old dear, you take the real world for what it is so you're able to see the credit as well as the deficit. But your Cousin Felix – ' the furrow between her brows deepened again – 'oh, he's very strong and controlled, he's got a keen sense of integrity and a scrupulous sense of honour – but he expects the ideal, he demands perfection. And when, of course, he doesn't find it – well, he's cynical about the rest of humanity but he's hardest of all on Felix de Lisle. So because he can't be perfect he can't allow that you could love him, because in loving each other you might also from time to time hurt each other he'll spare you both the pain by denying love exists at all.'

The tears began to stream down my face in sheer frustration. 'But this is painful, now. It's painful beyond all measure.'

'Yes, dear thing, I know. That's what makes his antics so dotty. Oh, I'll grant love between mere mortals is jolly difficult. Why, Robbie and I, two extremely ordinary mortals who rub along pretty well together as a rule and who'd be quite at sea apart, can nonetheless deal each other the most horrendous wounds over matters of such monumental gravity as whether a hand of eleven clubs constitutes grounds for attempting a Grand Slam. But, imperfect as ordinary mortal love is, it's all we've got. And it's pretty jolly grim trying to live without it.'

I blew my nose. 'How do I persuade Felix of that?'

Dilly smiled. 'I'm sure you won't have to. He can't be entirely potty, whatever we've said. He must know, despite himself, that love's the joy of things, the purpose of being alive in the first place. Oh, I agree we live in a rotten old world. And I agree love's a much misused word – why, people have been killing each other for love of something or other, religion, country, honour, principal or any high-sounding ideal you can make stand for plain old self-interest, since time immemorial. But love in its true meaning – the ordinary mortal love of one fallible human being for another, that's another business entirely. It's the one decent thing we've got, as long as there's one drop of it left, it's still an antidote to all the poison in the mixture. And I can't believe your Cousin Felix doesn't understand that in his heart of hearts.'

She put her arm around my shoulder and kissed me. 'Oh Christie, he's certain to come round. Because it's difficult, because he's ill and depressed and having a down on himself – that can only mean he needs you more, not less. It's probably the shock that did it, finding out everything he's believed for twelve years isn't true. I bet you he's lying there at this very minute feeling an absolute worm for having been so vile to you. I bet you he'll telephone or send a message tomorrow morning begging you on bended knee to forgive him. It'll be all right, you'll see.'

But he didn't telephone or send a message, not the next day or the next. The days drew into a week and then into weeks; days, weeks filled with emptiness and silence. I thought at least Tarantin or Stenko might call but even they seemed to have deserted me. It was as if I had been lopped off from the life of Cheyne Walk like a redundant branch. It was over.

Life in the desert is no easier for the second time of being there. The same things still made me cry, I still thought I saw him sometimes in the street although I knew it could not be him, still cherished the same foolish hopes although I knew there could be no hope left. I tried not to be angry with him, tried to understand. But every so often I would see a pair of cool grey eyes surveying me quizzically, lips curved in a half-mocking smile, would smell the sweet warmth of familiar skin, and I would have to jam my knuckles into my mouth to stifle the pain. I did not think now that he would give up to the verdict of the doctors, could not imagine, however much it cost him in pain and endurance, that he would submit willingly to the existence of an invalid while he still had the strength to resist; rather, I agreed with Dilly that his physical difficulties had been, even if unconsciously, a pretext and that his giving up was of a different, more fundamental nature, a failure of faith, of trust both in himself and in me. Perhaps indeed he was right and I had never truly known him. Had there not, after all, been always two Felix de Lisles, the familiar, loving face and that other looking-glass image, the face that was like mine and not like it, that was scarred from other wounds than those the Kaiser had inflicted? 'Love is a word I've always feared, little Christie. You were like some bright dream of innocence I've always longed for but must not have. Anna's way is my way, I accept what I am.'

I too must learn acceptance. The absorbed, gentle, loving face was gone for ever and there only remained the image in the glass, the Felix de Lisle who was too irreparably damaged to give love or receive it, who came from Rostova's place. I thought of him somewhere in the future, at a party perhaps or at dinner, my brilliant, beautiful Cousin Felix, elegant, detached, surveying the room through the curling smoke of a Muratti, his smile charming but his eyes opaque, an observer merely whom life no longer touched, whose cool control concealed not energy or passion, but emptiness, who, though he still relied upon his cane, was crippled not in body but in all the closed places of his heart and soul. I saw him thus and my tears welled up involuntarily for him, and for all the potent, whirling life that had been lost.

Yes, I tried not to be angry but to understand. After all, when I thought of my mother's marriage to Montague Ward, thought of mine to Archie, and of the bleak faces of the unemployed and of Sally Mullins lying in the road like a bundle of rags for the pawnshop and of Rostova and of the fat abortionist with her little shell-like nails, it seemed that perhaps Felix was right, that humanity was only capable of inflicting himiliation and pain. And Aunt Jessica, with whom so much of the wretchedness had started, hadn't she too known all along that the odds are on the side of evil not of good; for hadn't she known, she who had never really let Montague Ward go, she who would have taken pains to find out how and why he had died, hadn't she realized that I, with my flaming red hair and inconvenient birthday, could not have been his child? Wasn't that perhaps the true reason for her hatred of me, wasn't that her reason too for triumph even in death, for she must have been certain, with the diaries gone, that if she told Felix only half the truth it would stick as if it were the whole, for there could be no way in which we might prove it otherwise? What good was Dilly's tiny drop of salve against the poison of that? What good was Dilly's hope for the world when every day on the wireless and in the newspapers now there was talk of rearmament and germ warfare and Hitler's growing military power and Mussolini's bellicose intentions towards Abyssinia? Was not Felix right that all the passionate force of man, all his potential, was directed not to create but to destroy – and what hope was there for Dilly's frail, simple notion of love against the might of that destructive impulse? But then I thought of Mrs Burton, and Stenko and Tarantin, and Rosa Schumacher and Mrs Wix and of Dinu, my father, and of my sad, gentle mother and of Dilly herself, and knew that Felix was wrong. Though it wasn't Dilly's love that drove the world, that love, with all its faults and failures, that love with its small victories and simple generosities, that ordinary, extraordinary love of one individual for another was the single force for good we had.

The weeks at Berkeley Square drifted by and I began slowly to thaw from frozen anguish to a state of painful but tolerable sensation. I had survived before and now I must learn to survive again. One miraculous thing had happened to me; perhaps as my only means of obliterating misery, I had begun to play the piano again, feverishly, obsessively, as if to make up for all the years I had neglected it, working six or eight hours a day until my eyes burned with fatigue and every muscle of my body ached. And gradually, oh only for a few bars here and there, but occasionally, triumphantly, nevertheless, I had the sense not of fingers fumbling for notes, of technical problems taunting me with my inability to surmount them, but of the music itself, clear, pure, abstract, flowing out from my touch, carrying me with it till, beyond the room and my hands upon the keyboard and my aching body, in limpid bright cascades, it sang of hope.

Dilly was to return to India in the second week of October and so I too must make some practical plans for the future. I wrote to Mrs Schumacher, explaining my intention to concentrate seriously upon my piano studies but asking if, perhaps on a part-time basis, I might have my old job back. She replied that since she now regarded me as a friend she could not countenance my coming to New York as her employee; but, as Barrymore had become quite a shadow of himself without my company and as, in any case, she had far too much money for one crazy old woman, she would consider it a personal favour if I would allow her to sponsor my studies. And, after much agonized debate, I swallowed my pride and wrote back accepting her absurdly generous offer. So it was settled. I had not seen Felix for six weeks and on October 7th I should sail for New York, never to see him again. I told myself how lucky I was to be given such an opportunity for a fresh start in life, and tried not to let my mind dwell on all that was past.

As the weeks drew by I observed Dilly from time to time glancing at me sideways with eyebrows raised. One day at the end of September, when my ticket had been bought and plans for packing up the household were considerably advanced, she came in while I was practising, waited for me to stop, seemed about to speak, hesitated, then surveyed me with a sigh.

'You know, Christie, I can't help feeling you should write to him or telephone or something before you do anything drastic.'

'Oh Dillo,' I said, 'don't you think I have to screw myself down, take a grip of myself every day to stop myself doing precisely that?'

'But should you? I agree he's been entirely horrid, but nevertheless – he's probably got over his lunacy by now. And while you're here thinking he's stopped loving you he may be thinking exactly the same, only vice versa. One teeny telephone call can't do any harm.'

I felt, with irritation, the tears spring to my eyes again. I bit my lip. 'Dillo, I can't. It's been six weeks. I can't – force myself on him. I just can't.'

She sighed again, then shrugged her shoulders. 'Oh well, if it were Robbie and me . . . But then I always forget about your family and its dotty pride.'

Though I could not do as she suggested, I was taken aback. I had ceased to think of myself as part of the family, could no longer imagine I shared any trait with either the Cavendishes or the de Lisles. I was alone now, rootless, about to go into permanent exile unencumbered by any baggage apart from what little musical skill I possessed and the duty I knew I owed to myself to survive. From henceforth I should not look or be like anyone else; I should simply be me. Only one aspect of this cutting loose filled me with a sharp regret: I had not been able to bring myself to visit Dinu a second time without, as I had promised, taking Felix, and now it seemed that, having after all these years found him, I should lose him again. I knew I should write to him to tell him of my impending departure for New York and make some excuse for my behaviour, I thought my silence probably hurt him and the idea added to my anguish. But I could not do what I knew I must. In all my sensible planning, the issue of telling Dinu hung suspended, too painful to face.

CHAPTER FIFTY-THREE

On October 2nd, the six o'clock news on London Regional announced that Mussolini had invaded Abyssinia and Italy had been mobilized. I had just switched off the wireless when Dilly appeared to say that my cousin had called to see me. I stared at her.

'Oh Lord, Christie, I'm sorry! I didn't mean him. The other one. Your Cousin Meredith.'

Meredith had been shown into the morning room. As he turned towards me I was shocked by how he had aged. His flesh, mottled, gross, seemed to hang from him, boneless, as if the burden of his responsibilities, his political success, had grown upon him like a physical encumbrance. His eyes were rheumy and shot with broken veins, his hands shook, the smallest movement appeared to engage him in an enervating battle for breath. Looking at his face, that face we all shared, and seeing its similarities obscured forever by the folds of pendulous flesh, I wondered how much longer his heart would continue the unequal struggle of pumping life into it.

I expressed my surprise at seeing him after so long. The jowls quivered with embarrassment.

'Well, bad business, divorce. Sybil, y'know, woman of high principle . . . Still, tend to take a broader view myself. Family got to stick together, bygones be bygones, eh? Didn't know where you'd got to, anyhow. Only found out today, from my dear brother.'

Despite myself, my heart lurched. 'Felix? You've seen him? Oh Meredith, how is he?'

'Lunched with him at my club. Seemed – d'you know, as a matter of fact the whole thing was dashed odd.'

'But he wasn't – was he well?'

The earnestness of my question seemed to surprise him. 'Now you mention it, he was a touch lame. Souvenir from Jerry still giving him gyp. Said he knew some quack in Paris who could fix him up, one of the reasons he's going back there.'

So he, like me, was leaving England. I tried to feel only happiness that he was better, not a selfish sense of loss at a departure which, after all, no longer touched me.

'But that wasn't what was odd,' Meredith was saying. 'Seems he's trying to settle his affairs before leaving. Told me a most peculiar story about his being a bastard and believing for a while you were his sister. Said he'd felt dishonourable about not coming clean before but he'd had to keep mum to protect you. Must say, I found the whole thing jolly dashed confusing.'

I tried to smile. Here it was again, that rigid sense of honour, punctilious, unsparing to the last. Something in its very fastidiousness made me, quite irrationally, feel like weeping.

'Proud blighter, my brother. Got to admire him, in a way. Thing like that, can't have been easy for him to come out with it.'

'No,' I agreed.

'Anyway, still Cavendish blood, eh? Shan't mention it to Sybil, least said the better, but – well, it explains a lot. Perhaps he's not quite the bounder I thought he was.'

'No,' I said softly. 'Felix was never a bounder.'

'And you, m'dear. Made me think. Family's been a little hard on you, leaving you to sink or swim. Blood thicker than whatever, y'know. Thought I'd better take a look at you. Which reminds me – ' even the effort of reaching into his breast pocket seemed to aggravate his struggle for breath – 'Felix said if I was coming here to give you this.'

I stared at the envelope he held out to me. A great confusion of the senses assailed me as I took it, a leap of my heart so that the room seemed to spin around me. I wanted to tear the letter open there and then, but I needed privacy for that, I could not read it in front of Meredith. I gazed helplessly at the crisp blue of the paper between my fingers and wished that he would go.

There was something in his heaving and puffing, however, in his uncomfortable shifting of flesh within the confines of his chair, which suggested that, far from accomplishing the purpose of his visit, he was only just working up to it.

'Thing is, m'dear – whatever else, we're all Cavendish blood in the end. My mother . . . Whole family could have done more for you. Perhaps we shouldn't have forced you into marrying young Cadwallander.'

'You didn't,' I said.

'And the divorce. Blame on both sides, I gather. Cadwallander's not a bad chap but – well, did hear something discreditable about an accident, truth hushed up at the inquest. New rich, y'know, come up from trade, don't have the values a family like ours has.'

I stared at him, perplexed, now seriously wondering what he could be leading up to. His jowls quivered.

'Seems my brother has some odd scruple about not being entitled to the money Pater left him. Told him it was rot, of course. The Pater always thought highly of Felix and – ' the jowls quaked as if he were attempting to swallow some indigestible emotion – 'wishes of the dead, y'know, whatever I might feel about my blasted brother. But he did mention – ' here again he succumbed to that curious consternation of the flesh – 'he did say he'd once thought of settling the money on you – '

I felt myself grow cold. 'And I turned him down,' I said.

'Still, he's got a point, m'dear. Family should have done more for you. Question of duty, y'know. And if he wants to give his money away – '

The coldness grew into a tight anger. 'Did he suggest you spoke to me about it?'

'Not in so many words, but – '

I looked down at the letter in my hands. 'Is that what this is about?'

'M'dear, I – '

'It is, isn't it? That's what it's about.' All the excitement I had felt at receiving the letter had suddenly evaporated, in its place had come something leaden, deadening. I tore open the envelope. And no, it was not the message of love my foolish hopes had conjured up, but four lines scrawled upon the writing paper of Meredith's club, four cold, impersonal lines.

My dear Christie,

Could you meet me briefly tomorrow? May I suggest 11 a.m. in Berkeley Square at the gate near the fountain? There is no need to reply to this. I shall arrange to be there and if you do not come I shall, of course, understand.

F.

I stared at the paper and then at Meredith. Not a message of love but a business letter. In the settling up of Felix's affairs I still remained an untidiness. There they were, the de Lisles once again. Not enough had been done so, however I resisted, I was to be paid off. A question of duty. Duty, honour, family solidarity, all cemented with money, never with love.

'You may tell Felix,' I said, 'that he may leave me out of his accounts. My particular ledger is closed.'

My tone seemed to have its effect on Meredith who, panting and wheezing, became purple with embarrassment. 'M'dear, I simply meant – Women of the family, doesn't look right, y'know, not to make sure they're taken care of. I'm a bit strapped, but if my dear brother could see his way – '

'I don't expect or want anything from the de Lisles!'

'Steady on, m'dear. Just trying to see duty done – ' He was puffing now like a grampus, so that no further words would come. Looking at him, his eyes running, his chest heaving, his fingers fumbling in his pocket for his inhaler, I felt my anger drain away. What had happened between Felix and me was not of his making. In his own curious way he meant well. It was not his fault if he had inherited with Sir Arthur de Lisle's sense of family duty a certain weakness of heart.

'It's kind of you to be concerned, Meredith,' I said, more gently. 'But I'm going to America in four days' time. The family has never had any obligation towards me, not in my eyes anyway. And now I'm going it can stop worrying about me for good.'

His breathing became easier, the purple faded to a mottled red. 'Oh well. So long as you don't feel – One's never certain one's done enough. . . .' He passed his hand over his forehead with evident relief. 'Better be off, I suppose. Driving down to Bournemouth, Party Conference tomorrow. This business of the Duce walking into Abyssinia's bound to come up, of course. Damn bad show, requires those of us in Government to take the strongest possible line.' He began upon the difficult process of levering himself from his chair. 'What's needed is a carefully worded motion to Conference supporting old Haile Whatsisname of Abyssinia and condemning the Fascists in the sternest terms. That'll make the blighters sit up and take notice. Got to do one's duty, man in my position – never can be certain one's done enough.'

I had read and re-read Felix's letter. I was certain from its tone, from his very choice of a meeting place, that he was coming to say goodbye. The goodbye was a tidiness on his part and the choice of the square the desire for neutral territory, beyond Dilly's critical gaze, somewhere there could be no tears and recriminations. I need not meet him, I would not go. I did not think I could bear the pain of it and Meredith's suggestion that he intended to bring up the matter of the settlement again rankled like an insult: I had reluctantly agreed to accept Mrs Schumacher's support, but that was offered with great generosity and love; this was money instead of love, given because it was the only thing left that could be given. I did not mention the letter to Dilly, I resolved to be strong, to pretend I had never received it. And yet something, perhaps a desire for tidiness myself, told me I should walk into Berkeley Square at eleven o'clock, nevertheless.

There was a sharp wind in the square which set the fallen leaves from the plane trees scurrying in little whirls and eddies. I had not bothered with hat or gloves but at the last minute had pulled on my moleskin jacket. Yet, despite its warmth, I shivered. Autumn: leaves russet, dying, a sense of things ending. Two stunted and sooty geraniums withered in a stone urn. From the water jug borne by the naked-breasted naiad of the fountain trickled only a small, sluggish, spasmodic stream. On the corner of Fitzmaurice Place and Charles Street, the billboards at the newspaper-seller's booth announcing Mussolini's occupation of Abyssinia screamed with stark directness the one word 'WAR!'.

I looked at my wristwatch. It was three minutes to eleven. A nursemaid came past with a pram. An old, ragged man plotted a steady course round the pavilion, picking up cigarette butts as he went. On the corner of Berkeley Street a taxi screeched to a halt, and from Bond Street came the distant honking of traffic.

Then I saw it, the long, dark-green snout of the Bentley with Anatole at the wheel, edging out of Bruton Street and round the square towards me. It pulled up at the gate and Anatole jumped out and went to open the passenger door. I did not move but remained where I was on the gravel path beside the statue. He climbed out slowly, painfully, his hand going back for the stick, my Cousin Felix, straightening himself, pausing for a moment, his coat draped over his shoulders, his head bare, walking towards me now across the gravel as I had seen him that very first time when he had returned from the Great War, the war to end all wars, a tall, lean, proud figure, hand clenching on the stick, walking stiffly, carefully, as if he held himself erect by an indomitable effort of the will.

Anatole climbed back into the car and it moved off slowly, round the square. When he reached the statue, Felix paused. There was a space of about two yards between us, but neither of us moved to close it. Though he was pale and unsmiling, he looked better I thought, no longer haggard. An uncomfortable knot formed in my throat. I closed my eyes and swallowed hard. I was going to America to start a new life and this was just a necessary formality, one small but important neatness, before new things could begin.

I glanced towards the empty seats of the pavilion, as I did so glimpsing out of the corner of my eye the green Bentley, not turning off but slowly circling the square. I willed myself to smile. 'Why don't we sit down?'

He shook his head. 'Before anything else, I must give you a message from Teddy. He's sorry neither Stenko nor he has been to see you, but he's sick and tired of making excuses for me. He's missed you, but he's been quite adamant on the subject.'

The Great God Tarantin. I should miss him too, for he had, after all, proved to be a friend. I should be sorry not to say goodbye to him, and to Stenko too, before I left for New York. I was aware once again of the slow peregrinations of the Bentley, but tried to shut my mind to them.

'How are you?' I said.

'A great deal better – physically, at least. And I've begun to work again.'

'I'm glad.' I paused. My mouth had become very dry. 'Meredith tells me you're going back to Paris.'

'I think so, yes,' he said. 'And you're joining Rosa Schumacher in New York.'

I glanced at him, surprised. 'How do you know that?'

He smiled. 'I received a letter from Silberstein Hayman two days ago saying they had instructions to send a painting to me and asking whether they should despatch it to Southampton or Le Havre.'

'Oh.' I was sorry poor Mrs Schumacher had had to lose her painting. I looked up at him, but could not think what to say. The smile had been fleeting and his face was grave once more. He too seemed to be struggling for conversation. I saw that the Bentley had passed Bruton Street and was sliding round Berkeley Square into Charles Street again.

'Why here?' I said. 'Why outside in the square?'

His lips curved sardonically. 'Because, my dear Christie, I don't trust myself. Because I want to be able to say what I've come to say and then, if need be, get into the car and simply drive away.'

Any vestiges of hope I might have cherished faded. My assumptions had been right, this was the last I should ever see of him. I swallowed hard. I accepted it, it did not matter. I must stop my hands trembling and my eyes burning dangerously.

The Bentley was rounding the top of the square again. Felix seemed to hesitate as if once more he were searching for further conversation. Suddenly I did not want the anguish prolonged. It was no use, we had nothing to say to each other, I did not want a practical discussion of how loose ends should be tied. I did not want to argue about the settlement, I wanted to short-circuit it all, stop it now.

'Christie, I – '

'Felix, please, I don't – '

We both stopped, embarrassed.

'Felix,' I said, with determination, 'once and for all, I won't take the money – '

'Money?' He stared at me in amazement.

'Meredith said—'

'Damn Meredith!' he exclaimed with unexpected violence. 'I don't understand why I seem so incapable of—' He paused, then began again, all at once speaking very quickly. 'My dear little one, I'm a fool. A bloody, pig-headed arrogant fool. I've spent the last six miserable weeks convincing myself this was for the best, that even if I made any kind of recovery I couldn't— I told myself the pain of separating would save us both hurt in the long run, that I was only being cruel to be kind. And then two days ago, when the letter about the painting came and I knew I'd got what I wanted, that I'd lost you, that I'd managed to kill—'

I stared at him bewildered. He had gone very white and the hand that held the stick trembled violently.

'Oh Christie, I had the world and I threw it away. Cruel to be kind? Just cruel. Cruel and blind and egotistical to take everything upon myself, to leave you out of count, to pour contempt on the most precious gift I've ever been given. You said yourself I obliterate you – '

'Yes,' I said. 'Sometimes you do.'

'Then I understand, I—' He stopped, seeming to fumble helplessly for words. I continued to stare at him. I had never seen him like this before, my cool, impenetrable Cousin Felix, disorganized, incoherent, his face suddenly opening to me as if all its fine and carefully-wrought defences were one by one falling away so that I had the sense of something in it chastened, younger, almost boyish, so that I remembered the time all those years ago I had first gazed upon it unguarded in sleep and had been overwhelmed by such poignant tenderness for him.

'I have what I deserve,' he said. 'A painting, a shadow. Yet you offered me – to throw away something beyond price and now, when it's too late, to understand what a coward I am – still to be a coward, for two days to dread what I know you must tell me so that I can't—Oh, dear God, I wasn't sure you'd even bother to meet me, the car is here so I won't cause you more pain by begging and screaming and making a nuisance of myself, I know I've forfeited the right to ask anything of you, but —Christie, it's not a dream that I love you, there's no dream in this appalling sense of something dead, in knowing I've wantonly destroyed all that I—Oh, my darling little one, could you ever forgive me? Could there be any hope for us?'

I gazed at that struggling, boyish, infinitely naked face. Its image seemed to blur for a moment, then become clear again.

'Do you think there is?' I asked in a whisper.

'If there is not,' he said softly, 'then I think there is no hope for me.'

I opened my mouth but no sound came out. There seemed, I remember, an instant of utter silence. Then suddenly, in a tangle of overcoats, in a flurry of lips and flying hair, without knowing at all how I got there I was in his arms and he was holding me to him, holding me so tightly I was giddy with it, and he was kissing my mouth, my eyes, my throat, and the sky, the plane trees, the dilapidated fountain, the whole square seemed to be spinning, whirling in a reckless, uncontrollable, lunatic dance.

'Little one, I may never get rid of this stick, you may never succeed in turning me into a human being, I think I have nothing to offer you – '

'Only that you, just as you are, happen to be the joy of my life.'

'Then teach me somehow to deserve you.'

'Oh my dear, dear impossible Cousin Felix!'

'My funny little skinny cousin – why are you crying? Crying and laughing at the same time. My beautiful crazy little one! I've been a fool and a brute and I've no right to a second chance, but dear God, if I am ever idiot enough to lose you again – Oh, my love, and we have missed so many years, so much time!'

'We'll make up for it,' I said. 'We'll make time run to catch us.'

'We'll make love till we're both driven insane with it.'

'We'll have hordes of children.'

'We'll work. And you'll never give up the piano.'

'We'll go to Paris.'

'We'll go to New York and tell Rosa Schumacher she must keep her painting.'

'We'll take Teddy and Stenko out for the most extravagant champagne dinner that's ever been had.'

'Not forgetting your friend Dilly.'

'Oh my darling, we'll make the world spin!'

'And never stop feeling dizzy with it!'

'And please, Felix – ' suddenly I was serious again – 'you will come and see my father?'

'Yes, my darling, of course I will. But first, before any of those things – ' he looked at me for a moment with that tender, half-mocking smile of his, then bent and gave me a long, slow kiss that seemed to spread with a great aching warmth to every region of my body – 'first of all, my dear, dear little one, we shall stop providing that tramp picking up dog ends over there with the finest entertainment he's had for years, climb into the car with Anatole, and go and find the fastest way in London we can be married.'

My mother, as I have said, wrote no further in her diary, except for this last brief entry three days before my birth.

Diary of Adele Ward.
Silver Strands Boarding House, Weymouth.

31st October, 1905.

Oh, dearest D, though I hate myself for the shameful thing which occurred between us, I cannot hate you. Sometimes I try to recall your face, that strong face with its gentle smile, those grave, clear eyes with their boyish lashes. But, after a while, it seems only to blur into M's, M's as it used to be when I had so many dreams and he sought to steal a kiss in Mamma's rose garden. Oh D, were you real, or only a dream too? Sometimes I wish –

But I must be very near my time now; I can feel the child quickening within me, like a bird fluttering and beating its wings, yearning to be free. I no longer visit M in his incarceration, for he does not know me and I cannot bring this living thing I carry into that place of death. I have written to Sir Arthur to apprise him of my circumstances for, if things should go badly with me, there must be someone to care for the new life that is to come; and I cannot believe, however J may hate me, she will but feel tenderness and compassion for a poor, innocent child. For there is in the child joy and hope and yes, oh yes, D, after all, love.

Belva Plain

– the best-loved bestseller –

Evergreen £2.50

A rich and tempestuous story of Anna Friedman, the beautiful, penniless Jewish girl who arrives in New York from Poland at the turn of the century and survives to become matriarch of a powerful dynasty.

Random Winds £2.50

The absorbing and poignant story of a family of doctors – Dr Farrell, the old-fashioned country doctor who dies penniless and exhausted, his son Martin who becomes a brilliant and famous brain surgeon, but is haunted by his forbidden love for a woman, and Martin's daughter Claire, headstrong, modern and idealistic, whose troubled romance with the unknown Englishman provides a bitter-sweet ending.

Eden Burning £2.50

A romantic saga set against the backdrop of New York, Paris and the Caribbean. The island of St Felice holds many secrets, one of which is the secret of the passionate moment of abandon that threatened to destroy the life of the beautiful fifteen-year-old Teresa Francis. A story of violence, political upheaval and clandestine love.

FONTANA PAPERBACKS

Victoria Holt

The supreme writer of the 'gothic' romance, a compulsive storyteller whose gripping novels of the darker face of love have thrilled millions all over the world.

BRIDE OF PENDORRIC £1.75
THE CURSE OF THE KINGS £1.35
THE DEVIL ON HORSEBACK £1.75
THE HOUSE OF
A THOUSAND LANTERNS £1.75
KING OF THE CASTLE £1.75
KIRKLAND REVELS £1.50
THE LEGEND OF
THE SEVENTH VIRGIN £1.75
LORD OF THE FAR ISLAND £1.75
MENFREYA £1.50
MISTRESS OF MELLYN £1.50
MY ENEMY THE QUEEN £1.65
ON THE NIGHT OF
THE SEVENTH MOON £1.35
THE PRIDE OF THE PEACOCK £1.75
THE SECRET WOMAN £1.75
THE SHADOW OF THE LYNX £1.25
THE SHIVERING SANDS £1.75
THE SPRING OF THE TIGER £1.50
THE MASK OF THE ENCHANTRESS £1.75

FONTANA PAPERBACKS

Catherine Gaskin

'Catherin Gaskin is one of the few big talents now engaged in writing historical romance.'
Daily Express

'A born story-teller.' *Sunday Mirror*

THE SUMMER OF THE SPANISH WOMAN £1.95
ALL ELSE IS FOLLY £1.65
BLAKE'S REACH £1.75
DAUGHTER OF THE HOUSE £1.50
EDGE OF GLASS £1.50
A FALCON FOR A QUEEN £1.75
THE FILE ON DEVLIN £1.50
FIONA £1.75
THE PROPERTY OF A GENTLEMAN £1.75
SARA DANE £1.95
THE TILSIT INHERITANCE £1.95
FAMILY AFFAIRS £2.50
CORPORATION WIFE £1.75
I KNOW MY LOVE £1.75
THE LYNMARA LEGACY £1.95
PROMISES £2.50

FONTANA PAPERBACKS

Victoria Holt also writes as
Philippa Carr

Some of the novels in a series that will follow the fortunes of one English family from Tudor times to the present day.

THE MIRACLE AT ST. BRUNO'S £1.50
THE LION TRIUMPHANT £1.50
THE WITCH FROM THE SEA £1.75
SARABAND FOR TWO SISTERS £1.65
LAMENT FOR A LOST LOVER £1.50
THE LOVE-CHILD £1.50
THE SONG OF THE SIREN £1.50
THE DROP OF THE DICE £1.75

FONTANA PAPERBACKS

Contemporary Romances

Once a Lover £1·75 **Diana Anthony**
Set in New York and San Francisco, *Once a Lover* is the moving love story of Lainie Brown, a young artist, and Jean-Paul Vallier, a blinded sports superstar. Then he regains his sight and Lainie fears she will lose his love. But she learns painfully, and joyously what she is, and why she is so worthy of Jean-Paul's enduring devotion.

Celebration £1·50 **Rosie Thomas**
Bel Farrer, a wine columnist, was a high-flying career girl – quick, clever and beautiful. But beneath her glittering professional appearance was a vulnerable heart. Both the titled aristocrat bound by an ancient code of honour, and the reckless, carefree playboy, claimed her heart and she had to make a choice.

Perfect Dreams £1·75 **Carolyn Fireside**
The world of high fashion, Hollywood and the jet set is the backdrop for this rich love story. Gabrielle Blake, a photographer's model, is independent, intelligent and lovable. Among the rich and famous men who fall in and out of Gaby's life is Terry Baron, a young journalist who finally rescues her when her career collapses but is it too late for them to rescue their love for each other?

Perhaps I'll Dream of Darkness £1·35 **Mary Sheldon**
In this compelling and beautifully written story of love and obsession the lives of a teenage girl and a burned-out rock star entwine fleetingly – with disastrous results. Probing deeply into her characters' inner lives, Mary Sheldon creates an unforgettable portrait of frustrated passion that leads ineluctably to tragedy, and captures both the grace and the terror of obsessive, idealistic love.

FONTANA PAPERBACKS

Fontana Paperbacks

Fontana is a leading paperback publisher of fiction and non-fiction, with authors ranging from Alistair MacLean, Agatha Christie and Desmond Bagley to Solzhenitsyn and Pasternak, from Gerald Durrell and Joy Adamson to the famous Modern Masters series.

In addition to a wide-ranging collection of internationally popular writers of fiction, Fontana also has an outstanding reputation for history, natural history, military history, psychology, psychiatry, politics, economics, religion and the social sciences.

All Fontana books are available at your bookshop or newsagent; or can be ordered direct. Just fill in the form and list the titles you want.

FONTANA BOOKS, Cash Sales Department, G.P.O. Box 29, Douglas, Isle of Man, British Isles. Please send purchase price, plus 8p per book. Customers outside the U.K. send purchase price, plus 10p per book. Cheque, postal or money order. No currency.

NAME (Block letters)

ADDRESS

While every effort is made to keep prices low, it is sometimes necessary to increase prices on short notice. Fontana Books reserve the right to show new retail prices on covers which may differ from those previously advertised in the text or elsewhere.